THE RED Zone

BETH BOLDEN

PROLOGUE

BETWEEN THE REFEREE'S WHISTLE and the snap of the football, there was always an eerily silent, utterly static moment.

That split second of time, so quick you could nearly blink and miss it, was almost solely responsible for Spencer Evans falling in love with football all those years ago. Anything was possible in that moment. A hundred thousand possibilities, only defined by the athleticism of everyone on the field. Anything could happen, if only he could *make* it happen.

To anyone else, Spencer was sure the silence and that strange stillness didn't exist.

After all, there was the raucous noise from the crowd full of fans—slightly tempered, if it was a home game, but indisputably still loud. The creaking of cleats digging into the turf. The nervous twitch of the offensive lineman's eyes as he stared Spencer down from behind his helmet. The flash of blue of a wide receiver—probably Chase Riley, if Spencer guessed —switching sides, trying to find an open slot so he could move down the field unchecked.

In that moment there was nothing, and there was everything.

Spencer inhaled, and then, just as he was about to exhale, the ball snapped and he didn't even think, just let years of well-honed instincts hijack his body and use it for their own end goal.

The end goal?

To disrupt the play unfolding in front of him.

To slough off the offensive linemen converging on his position.

To reach the quarterback and make sure he didn't have even the handful of seconds he needed to throw the ball downfield.

Especially that he didn't have the handful of seconds he needed to throw the ball downfield to Chase Riley.

One lineman, big and bulky, with a determined set to his shoulders even under his pads, faced off in front of him first, but Spencer had been dealing with this asshole the whole game so far, and up til now, he hadn't managed to stop him, and he wasn't going to stop him this time either.

Spencer thrust out his arm and skirted around him, smashing his palm right into the center of his jersey, keeping his center of gravity low and steady, using all the strength in his legs to keep them churning, keep them moving. He rounded the corner around the first guy, and *of fucking course*, there was a second guy there. His sole job was to back up the first guy; make sure that Spencer didn't break through.

It was only a matter of time before they'd start to double-team him, and the very first play of the second half? It was exactly what Spencer would have told them to do. But it was hardly unexpected, and Spencer had already anticipated it.

It was a good plan, in theory. The problem was in reality, Spencer totally outmatched the second-string tight end, who was big and probably pretty fast, but not nearly smart enough to be the starter.

Spencer knew this because he wasn't quick enough to anticipate Spencer's sudden dodge to the inside. He'd expected him to go to the outside, where there was empty field and a clear, easy path to the quarterback. Sam Crawford had had the ball in his hands for approximately two point four seconds at this point, and Spencer knew he could get to him, could feel it deep down, in his bones, in his tiring, overworked muscles, as he strained to whip around one last player, and suddenly, unexpectedly, everything stopped.

The *pop* was jarring. It didn't hurt, not exactly, not at first, but the unexpected sensation stopped him, moored him in place, and he found himself dropping to his knees. There was a roar in his ears and everything went fuzzy, but it took another few seconds, and then, finally, the pain hit.

Spencer had experienced a lot of pain in his years playing football. He'd broken a leg once; he'd sprained both ankles numerous times. He'd had his nose shattered and then put back together—his aunt Pru thought he looked more distinguished with it listing slightly to the right now, anyway—but he'd never experienced anything like this.

The pain was centered around the lower half, right above his heel.

Spencer knew what it was, without a doctor examining him, without a single consultation.

At thirty-two, his career wouldn't be over by a long stretch, but it had sure gotten a whole lot fucking harder.

He breathed in and then out again as Sam Crawford threw the ball, landing it perfectly in Chase Riley's hands as he ran for a solid twenty-yard gain.

Spencer hadn't stopped Crawford. Hadn't pounded him into the turf like he'd done already twice this game.

Nope. Spencer's body had done all the stopping on this play.

He rolled onto his back, grinding his teeth against the consuming pain.

The referee blew the play dead.

Everyone around him got up, starting to head towards the new *first down* marker, established by Riley's catch and run.

But Spencer stayed.

He supposed he could try to get up. Try to hobble over to the bench. He would probably get a load of crap later for staying put. That was just the kind of passive-aggressive shit that the dumb-asses in his locker room would try to pull.

Somehow even being a two-time Defensive Player of the Year winner was not enough to prevent anyone and everyone from calling him a pussy.

At any other moment, Spencer would have cared. He'd have dragged himself up. He'd done it enough times, in that never-ending cycle to be the tough guy who wasn't any less of a man just because he liked men in his bed.

But this was different.

Shaughnessey stopped at his shoulder. Just out of visual range. But Spencer could hear him. Feel him. When someone was a threat, you learned to *sense* them.

His own teammate shouldn't have been one. It should have been the aqua and blue jerseys on the other side of the field that were the threats, but Spencer had discovered nine years ago that sportsmanship wasn't as cut and dried as those ESPN documentaries tried to make it.

People were shitty. And Shaughnessey was the worst of the bunch.

"Hey, dickwad, you slackin' over here?"

Spencer didn't move. Didn't even blink.

Figured his non-response was enough of an answer.

Another player jogged up. It was Blaze, and he actually looked concerned.

"You okay, big man?" Blaze was one of the semi-decent guys on the team. A long, lean corner, he could pluck a ball right out of a wide receiver's hands, or stretch himself out, full length, and prevent them from ever feeling it brush their fingertips.

He was real good, and even more importantly, he was not like Shaughnessey.

"Achilles," Spencer said tightly.

"Oh, fuck," Blaze said. Spencer saw him wave to the sideline, and a few medical personnel jogged out.

"Get your ass up," Shaughnessey barked. "We ain't no pussies here. This is our city, goddamn it, and we're gonna punish Crawford for ever thinkin' he can play here."

"Fuck off," Blaze told him succinctly. "Spence is hurt."

Shaughnessey rolled his eyes and turned away. It wasn't all that unexpected, but it would be easier, Spencer told himself, if he wasn't around for this next part anyway.

The medical team stripped off his shoe, his sock, and the tape around his ankle, Spencer straining against the pain of it as it ripped across the back of his calf, right where the agony lived.

"Let's get you up," one of the guys said, "we need to get you to the locker room. Scan time."

They helped him up, and as they walked off the field, Spencer being assisted by two guys half his size, he heard the roar of the crowd echoing in his ears.

He'd been booed before, after an injury. But the Riptide fans were *classy* that way. Or maybe they were just happy that in the annual Battle of Los Angeles game, one of the most important pieces had just been removed.

They didn't know—couldn't know yet—but Spencer already did.

He'd be sidelined for some time to come.

· · ● · ● · ● · ·

Spencer squirmed on the examination table, the paper crinkling under his big body. It had been the longest three months of his life since he'd torn his Achilles. He was more than ready to get on with the rest of his recovery.

"I bet you're ready to get this cast off," Mary said, her hands competent as she manipulated the heavy sharp shears that cut through the plaster surrounding his calf like it was sopping wet paper.

"I could do with a bit more breathability," Spencer admitted wryly.

He'd never worn a full plaster cast before—he'd gotten lucky enough that he'd only ever been in boots. This cast business? He hadn't anticipated just how crappy an experience it was.

"Could also do without using a coat hanger to scratch every itch," Spencer added, because the sutures, while healed, had itched like a *bitch* while they'd been turning into scar tissue.

And that didn't even take into consideration the horrible cramps he'd experienced, running all up and down his calf while his torn Achilles tendon had healed.

Shaughnessey would have delighted in calling him every name in the book if he could've seen how Spencer mashed his face into his pillow and just screamed, unable to move his leg to alleviate the cramp, or the debilitating pain that followed after.

Out of all the injuries he'd ever experienced—and he'd experienced his fair share, because what NFL player *hadn't*—this was definitely ranking up there as his least favorite.

Mary peeled off the rest of the cast, and Spencer grimaced at the sight before him.

His lower leg, which hadn't seen sunshine or fresh air in three months, was a sickly jaundiced yellow. The muscle tone that he'd always taken such pride in honing, until he was a well-oiled machine, had withered away until his calf resembled a stick figure and not the muscular tone of his other leg.

"Looks pretty gruesome, doesn't it?" Mary said with commiseration in her tone.

It did look terrible, but it was more than that. Spencer looked at it and saw all the many months he was going to have to spend recovering. And he'd already given three months of his life.

Three precious months of the off-season, because the injury had happened in late November, at the tail end of the season. He'd be lucky if he made it back in fighting shape by April, when OTAs—optional training sessions—officially began. And because Spencer was Spencer, stubbornness ingrained in him, he'd never missed a single one. Even though sometimes he had a love-hate relationship with football, being the best was important to him. A point of pride.

"I didn't expect . . ." He trailed off. He had expected recovery to be hard. He hadn't expected it to be *this* hard.

"You've never been in a real cast, have you?" Mary asked sympathetically.

Spencer shook his head.

"Well, Doctor Chandarana will be in shortly, to discuss PT options with you. But I think she's going to be happy with how it's healed."

"Really?" Spencer couldn't help his skepticism.

Mary shot him a frank look. It was one of the reasons he'd liked her so much. "For a lot of people, this injury would've ended their career," she said. "You know that, Spencer."

He did know it. It was what he'd feared, all those long December nights, when he'd lain awake in bed and wondered what he was going to do with his life if that was the case for him.

And those thoughts always, inevitably prompted others.

Ones that asked, *And what've you been doing with it so far?*

Questions he'd never been able to answer.

"I know," Spencer said.

It was too hard, usually, to think about if things had been different. If he'd made a different choice and not come out of the closet. If he'd been drafted by a different team. If the team he *had* been drafted to had been different.

But it wasn't different.

He couldn't change the past.

But, a voice in the back of his head echoed, *you can change the future.*

It wasn't like Spencer had never considered it. It would be impossible to live the life he'd lived for the last nine years and not ever think about what he could change.

There was a soft knock on the door and Dr. Chandarana walked in, her expression no-nonsense. She was one of the best orthopedic surgeons in Southern California, but he'd have selected her despite that, because from the first moment, she'd been brutally honest, with none of the usual bullshit hedging that made him crazy.

"Hello, Mr. Evans," she said briskly, immediately walking over and examining his ankle carefully, not touching it yet. "How are you feeling today?"

"Glad to have the cast off," he admitted.

She pulled a pair of gloves on, and he flinched the moment she touched his ankle. It was unbelievably stiff as she manipulated it around.

"It will take time," she said, "to break up the scar tissue and regain your flexibility."

"And my muscle tone," he said ruefully.

"Yes," she agreed. "But I know the best physical therapist in the city. Mary will get you their card. And you'll work hard."

She stated it like fact. And yes, most football players he knew would work hard. But she'd gotten to know Spencer, and he figured she knew by now that he'd be committed to working the *hardest*.

Spencer nodded. He'd already known the recovery from this injury would be long and grueling. He just hadn't anticipated it being *quite* so long or *quite* so grueling.

"When do you think I'll be back?" he asked, even though he knew she wouldn't give him a solid answer. So much depended on his devotion to the PT work, and so much depended on factors that he couldn't control, like how well his Achilles had been repaired.

She pursed her lips. "You know I can't answer that, Mr. Evans," she said. "But if you commit to your PT like I hope you will, I don't think playing this season is out of the question."

"I don't want to just play this season," Spencer said. "I want to play the whole goddamn season."

"The sky is the limit, as long as you are willing to put in the work," she said, a glimmer of a smile appearing on her face for the first time. "And you're certainly not afraid of that."

He wasn't.

There were other things he was afraid of.

Things he didn't talk about.

Things he barely let himself *think* about.

Things that couldn't be changed unless he was willing to blow up his whole life.

He'd never been willing to do that before, but now?

He'd gotten a taste of what it would be like if he lost football. That long, lonely, miserable, interminable winter. And on the other side of that black hole, the risk no longer looked as terrible as it once had.

Maybe . . . Spencer thought . . . *maybe*.

Chapter One

"Mr. Mitchell, you've got a visitor." Over the intercom, his assistant Kyle's voice echoed throughout Alec's cavernous office.

He was right in the middle of reviewing a contract, lost in the tricky legalese of a particularly thorny, particularly important paragraph and, impatiently, he pressed a button to call Kyle back and tell him that he was too busy and whoever it was could wait.

But before he could open his mouth to tell his assistant just that, the door opened, and the shadow of a large man fell across Alec's gigantic Brazilian cherry desk.

"Hello, Alec," Spencer Evans said, walking in like he had been invited. Alec decided he was going to need to have another talk with Kyle about what *do not disturb* really meant.

"I see Kyle let you in," Alec said, leaning back in his chair.

Out of all the visitors he received, and being one of the foremost sports agents in the business, he received a lot of foot traffic, supposedly carefully monitored by Kyle, Spencer Evans was possibly the most unexpected guest he'd ever had.

Spencer sat down at one of the custom chairs across from his own. Without an invitation. But then that was Spencer. All brash confidence.

It was a good act. Not many people realized that was what it was, and even fewer knew that there was anything else going on underneath.

Alec thought he might be one of the only ones.

"What can I do for you?" Alec asked when Spencer didn't say anything immediately.

Spencer had torn his Achilles tendon in a game—in the Battle of LA, one of the most important games of the year, when the Los Angeles Riptide and the Los Angeles Stars played each other. He'd been in one of the luxury suites, watching, as he had a number of players he managed—and *friends*—who played for the Riptide.

But even though Spencer played for the Stars, he'd felt his own sharp intake of breath when Spencer had gone down, echoed by nearly everyone in the stadium.

Spencer Evans was a once-in-a-generation talent. He was the kind of player where just being on the field changed everything about the game.

The injury had looked bad and *was* bad. No doubt he'd had a long recovery from his Achilles tendon tear, but he'd walked in here with no crutches, and no noticeable limp. He'd been working hard, then.

But then, that was exactly what Alec would expect out of Spencer Evans.

"I want you to be my agent."

It was the last thing that Alec expected Spencer to say.

Only a decade of being an agent plus law school before that gave him the ability to keep his expression neutral.

He and Spencer had circled each other for years. For many reasons.

There'd been a time, way back in the beginning, when Alec had been certain that Spencer would hire him to be his agent.

It had never happened.

He'd never *expected* it to happen.

Especially not now, not when Spencer was so entrenched in his whole "prove to the world he was the least gay man of all gay men" persona.

"You look surprised."

Alec guessed he hadn't managed to control his expression all that well.

"Well, can you blame me?" Alec said. He stood and began to pace behind the desk, in front of the huge bank of windows.

"I want you to be my agent, and I want you to get me traded." Spencer paused. "To the Riptide."

Alec swiveled and looked straight at him. Something he didn't usually do. For reasons that had nothing to do with the fact that he'd never been able to count Spencer as one of his clients. "You want me to get you traded to the Riptide," he repeated, disbelief creeping into his voice.

"If anyone can do it, it's you," Spencer said, which was *probably* true, but Alec didn't particularly feel like giving him the satisfaction of agreeing.

"Decided things aren't going so great, huh?" Alec asked.

It was Spencer's turn to look surprised. "What do you mean?"

Alec waved a hand. "It's obvious, isn't it? You had a serious injury. You spent weeks— months—in recovery. All that time to think. Clearly you finally decided that it isn't worth it to try to be as toxically masculine as everyone else in that locker room."

"It's . . ." Spencer's brows pinched together. He looked unnaturally distressed.

It was only then that Alec realized what coming here must have cost him.

Yes, he was admitting he'd been wrong. But then Alec had asked him to rub his own face in it.

It was why, ultimately, they would make a terrible team.

It was why after so many fucking years, Alec had decided, ultimately, that it was good that Spencer had never hired him.

And that, he reminded himself, was something he still believed. Even as he felt his resolve begin to weaken. *You want to do this, you've always wanted to do this.*

How much he wanted to do it was reason enough to turn Spencer down.

Nevermind all those other—much more personal—reasons.

"No," Alec said succinctly.

"Excuse me?"

Alec leaned over the desk, hands braced on the edge. "No," he repeated.

"*No*, you wouldn't be the best agent to get me traded to the Riptide, or *no*, you won't do it?"

Alec contemplated his answer. He could lie. Spencer wouldn't believe him. But it would save face.

"No, I won't do it," Alec said. "I'm not taking on new clients right now," he tacked on, as a way to soften the blow.

But from the way Spencer was staring at him, shock in his eyes, it was clear the blow had not been softened. He had come here, fully expecting that Alec would jump all over the chance to *finally* be his agent.

Any agent would fall over themselves for even the *chance* to be Spencer Evans' agent.

"Is this because of Riley?" Spencer asked.

It was easy to see why he might jump to that conclusion. Chase Riley was one of Alec's other clients, and only a year earlier, he and Spencer had had an ugly confrontation. Spencer had eventually apologized for his judgmental comments, but Alec knew they'd bothered Chase for some time.

It would be easy to blame his reluctance on Chase.

But other than being angry on Chase's behalf—because he genuinely *liked* Chase, a lot—he'd not been particularly surprised. Spencer's experience as an out gay man in the National Football League had been so different from Chase's. Alec knew he wasn't even aware of the extent of Spencer's situation, and he still felt sorry for him.

However, he didn't feel sorry enough to take on Spencer as a client.

"No," Alec said firmly. "I just think it's a bad idea."

"It's a bad idea for me to finally do what you've been wanting me to do since I was drafted?" Spencer's tone was incredulous.

"I haven't wanted you to do anything."

It was a lie. He wished he didn't feel the way he did. He'd spent nine years pretending that he didn't.

It was those ten years that stopped him now, along with his deep-seated suspicion that Spencer didn't really *want* to change. He'd been doing this for so long now that it would be far easier to just keep doing it.

The only thing worse than not helping Spencer would be to watch him try and fail.

Spencer stood, suddenly. His honey brown eyes were wild and angry. "I can't fucking believe you. You stand there, judging me every fucking day, and when I finally say, *sure, let's do it your way*, you tell me *no*."

"I don't . . ."

But Spencer didn't let him finish. "What you're really trying to say is that you *can't* do it."

That wasn't what Alec was saying at all. Of course, any team would want at least a chance at Spencer Evans. In the end, it might not work out between him and the Riptide but Alec was pretty confident in his own abilities to at least get Spencer on a team that appreciated him. *All* the parts of him.

But Alec's abilities as an agent had never been the problem.

It was the part of him that wasn't an agent that was the biggest roadblock—the part of him that was a man.

"If I *wanted* to, I certainly could," Alec retorted.

Spencer's eyes narrowed. "So, this *is* about Riley."

Alec, who considered his intellect particularly suited to the chess match that was professional athletics, was taken aback. Had Spencer just played *him*?

"It's about . . ." Alec knew how flustered he sounded.

"Yeah, it is," Spencer said, sitting back down again. "What can I do to make it right? I apologized. I can apologize again."

Alec stared at the man across from him. He was dwarfing one of the custom-crafted chairs that he'd ordered from Italy. But he looked comfortable. Comfortable enough that he wouldn't be moving for some time.

Alec needed him to get out of his office, before he ended up convincing him to change his mind.

"You don't have to apologize again."

"Clearly you think I do," Spencer said. "And I can. I . . . I feel bad."

"You already apologized last year," Alec said in a clipped voice. "Now, unfortunately, despite what that idiot Kyle told you, I *am* actually busy, and . . ."

Spencer raised an eyebrow. "You're kicking me out of your office?"

Yes, yes he was.

It was all self-preservation, but there was no way that Spencer could know that.

"I'm busy," Alec said.

The corner of Spencer's mouth quirked up. "You could be busy with *me*," he said.

For a split second, Alec was sure that he'd misheard.

Spencer wasn't . . . *no*, they'd agreed so many years ago they couldn't, they wouldn't ever, he'd been *so* fucking clear.

But then Spencer flushed, like he'd just realized the implications of his statement. "I meant, *busy with my career*," he corrected.

"Right," Alec said, clearing his throat. It was probably pointless to hope that Spencer hadn't noticed his shock. Or his undeniable interest. He could still feel it, the arousal spike in his blood, the awareness he'd felt of Spencer's bulk and his very presence from the moment he'd walked into his office blossoming into something more.

Something much hotter.

But Alec shook it off because goddamn it, he was a professional.

"Think of how much money I could make you," Spencer said slyly. Like he didn't already know why Alec did this job. The money was undeniably nice. But the impact he'd made? That was why he still got up every morning, way too early, and dragged his ass to the office. It was why he still worked far too late, and way too many weekends.

Spencer Evans, the player, *would* be a jewel in his crown. Especially if Spencer turned out to be half the man that he promised, behind all those walls and underneath the stupid tough-guy act.

He was almost tempted to change his mind. But that was exactly why he'd tried to get Spencer out of his office. He wanted him. He'd always goddamn wanted him.

As a player you manage, Alec mentally tacked on. But who was he fucking fooling anyway?

"You'd make me a fortune, to bank right alongside my other fortune," Alec said. "Unfortunately, I'm only in the market for one fortune right now, thanks."

Spencer stared at him, those sugar brown eyes wide and disbelieving. Like he'd really thought if he got his ass in the building, in the chair opposite Alec, that all the pieces would fall into place, and it would be *easy*.

Alec wasn't stupid enough to think anything in this business was easy, and frankly, neither was Spencer.

He knew better.

He'd . . . well, Alec could only suspect that he was a little desperate and that . . .

"You have to go," Alec said, some of his own desperation creeping into his voice.

Spencer didn't move.

"Listen," Alec said. "I know someone. I can ask them. Real good agent. He's Jamie's agent. You've probably . . . well, I guess you probably wouldn't have met him, but Grady, he could probably at least get you a meeting . . ."

"I don't want them," Spencer said in a hard voice. "I want you."

How many fucking times had Alec dreamed that he would say those words? Say them and mean them?

He'd lost track of how many times.

That was exactly why Spencer *had* to go.

"I'll have Kyle get you Grady's number," Alec said. Not that Spencer couldn't get ahold of Grady if he wanted to.

He could have any agent in this business, but he'd come here. Likely because Alec repped a number of guys on the Riptide and had a pretty open line of communication with their VP of Player Personnel, but also because of their shared history.

So many moments over the years. They flickered through Alec's mind, one after the other. Starting with the first time they'd ever met, at the opening night of the NFL Draft. When he'd leaned over, and Spencer had looked up into his eyes, fear and determination mixing in them, along with an undeniable attraction.

It had been an intoxicating combination, and unfortunately for Alec, nine years had not dimmed Spencer's ability to lead him around by his dick—and his heart.

"You really . . ." Spencer took a deep breath and continued. "You're really saying no."

"I'm saying no," Alec said, as gently as he possibly could.

"I just . . . I thought . . ." Spencer stared at him. Alec wavered, almost opened his mouth to tell him that he'd changed his mind, that he could never really say no to someone like Spencer, someone who'd needed help for so long and was finally brave enough to reach for it, that he could never say no to *Spencer*. But before he could, Spencer stood and walked out.

Nine Years Ago

Spencer had never been so nervous in his whole goddamned life.

He was either going to throw up or pass out, and if he did, everyone would know what he was secretly sure they suspected anyway: he was *weak*.

So he gripped the edge of the table, underneath the white and gold-trimmed tablecloth, and held on for dear life.

Prudence, his aunt, was chatting happily to another mother, next to her, and had somehow missed that Spencer was increasingly sure that he was going to embarrass himself.

In thirty minutes, the NFL Draft would begin, and he would be both hoping to hear his name called and dreading getting up on the stage.

What if the wrong team drafted him? What if he fell to the bottom of the first round? What if he fell all the way to the second? What if Roger Goodell never called his name at all? What if he was left in the green room, by himself, while teams took everyone else around him?

He'd worried that coming out of the closet hurt his draft stock, but Lawrence Nicholson, his agent, had promised him that wouldn't happen. "After Colin O'Connor came out two years ago, everyone's all excited about the new version of the NFL," Larry had promised him.

It wasn't like he didn't trust Larry. He did, as much as you could trust any agent—considering most everyone knew they weren't in it for charity, they were in it for the fortune and the fame.

He'd thought the hardest moment of his life had been facing the Ohio State locker room after announcing that he was gay, but this was so much harder. It wasn't just a locker room watching him now; it was an entire sport.

The entire world.

Larry had stopped by a moment ago, giving him a few words of encouragement and a last-minute thumbs-up. "You've got this," he'd said, "lots of interest in you, kid." He'd left then, to make the rounds of his other clients waiting to see where they'd be drafted.

Spencer knew he should be feeling good. Lots of people said he was the best defensive end in the draft. Even Mel Kiper had said it. Both his Pro Day and his appearance at the combine had been exactly what he needed, at least according to Larry.

He'd lined up all his ducks, now he just had to wait.

And truthfully, Spencer was utter shit at waiting.

"Hey, you must be Spencer Evans."

Spencer glanced up from the hole he was probably wearing into the tablecloth with his intense stare, and nearly swallowed his tongue.

He'd been out since his junior year of college, and he'd had a boyfriend and a handful of hookups during high school and his time at Ohio State, but he'd never gotten used to talking to cute guys.

And this guy?

He wasn't just cute.

He was stunning. Utterly handsome. Bone-meltingly hot. And about a hundred other adjectives that Spencer couldn't formulate in his short-circuited brain.

"Yes." The word barely tumbled out of his mouth. "That's . . . that's me."

The man was one of the few in the room who was wearing a suit, instead of the suit wearing him. Spencer wouldn't have guessed he'd have found such formal clothes so incredibly hot, until this moment. But right now, he wanted to peel each flawlessly tailored piece off his body. The gray and purple striped tie brought out the stormy bluish-gray of his eyes, and his dark hair was styled perfectly, setting off his freaking gorgeous face in a way that Spencer could never hope to replicate.

"Alec Mitchell," he said extending a hand. "It's great to meet you."

Alec Mitchell.

Spencer was suddenly kicking himself. During his senior year, he'd been swarmed by agents and their informational packets, all of them making grandiose promises, almost all of them painfully transparent.

But he remembered Alec's packet specifically. He also remembered declining to meet with him, because he was a newer agent and he'd never had a client taken in the first round of the draft. He didn't think Alec had any players who'd even been drafted.

The other deciding factor had been Alec's sexuality.

He was the only agent who had pursued Spencer who'd been gay. At least the only one who would admit it.

And Spencer, terrified that he might be judged for his sexuality, hoping to downplay it as much as possible, had dismissed Alec almost immediately for that reason.

He was already gay, thank you very much. He didn't need a gay agent to drive the point home.

Now he couldn't help but regret throwing Alec Mitchell's packet away and refusing to meet him in person.

He reached out with his hand, wishing that he'd gotten a chance to surreptitiously wipe the dampness of his palm on the tablecloth or control the trembling of his fingers, but neither issue seemed to bother Alec, who shook his hand enthusiastically.

"It's just such an honor," Alec said, and to Spencer's shock, he *sat down.* "Your footage from Ohio State was incredible. And your stats at the combine? I was standing with a GM when you ran your forty, and he couldn't believe how fast you were."

Spencer considered asking which GM it had been, but he didn't know if that was allowed. There were so many rules—and so many of them unspoken—and he didn't want to say or do the wrong thing. That was part of why he was sitting here, sweating through his own suit, while Alec looked not only cool but annoyingly, impeccably pressed.

"I was actually hoping," Alec continued, like Spencer's non-answer was totally acceptable, "to meet you before all this." He waved around.

Spencer swallowed hard. "Yeah, I remember your packet," he said.

Alec smiled, the corner of his eyes crinkling, and it made him not only unspeakably attractive, but *approachable.* Like he wasn't a hundred million miles out of Spencer's league.

"But you didn't call me," Alec said conversationally, like this hadn't disappointed or upset him at all, but Spencer found that difficult to believe.

"I didn't," Spencer said cautiously. "I'm working with Lawrence Nicholson."

"Larry's a great agent," Alec said.

"He has been so far."

"I'll be honest, I was really hoping to work with you more closely," Alec said, leaning in, all disarming charm that flustered Spencer. Or maybe that was the whiff he'd gotten of his cologne. It was rich and sweet and intoxicating. Sandalwood and the barest hint of lavender. Spencer imagined he was back in Ohio, in his aunt's garden, and he was pressing Alec into the grass right by the lavender bed, the purple of its flowers reflected in Alec's eyes. The undeniable eagerness in them. Spencer could lean down, and their lips would brush and nothing would be the same after that.

Spencer's heartbeat accelerated. They were sitting here in the green room of the NFL Draft, and yet he swore he was back in that garden. "Why?" he asked even though he already knew the answer.

It wasn't because Alec had taken one look at him and wanted him—not the way Spencer wanted, anyway. It was because Alec was gay and there was a rumor he was trying to encourage more players to come out. That he was "collecting" queer athletes.

He'd wanted Spencer because he was about to make history and be the first out gay man to be selected in the NFL Draft.

"I think it's fairly obvious," Alec said deprecatingly. "I was on my way to being the youngest associate at the best law firm in Boston. I quit, the day Colin O'Connor came out, because he was doing something great, and I hoped other players would too, and I didn't want them to get screwed over just because they're not like everyone else. What I want is to change the National Football League. And I think you do too."

He didn't.

Nobody believed him. Not a single team in the interviews he'd done at the combine had taken his answer about coming out to prevent more gossip and questions—and *blackmail*, he'd thought but not actually said out loud—and believed it. He'd seen the look in their eyes. Like Alec, they all thought he was the younger version of Colin O'Connor.

He wasn't. He just wanted to keep his head down, play the game, do what he could to help his new team win. He wasn't here tonight to make history, even though he probably would.

"I just want to play football," Spencer said.

"Right, of course you do," Alec said, unexpectedly patting him on the arm. "Of course you do. But think of what it'll mean when you do."

Spencer didn't want to think about it. He just wanted to be fucking normal, that was all. Just another guy on the team.

Not some kind of fucking after-school special.

Not the next *30 for 30* documentary airing on ESPN.

Not another weapon in Alec Mitchell's arsenal.

"I'm here for football." *And to flirt with you, if you'd ever let me.*

But the chance of that happening was slim to none, especially when the realization dawned on Alec's handsome face.

"You didn't call me because I'm gay," Alec said, dumbfounded, like he couldn't quite believe it.

Spencer shrugged. "I want to be that really great player, the one the offensive line worries about in practice, not that *gay* football player."

"Why can't you be both?"

There was a part of him, buried so deep down, that craved that. That wondered, in the dark of the night, when he couldn't sleep, if he was making a mistake.

But then Spencer remembered all the microaggressions he'd experienced at Ohio State. Nothing he could actually go to the coach about, nothing he could take to the athletic director's office. And how, when he'd kept his head down, and played extraordinary football, they had mostly stopped. Like it wasn't worth losing to continue harassing Spencer. That a national title might make it worth having *that* guy on their team.

"Because that's a fucking fairy tale," Spencer said in a low, hard voice, "and you know it, but you just haven't faced it yet."

Alec stared at him, those fairy-tale eyes wide.

He was so beautiful and so fucking *clueless*.

Spencer was living in the real world, and he'd keep living in it, long after Alec gave up his quest to change the NFL and the world.

"I'm sorry," Alec said, suddenly straightening, and standing. "I've taken up too much of your time."

Then he was gone, leaving only that hint of sandalwood and lavender behind. Spencer's head was swimming with it.

Forty-six minutes later, Roger Goodell stood on the stage, and called his name, drafting him third overall, to the Los Angeles Stars. Spencer stood, his aunt Prudence reaching out to hug him. Larry shook his hand, uttering a string of meaningless praise and assurances. As he walked towards the stage, towards the next stage in his life, he swore he saw Alec watching him, clapping along with everyone else as he made sports history.

But deep down, it didn't make him feel any less uneasy.

CHAPTER TWO

If ALEC THOUGHT HE was going to give up that easily, he was delusional.

Spencer was mad. Actually he was really fucking pissed off. No doubt about it. He stomped down the stairs, taking them instead of the elevator because he'd missed a morning in the gym coming to Alec's office in Malibu. But at the time, he'd decided it was worth it.

After going back and forth for months, he'd woken up this morning and felt like today was the day. Today, he could get in his car and drive to Alec's office and throw himself on his mercy.

Most days, he felt like that for only a moment or two, but the fear of rejection always crushed him before he could do it.

But this morning, the sky had felt like the limit, like he'd finally emerged from the months-long rut he'd been in. He could walk normally, he was even running, and he was finally lifting again. While his physical therapist, June, was a not-so-closeted sadist who enjoyed torturing him, the pain and even bone-deep exhaustion made him feel alive again.

The more alive he felt, the more ready he felt to leave his shitty situation behind. He'd tolerated it for so long, had believed that there was no fixing it, even if he wanted to, but he'd realized over those long, dark months when he'd had only his own ugly thoughts for company that he'd never really *tried*.

Sure, he'd listened, likely with way too much trust, when Stars management had told him that there were going to be changes happening.

The changes had only been surface level, and he'd never fought harder. Even though he'd known he should have.

He'd told Alec once that staying on the team made him a better player. He'd believed that then. He didn't disagree with it now. But he'd become one of the best defensive players in the NFL. Some people said he was one of the best who'd ever played.

He had no excuses left, and he couldn't take any of this sitting down any longer.

And if Alec freaking Mitchell thought he could sit there, in his luxurious office, with that ridiculous desk and those spindly designer chairs, with all his experimental art on the walls, and tell him *no*, he was going to experience a rude awakening.

His feet pounded down the concrete steps of the staircase. He felt his calf twitching and pulling, and he almost stopped short, but he remembered what June had said, "It's gonna hurt, dude, but it's not gonna break," and he kept going.

By the time he reached the ground floor, his flare of temper had calmed enough that he could think clearly.

Once he thought clearly, his next step was obvious.

He couldn't go back to Alec again. Not yet. He needed to get someone on his side. One person, *specifically*.

Before his injury, the idea of going to beg forgiveness from Chase Riley would have been too painful to contemplate. And *that* was taking into account that he'd already done it once. Except, Spencer realized, it must not have worked—at least not the way Spencer needed it to—because if it had, then Alec wouldn't have turned him down.

He wouldn't have said yes immediately, either, because Alec was one of those insanely-smart chess types, who never made a move that he hadn't contemplated ten moves ahead, but he would've eventually come around. He'd have made Spencer wait and sweat it out. Probably, and almost certainly fairly, for the bullshit that Spencer had said and done over the years.

But he would have eventually said yes.

He's still going to say yes, Spencer told himself with conviction.

Because once he'd settled on this path, nothing was going to sway him from it.

The only question was how Spencer could manufacture a meeting with Chase. He'd never take a phone call. He wouldn't respond to a text. Email? That was totally out of the question.

He was going to have to run into him organically, and he could think of only one place where he might be able to do that.

• • • • ● • ● • • • •

It wasn't exactly a hardship to sit in the picnic area of the Food Truck Warriors, a food truck lot on the other side of town, but Spencer was still uneasy. There were ten trucks circling the outside of the lot, all with brightly colored signage, each menu sounding more delicious than the next. And all of them, without fail, had a rainbow flag flying. This was a safe place, more than one sign declared, where there was not an ounce of discrimination tolerated.

Spencer could understand why Chase had felt so comfortable here, and also why he'd allowed himself to make the choices he did. This place, where he must spend a lot of his free time when he wasn't on the field or preparing to *be* on the field, would make anyone feel free.

Chase, it seemed, was even dating one of the food truck owners. Spencer had dug deep into his memory, and he was pretty sure that his was the one with the dripping cheese painted all along the front side of the truck. *Say Cheese* it proclaimed loudly, in several different shades of turquoise.

But even though he'd wanted to, he hadn't ordered either a grilled cheese or one of the delicious-sounding macaroni and cheese variations outlined on their menu.

He was still watching what he was eating carefully, as they weren't ramping up his exercise regimen to its normal levels quite yet, so he'd examined each truck in turn, and ended up ordering a full chef's salad from a truck named Basket. The portion was huge, with lots of fresh greens, topped with pickled veggies, smoked shredded mozzarella, sliced smoked turkey, and even a deep-fried deviled egg perched on top.

Spencer could have told them to forget the egg, but he figured that he was going out of his way to make a healthy choice, so it wasn't going to kill him.

Plus, he thought as he bit through the crunchy exterior to the creamy, lemony, herby filling, it was *delicious*.

No wonder Chase had started working out like a maniac in the off-season. If he spent a lot of time here, he'd need to.

He'd taken his salad back to a table closer to the truck that Spencer was pretty sure Chase's boyfriend owned. He might not show up to today, Spencer reasoned as he drizzled the dressing over the greens, but he would at some point. Plus, it wouldn't exactly be a hardship for Spencer to spend a few afternoons hanging out here.

There was a flyer on the table he was sitting at, proclaiming live music at four today, and on the opposite side of the paper, it listed various bands playing all through the weekend. From the fairly professional-looking stage setup at the front of the lot, it looked like not only had the group carved out a great food destination but a live-entertainment mecca as well.

With the location, in a quasi-industrial area, with lots of lunch business, and likely almost no one around at night to complain about noise, it really was the perfect spot.

Spencer took his time eating his salad, enjoying every bite in a way he didn't usually, hoping that before he finished it, he would spot Chase's distinctive blond hair. But he didn't.

He lingered for another twenty minutes after he threw the biodegradable container in the recycling bin by going through his email, even though he usually avoided his inbox like the plague. But Chase didn't show up then, and Spencer resigned himself to spending the rest of this week's lunch hours here.

Theoretically, he could always go up to the Say Cheese truck, and ask to speak to Chase Riley's boyfriend. But Spencer assumed that Chase Riley's boyfriend would know exactly who he was, and that the chances of him being willing to open a line of communication were slim to none.

He'd just have to come back tomorrow.

The next day, Spencer ordered lunch at the wrap truck, the yellow and orange script proclaiming it *Wrap it Up*. He ordered a Thai chicken wrap, and carried it back to the same table he'd sat at yesterday, watching for the next hour as tons of people stepped up to the cheese truck and ordered, but none of them had Chase's distinctive blond hair.

The salad had been delicious, but somehow, impossibly, the wrap was even better, and he had to restrain himself from going back and ordering another one.

June sent him a text forty-five minutes into his second vigil.

Hey, soft guy, her text read, **haven't seen you at open gym this week, you finally give up?**

Spencer couldn't help but chuckle. He'd been working out on his own at the gym in his house, as the open gym hours at the PT clinic that June owned conflicted with what he considered the prime time for Chase to come see his boyfriend.

It hadn't been ideal, because he'd felt like he'd finally found a good groove with seeing June and letting her push him to the next level of his recovery. But the draft was coming up soon, and if he was going to be traded, this was the right time for it to happen. If he wanted to leave the Stars, he was going to have to make his move now. And without Alec, that couldn't happen at all.

He supposed that if he didn't end up convincing Alec, he could always ask Larry to see what he could do. In the nine years he'd been in the NFL, Larry hadn't exactly been a terrible agent. But then, he hadn't really been a great one either.

It wasn't that he hadn't done the job that Spencer had needed him to do because he had. But it had never been quite good enough, and he'd never been dedicated to helping Spencer get out of his shitty situation either. He'd passively accepted that this was the way things were, and he'd never tried to convince Spencer to leave.

Not like Alec had.

Alec had always wanted better for Spencer, when even *he* hadn't thought he deserved better.

Spencer couldn't believe that had changed so completely. Alec would come around—surely he'd do it when he fixed things with Chase.

If he had to come here for *weeks*, he'd be here every single day, though he sure hoped that Chase showed up earlier than that. He had a season to get ready for.

Just busy with something, but doing a lot of work on my own. Don't worry. I'll be back, and then you can keep kicking my ass, he texted back to June.

But by the third day, Spencer was beginning to wonder if the gossip he'd heard was wrong.

Maybe Chase and the food truck guy had broken up.

Spencer finished eating his meatball sub—the smell of the garlic and the herbs and the roasting meatballs had called him from across the lot today, and he'd been helpless to resist that delicious scent—and after wiping his fingers, opened up his Instagram app.

It was easy enough to find Chase, even though he didn't personally follow him. The first picture on Chase's feed was of him working out, all moody black and white, something about prepping for the season—and it made sense, Spencer thought, he was supposed to be doing the same thing, not helplessly chasing after Chase's forgiveness—but the second photo was of him and another guy, and this one was in color. It had been posted two weeks ago, and the way they were staring at each other made it pretty clear that there hadn't been any breakup. So, where was Chase? Why was he not here, staring gooily into his boyfriend's eyes and grabbing lunch while he was at it?

Spencer sighed. And before he could change his mind, hit the follow button on Instagram. He spent almost no time at all on social media, but Larry had convinced him to create an account a few years back. He followed almost nobody, only his aunt Pru, who posted about her garden and her knitting projects, and a handful of guys on his team. The ones who never made any snide comments about how Spencer liked to take it, anyway.

And now he was following Chase Riley, who had a mind-boggling number of followers, and probably wouldn't even notice that Spencer had clicked that little blue button.

He'd hoped that he'd only have to come back a few times, at most, to run into Chase, but by the fourth afternoon, he'd given up on that pipe dream, and now just hoped that he'd be able to see him at all.

Today, he headed back to the picnic-themed truck, and throwing his careful diet out of the window, ordered the fried chicken special, complete with coleslaw, potato salad, and a sweet potato biscuit that smelled even better than it looked, dripping with honey and butter.

He'd just shoved a delectable crumb of spicy, savory breading into his mouth when a shadow appeared over his table. He glanced up, and there was Chase Riley, his hair tied back, and a confused wrinkle between his blond brows.

Spencer chewed and swallowed, but before he could finish, Chase sat down opposite him.

"Do I need to kick your ass?" he asked.

"What?" Spencer wasn't sure he understood.

"My boyfriend says you're stalking him, and I don't share. And I definitely don't share with you. And then you *followed* me on Instagram. You realize you only follow like ten people, right?"

"Yes," Spencer said. Not sure which question he was answering. Maybe both.

"Yes, you know I don't share, or yes, you only follow ten people?"

"Well," Spencer said, setting his fork down, "both, really. I'm not here for your boyfriend. I've been coming here, hoping to run into you."

Chase raised an eyebrow. "You've been coming here for *me*? I'm sorry, dude, but *no*. Tate doesn't share either. And I'm not interested."

Spencer willed his flush to recede. Maybe if he'd had the kind of coming-out experience that Neal Fisher and Sam Crawford and now Chase Riley had had, he wouldn't feel like someone assuming he was sexually interested was an accusation he needed to refute as quickly as possible.

Maybe he wouldn't feel that momentary surge of terror. Like he'd just been found out.

"I'm not *interested*," Spencer said, forcing his voice to remain calm. "I just want to talk to you about something."

"You could've just sent me a DM," Chase pointed out. "'Cause I followed you back. Mostly out of insane curiosity, but I still did."

"DM?" Spencer was confused.

Chase rolled his eyes. "Direct message. If we both follow each other, we can exchange direct messages, privately."

"Oh." Spencer hadn't ever considered doing that. "Would you have answered me?"

Drumming his fingers on the table, Chase didn't answer right away, just looked at him, like he, just like Alec, could see right through him.

"I don't know," he finally answered. "I don't think we're ever going to be friends, if that's what you're asking, but I'd have been curious what you wanted. So maybe."

This was it. The moment of truth.

Spencer had practiced this second apology, knowing that it had to be good enough that Chase would not only forgive him, but also persuade Alec to help him out.

"I wanted to reach out and apologize," Spencer said. "I know the first time we talked, I was . . ."

"A total asshole?" Chase supplied helpfully.

"Yes, a total asshole," Spencer said. It didn't feel good to admit it. It didn't feel good to *know* it either. "I judged you, and I shouldn't have. I haven't always had the easiest time, and I let that get in the way."

"That's what Alec said," Chase said. He couldn't possibly know that he'd just brought up the main reason that Spencer had come here at all, but it felt serendipitous. "And that's what you said, too, last time you apologized."

"I wasn't lying then, and I'm not lying now," Spencer said. "And that's another thing I wanted to talk to you about . . ."

"Alec?" Chase leaned back, crossing his arms over his chest. Spencer hadn't precisely been following him, not the way some people did, but he was surprised to see the change in the guy. He'd actually gotten *protective*. A personality trait that he'd never expected to see Chase Riley display—but he'd clearly been wrong about him before, and maybe was *still* wrong.

Maybe there was a lot more to Chase than he'd ever imagined.

"Yes, Alec." Spencer paused, feeling breathless at the anxiety suddenly rocketing through him. If he couldn't convince Chase . . . *No*, he stopped himself, *you're gonna do it, and he's going to talk to Alec for you.* "I want you to help me convince him to take me on as a client."

Chase didn't have the greatest poker face that Spencer had ever seen, and he didn't—or *couldn't*—hold back his surprise at the request. "You want *me* to put in a good word for you? With Alec?"

"I know it's unlikely, especially after how much of an asshole I've been. But I want something different for the rest of my career, however much of it is left, and I think Alec can get it for me."

"You really think after you were so shitty to me, I'll just roll over and give you what you want?"

Spencer had known this would be an uphill battle. He *had* been shitty to Chase. Blinded by an avalanche of regret, bitterness, and more than a little self-loathing, he'd taken all of his negativity out on Chase. Said things that he'd only thought, deep down, in the dark of the night, when he lay there and couldn't sleep, and wondered what his life might have been like if he'd been drafted to another kind of team.

To his eye, Chase's path had been so painfully easy. He'd just *announced* his queerness on Twitter, no worries about repercussions, no angsting about his teammates' judgement, by talking about his boyfriend's food truck.

It was everything that Spencer had ever wanted, and nothing he'd ever gotten.

"I don't think it's going to be that easy, no," Spencer admitted.

"But you still came here."

"I had to do something."

Chase sighed. "I'm assuming you already talked to Alec, and he told you to take a fucking hike."

"Not...not precisely like that." From a few things that Spencer had gleaned from his conversation with Chase, and a few of the comments Alec had made over the years, he was pretty sure that Chase had no idea of their history. He couldn't blame Alec for not sharing. It wasn't anyone's business but their own, anyway.

"So he told you to fuck off," Chase said, like Spencer hadn't spoken at all, "and you thought you could come here and beg me to put in a good word. Get him to listen to you."

"Despite his answer, he *did* listen, and no, not *beg*, not exactly," Spencer said.

Chase smiled slyly. "You really think I wouldn't make you beg?"

"I was sort of hoping you might accept my apology and take it easier on me." He'd known reality would probably be different, but he hadn't known *how* different.

"I do accept your apology," Chase said, surprising him by sounding completely sincere. "I do believe that you experienced something totally different than what I did, and you probably resent the hell out of me for it. I can't blame you for that."

"But?"

"How do you know there's a *but*?"

Spencer barely refrained from rolling his eyes. He was supposed to be winning Chase over, not patronizing him. "There's always a *but*," he said, picking up his fork again and digging into his fried chicken. If Chase was going to keep him here, forever, *begging*, then he was going to at least eat his food before it got cold.

Chase was silent for a moment, watching him eat. "You're really serious about this," he said finally.

"What gave it away?" Spencer retorted between mouthfuls of the most tender chicken covered in the crispiest coating. "Me coming here for four days straight? Or apologizing again? Or me actually *telling* you that I was serious?"

"I'm just surprised," Chase said, sounding defensive. "I thought you were all busy getting back into *world domination* shape after your injury."

"I have been. But I'm capable of doing more than just working out." The coleslaw was tart and sweet on his tongue, the cabbage still the tiniest bit crisp.

"I'm sure you'll make sure to rob me of at least one touchdown next season," Chase grumbled.

"What if I didn't?" Spencer hesitated. It was becoming clear that Chase wasn't just going to shrug his wide shoulders and put in the word with Alec that he needed him to. Maybe it was even more complicated than that. It wasn't like he and Alec had ever been particularly simple, and it made sense that this wouldn't be either. "What if I *couldn't*?"

Chase's eyes narrowed. "What do you mean?"

"I want to play for a different team next season. Maybe I want to play for *your* team. For the Riptide."

There was no *maybe* about it, but it seemed that Spencer's words had their desired effect anyway, because Chase looked stunned.

"You want to play for the Riptide."

"I just said I did, didn't I?"

"You did." Chase shook his head. "I'm just . . . I'm trying to wrap my head around this."

"I'm not going to play for the Stars again. I'm done. If I can't get them to trade me, I'll retire." As soon as the ultimatum was out of his mouth, Spencer realized it was true. He wasn't going to step onto the field wearing their uniform, one more time. He couldn't do it.

All the slights and the insults and the "jokes" from so many years coalesced into one hard, tight ball of resolve, deep inside of him.

"No way, you're not gonna retire. You're in your prime," Chase said. His mouth was still hanging open, like he couldn't quite believe what Spencer was saying.

A year ago, Spencer would have agreed with him. But having your career almost derailed by an injury put everything into perspective.

He felt like he was seeing clearly for the first time in way too many fucking years.

"If the Stars won't trade me, then *yeah*, I'll retire," Spencer said.

"You told Alec this?"

"Some of it," Spencer admitted. "But I said enough. Enough he should've listened."

"And he didn't?" Chase frowned.

He'd known it before, but clearly Chase did not know his history with Alec.

No doubt Chase's experience with the agent had been totally different—but then, Chase was totally different. His coming-out had been different. He'd played his entire career for a team that supported and encouraged him.

He couldn't imagine the shit that had shaped Spencer, and that had placed him and Alec at opposite ends of every issue that mattered.

"He doesn't think I'm serious," Spencer said simply. "He thinks I'm just fucking around, and he doesn't want to be here for that.

Or, possibly, he's still angry with me over what happened between us last year."

"No way," Chase scoffed. "He's the one who encouraged me to talk to you, to accept your apology. He fucking *defended* you." He hesitated. "Which, that was weird, I thought at the time it was super weird, but he wouldn't talk about it when I asked him. Is there . . . is there any chance there's something going on between you two?"

Chase was so much smarter and more intuitive than anyone gave him credit for. But luckily, Spencer didn't have to lie at all.

"No," he said.

"Well, you can't be surprised that I wondered. It *was* weird. But I know he didn't turn you down because of me," Chase said.

The food was delicious, but it suddenly tasted like ash in his mouth. It occurred to Spencer then that all this had been a colossal waste of time, because Alec hadn't said no to him because of Chase. He'd said no because of *Spencer*.

His stomach churned, and he set his fork down.

The realization was not only inevitable, it hurt like hell.

He'd done this to himself. He couldn't change who he was. Or what he'd been through. Alec had always seemed to be understanding every time they'd run into each other, but at some point, at a moment Spencer couldn't pinpoint, that empathy had changed and warped.

Somehow, he'd crossed the point of no return, and he hadn't even known it.

"But," Chase continued, like everything wasn't falling apart, "I bet you we can still convince him to take you on."

Spencer shot him a disbelieving stare. "You really think so?" He wasn't convinced. Not anymore.

"Yeah, of course. He listens to me. Not always, but enough. Enough that I think I can get him to sit there with an open mind. And then you just need to tell him exactly what you told me."

"I already . . ."

"No," Chase said, and there was that steel resolve that Spencer had seen flashes of before on the field. "No, you really didn't."

"You weren't there."

"Maybe not, but you also weren't desperate when you went and saw him."

"And you think I'm desperate now?" He *was*, it was plain as fucking day.

"You came here," Chase said, tapping the table between them with his fingertips, "you came here for *four days* in a row. I know the food's good, but it's not *that* good. And you even followed me on Instagram. You only followed *nine people* before me."

"I'll have to take your word for that one," Spencer said dryly. "I don't spend a lot of time on Instagram."

"Exactly," Chase said. "Exactly my fucking point."

"Okay, so I didn't tell him everything," Spencer finally conceded. "I don't . . ."

"Just leave the openness part to me," Chase interrupted. "He'll listen. He'll really listen. I promise. But you've got to tell him the truth. The whole truth."

Spencer didn't think he'd be telling Alec the whole truth—it was too thorny and too difficult to reveal it all now, so many years later—but he could tell him enough of it.

"Okay," Spencer said.

"One more thing," Chase said casually. "I want you to promise me something."

"Anything." It was a little stupid to say it, because this was Chase Riley and he could still be reckless. At least comparatively. But Chase was right about one thing: Spencer *was* desperate.

Sometimes it felt like the only reckless thing Spencer had ever done in his life was come out of the closet, and even then, he hadn't done it because he'd wanted to.

"I want you to take some time, in the next few months, to figure out who you really are, underneath all that . . ." Chase waved his hand around in Spencer's general direction. "All that crap you put on for your stupid teammates."

"All *what* crap?"

Except Spencer knew exactly what he was talking about. But knowing was one thing, and admitting it, especially to Chase Riley, was entirely another.

"You know," Chase said. "That macho, tough-guy, *you wouldn't even check out a hot guy if he passed by, butter wouldn't melt in your mouth*, attitude. That wasn't the shit I was dealing with, not by a long shot, but that doesn't mean I didn't have different shit." Chase's voice had suddenly gone shrewd, and Spencer was unpleasantly reminded that he was smarter than he let on.

"How do you know I wouldn't check out a hot guy if he passed by?"

Chase shot him a look. "Listen, dude, I've seen enough and heard enough to know. The point is that *you* don't even know. You gotta find out who you really are, away from those assholes on your team. You want me to help you with Alec, that's my price."

"Seriously?" Spencer couldn't hold back his disbelief. "You want me to . . . what exactly?"

"Soul search? Experiment?" Chase shrugged. "You know what, *Alec* would be perfect for this. He'd know exactly what to do."

"I'm not going to Alec about this," Spencer said. The very idea of it was humiliating in the extreme. He could never go to the man he'd had impossible feelings for forever, and say, *oh by the way, I've been pretending for years to be someone else, to be someone that my teammates accept. Pretty please help me figure out who the person underneath all of that is?*

He already had plenty of Alec's pity, thank you very much.

"You want my help?" Chase's eyes gleamed. "Yes, you will."

Spencer stabbed his chicken over-enthusiastically with his plastic fork, imagining it was Chase's hard head he was spearing. "What's stopping me from telling you that I will, and then never doing it?"

Chase crossed his arms over his chest and grinned. "Your unimpeachable honor."

"You're counting a lot on something that you aren't even sure exists, considering that apparently I don't know who I am."

"I know *it* exists," Chase countered, and leaned forward, resting his elbows on the table. "In the Battle of LA three years ago, you helped Rashad to the sideline, when we didn't know he was hurting. You didn't have to do that."

"I'm pretty sure that I'm the one who rung his bell, so . . ." Spencer said wryly. "It would've been shit of me not to help the guy out."

"Do you think Shaughnessey would've done it? Or Graves?" Chase asked pointedly.

He knew they wouldn't have. Knew because at halftime, they'd given him crap about it. Just another way they thought he was a soft pussy. And other names that he chose not to remember.

"No," Spencer ground out.

"I know I'm right about you. I didn't like you at first, but . . . truthfully, you're growin' on me," Chase said. "Maybe I don't know everything, but I know enough to know changing teams is just a superficial fix. You're gonna be the same guy, underneath the uniform colors. And as someone who just went through this shit, I promise it's important. You need to do it."

"And you want me to ask Alec to help?" The embarrassment was already surging through Spencer. What if he said no? What if he turned him down flat? What if he didn't want to spend any more time with Spencer than he needed to, professionally?

Alec had already told him that once before and it had taken months for the sting of it to go away.

"Yes." Chase nodded enthusiastically. "It's a great idea."

"It's a fucking terrible idea," Spencer muttered back.

"But you're gonna do it," Chase stated.

Spencer glowered. "I'm gonna do it."

"Let's shake on it," Chase said, extending his hand.

"Fine," Spencer said, sighing as he took it and they shook hands briskly.

Chase stood. "I'll talk to him, and let you know the plan," he said. "Check your DMs and finish your food. Wouldn't want a good Basket lunch to go to waste."

CHAPTER THREE

SPENCER WOULD RATHER HAVE died than admit it to Chase, but he wasn't sure *how* to check his DMs.

But he also wasn't willing to leave anything to chance, so after his workout with June the next day, he looked it up on Google.

He also learned a whole bunch of verbiage that maybe if he was a normal, social gay guy, trolling for hookups and posting thirst traps, he might actually *use*, but if he'd ever had the inclination, the desire to be that person had been burned out by all the shit he'd been through over the years.

Now technically knowing how to go about it didn't make him want to do it—but it did help him understand the little red icon in the upper right-hand corner of his Instagram app the next morning.

Chase had sent a message. **Be here at 2 PM tomorrow**, the message read, **and be ready.** The address followed.

The very first thing he did was google the address.

It wasn't that Spencer didn't *trust* Chase. He trusted him just about as much as he trusted anybody, he supposed. He'd apologized and asked for his forgiveness, and Chase had given it. That was more than Spencer had gotten with some of his teammates over the last nine years.

It was the address for a shelter, specifically the headquarters of an organization that specialized in cat rescue. And tomorrow, Spencer read, they were having a charity event. There, right on their web page, was Chase's smiling face. He was the big draw at the event, apparently.

Spencer had no fucking clue how *cats* were supposed to convince Alec to listen to him.

He leaned back on the couch in his living room, staring at the charity web page on his phone, like the more he looked at it, the more sense it might make.

Finally, he gave up, and switched apps, back to Instagram.

I'll be there, he sent to Chase, **but I don't get it.**

Chase's response was almost immediate. **You allergic?**

To cats?

Yes, to cats. Spencer could practically *hear* the eye roll in Chase's words.

No, Spencer typed back, **but I'm still trying to figure out how this helps me.**

You will, was all Chase responded with.

Spencer tossed his phone on the cushion next to him in frustration. Maybe it had been a mistake agreeing to accept Chase's help. He was kind of a wild card, still, even though over the last two years, he'd become steadier and calmer, and the batshit antics had stopped entirely. Of course, Spencer wasn't sure yet if this crazy idea of him asking Alec to help him "discover himself" was Chase regressing.

But you trust him, a voice inside Spencer said. *That's why you agreed at all. Why you shook on it.*

It sounded suspiciously like Alec's.

And I trust him, which is the whole point, that voice added with amusement. *If he thinks I can help you, then I can.*

It was undeniable. No matter how Spencer felt about the wide receiver, he couldn't deny that Chase was close to Alec.

Might even know what made him tick better than Spencer himself.

After all, they'd never gone on that date.

Maybe if they had, Spencer might know why cats were instrumental to buttering Alec up.

•　•　•　●　•　●　•　●　•　•　•

The cat shelter was a short, squatty brick building about a mile from the food truck lot that Spencer had waited for Chase at.

It was not completely insane to think that this was how Chase had ended up doing work for them; as far as Spencer knew, Chase didn't even *have* a cat.

Spencer pulled into the nearly full parking lot and then nearly pulled back out again. He didn't usually show up at charity events. He sent checks, big checks typically, but the in-person thing was not his normal MO—but Chase? Spencer could see him being an active participant.

He parked next to Chase's ridiculous aqua blue car, and promised himself, as he took one last deep breath to brace himself, that if he did manage to get traded to the Riptide, *and* he found out who he was, deep down, he wouldn't start driving a turquoise car like Chase.

Black was perfectly fine, thank you very much.

He could do white.

Eighteen months ago, he'd even gone wild and bought the latest Ducati motorcycle, and specifically ordered the candy apple red version.

But aqua? No, thank you.

You're stalling now, that voice said with wry amusement. *Get your ass in gear.*

Spencer got out of the car. There was a gigantic balloon archway over the front door, all done up in various shades of blue, with a few white accents. Riptide colors.

If Spencer had thought he was at the wrong place, that would have set him straight immediately.

He approached the front door and a woman with auburn hair pulled back in a high ponytail greeted him. "Hey," she said, "you here for the adoption day?"

"Adoption day?"

"Yeah, we're having a special adoption day," she said, passing him a clipboard, and a pen. "If you're looking to adopt, you'll need to fill this out first."

"Oh good, you're here." Suddenly Chase was there, smiling widely like this was the greatest moment of his life. Like watching Spencer squirm at the thought of adopting a cat was even better than winning a Super Bowl.

You've never won a Super Bowl, you've never even played in one, that voice said dryly, *so maybe it is.*

"I'm here," Spencer said, and added in a lower voice, "But what the *hell* is going on? I'm not going to . . ."

"Yes, you are," Chase said, wide smile still in place. "You absolutely are. You said you weren't allergic."

"I'm *not*," Spencer retorted, "but that doesn't mean I want to adopt a cat!"

"You want Alec to listen to you? To think you're really serious about this?"

Spencer frowned. "Of course I do. You *know* I do."

"Then," Chase said, plucking the clipboard from the woman's hands and pushing it firmly into Spencer's chest, "you need to fill this out."

Spencer shot him a disbelieving look, but when the smile on Chase's face didn't waver even once, he finally decided that he might as well.

A cat might be nice, right? Sometimes he thought his house was a little big and lonely and quiet. He'd considered getting a dog, but with all the traveling he did during the season, he hadn't wanted to have people he didn't know coming into his house. He hadn't considered a cat.

But it appeared the time for consideration had passed.

"Fine," Spencer said, grabbing a pen from a cup on the table by the door. "I'll fill this out."

"Excellent," Chase said, rubbing his hands together. "I'll take you to the back as soon as you're done."

"The back?" Spencer asked absently as he scribbled down the answers to the questions on the form. They were fairly straight-forward: name, address, phone number, email address, emergency contact . . .

"Yeah, where the cats are," Chase said. "So you can meet them."

"Right," Spencer said, writing his aunt Pru down for the emergency contact. She lived in Ohio still, but she'd probably be thrilled to find out he was adopting an animal.

"You done?" Chase actually sounded *excited* about Spencer adopting a cat. Definitely more excited than Spencer was, that was for sure.

"Almost."

He was sure, on top of the form, that he would be writing a large check. He should have just told Chase that the large check was the beginning and the end of his involvement. He didn't need to actually *adopt* a cat.

And yet, there he was, handing the clipboard to the woman and following Chase down a narrow hallway. He could hear the cats now, if he listened hard, and when Chase led him through a doorway, into a big open room lined with cages, it was unmistakable.

So much meowing.

At least, his house would be a hell of a lot less quiet, anyway.

"Well?" Chase said, raising his arms. "You gonna meet all the little guys and girls?" He'd already walked over to one of the cages, where a calico kitten was fully outstretched, trying to climb the front of the cage.

Spencer watched as Chase stuck a finger between the bars of the cage, the kitten immediately latching on to it instead. "See," Chase said softly, "they just want a little attention."

"This why you brought me here? Thought you could work on Alec's heartstrings?" Spencer approached the cages on the other side of the room. Not all the cats in them were kittens, like the one Chase was playing with, some of them were older.

"Something like that," Chase said.

Spencer scanned the cages, not sure what he was supposed to do, or how he was supposed to do it.

"Feel free to meet any kitten you like," Chase said. "You can open the doors, too. Hold them. Though I often find that the cat chooses the owner."

"You have one of these?" Spencer asked, raising an eyebrow.

"Three," Chase said.

"I didn't realize you were such a devoted pet owner."

"It's Rachel, my boyfriend's sister. She's a big volunteer here, with her girlfriend. And I started coming with them, sometimes, and I got hooked. I shouldn't keep adopting them but well . . . I'm sure your house is pretty empty too, right?"

Spencer nodded. He had noticed a cage at the very bottom of the stack, with only a single cat in it. Black, with fur dark as the night, and as he crouched down closer, he noticed the cat was missing an eye. From the neat line of stitching where it had been, Spencer could tell the cat hadn't been born that way; the eye had definitely been removed.

"What's this guy's story?" Spencer wondered, before he could stop himself.

"Bad eye infection when they caught him," Chase said, coming to stand near Spencer. "His name's Ignatius."

"Ignatius?" Spencer raised an eyebrow. "For a cat?"

But the way Ignatius was looking at him, through just the one eye, solemn and yet mischievous, Spencer thought the name actually suited him.

"We've got to be careful about the black ones, too, and people don't always want them," Chase explained. "And then there's the eye."

"You mean, people don't want to adopt him because he's black and he's missing an eye?" Spencer shouldn't have been shocked, because it wasn't like people didn't shy away from *him*, just because of who he wanted to love, who he wanted in his bed, but it affected him more than he wanted to admit to that they'd rejected this poor cat for similar reasons.

For reasons neither of them could prevent.

Spencer opened the cage, and Ignatius leaned out, sniffing his finger cautiously, and then, all of a sudden, he rubbed against it, pressing his whole head against Spencer's hand, and that was it.

He knew he was going to bring this cat home.

• • • ● • ● • ● • • •

The last thing Alec expected to see when he walked into the cat shelter was Spencer Evans with a long, lean black cat draped across his shoulders, and the brightest smile he'd ever seen on his face.

He turned to the man next to him. "Do you really think I'm that easy?"

Chase grinned. "Aren't you?"

"No," Alec said with a scowl. "Not even remotely."

Except he was, and obviously Chase knew it, though *how* he knew it was unclear.

Though, Alec supposed that he had to give Spencer at least a *little* bit of credit. He hadn't just taken his rejection and gone to lick his wounds. Instead, he'd sought out the one person who had plenty of reasons to also turn him away, and had actually convinced him to help.

That was the thing about Spencer though. He was dogged, determined, and irresistibly charming, when he chose to be.

Alec watched as the black cat rubbed his face against Spencer's face and he laughed, clearly delighted with the animal. He couldn't remember ever seeing Spencer so happy, except maybe on the football field.

He felt his resolve waver.

Which was, no doubt, why Chase had picked this specific venue for them to run into each other again.

"Come meet Spence's new kitten," Chase said encouragingly. "His name is Ignatius and he only has one eye."

Spencer glanced up and for a moment, when their gazes met, he felt the surge of attraction and also, inevitably, the clang of warning bells.

"He only needs one eye," Spencer said staunchly. "He's better with one eye than you are with two."

"Spencer, imagine running into you here," Alec said dryly, reaching down and giving Ignatius' dark head a quick rub. That was as close as he was physically getting to Spencer today—or anytime in the near future. "I'm shocked and surprised."

Chase grinned unrepentantly. "I'm just recruiting other people to help spread the word."

"What you really mean," Alec said, "is that you're at maximum cat capacity in your house, and you need to find other people to adopt all these animals."

"Listen, my house is huge. I'm not even *close* to maximum cat capacity," Chase said.

"Okay, then what about Tate? Surely he doesn't want to share you with a horde of furry creatures?"

"Let me guess," Spencer said, rising to his feet, "you don't have a cat."

"He doesn't, despite all my attempts to convince him," Chase chimed in.

"I travel a lot," Alec said. "No time for an animal." He turned to Chase. "Don't worry, I'll write a big check."

"I wasn't worried about that," Chase said. "You're always generous. But these guys need homes. Not checks."

Alec ignored the pulse of guilt that resonated through him. It wasn't like he didn't agree with what Chase was saying—or what he was doing. But a cat? What would he even do with a cat?

Of course, he had a feeling that Spencer's thoughts had run a very similar direction from the moment Chase had suggested it, and yet here he was, tucking Ignatius under his arm, just like a football.

"We both know that Spencer isn't here for himself, so we'll say I'm responsible for Ignatius' adoption," Alec said.

"You should at least cuddle with some of them," Chase said. Shooting him a reproachful look. "They need love, too, and so do you."

Alec wasn't dim enough to miss the way Spencer's eyes slid away from his own at Chase's suggestion.

Did he need love?

Alec didn't know. He'd lived without it for a long time now, and it wasn't like he was unhappy with his life. When he'd quit halfway through his first year as an associate at one of the most prestigious law firms in Boston, he'd had very specific goals, and he'd accomplished all of them. There was satisfaction and a kind of happiness in that.

And he had friends. People he cared about, who cared about him.

That had always been enough.

Except when you run into Spencer Evans, and then you spend way too much time thinking of what could have been.

"Fine," Alec said, and approached a cage full of mewling kittens. He opened the door, intending to pluck one out, and let it get its white hair all over his gray suit, but instead he ended up with three. He settled down with them in the chair in the corner, letting them climb all over. The rest of his day was free, no meetings, and if he ended up covered in cat hair, it wouldn't be the end of the world.

Alec could feel Spencer watching him, even as he sat down on the floor with Ignatius. Chase disappeared out of the door, predictably leaving the two of them alone.

"You surprised me," Alec finally said, as a set of needle-edged claws picked its way up his leg. No doubt leaving tiny pinpricks in the expensive fabric. He plucked the white kitten off and settled it on his chest. It purred loudly as Alec scratched it under the chin, the sound louder than he could've expected to come from such a small creature.

"Me adopting a cat?" Spencer asked, obviously to keep up the facade that he'd come here to do that, and not to convince Alec to change his mind.

Alec shook his head. "You must have constructed some kind of apology, to get Chase to help you."

"Actually . . . not really," Spencer admitted. "I just asked. Told him what I wanted."

Alec sighed. "Sounds like Chase. The man doesn't hold a grudge."

"He doesn't seem to."

"I guess you're lucky that way," Alec said.

"The only way I'm going to be lucky is if Chase's help gets me what I want." Spencer's gaze was dark and intense. "I want to change. I want you to help me make that change."

"There's other agents I could . . ."

"No, it has to be you," Spencer said firmly.

"You know why it's a bad idea for it to be me," Alec said. "I'm not sure I can be . . . as objective as you need me to be."

Alec plucked a cat off his shoulder and set it on his knee, flinching as it kneaded its paws into the fabric of his pants. He'd given up on this suit; he should've known better than to wear one of his favorites to the cat shelter.

When he glanced over at Spencer, his gaze burned him. "I don't want you to be objective," he said. "I'm counting on you not being objective at all."

"You're really not going to give this up, are you?" Alec said, beginning to be resigned. Surely he could manage to shove Spencer into the "client" box? It wasn't like anything had ever happened between them, no matter how much he'd wished it would. How hard would it be to just shove all those feelings he already pretended didn't exist into a deep place where he didn't ever think about them?

If it meant that Spencer could keep smiling like he was right now, as he played with Ignatius, then it would be worth it.

"No," Spencer said. "What gave it away?"

Alec rolled his eyes. "Okay, we'll talk about it."

Spencer smiled, slow and sure, and it was a heady feeling, that it was *him* that had done that. "Talk about it?"

"There's . . . issues," Alec said. "We need to go over the parameters. What I think I can do for you, compared to what you want me to do. It might . . . it might not be a good fit."

"It's gonna be a perfect fit," Spencer said, and Alec couldn't help himself. He wanted to know just how flawless it really was; he'd *always* wanted to know what it would feel like to have Spencer wrapped around him.

It turned out it was going to be tougher than he'd imagined to dismiss those thoughts.

"I'm not as confident as you. Why don't we set up a meeting for next week to discuss it further," Alec suggested.

Spencer frowned. "Next week? I didn't think you'd want to wait that long."

"You do realize that I've got other clients," Alec said. And most of them didn't ever quibble when Alec said something. They sat back and let him do his thing, but it was already clear that Spencer was not going to be that kind of client.

"Then fit me in for dinner," Spencer said, and he grinned, wild around the edges, like he was remembering their aborted bet from the Super Bowl a few years back. "Surely you've got to eat."

"I guess I could." Alec was rapidly mentally scrolling through the restaurants he liked to go to, at least the ones that would seem less *date*-like. With another client, he'd never worry about that, but with Spencer? It was going to be a problem. "We could . . ."

"I'll handle the arrangements," Spencer said. "Don't worry about it. Monday? At seven?"

Alec opened his mouth and then snapped it shut again. He hadn't expected Spencer to take this kind of initiative, and all he could do was nod in agreement. "Let me check my phone, but I think my schedule's clear."

"Good," Spencer said with a sharp nod. "I'll text you the details."

Of course he would. And just the act of getting a text from Spencer, again, after all this time, would inevitably make him think of all those other texts. The quasi-flirtatious ones, when they'd discuss Alec's appearances on *Good Morning Football* and dozens of other things. When Spencer would say something like, *you should wear that tie more often, makes your eyes look amazing,* and Alec would float around on cloud nine for a week, even though he already knew nothing was going to happen.

But the compliment was all it took.

After the Super Bowl, when Alec had shut down the idea of a single date, Spencer had stopped responding to Alec's texts, and after a few overtures that hadn't gone anywhere, Alec had given up.

It had hurt more than he'd imagined it would, losing that last tie to Spencer, but he'd gotten over it, eventually. But now? Spencer was the one reaching out, and truthfully, Alec was helpless to resist.

He'd wanted more for so long. Spencer as a friend. Spencer on a team that actually appreciated him. Spencer losing his bone-deep fear of being queer. Spencer *happy*.

It's going to be worth it, that would be worth anything, especially if it's you that makes it happen.

"You gonna adopt one of those?"

Chase was back with another group, who were currently cooing and giggling over the kitten cuteness, and he'd directed his question towards him.

It was not a huge stretch. After all, he did have three kittens currently making holes all over his custom suit.

"Not today," Alec said, and to his own surprise, he sounded rather reluctant about it. Maybe he should consider what Chase was suggesting. Marie, his housekeeper, could always care for the animal when he was out of town . . .

He gathered all the kittens up on one arm, and returned them to the cage before he changed his mind about anything else.

He'd let Spencer back in.

That was enough for now.

SEVEN YEARS AGO

THE AIR WAS STILL hot and sticky, even though the sun had gone down hours earlier. Alec pressed his bottle of Corona, still cold-ish, against the side of his neck.

The beach was full of players and their partners, other agents like him, and plenty of NFL officials, making sure that the big luau celebrating the end of Pro Bowl week didn't get too rowdy and out of hand.

Alec hadn't wanted to come to Hawaii, even though once he'd been invited, he knew he should. Still, despite his reservations, it had been a good week. He'd spent most of it talking and schmoozing potential clients, his least favorite part of the job, but it had paid off, because he had tentative agreements from three current players, and promises from several others.

And, with careful planning and execution, he'd avoided Spencer Evans.

Spencer, if he'd thought about it at all, was probably relieved. Probably assumed it was because Alec didn't like him. Probably believed that Alec wasn't interested in a guy who, despite being out of the closet, spent an unbelievable amount of time and energy proving he was the toughest guy on the field. Proving he was the *straightest* gay guy in the world.

It wasn't like Alec didn't know why. He'd heard the rumors about the Stars locker room and its toxicity, and how the coaching staff and ownership actually believed that it made their players better on the field.

When he let it, it broke his heart that Spencer had all his worst beliefs reinforced by the team he'd been drafted to.

If he'd gone someplace else, Alec wanted to believe that Spencer would have eventually changed his mind. But now? There was no hope for it.

It would be so much easier if he could treat Spencer as just another player, just another guy in the NFL who needed representation, but from the very beginning, Spencer had always been more than that to Alec, and in the last three years, nothing had changed.

So instead of becoming casual, friendly acquaintances who didn't care about each other, Alec avoided him.

He'd originally planned to not attend the luau tonight, because Spencer was certain to be here, especially considering this was his first Pro Bowl invite.

Yet he'd come anyway. Alec sighed. He'd even caught himself scanning the crowds more than once, looking for that all-too-familiar head of dark hair. Spencer was easy to spot in a crowd, because he was so tall, but Alec hadn't seen him yet.

Maybe he hadn't come after all.

He was definitely *here*, in Hawaii, because Alec had seen him from a distance a handful of times over the last few days, and had watched him play in the actual Pro Bowl.

Making one last quick scan, trying not to be too obvious that he was searching for someone in particular, Alec turned and nearly walked right into Heath Harris.

"Hey, it's Alec, right?" Heath said.

Alec could still hear the remnants of Heath's Texas drawl in the edge of his voice even though he'd been in California for years now.

Like Spencer, this was his first Pro Bowl.

Unlike Spencer, Alec didn't know much about Heath.

"Yeah, Alec Mitchell," Alec said, extending his hand, and they shook briefly. Heath had a good grip, a strong handshake and a way of looking a man in the eye that Alec appreciated.

There were some outdated assholes who continued to look down on him, didn't want to shake his hand, didn't want to touch him at all, like that would mean they'd been infected with his gayness or some other stupid bullshit.

It wasn't that he didn't know exactly what Spencer had been talking about three years ago, on that night of the draft. He knew. He'd seen it, firsthand. He simply believed there was hope in spite of the persistent pockets of ignorance and homophobia.

"Good to meet you. Sorry to nearly run you over." Heath chuckled self-deprecatingly.

Alec looked him over. He looked uneasy, holding himself tightly, when everyone else on the beach was obviously relaxed and having a good time.

"No harm, no foul," Alec said. "Enjoying the festivities?"

It was impossible to miss the flash of unease in his expression. And then there was the way his fingers were clamped, white-knuckled, around the bottle in his hand. He was not enjoying the festivities.

"Oh yeah," Heath said, clearly lying. "It's been great."

Heath had been drafted during Alec's first year as an agent, and he'd been in massive demand, a dozen or more agents vying for his attention and his signature on the bottom line of their contracts. That was usually how it went with quarterbacks.

Alec hadn't even bothered approaching him. Heath wasn't the kind of player he was looking for anyway—back then, anyway, and honestly, not much had changed. It wasn't as if he *only* represented the guys in the NFL who wanted to come out or who had already come out. If he restricted himself to that list, it was going to be small. But those were the ones Alec tried to focus on.

He'd never heard even the tiniest hint that Heath Harris was queer. In fact, once Alec thought about it, he'd heard almost no rumors about him at all. Women *or* men.

Now that he considered it, that *was* interesting.

"Glad to hear it," Alec said. He couldn't help but feel sorry for the guy. Heath was clearly not comfortable in social situations, and unfortunately for him, it often felt like the NFL was one big, long social situation.

"Neal said you were great," Heath said, awkwardly changing the subject. "Neal Fisher?"

Right, how could Alec have forgotten? If he hadn't been so annoyingly preoccupied with Spencer, he would have immediately made the connection that Heath and one of his favorite clients, Neal Fisher, both played for the Los Angeles Riptide.

"Neal's the best, isn't he?" Alec said. He hadn't heard a whiff of a rumor about Heath Harris, and he certainly hadn't heard anything about Harris looking for new representation, but maybe Neal could put in a good word.

Neal wasn't exactly out of the closet yet—but he wasn't hiding either, which at this point, Alec was taking as a win.

"He is," Heath agreed, and his face relaxed just a fraction. "Great kicker, too."

"Well," Alec said, "if you ever want to talk about what I've done for Neal, and what I could do for you, too, just let me know."

Heath looked surprised. "No hard sell?"

"I'm not that kind of agent," Alec said wryly. "I'm sure Neal's mentioned that to you."

"A handful of times, yeah," Heath admitted. He hesitated. "Well, I'll think about it. I'm glad I ran into you."

It sounded like he actually meant it, and when he walked off, Alec swore he saw a hint of a smile on his solemn face.

If he could actually *get* Heath Harris as a client, and maybe also figure out a little of why he always looked so sad and uncomfortable, maybe . . .

Alec was so busy planning his conversation with Neal, and formulating a strategy for convincing Heath that what he really needed was a new agent, that he almost missed that he'd managed to pace all the way down the beach. He'd ended up in a quieter area, with only a few people hanging out in pockets here and there.

He looked up and there was the last person he'd expected to see.

Spencer *was* at the party. Technically, Alec supposed, if a piece of driftwood all the way down the beach still counted as the party.

Their eyes met, and Alec felt that same jolt of electricity he'd felt that first time, when he'd approached Spencer at the draft, thinking that they'd just exchange a few friendly words. That he'd just say hello. Introduce himself. Except it had been so much more than that. The fascination that Spencer Evans had held for Alec before that moment—all the time he'd spent reviewing his history, watching the footage of his playing time at Ohio State and then at the combine, and finally his frustration when his careful overtures had gone unanswered—had blossomed into something unexpected.

He'd never imagined that all that time, what he'd felt was not only respect and admiration for a great football player, but *attraction.*

Because he'd definitely felt it, that night of the draft.

When he'd leaned in, hoping to keep their voices low and their conversation private, it'd hit him like a sledgehammer, shattering all his good sense and all the promises he'd made himself that he wouldn't ever get involved with a player.

But then, he'd never been attracted to one before.

Unlike the way some assumed that a gay man working as an agent in the NFL would be like a kid in a candy store, Alec had always prided himself on his professionalism and self-control.

If he'd wanted to be taken seriously, he hadn't had any other choice.

But Spencer Evans made him want to throw all his rules away, with both hands.

"Hey," Alec said, after the silence had stretched out too tightly between them. "Not interested in hanging out at the party?"

He knew they were both thinking of that night at the draft. Maybe Spencer was embarrassed. Maybe he was even angry that he'd run into Alec again. They hadn't exactly parted well, and they hadn't spoken since.

"Not particularly," Spencer said.

It wasn't precisely an invitation, but then Spencer hadn't told him to fuck off either, so Alec threw away the rest of his good sense, and went and sat down next to Spencer on the driftwood log, careful to leave at least a few inches between them.

He didn't know if Spencer was attracted to him too, but he wasn't going to make any assumptions. And even if the attraction was mutual, it wasn't like Alec was going to let anything happen.

He just wanted to talk. That was all.

"Any reason why not?"

Spencer shot him a disbelieving look. Like he couldn't believe that Alec would have to ask.

Alec let his gaze drift over Spencer's body. He was an undeniable force, with thick thighs and thick arms, and a defined chest that he could barely make out through the fabric of his clothes. He was wearing a pair of blue and white striped board shorts with a plain red t-shirt—not something with the Stars logo on it, but the color was similar enough to the rest of the team merchandise that unless you were looking for the logo, you wouldn't notice it was missing.

But Alec noticed, because he was looking for it, and because he suspected the reason Spencer wasn't enjoying the party was related to the fact that he'd chosen not to wear something with his team's logo.

"You should be with your team," Alec said gently, "or meeting some of the other guys."

"Yeah," Spencer scoffed. "The game's over. Not sure what use I'd be to them now."

That was the clear flaw in Spencer's plan to keep his head down and just play football. When the games were over, he believed he was irrelevant.

Maybe the others treated him that way. Maybe they didn't, and the negativity was all in Spencer's head. Alec didn't know. He didn't have any clients in the LA Stars locker room, but he had a feeling that wasn't coincidental. He'd heard . . . things. Every time one of those ugly rumors cropped up, he always thought about Spencer, so determined three years earlier to be seen not as a gay football player, but just a football player.

"Listen, there are plenty of decent people here," Alec said. "I'd be happy to introduce you to some of them."

He glanced over, and Spencer was gazing at him, intently. "No, thank you," he said quietly. "I'm fine, right here."

"Are you . . ."

But before Alec could finish asking his question, Spencer interrupted him, finishing it for him. "Am I sure?" The corner of his mouth tilted up into half a smile. "You're not a decent person, then?"

Was Spencer saying what he thought he was? That he wanted Alec to stay here, and hang out with him? Alec thought he might be.

"Well, yes, I like to think so. And . . . thanks." Alec found himself smiling back.

"I should apologize for how shitty I was at the draft," Spencer said after a long moment. "I *am* sorry."

"Apology accepted. But you still don't think I'm right," Alec guessed.

"I don't know," Spencer said, shrugging. "I want you to be right. But my experience? It sucks to be gay and playing football. I'm not sure that's ever going to change."

"I'm still working on it." Alec couldn't help the guilt he felt. He'd always known he couldn't change opinions and attitudes overnight, but he'd hoped anyway that Spencer wouldn't end up experiencing the rotten end of the spectrum.

"I know," Spencer said, in a way that made it obvious that he'd been following everything that Alec had been doing.

"You're only a year or two away from your rookie contract ending, you could go to a different team."

"I could," Spencer said. "But would I be the player I am today without the team I'm on? The coaching staff? I don't know. I'm not sure I'm willing to find out. As shitty as they can be, they pushed me to be the best. And that's all I ever wanted to be. The *best*."

"Oh." Alec shouldn't feel that twinge of disappointment. He wasn't responsible for Spencer's choices. Yes, the Stars were exceptional on the defensive side of the ball. But was it worth *this*?

"Don't feel sorry for me," Spencer said. "I chose this."

"You didn't choose the Stars; they picked *you*," Alec pointed out.

"Yeah, but it's my choice to stay. To keep playing." He gestured around. "And look where I ended up."

Alec knew he couldn't argue with the results. In three years, Spencer had gone from an exceptional talent with a lot of upside to one of the most dominant defensive ends in the National Football League. But he sure as hell could argue with the method.

"I really am glad you got where you wanted to be." Alec meant every single word.

"You know," Spencer said, that half-smile emerging again, "I kinda think you *are*."

"You had the talent. If you only knew how much I watched your college footage tape," Alec said wryly.

Spencer stretched his feet out, pushing sand as he went. "Really?"

"Really." Alec didn't know why he'd made that particular confession, but he hoped that Spencer wouldn't ask him why.

Of course, at the time he thought he was doing it because he wanted to be Spencer's agent. It was only later, when they'd actually met in person, that he'd realized the other reason why he hadn't been able to stop.

Why he *still* wasn't able to stop.

In weak moments, he still occasionally watched it. He wasn't proud, but he hadn't been able to help himself. There was something about that dominant, powerful frame and the way it ran over men almost as big like they didn't exist. A singlemindedness that shouldn't have been such a turn-on, but *was*.

Alec glanced down. Even in the darker end of the beach, with the sun setting hours earlier, he could still see the powerful muscles of Spencer's thighs, outlined in the striped material of his shorts. He swallowed, hard. Definitely turned on. Not wanting to be. Afraid that Spencer didn't feel the same. Even more afraid that he *did*.

"I'd ask you why," Spencer said, his voice somehow dropping impossibly lower, to a register that Alec felt in his fucking gut, "but I think it's probably the same reason why I started watching *Good Morning Football* every day."

Alec's fingers dug into his own thigh. He hadn't expected Spencer to start watching the one television program he appeared on on a semi-frequent basis. Even if he had, he certainly hadn't expected Spencer to confess that particular fact.

"I could send you a schedule so you're not forced to watch every single episode?"

Alec won a full-blown smile this time. It made him breathless. Spencer Evans was a handsome man, at any place, any time, but like this? He was breathtaking.

"That's what DVR is for," he teased. "But sure, if you wanna give me a heads-up you're gonna be on, I wouldn't exactly be complaining."

Alec swore that Spencer swayed nearer, their shoulders almost brushing. Had they somehow grown closer over the last ten minutes? He wasn't sure, but it felt like they had. He could feel the heat of the man next to him, burning like a brand, right through the cotton of his designer polo.

"If I had your number, I could," Alec said.

Spencer looked amused. "Is that what you'd use it for?"

God, Alec wanted to use it for all kinds of things.

He'd vowed he'd never do this. But what could the harm be? Spencer was never going to be a client. He'd made that clear enough. Alec found himself weakening on the one stance that he'd sworn he'd never budge on, and why?

Because Spencer was hot, and here, and obviously interested. And even more, Alec was tired of pretending that he didn't want him.

"It depends," Alec said.

He felt Spencer's fingers brush his on the log, warm and sure and calloused. "On what?"

Alec could stand up right now and suggest that they go to his room. It wasn't very far away. They'd be in private, and could do anything they wanted and nobody would ever be the wiser.

What was stopping him?

The remnants of honor? Some displaced sense of romanticism that believed, despite all the evidence Alec had heard—or not heard—of Spencer's hookup habits, that he deserved someone who wasn't just going to fuck him in a dark, impersonal hotel room and leave the next morning?

Alec realized suddenly that he didn't want that dirty, impersonal fucking.

Whatever happened with Spencer—and he was beginning to think that nothing could—it was going to be personal. One hundred percent committed and personal.

The problem was, that wasn't how Alec usually handled his business. When he needed sex, he found it, and then he moved on. He assumed that Spencer dealt with his own urges the same way.

Except he'd never heard once of a boyfriend, or even a regular hookup partner, or even a friends-with-benefits arrangement. His shit, whatever it was, was locked down tight, even though it didn't need to be.

Spencer was out. He could parade a hundred guys around if he wanted to. But he didn't. Alec knew he wouldn't, because that was the choice he'd made. And while Alec had his own set of hookup rules, they weren't in place because he was terrified of anyone figuring out that he *actually* liked men. Liked fucking them, being fucked, the whole nine yards.

What did Spencer like? Alec doubted he even knew. He'd never given himself a chance to find out.

"It depends on what this is," Alec said, kicking himself the whole time.

He'd thought this could just be sex. It could never just be sex. His feelings were already involved; he already knew that much. Should have realized it way earlier than this moment, but he hadn't.

Why couldn't he just take the good things that came and let go of the rest?

"You know," Spencer said casually, like they weren't indulging in a conversation that resembled a whole freaking minefield, "the first time we met, I thought you were the hottest guy I'd ever seen."

Alec smiled. It would be so easy to just lean over, to find out how good Spencer Evans tasted.

You want to, you've wanted to since you saw him the first time. His picture, on your news feed, right after he came out of the closet.

You wanted to even more, when you met him and he told you that you were living in a fairy-tale world.

He still wanted it. More than anything in the world.

But it was hard enough, a fucking uphill climb, to be a queer agent in the NFL. He was barely accepted. Scraping by, some of his clients still nervous that associating with him would brand them as queer, too.

This thing with Spencer, it wasn't going to just be sex. And that meant it would be something more. Like a relationship. Alec already knew there was no way he could ever, not in a million years, get involved with a player. The tentative connections he'd begun to forge would drop, instantly.

He'd become persona non grata.

"That's me, such a Prince Charming," Alec said wryly.

For a moment, Spencer looked confused, but then Alec watched as he remembered the memory. "Just because I thought you were wrong, doesn't mean you didn't make my palms sweat."

"Three years older, do I still do it for you?"

Spencer eyed him up and down, his dark eyes intense and focused. Like he was sizing up an opponent. A quarterback he was about to smash. Or a man he desperately wanted to fuck.

"Yes." His voice was low and dark and belonged somewhere a lot more private than this very public beach full of football players.

It was the feelings. All those fucking feelings.

Alec was disgusted with himself.

But somehow the regret felt even worse.

"You'd fuck me but you don't want to talk to me," Alec said before he could change his mind. Could try to figure out how to make this work, anyway.

"No?" Spencer looked puzzled now. Like he couldn't quite figure out how they'd gone from that to this.

That makes two of us.

"I'm talking to you right now," Spencer continued, an edge of hurt in his voice. Alec could hear it and he hated himself.

"But you shouldn't be," Alec said, and stood up.

And that, Alec thought with a resigned sigh, was why he was going to be spending tonight alone, in his impersonal hotel room, with only his right hand and his imagination for company.

Spencer looked eager for a second, but then he must have seen the resignation on Alec's face, because his expression changed. Closed right up, but not before Alec could spy another flash of pain in his eyes.

It was the same emotion he'd seen three years earlier.

This was why he'd avoided Spencer Evans. No good could come from them being friendly—or wishing for things they couldn't have.

"Where are you going?" Spencer stood too, and Alec could see his fingers twitch, like he wanted to reach for him, desperately. For a second, an almost blissful second, Alec imagined Spencer stopping him the way he really wanted to be stopped.

With a kiss. With a steamy, heart-stopping, ro-mantic-as-all-hell, line-drawn-in-the-sand, both literally and metaphorically, kiss.

But he didn't, because he was Spencer Evans, and in the end, Alec was actually glad, because it would have been an epic mistake.

"I'm going back to my room," Alec said. "Alone."

Spencer frowned. "What? Why?"

"Because this is a bad idea." But because he couldn't just leave well enough alone, Alec reached for him, plucking his phone right out of his pocket. For a split second, he felt the slippery board short material, warmed by Spencer's body, and he nearly changed his mind. The way Spencer's eyes darkened and he leaned into the touch made it even harder. But Alec was one of those people who once they made a decision, didn't often reconsider.

But he was willing to do this one thing. He pointed the phone at Spencer's face and it unlocked. Pulling up the texting app, he ignored every other message and typed one of his own. To himself. So that going forward, Spencer would have his phone number, and he would have Spencer's.

If, for example, he wanted to let him know that he'd be on *Good Morning Football*.

Finished with the text, he sent it, and offered the phone back to Spencer.

"That's not usually why men go digging in my pocket," Spencer said.

He'd matured in the three years since the NFL Draft. He'd been terrified and unsure back then, and Alec wasn't sure he was really *less* of those things now, but he'd found some confidence. At least in this.

Maybe Alec still made his palms sweat, but he'd learned to flirt, and he could do it well enough that *Alec's* palms were sweating.

Or maybe that was just the sweltering heat of Hawaii.

Except Alec knew it wasn't. It was all those possibilities. Hazy, future possibilities. Impossible possibilities, but impossible or not, they were still mesmerizing.

"I bet not," Alec said.

"Why?" Spencer wanted to know.

It was a question that could have meant so many things. Alec wasn't quite sure he knew which question Spencer was really asking. Maybe Spencer didn't even know.

But there was only one answer Alec was truly willing to give.

"Because you should never rely just on your DVR for *Good Morning Football*," he said, and turned and walked away.

Chapter Four

"You look awfully fancy for breakfast," Neal said, gesturing towards Alec's three-piece suit as the waitress poured coffee for both of them.

"I always look like this," Alec argued, even though that wasn't technically true.

He had a full day of meetings, starting with his breakfast with Neal, and ending with the dinner he'd be sharing with Spencer, and he'd wanted to make sure he not only looked good, but that he looked legitimate. *Professional. Untouchable.*

As a result, he'd spent a good twenty minutes in his walk-in closet, debating which suit, which shirt, which tie, until he'd almost been late.

"No, you don't," Neal said, leaning back, smiling. "You've got something up your sleeve. I know you do."

Neal was an observant guy, but there was no way Alec's suit choice this morning was enough to tip him off.

"Chase talked to you," Alec said, flattening his palm against the menu sitting on the vinyl tabletop. Neal liked this old-fashioned diner for breakfast, and because Neal was a client *and* a friend, Alec tolerated its idiosyncrasies.

"He might've," Neal confessed. "But you representing Spencer Evans is big news."

"It isn't official yet." Alec stirred a spare teaspoon of sugar into his coffee. Wished he had something a hell of a lot stronger. He should've guessed that Chase would tell everyone, especially considering that he was close friends with many of the other current and ex-players he represented.

"Why not?" Neal looked more interested in this conversation than Alec felt comfortable with. "This is a *big deal*. This is Spencer Evans who . . ."

Alec did not want to hear a recitation of all the things Spencer had done and said over the years—everything he could fix that would undeniably make him a feather-in-the-cap kind of client—and held up his hand. "No, please, I beg you. *Stop.*"

"You've always been weird about Evans, but this is a new level of weird."

"Did I interfere when you started dating Jamie?" As soon as the sentence was out of his mouth, Alec realized he'd made a major misstep. Spencer was going to be a *client*. He wasn't going to be dating him. And comparing their situation to Neal and Jamie, who were head over heels, madly in love with each other was not only massively inaccurate, it would give Neal totally the wrong impression.

Or the right one, his conscience added slyly.

"Not anything we can specifically count as *interference*," Neal said, a slow smile emerging across his face, "and what does me dating Jamie have to do with you signing Evans as a client?"

"Nothing," Alec said brusquely. Wishing fervently that the waitress would come back so they could order and Neal's train of thought could hopefully be permanently derailed.

"Hey, *you* brought it up," Neal said. "You said it was like me and Jamie. Which, for the record, only makes me think something else is going on between you two. Is there something else?"

"No," Alec said. It was the truth, but he still felt guilty because Neal was his friend. Maybe he should have confessed long ago that Spencer Evans did it for him, in every way that mattered, even when he hated how Spencer had chosen to live his life. But he hadn't said anything, because Neal was also a client, and he'd tried to keep a firmly professional line between them. But over time, despite all his good intentions, the line had faded, especially once Alec had started gaining other members of Neal's circle as clients.

First there'd been Chase. Then Rashad Green, the running back for the Riptide. And finally, what he'd always thought would be the crowning achievement of his career as a queer agent: Heath Harris. Even retired, Heath was a major accomplishment. He hoped, with time, he might even be able to win over Sam Crawford, Heath's boyfriend and the current quarterback for the Riptide.

Spencer had been one hundred and ten percent right when he said that Alec had a good in with the Los Angeles Riptide.

"Well, you can't blame me for asking," Neal said. "You're so weird about him. Always have been."

"I am not *weird* about him." Except Alec knew he was. There was the undeniable attraction. The way they'd circled each other over the years, almost-but-never-quite doing anything. Then there was the way the stuff that Spencer did bothered him more than it should. The uber-masculine, uber-tough-guy shit Alec *knew* wasn't who Spencer was.

And why was that? Oh, that's right. Because Alec had to be stupid enough to go and get himself feelings.

"I . . ." Alec sighed. Neal was a friend. Undeniably. And also undeniably, it turned out that Alec was in the right mood to confess. "We've known each other since he came out, nine years ago. Almost ten, now. But . . ."

"But," Neal prompted. Alec would have to be a lot blinder to miss the gleam in his friend's eye.

"But it wasn't ever going to work out. It wasn't ever going to be just a few hookups."

"Oh?" Neal looked intrigued. "Why not?"

Alec glowered at him. "You know why not."

"Oh, so you've got feelings. For Spencer Evans." Neal looked contemplative now. "Huh. I wouldn't have guessed."

"Well, that's exactly the point of it," Alec said. "You weren't supposed to."

"And what does Spencer have? He feel the same?"

Alec shrugged. He didn't know; rather, he'd never asked. Only because that way lay disaster. If he thought about it—and he rarely let himself go there—he'd probably guess that Spencer felt the same way he did.

But Spencer, despite his bitterness about football and queerness, had always been a little naïve. Had he realized that Alec could never date a player?

Alec honestly wasn't sure, but there it was.

He couldn't do it, not in his job, not with the kind of connections he'd formed, and that had always stopped him. Well, not really stopped him, because he'd slipped up enough times, desire overwhelming even his good sense, but he'd always held back, in the end.

"So you've never told him," Neal guessed.

"About the feelings? No, of course not."

Neal rolled his eyes. "Of course not. You're not very good at this, you know."

"Not very . . ." Alec gaped at his friend in shock.

"You," Neal pointed to him, "need to tell him."

"It's not a good time, we've got this deal . . .I don't want to . . ." Alec glared at Neal, feeling exasperated. "You know how it is in the NFL. I start dating a player, I lose my credibility."

"Ten years ago, maybe," Neal admitted. "But not now."

"You're wrong," Alec said. He wanted Neal to be right, but honestly, Neal could be naïve in his own way.

"I think . . .I think you've forgotten how far we've come in this," Neal said softly. "I think you should tell him. Stop pushing him away . . ."

Alec opened his mouth, to argue reflexively. He hadn't been pushing Spencer away . . .

Or had he?

Maybe it was self-preservation, but he had.

He knew he had.

"I'm busy," Alec said. "I'm trying to get this goddamned deal done."

"Are you really going to get him traded to the Riptide?" Neal seemed fine with changing the subject. Like he knew he'd gotten all he was going to out of Alec about this.

Frankly, Alec was astonished he'd gotten that much out of him. He usually didn't share, even with friends.

"That's what he wants."

Neal tapped his fingertips on the table. "You really think that's a good idea?"

"I don't think it's a *bad* idea. The guy's spent nine years on a team that turned him inside out, trying to be someone that he isn't. Shouldn't he have a chance to be accepted by his teammates?" Alec arched a brow. "Like *you* and Jamie and Sam and Heath were accepted? Like Chase was accepted?"

But Alec could tell Neal wasn't quite convinced. "You really think Heath's going to be okay with this? After Evans pulled that stupid bullshit with Chase?"

"Chase is *helping* him," Alec pointed out.

"Yeah, but Chase doesn't even know how to hold a grudge. You know that. On the other hand . . ."

"Heath totally can and will hold a grudge. Especially if someone did something to someone he cares about." Alec sighed. "Leave Heath to me, I'll deal with him. It's not like he's technically *on* the Riptide anymore. He's a coach."

"No, but as much as the locker room follows Sam now, Heath is the heart and soul of the team. Everyone looks up to him."

Alec knew Neal was right. If Heath was against the idea of Spencer Evans being on the Riptide, it wouldn't ruin Alec's plans, but it would certainly make them tougher.

"Maybe," Neal continued, "you should just convince him to join a different team. He's fucking amazing. Surely just about every team in the NFL would jump on the chance to have him play for them."

"It's the Riptide he wants. He's not taking any chances."

"What about the Piranhas? They still have all those ties to Colin O'Connor."

Alec shot Neal a look. "You're an analyst, you should know exactly why Spencer doesn't want to play for the Piranhas. They won *two* games last year. They're in major rebuilding mode. He doesn't want to start over from scratch. He wants to win a Super Bowl and do it for a team that doesn't pretend that he's someone else."

"I get it, I do, but I think you've got your work cut out for you, that's all," Neal said. The waitress approached their table. "Let's order, and you can tell me all about the insane offer ESPN just made for me."

"It's not insane," Alec said, even though it kind of was, "it's only half-insane, and you don't even want to do it. You want to stay where you're at, trading quips with Terry Bradshaw."

"Yep," Neal agreed, "but it's nice to be wanted, you know?"

As Alec watched his friend and client order, he knew it *would* feel good for Neal, who, after missing the winning field goal in the Super Bowl, had been summarily dumped following an illustrious career with the Riptide. With recovery time under his belt, and finding a new job that he loved, he'd moved on, but Alec wondered if anyone could truly move on from an experience like that.

Even after Spencer ended up on a team that accepted him, would he ever *really* feel accepted?

Alec realized uneasily that he wasn't entirely sure.

• • • • ● • ● • ● • •

When Spencer texted Alec his address for their dinner tonight, he'd fully expected the agent to balk and insist they go to one of the many high-end restaurants he liked to patronize.

But he didn't. He just said he'd be there at seven, ready to discuss the terms and complexities of their professional relationship.

Spencer wasn't stupid; the wording had been too pointed to miss.

He shouldn't have been surprised at all when Alec showed up in a three-piece suit—it was *May* in Los Angeles—and with a bottle of fancy wine.

"Hey," Spencer said, opening the door just a fraction. "We gotta be careful. Iggy keeps trying to escape."

Alec raised an eyebrow. "Iggy? And he's already trying to leave you?"

"You wanted me to keep calling him Ignatius?" Spencer asked, checking to make sure the cat hadn't heard the voices and come to see what was going on. He'd caught him, three paws out the back door just ten minutes ago, and half a dozen times in the last twenty-four hours alone.

He opened the door another fraction. "Come on in," Spencer said, "and *no*, not escaping exactly, just keeping me on my toes."

"I should have suggested Chase convince you to adopt a cat ages ago," Alec said, sliding through small space with a surprising amount of grace. "You've needed someone or *something* to keep you attentive forever." He extended the bottle of wine. "I wasn't sure if you were cooking, or *what* you were cooking, but I thought this red blend would go with just about anything."

Spencer didn't take the bottle. "I don't drink wine," he said before he remembered that not only did he need to convince Alec to take him on as a client, he needed to convince Alec to take him on as a freaking *life project*.

Ugh.

Chase had texted him this morning, reminding him of their agreement, as if he could have forgotten about the deal they'd made.

"Oh."

He swore Alec looked disappointed. "But you're free to open it for yourself," he added quickly, hating that he felt guilty. Alec had gone out of his way to emphasize that all they had between them was business. "I'm grilling. Rosemary lemon chicken, it's one of my aunt Pru's recipes. She swears it's a no-fail."

The foyer of Spencer's house opened up into a living room, with the dining room at the far end, next to the kitchen. When he'd bought it, he hadn't wanted to hire a designer, so Pru had come out and helped him painstakingly pick out everything for the house. In the end, maybe it wasn't as elegant or put together as it could've been, but Spencer was happy with it. He felt *comfortable* and that had been a requirement. He already felt like an interloper so much of the time. He didn't want to come home and feel like he was still trespassing.

"You have a lovely home," Alec said stiffly, still cradling his wine in the crook of his arm. He hadn't even unbuttoned his jacket.

Spencer, who was wearing a t-shirt and shorts, felt annoyingly underdressed.

Alec had made it plenty clear they were going to be discussing business and only business—but did they have to be uncomfortable doing it?

"Thanks," Spencer said. "I thought we'd have more privacy here than someplace else, like a restaurant."

That *was* true, but Spencer, who was already inwardly sweating at having to ask Alec what he'd promised Chase he'd ask, hadn't wanted to do it with any kind of audience.

Especially if Alec turned him down.

"What about my office?" Alec questioned.

"That didn't go so well for me last time." It was a weak joke, but he hadn't wanted to go back to the office. That felt so . . . formal. Constrained. And in his office, Alec held all the cards. Here, at least, they felt like they were on more equal ground, and he felt like he could at least broach the subject of Alec helping him out.

"I told you that we would discuss it," Alec said.

"Feel free to sit down, relax. I'm just about to put the chicken on," Spencer said. He'd already set the table. The potato salad Pru had walked him through was in the fridge, chilling, and the broccoli was in the oven, roasting, and even though he almost never hosted anyone at his house, he found he was almost enjoying himself.

He'd imagined Alec in his house so many times. And not just in his house, *in his bed*.

That wasn't happening, but it still felt like a dream come true to watch him walk around the living room, taking in the awards on the built-in bookcases, the few pictures of him and Pru that he'd put up.

"Your aunt?" Alec asked, pointing to one of the silver frames.

Spencer nodded. She was smiling in this picture, at his Ohio State Senior Day.

"You ever hear from your parents? Your mom, right?"

"No," Spencer said. "Not a word." He didn't have to say that he was grateful that his mother, who'd abandoned him to her sister as a baby, had never come back around. Pru was his mother now, in every way that had ever mattered.

"You're lucky," Alec said.

Spencer didn't have to know who he was thinking of—Heath Harris' situation with his father was well known around the league.

"Yeah, I really am," Spencer said. "Can I take your jacket? Open your wine?"

"If you have an opener and a glass, I'd appreciate it," Alec said, still stiff. Too formal. No matter how Spencer tried to get him to relax.

He'd been worried that *he'd* be the nervous one, because of what he was going to ask Alec to do, and also the fact that he was hosting Alec Mitchell, at his house, *finally*, after all these years of wanting to. But compared to how uptight Alec seemed, he felt positively laid-back.

If he was going to do this, the way Chase wanted him to, then Alec *needed* to relax.

Pru liked a good white wine or rosé in the summer, so he knew he had an opener. He dug through two drawers before finally finding it, and pulled a glass from the cupboard. He knew the bare bones about wine, and knew there was a "right" glass for every type, but he had no idea if this was the correct one. He *hoped* it was, because if he could convince Alec to have a glass or two of wine, surely he'd be more receptive.

"Thanks," Alec said as he set the wine down on the eating-bar side of the long kitchen countertop. There were four fairly comfortable barstools set there—Spencer knew how comfortable they were, because that was often where he ate his own meals, usually alone—and he hoped that Alec might sit down in one of them, maybe even unbutton his jacket.

Spencer went and grabbed the marinating chicken from the fridge, and out of the corner of his eye watched as Alec opened the wine, doing so with a few expert movements. He poured a healthy amount into the glass, not fussing about which kind it was, for which Spencer was grateful.

He wasn't as sophisticated or cultured as Alec was; he didn't *want* to be, necessarily, but he'd also never gotten a chance to find out.

But this is your chance, he reminded himself. *This is why Alec Mitchell is sliding onto one of your barstools. He's going to make it possible for you to find out.*

For the first time, Spencer was actually happy that Chase had made him promise to do this.

"Where's your cat?" Alec asked, breaking the silence between them.

"Probably causing trouble," Spencer said dryly. "He's destroyed three rolls of toilet paper, a book, four Post-it notes, a notepad, and an empty Starbucks cup. *Today.*"

"He likes paper, then," Alec said. "One of Chase's beasts does too. Best to give him lots of stuff you don't care about him ruining."

"I figured that out after the first day," Spencer said. "But he also played for hours, so he might be napping."

"Best we don't wake him up, then," Alec said. Still so goddamned formal. Like somehow Iggy's appearance was going to make this all a little too personal.

"I wasn't planning on it," Spencer said. "I'm going to go get dinner on the grill." He motioned to the large patio outside the floor-to-ceiling windows that lined the back of the house. "Come with me and you can tell me all about how you're going to get me traded."

Yes, he'd just got Alec *finally* sitting down, but he was still wearing the jacket, and if he got him outside, it was warm, especially by the grill. He might get him to ditch it, if he was lucky.

"Sure," Alec said. He picked up his wine and followed Spencer outside.

The grill was hot, a few tendrils of smoke rising through the air as he opened the lid. The chicken sizzled satisfyingly as he used a pair of tongs to add it to the grate.

"You have a nice place here, really," Alec said, as he looked around the secluded backyard. "I thought you'd live in one of those soulless luxury condos or something."

"No," Spencer said. He had, at first, when he'd come to LA. But he'd hated it. Hated not being able to go outside and enjoy the fresh air. Hated all that steel and glass. It *had* felt soulless. And he'd already felt his soul being eaten away one practice at a time, anyway, so he'd bought this house as soon as he'd found the right one.

He watched as Alec took a long sip of wine, his Adam's apple bobbing as he swallowed. Spencer's fingers tightened around the tongs. This would be so much easier if he wasn't still crazy about the guy. If just being in the same room with him didn't make him want to fall to his knees and beg. For anything. *For scraps.*

"I lived in one for awhile, but it wasn't for me either."

Spencer didn't know where Alec lived—only somewhere near the ocean, from an offhand comment he'd made in a text message years ago.

But now, Alec was going to be his agent. He *could* ask without sounding creepy, like he wanted to unexpectedly show up at Alec's house.

"Somewhere by the ocean, right?"

"Near Venice Beach, yeah," Alec said. He turned towards Spencer. "How did you know?"

Spencer pretended to be very busy with the grill, even though all he had to do was put the chicken on and then flip it after five minutes. Pru had been very specific about not touching it during this stage of the cooking process. "You mentioned it, once," he said, hoping that Alec would let it go.

He remembered exactly when and how Alec had mentioned it, because it had been impossible to forget Alec talking about sleeping with the window open, so he could hear the sound of the waves and smell the salt in the air.

Back then, it had been impossible not to imagine himself in the bed next to Alec. Feeling the breeze, hearing the ocean, and experiencing what it would be like to be wrapped up around each other, *finally*.

It had never happened, but he'd wanted it for so goddamn long.

"Dinner will be ready in a few," Spencer continued. "You wanted to have this meeting, you should kick it off."

"I did," Alec said. "I know you came to me because you think I can get you traded to the Riptide, but I can't guarantee that."

"I'd have a better chance with you than with someone else," Spencer pointed out.

"Possibly," Alec conceded, tilting his head. "But I can promise that wherever you end up going, you'll be treated better."

"Larry promised that too, with the Stars, with the second contract I signed."

"No offense, but Larry is Larry and I'm me," Alec said steadily. "That's not going to happen this time around."

"He claimed that they made promises they didn't have any intention of keeping," Spencer said, flipping the chicken carefully, just like Pru had told him over the phone.

"The problem," Alec said, leaning against the back of one of the lounge chairs, "was that the Stars were never going to change. Locker room culture is pervasive, and it comes from the top down. Larry should have known that, and known that any promises they made were empty."

Spencer had figured that out, too, eventually. But it had been a source of contention between him and Larry, and when the fallout had happened, he'd known that eventually he'd need to find a new agent.

In the back of his mind, he'd always known it was going to be Alec he went to.

"And you know who won't make shit up to get me to the table?" Spencer asked archly.

Alec nodded. "Anything I can do to help?"

Spencer shook his head. "This is all really simple. I just need to grab the sides, and then we can eat."

Spencer tested the chicken with the meat thermometer Amazon had delivered yesterday, then, satisfied it was done all the way through, pulled it off the grill and onto the serving platter, and gestured towards the door. Alec smoothly reached over and pulled it open.

After setting the chicken on the table, Spencer grabbed a beer from the fridge with the potato salad. Last thing was to grab the roasted broccoli, and when he pulled it out of the oven, switching the heat off, he thought it looked just like Pru had told him it should.

"This looks delicious," Alec said when Spencer sat down with him. "I didn't know you could cook."

"I don't, normally, but my aunt walked me through it," Spencer admitted as he served himself a piece of chicken. It looked good, sure, but he doubted it was as impressive as Alec said it was. Especially considering that he knew Alec liked to patronize expensive, fancy restaurants.

One of the reasons he'd done this was because he'd never tried cooking before, because it had always seemed like an uncomfortably domestic task that he didn't want anyone to catch him doing.

But now that didn't matter, and he'd hoped that by trying this, he'd show Alec that he was willing to take the risk. Willing to change. *Wanting* to change.

As Alec cut into his chicken, Spencer decided this was as good a moment as any.

"Actually, I don't want you to just be my agent," Spencer said.

Alec glanced up, shock on his face.

"No, not *that*," Spencer said awkwardly. Wishing he was more charming, like Chase. Could convince someone to do something just because he was the one asking. "It's not really part of the agent thing, more of a favor to me, I . . . well, I don't want to just change teams. I want to be . . . different."

"Different," Alec stated, and that frosty formality was back. "Why don't you tell me what you want me to do for you?"

"It's a bit more complicated than grilling you some chicken." Spencer took a deep breath, praying that Chase had read this situation right. "I know it's not just as easy as switching teams, wearing a different uniform. I'm gonna have all the same problems, underneath it."

"Of course it won't be that simple," Alec agreed. "But I'm not sure what *I* have to do with any of this. I said I'd be your agent. Get you on a different team. Hopefully the Riptide, but no promises."

"What I need is your help." It was harder than Spencer had anticipated, baring his heart and his soul this way.

"You need a therapist. I'm an agent." Alec's tone was mild, not accusatory, but it still stung.

"Are you gay or not?" Spencer retorted.

"You're going to have to be clearer about what kind of help you're looking for, exactly," Alec said. "Yes, you know I'm gay. But there's a hundred different ways to be gay. I'm not going to be your gay tour guide."

"What if I haven't tried any of those hundred ways?" Spencer asked. He'd known he was desperate for Alec to agree to be his agent, but it turned out he was just as desperate for his help here, too.

Chase was so much smarter than anyone gave him credit for.

"You want the gay tour guide," Alec guessed.

"Not exactly," Spencer said. "I just . . . I don't know what I like, even? I've tried so hard the last nine years to keep my head down. Don't make any waves. Don't do anything that might make people think I'm not tough. You said it yourself . . . be straight," he added wryly, "without actually being straight."

Alec set down his silverware with a decisive click. "This is you asking this. *You* want to do this."

Spencer froze.

"You have to really want to do this," Alec said. "It's not going to be easy. In fact, I would argue it's going to be one of the toughest things you've done."

"Tougher than the shit I've been going through?" Spencer asked dryly as he cut through the chicken on his plate. It was just as moist and tender as Pru had promised. If this whole thing with Alec went sideways, at least he could say that he'd fed the guy an edible meal.

"Tough in a different way," Alec clarified.

"That isn't enough to scare me away."

Alec sipped his wine. "I'm not so sure about that. You know how to be tough. How to be the biggest, manliest football player on the field, so you don't have to deal with your teammates' crap. But I'm not sure you know how to be Spencer Evans."

"You might be right," Spencer said uneasily. He knew who he was, deep down, didn't he? Even all the homophobic assholes in the world couldn't erase that. But it was stupid stuff, like *did he like to cook? What did he like to wear? What did he like to eat? What did he like to drink?*

His life felt like a series of decisions that he'd made to placate everyone else.

Never to bring himself joy.

Alec shot him a chastising look.

Spencer cleared his throat. "How do you even know all of this?"

"Because I *know*. I know you."

It reminded Spencer, even though he didn't want to be reminded, of a time when they'd almost known each other a whole lot better. A whole lot more intimately.

"Then if you know all this, know *me*, why won't you help me change?"

"No." Alec shook his head forcefully. "*No.* I don't want to change you. I want you to be *you.* The Stars wanted to change you. What you need to do is reverse all the damage they've done over the years."

The chicken, no matter how moist it was, felt dry in Spencer's mouth.

"I'm not . . ." He swallowed hard. "I'm not *damaged.*"

He knew who he was. Didn't he?

Alec's gaze was painfully sympathetic. "Aren't you? Isn't that why you want to get away from them?"

Spencer forced himself to think this through. Logically. Unemotionally. What *were* those decisions anyway? Did what he liked to drink, and what he liked to watch on TV, what colors he liked to wear . . . didn't those things make up who he was as a person?

The answer was a lot more black and white than he'd anticipated.

"You're right," Spencer admitted. "I . . . maybe I am a little damaged."

"So to be clear, what you want is for me to not only succeed in getting you traded to the team of your choice, but also to help you discover who you really are, under all the hyper masculinity that the Stars forced onto you? That's all?" Alec's voice was wry.

That's all, Spencer told himself, except that facing it felt far more terrifying than he'd imagined. Of course he hadn't imagined that he'd have Alec by his side either, watching as he dug deep, pushing aside nine years of homophobic crap, trying to figure out who he might be under all that.

"I know you wanted to keep this professional," Spencer said cautiously, taking a drink of his beer. He needed a little liquid courage for this part. "But it might help if you were a little *less* professional. That's all I'm asking for."

"Did I say that I wanted to stay professional?"

"Not in words," Spencer retorted dryly, "but in everything else. I know *you* too."

"Fair," Alec conceded with a fleeting smile. "But who says this *isn't* professional? While you've spent the last nine years building a certain image, so have I. A very different image. Maybe I want to make sure that's preserved when you come on board as a client. Maybe that's why I'd agree to do this."

"What if I end up being just the same kind of tough guy underneath everything?" Spencer asked, the thought suddenly appearing in his head and terrifying him.

"You aren't," Alec said, his gaze full of annoying pity. "But if you are, then you are. There's nothing wrong with being a tough guy because that's who you are, Spencer. The problem is being a tough guy when you're not *really* a tough guy. When it's all an act so everyone conveniently forgets that you're gay."

Spencer wanted to argue that hadn't been what he was doing, but it was *exactly* what he'd been doing, so he couldn't. Alec had trapped him, neatly.

"I take it you'll do it, then."

Alec sighed. "I'll do it."

"Don't sound so enthusiastic about it." Spencer could hear the amusement in his voice. The undercurrent of excitement. It was always exciting to go into the unknown, but at least he wouldn't be alone. In that, Chase had been right.

"This isn't going to be easy."

"I told you, I'm not afraid," Spencer returned.

"Maybe you should be."

Maybe Alec was right, and he actually was. Maybe part of that fear was because he'd be exposing himself in front of the only man who had ever really mattered. That was scary on a whole other level.

But Spencer couldn't go into that. He *wouldn't* go into that.

"You cooked a great meal," Alec said, "you should eat it, before it gets cold. We can go over more details after."

Spencer glanced down at his food. He *hadn't* eaten much. Unlike Alec, who'd nearly cleaned his own plate. He picked up his fork again.

"Okay," he agreed.

Chapter Five

Alec had never imagined that Spencer wouldn't just want a new agent. That he'd want *more*.

He'd definitely anticipated that despite Spencer coming to a crossroads and deciding that he wanted a very different kind of life, that it wouldn't be quite so simple—and that it wouldn't be easy at all—to shed his misconceptions and his habits and make his dreams a reality.

The trade? That wasn't exactly straightforward to accomplish, and would likely take all of the knowledge that Alec had acquired over the years to pull off, but this part? The struggle for Spencer the man, not Spencer the player? It was not only so much harder, but it also happened to be the legacy that Alec had been trying, over the last ten years, to leave behind.

Athletes who weren't afraid to be themselves, who stood in the face of all the toxic masculinity perpetuated by professional sports and spat in its face.

He couldn't take responsibility for everything that had happened. He'd only been out of law school a year when Colin

O'Connor had come out as bisexual. Certainly, Heath Harris and Sam Crawford hadn't consulted him before their kiss at the Super Bowl victory celebration. When he'd become friends with them—and then Heath's agent—later, he'd realized that they hadn't even planned it out. Nobody had been given a heads-up that they were planning to come out. They'd just *done* it, because the thought of standing up on that stage and not being their true selves had seemed like the worst kind of lie.

But it wasn't easy to get to that place, and Alec wasn't sure Spencer was quite there yet.

He still cared what people thought of him.

But they could work on that.

"So," Spencer said as he stood at the sink, rinsing off their dishes, before loading them into the dishwasher, "what's the attack plan for getting the Stars to agree to trading me?"

There was a part of Alec that had hoped that of all the things Spencer could have asked, he would've wanted to know what Alec had planned for him *personally*.

Because he had plans and ideas. So many ideas. So many things he wanted to introduce Spencer to, and see his eyes light up with all the possibilities.

He'd never imagined any of this before twenty minutes ago, but the moment Spencer had brought it up, asking for something he never would have suggested himself, it had felt like the right choice.

Maybe it was a little self-serving to insert himself into Spencer's journey this way, but Spencer had *asked* and he had a feeling that if he didn't agree, Spencer wouldn't experience all of it. He'd struggle. Maybe he'd even get cold feet.

Everyone needed a little push sometimes, and also a whole lot of encouragement.

"I think you know what the best way is to get yourself traded," Alec pointed out. "You've been in the NFL long enough."

"Yeah, I do, but I wondered if you thought that would work."

"It will, with some variations. Before the draft, I want you to do a full interview. Tell everything. Say you want to be traded."

"You don't think that's gonna make me look bad?"

Alec had known Spencer still cared about what people thought of him, but it was another thing entirely to hear such undeniable proof come out of his mouth. He *ached* for him, and for the millionth time, wished that things hadn't turned out the way they had, all those years ago.

"I think we can make sure it doesn't reflect poorly on you," Alec said, "just the Stars."

"We're going to throw them under the bus, aren't we?"

"Could they use a little shaking up? Hell yes they could. I've been wanting to do it for years," Alec said. "This is the perfect opportunity."

Spencer frowned. "They're not the only team that hasn't been supportive to a player—either out or closeted. I know that much."

"No, but you were one of the first, and they not only wasted that chance you gave them, they treated you like shit because of it." Alec was actually looking forward to taking them to task—fully and completely. "They should pay for that."

"And you want me to be the one to do it."

"It's the easiest way," Alec said.

"I was worried you were going to say that," Spencer said, turning back to the sink. "I don't want to make this just some kind of moralistic crusade. What I really want is to play for a different team."

"You're hiring me because you believe I can do this," Alec said frankly, "and this is how it's going to get done. The only way it's going to get done, as far as I can see."

"Why can't we just say I want to play for a different team? That's what Aaron Rodgers did with the Packers."

"But everyone *knew* why he was pissed. Nobody knows why you're pissed. Why you want to leave. You're gonna have to tell them why. Spell it out."

Spencer closed the dishwasher with a decisive click. "I can see the benefit of doing it that way," he said, finally.

Alec watched as he walked over to the fridge and pulled out a second beer.

"You going to get drunk like the Super Bowl a few years back?" Alec asked, raising an eyebrow. He'd only ever seen Spencer tipsy that one time. He wasn't a big drinker, and Alec had suspected he was drunk when he'd sat down next to him, but it was only when Spencer had suggested a date that Alec had known it for sure.

"No," Spencer said.

"You should try my wine," Alec said, gesturing towards the bottle. "You said you don't drink wine, not that you don't *like* wine. And this is an easy drinking red, real fruit forward, not too many tannins on the back end."

"Is this how you want to do this?" Spencer asked suspiciously. "Make me try things I don't think I'm gonna like?"

"How will you know, if you don't try?" Alec hesitated, and slid his jacket off, hanging it over the back of one of the barstools. "Come over here. I'm not going to bite."

Spencer shot him a look, full of heat, and Alec remembered why it was probably better *not* to take his jacket off and why it was definitely better not to make jokes that could be taken in any kind of sexual context.

Well, he'd done it and he wasn't going to take it back. If they couldn't figure out how to make this work, then Spencer wouldn't get what he needed—and Alec wanted that more than anything else.

"Fine," Spencer said with a sigh. He skirted around the edge of the kitchen island, approaching hesitantly as Alec tilted the half-full glass in his direction.

"Isn't there supposed to be a special way I do this?" Spencer asked as he took the glass.

Alec raised his eyebrow. "A special way? You take a sip. Swallow it. Decide if you like it or not. Though, really, you should try it twice. The first sip will clear your palate from that god-awful beer you've been drinking."

"That's what I mean," Spencer said. "I don't want to do it wrong."

"Not drinking it, that's doing it wrong," Alec said, even though he knew what Spencer was referring to. But all of the swirling and the legs and the aroma, all the self-important recital that true wine connoisseurs participated in was only going to confuse Spencer. Alec just wanted him to fucking *try* it.

"Alright, fine," Spencer said, grumbling, and lifted the glass to his lips.

Spencer made a face, and Alec said, "Nope, not yet. Don't tell me you don't like it yet. You've got to clear your palate."

"How do I do that?"

Alec put his hand on Spencer's arm, stopping him from handing the glass back. "Take another drink," he instructed. "In a minute."

When he pulled his hand back, he could still feel the heat and solid strength from Spencer's forearm. He was going to have to get used to all this touching and personal connection, and hopefully when he did, it wouldn't affect him this strongly.

"Alright," Spencer agreed. "It wasn't . . . well, it wasn't what I thought it'd be."

"You didn't hate it," Alec guessed, leaning against the edge of the countertop.

"I thought I would," Spencer confessed. "Wine's just so fancy and complicated, and I'm not . . . I've never been either of those two things. And beer is fine."

"Beer is fine, sure. You might not dislike it. But what if you liked something else better?"

"I don't know," Spencer agreed. He hesitated, and Alec watched him closely, even though it almost hurt to look at him like this. So unsure and vulnerable and wanting so hard to do the right thing, the *best* thing. "It's why I asked you to do this."

"No," Alec said, because he'd been wondering *why* Spencer had asked him since he'd initially brought it up, and he was fairly sure, after thinking about it for a little bit now, that it hadn't been Spencer's idea.

Not that Spencer wouldn't *want* to ask, or that he didn't *need* his help. Alec could easily believe both of those things. But he didn't think that Spencer would have ever taken the leap and actually *asked*.

"No what?" Spencer asked, after taking a second sip of wine. "It's why I asked you."

"Yes, it is, but that's not why you asked."

"What are you saying?" Spencer paused. "I actually think I might *like* this."

"I've got great taste in wine," Alec said. "We'll try some wineries together. Figure out what you like. Start your cellar."

"I don't have a cellar," Spencer said, confused.

"But you *will.*" Alec couldn't help his smile. "Also, wine is not necessarily *gay*, you realize?"

"I know, I know it isn't, but . . . well, I didn't want to give some of my teammates the impression that . . . well, you know how they are."

"I do," Alec said. "Your new teammates won't give a shit, I promise. And speaking of new teammates, Chase sure is interfering, isn't he?"

Spencer flushed immediately, which validated Alec's assumption better than any words could.

"How did you guess?"

"He might have agreed to help you out of the goodness of his own heart, sure, but he wasn't going to do it without making a demand of his own, and knowing Chase, it was something he thought might make you sweat a bit, but would actually be helpful, in the end."

"You know him pretty well, then," Spencer said.

Alec wasn't sure how he felt about the fact that Spencer asking him to help him personally hadn't been his idea after all. Was he disappointed? Probably more than he should be, he decided.

"I do," Alec admitted. "Also, he enjoys being a pain in my ass, so there's that too."

Spencer frowned. "Is that why he wanted me to ask you? Because it would . . ." Alec watched as Spencer's frown deepened. He looked genuinely distressed. "Because it would be a pain in your ass? Because if it is . . ."

Alec didn't even let him finish, and because he was flustered that he'd made yet *another* rookie mistake concerning Spencer, put his hand back on his arm, and squeezed reassuringly. "No," he said firmly, "no, no, it's not like that at all. I wouldn't have said yes to either thing you wanted, if I didn't want to do this. You're not a pain in my ass. That's Chase and his interference."

"Alright." Spencer, however, did not look fully convinced.

Alec sighed. "I really am an idiot, sometimes, despite trying very hard to make sure nobody realizes it."

"You're not an idiot." Even insulted, Spencer was more loyal than Alec deserved.

"I kind of am," Alec admitted. "I didn't even realize you went out of your way to award yourself the bet I deprived you of, all those years ago."

"Now I'm lost," Spencer said.

"The bet. The Super Bowl."

Alec watched as comprehension dawned across Spencer's handsome face. "Oh, yeah. Well, this *was* dinner, but remember, you said *twice* that it was a professional meeting."

"We shared a glass of wine, Spencer," Alec said, "and you cooked me dinner. It was enough of a date to count."

Spencer grinned. "Does that mean . . ."

Alec didn't let him finish there either. Afraid, maybe, of what he might say. What he might suggest. What Alec might *agree* to.

"No, don't even think about it," Alec said. "You're my client now, remember?"

"And you don't get involved with clients?"

"Even when I'm tempted," Alec admitted, and even though he shouldn't have, the light that shone in Spencer's dark eyes made the purposeful slip worth it.

"Should I be flattered?"

Alec reached up, patted him on the chest, knew he would feel the heat of his body long after he left tonight, and decided that was worth it too, for the way Spencer's smile softened. "Absolutely."

"Then I am," Spencer said, and drained the rest of the wine.

· · ● ● · ● · ● ● · ·

"You," Alec said as he walked into his office, only to find Chase sitting in one of his designer chairs, his feet propped up on the edge of his Brazilian cherry desk, "have a lot to answer for."

Chase shot him a brilliant smile and slid his feet off. "Sorry, I forget you're a stickler for that."

"It's not just me," Alec retorted dryly, "and that's not *all* you have to answer for."

He sat down at the desk, and pushed the Starbucks cup towards Chase.

"Oh, Spence must have talked to you."

"Spence?" Alec raised an eyebrow. "I didn't realize you two were on nickname kind of terms."

"Why wouldn't we be?"

"Neal was right, you are physically incapable of holding a grudge." Alec drummed his fingers on the desk. "And as for you interfering, I'm not exactly thrilled about that either, but as much as I hate to say it, it was a good idea."

"You mean, I was *right*," Chase corrected, reaching out and grabbing his coffee.

"Yes," Alec said, incapable of holding back his own smile. Chase was that way; you could never stay angry or annoyed with him for long. Just the way he could never stay angry with anyone else.

"I didn't think Spence would tell you. Thought he'd just ask, like it was his idea."

Alec shot his client a look. "He *did* just ask."

"Oh. *Oh.*" Chase grinned again. "So you figured it out."

Alec nodded. "I've known Spencer long enough that it wasn't that tough to figure it out."

"You should be thanking me," Chase said.

"I should? Why?" Alec opened up his email. Chase had come here because he'd invited him to discuss the big news, but he'd been working with Chase long enough to know that until the subject with Spencer was settled, he wouldn't be able to move on.

"*Duh*," Chase said. "You've got a thing for him."

Alec's hand jerked, nearly spilling his coffee all over his desk and all over the newly printed contract between him and Spencer, the one that he'd be in tonight to sign.

"What?" he exclaimed, his voice sounding totally fake even to his own ears. "What are you talking about?"

Chase leaned back, all smug satisfaction. "I knew it," he said.

"You don't know anything," Alec said crossly.

"I know something about this, because I've been through it. You think you're the only guy who pined for years for someone they didn't think they could have? I've been there, I know how to recognize the signs."

"There are no signs," Alec retorted, except he was lying, because he knew there were. And yes, Chase could probably recognize them, because he'd been pining after his now-boyfriend for years, before they'd finally gotten together.

"I know the signs, I can spot them from a mile off, and you've got them," Chase said. "You really shouldn't have defended him so staunchly."

"I didn't. I defended you." At least that was how Alec—*mostly*—remembered it.

"Oh, you were on my side," Chase corrected, "but you made sure I knew why he'd said what he did. And for the record, I think you were right. Being on the Stars for that long, that fucked him up real good."

"It did, but getting away from them will be the first good step for him," Alec said, and then because he had no intention of divulging any of his plans or his personal business with Spencer to any of his other clients, especially any of the clients who considered him a friend, he changed the subject. "I got a call yesterday from *Sports Illustrated* magazine. It turns out they want to put not just me on the cover, but *us*."

"Me and you?" Chase's eyes grew wide. "That would be so cool."

"Not just me and you. Me and my clients. You and Neal and Heath."

"AKA your queer clients," Chase said sagely.

Chase could be a huge doofus sometimes, but when he applied his brain, he could be one of the sharpest guys in the room. "Yes," Alec said.

"What about Spence?"

"What about him?"

"He's becoming one of your clients, and he, despite all his efforts to prove otherwise, is definitely queer."

"And?"

"Shouldn't he be on the cover, too, then?"

"They didn't ask because they don't know about him yet." Alec tapped his fingers on the desk. Chase's question was the same one he'd been asking himself since the call had come through.

Should he put Spencer on the cover with the rest of his group?

It would look weird if he was left off, but he could always blame the timing.

But then, becoming Spencer Evans' agent had always been something he'd wanted, something he'd tried to make happen from the first article he'd read, about the best defensive player from Ohio State in ages coming out of the closet.

Shouldn't he be shouting his achievement to the skies?

"You should include Spence," Chase said stubbornly. "He's gonna be one of us."

"That's beside the point," Alec said. "I wanted to talk about it with you, if you were game."

Chase shot him a look. "Did you think I wouldn't be?"

"No," Alec said, "but they have a very specific aesthetic that they're going for, and it's not for everyone, so I wanted to talk to each of you one-on-one before I connected back up with Carla."

"Who's Carla?"

"The production designer at *Sports Illustrated*," Alec said, trying not to be annoyed. "But here's the thing, they want you—*us*—to be naked."

Alec had expected Chase to be surprised. Maybe not shocked, because this *was* Chase Riley, and during the heyday of his crazy antics, he'd have barely blinked at posing naked for *Sports Illustrated*.

Satisfyingly, Chase's mouth dropped open.

"What?" he exclaimed, leaning forward, with an uncomfortable gleam in his eye. "You're gonna get naked for a magazine cover?"

Yes, he was. Though he had mostly pushed that thought to the side, and had focused instead on making sure all of his clients were okay with the concept. That had seemed easier, anyway, than thinking about taking his own clothes off.

Alec nodded. "That's the plan. Can I let her know you're on board?"

"Hell yes, I am." Chase grinned. "If only because I can't wait to see you squirm once you're out of your three-piece suit."

"Great," Alec said weakly. "That's just great."

"Don't sound too excited. Think about it: you're gonna be surrounded by three—*four*, if you'll get your head out of your ass about Spence—awesome athletes. And we're all gonna be naked. *Exposed*."

Alec had already considered calling back the personal trainer he'd let go of two years ago because he hadn't been able to make the time in his schedule for him. Now? As soon as Chase left, he'd have to dig his phone number out.

"Right," Alec said. "That's the whole idea. We've bared our selves, and now we'll bare our bodies."

"Have you asked anyone else?" Chase wondered.

"Not yet," Alec said, "so *please* don't text them as soon as you leave, okay? I want to get everyone's opinion on this without being pressured. It's a lot to ask."

"For you, maybe," Chase said with a smirk. "The rest of us are in fucking fantastic shape. Even Neal."

"Don't remind me," Alec said wryly. And it wasn't like he was in *bad* shape. His clothes fit fine. He jogged, sometimes. He tried to do a round of pushups and sit-ups every morning, if he had the time. But he also wasn't a professional athlete either.

"You want me to help you out?"

"No, thank you, I'll be fine," Alec said.

"You will be if you get to see Spence naked," Chase teased.

"So that's a yes for you, then," Alec said firmly, changing the subject. He had spent nine years trying—and failing—not to think about Spencer naked.

It was testament to how poorly he'd done that when Carla had gone over the theme of the shoot, the possibility of being naked with Spencer had been one of his very first thoughts.

"It's a yes," Chase confirmed. "And about Spence . . ."

"No," Alec said firmly. "We're not talking about him anymore."

"Okay, fine," Chase said, "I give up."

"You never give up," Alec said, his gaze narrowing in on his client "*Never.*"

"Well, temporarily I am, because you won't give me anything," Chase said with a pout on his face.

"God forbid I don't share my personal life you," Alec said.

"Oh, so it *is* personal, then," Chase said, rubbing his hands together. "Neal said so but I wasn't sure."

"You're the worst, get out before I decide to shove you out in front of the camera without a modesty patch," Alec said, regretting opening his mouth at all. He'd made the same exact mistake with Chase that he'd made with Neal.

"Ooooh, *that's* an idea," Chase said, grabbing his coffee and giving Alec a quick salute before he walked through the door.

"Ugh," Alec said to himself, banging his head against the desk.

Then, before he'd even had a chance to catch his breath and start looking for his old personal trainer's phone number, Kyle's voice echoed through the intercom. "Rashad's here," he said. "He wants to talk to you about a problem."

That was the life of an agent. Even when you thought you had the day planned out and organized, there was always something to throw a wrench in.

FIVE YEARS AGO

THEY'D BEEN DOING THIS for two years now, it shouldn't come as a big surprise when his phone dinged with that particular tone that always set Spencer's heart beating a little faster.

Alec would never know that he'd given him his own distinctive tone, but he'd done it after one close call. He'd gotten one of Alec's texts while in the locker room once, after practice, and after reading the text, his smile had nearly given him away.

"Don't see you smilin' like that much," Shaughnessey had said to him. "You got a hot date? Gonna get into some poor dude's pants?"

He did have a hot date, but not in any way, shape, or form like Shaughnessey thought. It was a text date, and they were often the highlight of Spencer's week.

He'd learned his lesson, and set Alec his own tone, making sure to read whatever he'd sent when he was finally alone.

It became a ritual.

He'd settle down on his couch, in his comfortable living room, the one place he felt like he could really be himself—if he even knew what that was, anymore—and open his phone, and let the charm and humor and kindness of Alec Mitchell wash over him.

He'd always, from the first moment they'd met, thought Alec was insanely fucking hot. He'd wanted him that first night, at the draft. He'd wanted him even more at the Pro Bowl, a few years later. And now, two years after that, it was deeper than that.

He *liked* him.

And he wanted to believe that Alec felt the same way. After all, he was a busy guy. Had a whole bunch of successful clients. Surely he had way better things to do with his time than text with Spencer.

But whenever he reached out, the texts almost always morphed into a conversation.

They didn't talk on the phone. They didn't meet up in person—even though Spencer had plenty of fantasies about that—but they *did* text.

Got an appearance on Good Morning Football tomorrow, the message read, **and trying to figure out what I should wear.**

Spencer ignored how his fingers were trembling, and after thinking for a moment, typed back, **That blue shirt, the one that made your eyes pop last time.**

Didn't know you noticed, 'cause you never told me. Not cool. Alec's texts always came through so quickly, it was like he couldn't wait to answer, and they never failed to make his heart beat a little faster. Not just because of the inevitably flirtatious nature of the words, but because Alec obviously *wanted* to talk to him.

I noticed. He'd done a lot more than notice. Spencer wasn't proud of how far Alec could push him sometimes, but nobody needed to know that he'd watched that particular segment with his hand wrapped around his cock, imagining Alec crawling towards him, those unearthly eyes alight with pleasure and interest and affection.

Can't wear the same thing, even if you like it. What about this one?

The best—and the worst—were the selfies that Alec would send. This one was not only hot, with Alec draped in a silvery-gray shirt, a few little tantalizing glimpses of skin on display, his handsome face was warped in a silly expression, his tongue out.

Spencer would definitely be keeping this one for later, the ridiculous face and all.

Gray is so boring, though.

But Alec? Alec was anything but boring. He was interesting and funny, and *God,* he set Spencer's insides alight with all his fierce loyalty and the joy that was right there, just below the surface.

Not for the first time, Spencer considered just dispensing with the pleasantries, and saying, *let's meet up. Tonight. I can't do this anymore, you're making me crazy. I need to know what you feel like. I need to know what you taste like.*

But he didn't, because the chance of all of this ending, of Alec turning him down, was too terrible to contemplate.

If he lost him . . . even the tiny bit of Alec that he was privileged enough to know . . . Spencer didn't know if he'd ever get over it. Surely, Spencer thought, if Alec wanted something to happen, something would have happened.

No, he just wanted to text. So Spencer would text.

Is it boring on me, though? Another picture came through, this one with Alec batting his eyes adorably.

Spencer laughed out loud. Couldn't help himself.

Before he could overthink it, he switched apps, and took a short video of himself nodding vigorously, and then sent it off.

Alec's reply came back almost instantaneously. **You're the worst. No gray, then. What about dark blue?**

I like blue, Spencer texted back. *But not as much as I like you.*

Always with the blue, Alec responded, **don't you like anything else?**

The answer was easy enough. He didn't think about it too much before he typed it out and pressed send. It was simpler with Alec to not spend too much time and effort worrying about being too forward.

The only thing he couldn't do was take it *off* texting.

But for the last year, it hadn't just been him pushing them further, it had been Alec, too.

Yeah, give you two guesses what else, and the first one doesn't count.

Spencer was already hard and throbbing in his shorts, just at the thought of what Alec might say back. It was always a test of his self-control if he could wait to wrap a hand around his cock before their conversation ended.

He almost always made it, usually because he enjoyed talking to Alec just as much as, if not more than, he liked looking at him. Or fantasizing what it would be like if both of them lost their minds and they met up.

Purple shirts? Wearing nail polish? Watching RuPaul's Drag Race?

One of the reasons Spencer liked him so goddamn much was his wicked, sly sense of humor. It seemed impossible sometimes that all of Alec's sarcasm came from a face that could look so sweetly innocent.

Or low down and dirty, if he chose. There was a picture Alec had sent him ages ago, where he'd been sticking his tongue out and there hadn't been a silly expression to go along with it, and it had fueled Spencer's jerkoff sessions *forever*.

What's RuPaul's Drag Race?

Alec was also a saint, because he didn't ever judge Spencer when he asked stupid questions, questions that he should probably already know the answer to.

Bravo On-Demand, Alec typed back immediately, **check it out to your own detriment, because you'll never get anything done.**

Spencer reached for the TV remote and his fingers hovered over the power button, but he didn't click. Drag? Would he even like that? Why did Alec think he would? Because he was gay? Because he liked dick? A pulse of fear speared through him. It was stupid, and even downright silly, because he was in his own home, his *private* home, but what if someone found out? What if Shaughnessey . . .

Would I like it? It was rare for Spencer to worry about what Alec might say in response to one of his questions. And he hadn't been exactly clear, but Alec was so smart, he'd probably been clear enough.

You would if you let yourself, Alec's answer said. **And not because you're queer and so are they, but because it's a fucking great show.**

If it was that good, if Alec enjoyed it that much, he *could* check it out. Might give them something to chat about when they texted.

And, Alec sent another text before Spencer could even respond, his fingers still hovering above his phone, **for the record, I dig Marvel too. Just because I'm gay doesn't mean I can't**

enjoy all kinds of shit. You should know that better than anybody.

He knew it, but it was hard sometimes to *believe* it. Especially when it felt like he spent so much fucking energy trying to be the hardest, toughest, most badass motherfucker on the team. The only one who still fucked with him to his face was Shaughnessey, and someday, he'd retire or be traded and the rest of the jerks on the Stars would fall in line.

But until that point . . .

The waiting was hard. But things like his texting with Alec made it a little bit easier.

Instead of typing what he'd intended to, before Alec had sent the second text, Spencer changed direction.

So, Captain America or Thor?

This was exactly the change of subject they needed. Away from what a failure as a gay man Spencer was, and back to the flirty sweet dialogue they usually had.

Alec texted back almost immediately. **America's ass most definitely. I like them big and blond.**

Spencer swallowed hard. He was . . . well, he was big, definitely. And not quite blond, but in the summer, when he was outside on the practice field all the time, his medium brown hair could get much, much lighter. *Almost* blond.

Oh, so Thor isn't big and blond? It was so much fun to tease Alec. Maybe not as much fun as something else could have been, if they'd actually been together, and Alec was sitting on this couch with him. But Spencer had learned not to let his mind wander there. This was enough.

Who says I should have to choose? Alec texted back. **What about you?**

Spencer thought back to the last Marvel movie he'd seen. **I like the dark-haired one. The one with the crazy metal arm.**

You would, Alec said, **you're all about the dark, tormented ones, aren't you?**

And the fairy-tale princes. Spencer couldn't *not* say it. Because that's what Alec had been to him from the beginning. An unobtainable fantasy. But one that he couldn't resist, even if Alec was good and kind and maybe not *pure*, but worthy. The most worthy person Spencer had ever known.

Who else would have taken on the responsibility of trying to change a world that was steeped in so much dangerous hyper-masculinity? Especially when Spencer knew that Alec got just as much flack as he did, sometimes. But even if he did, he never let it show, never let it ruffle any of his feathers. His suits were always perfect, his hair flawless, his armor always complete, no matter what. Even when people insulted him to his face, he fought back with grace and dignity. All the things Spencer had never been able to find in himself.

Spencer was often torn between pure awe and a deep, visceral need to be the one to muss him up a bit.

Sometimes Spencer didn't know whether he wanted to *be* him or be inside of him.

It was a problem.

You still think I'm some kind of high and mighty king, huh?

No, Spencer replied, **you're a prince, and with those eyes, how could you be anything but a fairy tale?**

It was impossible to know exactly how Alec took his words; after all, he couldn't see Alec smile. But he *felt* it, even through the phone. Even if it was just his imagination.

Still putting me up in the tower, huh, Evans?

He was putting himself up in the tower, much as he might try to deny it. If Spencer had had his way, Alec would be down on the ground, *with* him. Under him, if he had anything to say about it.

Someday you'll come slumming with us. *With me.* Spencer's fingers hesitated over his screen. He should change it. Add the other two words. Make it clear that the slumming-it part would be, at least, crazy hot and insanely pleasurable. At least that was how it always was in his fantasies.

Only interested in your tower.

Spencer smiled, even though Alec wasn't even there to see it. Knew that he'd understood what he *really* meant, even though he hadn't typed it.

That, and so many other things, were what made Alec special. Made what they shared special.

It felt like nobody else understood him. Like he didn't *belong* anywhere. Not anymore.

Sometimes he even felt like an interloper in his own fucking locker room.

Someday, Spencer replied. *Someday my prince will come*, he thought to himself, the melody of the Disney song echoing in his head. And if he was watching Disney, he might as well fall all the way in, right?

I'm turning on RuPaul, but I'm warning you, if I hate it, I'm coming over and telling you in detail about it.

Alec sent a thumbs-up text.

Not addressing the elephant in the room, the *monster* in the room. Spencer would never come over, even if he loathed the show. He'd never been invited and he wasn't invited now. And the last thing he'd ever do was force his way in.

If Alec wanted him, he was going to have to say so. Explicitly. In small words that Spencer could understand now that all his blood had drained into his cock.

But he didn't, and he probably never would, and Spencer was just going to have to learn to live with that.

CHAPTER SIX

SPENCER DIDN'T KNOW WHAT kind of plans, specifically, that Alec had, but when he spent twenty minutes staring into his closet, wishing he had something else he could put on that wasn't just jeans or sweatpants, he hoped that clothes were part of them.

Normally, he wouldn't give a shit, but this was Alec and he was going back to his office, this time to sign everything that made their professional relationship official, and Alec had mentioned there could be pictures.

This was going to be the first step of his new life and he wanted to take it the right way.

Finally, he settled on jeans and a white polo, no logo, nothing. He wished he had anything in his closet with the Riptide logo on it, because that would give the Stars a reason to start sweating, but he didn't.

Maybe he'd remedy that for next time.

His brown hair was cropped painfully short, so there was nothing to do but run his fingers through it, and hope that it would lie mostly flat. Undoubtedly Alec was going to have something to say about the no-nonsense haircut he'd been getting for years.

He had a feeling Alec was going to have a *lot* to say about *everything*.

Spencer, for the first time, thought he might actually be looking forward to listening.

He considered driving his new Ducati to Alec's office, because he loved taking it out, but since they were meeting at seven, he'd be leaving right in the middle of rush hour, so he left it in the garage and took his Tesla instead.

The drive was long and uneventful, but finally Spencer parked in the lot next to Alec's office, and took the stairs up to the third floor.

Kyle was still at the front desk, looking harried. "Oh," he said when Spencer walked up. "It's you, already."

"Everything okay?"

Kyle shot him a look that spoke volumes. "Just a crazy day here." He paused. "Though that's nothing too unusual, actually," he admitted.

"Is he ready for me?"

"Uh." Kyle hesitated. "I think so? Let me double-check."

But while Kyle was calling over the intercom, Spencer decided he might as well just head into the office. Maybe even catch Alec unawares again. That had flustered him wonderfully last time, and there was nothing Spencer liked better than seeing a flustered Alec.

He opened the door before Kyle could stop him, and to his surprise, Alec was not sitting at his desk, like he had been last time he'd barged in unannounced, but on the floor *next* to the desk, with his jacket and tie off, in the middle of doing a pushup.

The joke here was clearly on Spencer, because even though Alec was also clearly surprised to see him, the most flustered person was clearly him.

He hadn't expected to see Alec as undressed as he'd ever seen him, slim but undeniably there muscles bunching as he finished the pushup and got to his feet. He definitely hadn't expected to be so affected by Alec's body all laid out like that, hips and waist and his undeniably curvaceous ass in those tight blue slacks.

"Well," Alec said, breaking the tension, "I see that you're terrible at following directions. I can't say I'm surprised."

"What were you doing?" It was stupid to ask, but there were no words in Spencer's head. He'd come in here so sure he'd be able to catch Alec off-balance for once. But instead, it was he who'd been caught.

Alec shot him a look as he sat down in his chair. Didn't reach for the tie, coiled on his desk, or the jacket, which was draped over one of the other chair backs. "I think you know what I was doing. If you didn't, I'd be worried. Maybe too many blows to the head?"

"No, I get you were doing pushups," Spencer said stupidly as he sat down in the jacket-less chair. "But *why*?"

Alec's gaze was steely. "You think you have the physical side of things cornered, huh? No need for me to stay in shape?"

"No," Spencer said, hating how much he was suddenly floundering and ill at ease. "I just . . . I didn't ever think about you doing pushups." But now he wouldn't be able to *stop* thinking about it. Which was definitely a state of affairs he wouldn't be confessing to his brand-new agent, even if his brand-new agent had admitted that he found Spencer tempting.

"Well, I do pushups," Alec said grumpily. "Though maybe not as many as I should."

"How many should you be doing?"

Alec's disgruntled expression melted into a lopsided, wry grin. "God knows. I certainly don't."

"Well, you're helping me," Spencer said, before he could think better of it, "so it only seems fair for me to help *you*."

"You want to tell me how many pushups I should be doing?" Alec barely looked up from where he was sorting through a whole stack of papers on his desk. Probably his new contract, if he had to guess.

"It's slightly more complicated than that," Spencer said. "But essentially, yes."

Alec glanced up at him and their gazes locked. The white shirt Alec was wearing made his eyes look lighter, almost purple. Captivating, like every fairy-tale prince that Spencer had dreamed of when he was younger.

Funny how since they'd met, nine years ago, every fantasy he'd had, both innocent and dirty, had those same cornflower blue eyes.

"What's complicated about it?"

"I'd need to know what you're trying to accomplish, what muscle groups you're trying to focus on, how much time you have to devote to the task," Spencer said, automatically ticking off the points that he'd been asked by personal trainers since he'd been a teenager, "and a lot more, but that's a good place to start."

"Let's sign this contract first," Alec said. "And then we can discuss my distinct lack of fitness to your heart's content."

"Alright."

Alec went through every single page, densely covered in legalese, explaining what it all meant in laymen's terms.

"This is more in-depth than the contract I signed with Larry," Spencer said as he initialed the bottom of a page.

"Like I said before, Larry is Larry and I'm me. I don't like to leave much to chance." Alec smiled. "Did you tell him?"

"I talked to him yesterday. He wasn't happy about it," Spencer said, "but I think he understood. Mentioned he thought you'd have poached me ages ago. I set him straight, that this was my idea, but who knows what he believes."

"I don't care what he believes." The hard edge of Alec's voice was a good reminder that he was a killer agent. That he was going to do whatever it took to deliver what Spencer had asked for.

What Spencer needed.

Truthfully, Spencer might not have cared what Larry thought either, but he'd made a few judgmental comments bordering on nastiness that he hadn't appreciated. He wouldn't tell Alec how far Larry had gone, but he could probably guess.

Like he could probably guess why Spencer hadn't just felt obligated to set the record straight.

He definitely wouldn't be telling Alec about how Larry had mentioned snidely that Alec didn't sleep with his clients.

Like that was the only reason Spencer was changing agents.

Like Alec himself hadn't made that abundantly clear over the years.

But it had still bothered Spencer. Like the only way he could get Alec in his life was to hire him to be there.

"I didn't want him running his mouth," Spencer said.

"Oh, he's going to anyway," Alec said with a wave of his hand. "He's becoming obsolete. There's a new kind of agent, and he knows it and it bothers him that he's incapable of being different than he is."

He pushed the last page of the contract across the desk, towards Spencer.

Spencer's pen hesitated over the final line. He'd sworn to himself that he'd never take this step, but now it felt as natural as breathing.

His resolve hardened, he put the tip to the paper and signed confidently. How much different would the last nine years have been if he hadn't been so stubborn about all of this?

"There." Alec gathered up the pages and straightened them. "It's done. Quick picture, because I'd like to post it once the press release goes out."

"Sure," Spencer said, holding still as Alec pulled out his phone and snapped a few pictures.

"What?" Alec said, "no smiles? I thought this was what you wanted."

It *was* what he'd really wanted. But until he was traded, to the team he wanted, it wouldn't feel like he'd accomplished anything. This was just the first step. Still, Alec *was* right, so he shot the phone in Alec's hand a tentative smile.

Alec smiled back, and setting his phone down, reached out a hand. "It's going to be a pleasure to be your agent, Spencer."

It felt so formal to be shaking hands. But what else could they do? He would have to settle for a handshake. He took Alec's hand and shook it. Was expecting the inevitable frisson of electricity up his spine, because it happened every time they'd ever touched—which, because of the reaction, wasn't very often. Alec must not have been though, because he froze, their hands still clasped together, his eyes wide and surprised.

Spencer tightened his fingers, and for a second, they almost felt like they were holding hands, across Alec's desk.

Alec tugged his own away after a long moment, turning away, clearly flustered. "I . . . where is Kyle? He was supposed to bring the champagne in."

"Kyle looked pretty overwhelmed, earlier, when I walked in," Spencer pointed out. "Maybe he's busy?"

"No, he's going through a bad breakup and that means he's a mess," Alec said with an annoyed huff. He hit a button on the phone on his desk. "Kyle? The champagne? You said you'd grab it from the fridge."

"We don't need champagne . . ." Spencer started to say but Alec fixed him with a hard look.

"All my clients get champagne to celebrate a new contract," Alec said firmly. "And it's even more important for you because God knows, you've probably never tried champagne before."

Spencer nodded sheepishly. "You'd be right."

"Well, then," Alec said. "Kyle!"

"I'm here, I'm here," Kyle grumbled as he walked through the open door, a stainless steel wine bucket in one hand and two glass champagne flutes in the other.

"Oh good," Alec said, as Kyle set the bucket and flutes on the desk. "You're alive."

Kyle shot him a good-natured glare. "I was busy," he said, then turned to Spencer. "And *you*, you keep waltzing in before waiting for me to buzz you in."

"That's probably going to be par for the course," Alec said with a sigh. "Expect him never to wait for you to check with me, and never expect him to knock."

"Hey, I knock," Spencer said as Alec wrapped a towel around the bottle and expertly twisted off the metal cage top of the champagne, and then began to twist off the cork. "Most of the time, anyway."

"Not today," Alec said as the cork made a soft exhale coming out of the bottle.

"Aren't you supposed to have some kind of fountain explosion thing with that?" Spencer asked, gesturing as Alec began to pour the champagne into the two flutes.

"No, no, no," Alec said, glancing up with an aghast expression on his face. "That *ruins* it."

Kyle, who was on his way out, turned and shot Spencer a pitying expression. "Totally kills the carbonation," he added.

"You'll like it much better this way," Alec agreed, extending one of the flutes towards Spencer. "Trust me."

"I am, aren't I?" Spencer muttered.

He'd surprisingly liked the red wine the other night, even though he'd fully expected he wouldn't. It had been rich and decadent on his tongue, sweeter and fruitier in a way he hadn't anticipated. He didn't know if he'd drink it all the time, but he hadn't hated it.

Now, he supposed he couldn't balk at trying the champagne too. In any case, Alec wouldn't let him beg off.

"What shall we toast to?" Alec said, lifting his own glass. Spencer picked up his, fascinated by the pale blond bubbles rising through the liquid.

"To the Riptide," Spencer said resolutely.

Alec tilted his head. "To success," he toasted, raising his glass.

Spencer clinked his against it, repeating Alec's words. "That's not what I suggested," he said before taking a sip.

He lifted the glass to his lips, and let the sparkling wine slide past his lips.

The red wine had been dark and delicious, but this was like sunshine and fireworks in his mouth, bright and cheery in a totally different way.

"No," Alec agreed, "but it was a more realistic toast. And encompasses more than just success on this front. I want this to be a productive partnership all around."

Spencer took another sip, because he didn't want to think about what "all around" could mean.

"You like it," Alec said, before he could respond.

"You seem pretty sure of yourself."

"This is a five-hundred-dollar bottle of champagne. I'm confident it's incredible," Alec said, the edge of his lips twisting into a smile.

"What?" Spencer almost dropped his glass. "It cost *what*?"

Alec just shrugged. "This is a momentous occasion. I thought it deserved something really good. Went through my cellar last night and found something I'd been saving for a big deal."

"You think this is a big deal?" It was hard to wrap his mind around the fact that Alec thought he was worth one of his prized bottles.

Alec's gaze was steady and so *sure*. "Don't you think so?"

"I . . ." Spencer hoped it was the end of one kind of life and the beginning of another, so obviously it *was* a big deal, at least to him, but he was still unsure why it would be a big deal to Alec. Of course he'd said more than once he'd always wanted Spencer as one of his clients.

Maybe that was why.

"Trust me, it's a big deal," Alec said warmly. "I know I wasn't a hundred percent on board at first, but this is a day I've been looking forward to for a long time."

"Nine years," Spencer said. Tilted his glass towards Alec's and drained it. Enjoying, with every sip, the cheeriness exploding on his tongue. "Didn't think we'd make it here either."

"So now that I'm officially your agent," Alec said, and the ink was barely dry on the paper but Spencer suddenly felt a surge of resentment because even though he'd wanted him to be exactly that, the words also felt like the end of something else he'd always wanted. "I wanted to make sure that your recovery is solid. Make sure you're going to pass any physicals that might come."

"It is, and I will. But if you want more info, you should talk to June." It made sense, Spencer told himself, that Alec would want to know. That he'd *need* to know. Because in a few short weeks, he was going to start shopping him—to the Riptide and to other teams as well. Spencer wasn't under any false impression about what Alec was going to do or how he was going to do it.

"June?"

"She's my physical therapist. Has more in common with a drill sergeant maybe, but she's gotten me back in shape for the season already. I'm ready," Spencer said. "For mini camps, for workouts, for anything anyone wants to throw at me."

Alec raised an eyebrow. "That's an impressive rate of recovery, even for you." He reached for the bottle, pouring them each another glassful of champagne.

"I work hard," Spencer said, even though it had been so much more than that. Everyone in the NFL worked hard. He'd practically killed himself getting back in shape for the season.

"You did more than that." Alec sipped his champagne. "You know I have a workout facility for my clients?"

"You do?"

Alec shot him a look. "You shouldn't sound so surprised. You'll destroy my ego."

"I'm not surprised, I just didn't realize."

"Yes, I know you picked me because I have this special 'in' with the Riptide, but believe it or not, I've got a lot to offer, besides just the Riptide VP of player personnel on speed dial and a closet full of expensive suits."

Spencer let his gaze drift to where Alec had rolled up his sleeves, at his slender forearms and at the trim waist where the shirt disappeared into those tight slacks. "I do believe you've got a lot to offer," he said.

Chuckling, Alec set his glass on the desk. "I suppose you probably do."

"I've got a great home gym," Spencer said, "and then there's the one June owns, though she keeps threatening to set me free, so I guess I'll go back to mine, or I could always try yours out."

"I think you should try out the one I've got, because it wouldn't be a bad idea to mend some fences."

Spencer could practically *feel* how diplomatic Alec was trying to be. Yes, he had probably really pissed off the rest of Alec's clients over the years.

"I mended it with Chase, didn't I?" he retorted. "I can do it."

"No offense," Alec said, "but Chase is physically incapable of holding a grudge. He's just not built with that particular gene. He forgives *everyone.*"

"I'm assuming your other clients aren't that nice." Spencer finished his champagne. Wondered if it would be weird if he wanted more. He was driving home, sure, but he only felt light and happy, and if he kept drinking, he might not have to worry about winning over some members (and ex-members) of the Riptide who might not be very happy to have him around.

Spencer could even anticipate who it was that might be the unhappiest.

Heath Harris would surely be at the top of that list.

"They're plenty nice but . . . maybe not to you," Alec said, reaching for the bottle and pouring the rest into Spencer's glass.

"I wouldn't be surprised," Spencer said.

"Yeah, but doesn't mean it's right."

"Who says it isn't?" Spencer retorted. "I was a douchebag."

"A douchebag with reasons," Alec said, tilting his glass in Spencer's direction. "You never set out to be a douchebag, and you definitely didn't *want* to be a douchebag. They should understand that."

Spencer gulped his champagne. "They don't have to," he said. "I'm not . . . I'm making this change for a reason."

"I know," Alec said, his expression warm, and his gaze even warmer. "I'm proud of you for doing it. It won't be easy."

"The most important things aren't."

"Well," Alec said, scribbling some notes down on a bright pink sticky note, "keep that in mind when you show up there tomorrow."

Alec reached out and stuck the note in front of Spencer. It was an address and a time.

"What's this?"

"Every Friday they hold a pickup game at my field," Alec said. "Well, *technically* it's not mine, but well, it's mine enough."

"Whose is it?"

Alec didn't answer the question though. Instead, he said, "Tell them I sent you."

"You want me to play against your guys?"

"Nope," Alec said. "I want you to play *for* them."

"You don't think they'll boot me out?"

This time it was Alec's turn to look him up and down, and then up and down *again*. Spencer couldn't help the way his blood heated with Alec's gaze on him. Admiring him. "You really think they can?"

"Not a chance," Spencer said. "And speaking of that, what's up with the pushups, anyway? Can't you get some of your guys to give you some advice?"

"I could, of course, but then I'd have to admit to them I need it."

"You do?"

Alec sighed. "In a month I'm going to be doing a naked photo shoot."

If Spencer's blood had been warm before, it was on fire now. "You're . . . you're doing *what*?"

Alec waved. "It'll be all classy and shit, I promise. No actual reveal of parts I don't want to reveal, but . . . I don't want to look bad."

"Trust me," Spencer said, hoping that Alec could hear the earnestness in his voice and believed it. "Trust me, you don't have to worry about that."

"Yeah, well, it's not that simple," Alec said. "It's going to be with all my queer clients."

"*All* your queer clients?"

"Yes, that includes you, if you're game," Alec said. "So now you get it? I don't look like you guys, like . . . well, like a freaking god."

"Trust me, I like you better for it," Spencer said, even though that was neither here nor there.

But Alec smiled at him anyway. "Thanks, that *does* help. But I want . . . I want to do something, at least in the few weeks I have."

"Well, I'll be happy to help."

Alec looked at him speculatively. "You will, huh?"

"I meant it, you don't *need* it, but I get why you might want to work out a bit," Spencer said. Purposefully *not* thinking about what it would be like to share a gym with Alec. What it would be like to watch him sweat.

"What about the photo shoot?" Alec smiled. "You game?"

He'd been so distracted at the thought of *Alec* being naked that he hadn't thought about himself.

"I'm . . ." Spencer hesitated. This wasn't the kind of thing he *did.*

"It's for *Sports Illustrated,*" Alec said. "The art director said something about equating exposing our souls and our bodies. I really like the idea. I think it'll be neat. A real example of how we're pushing professional athletics into a new, more inclusive space."

"And you want me to be part of it."

"You're one of my queer clients," Alec said bluntly. "The idea was for me to pose with *all* of them. But you *are* the newest one. If you wanted to skip it, I don't think it would be all that surprising."

"I don't want to skip it." Spencer surprised himself by how sure he sounded. "I . . . I wasn't expecting it, that's all." *Wasn't expecting to be included.* "Are you sure your guys aren't going to be pissed off that I'm part of this?"

Alec waved a hand. "I don't give a crap what they think. They can deal with it." He grinned. "Besides, you've got a month before the shoot. Don't think you can win them over?"

"I didn't say that." Spencer straightened. "I can do it."

"Good." Alec's smile was warm and supportive, and to Spencer's surprise, he did feel like he could do it. He could walk in tomorrow and play like a demon, like he'd always done. That had always won him approval in the past, even from homophobic assholes like Shaughnessey. "Maybe I'll stop by and see how it's going tomorrow."

"Make sure everyone is playing nice?"

"No, of course not, they're not going to give you a hard time," Alec said quickly. Too quickly. But then, Spencer thought, it wasn't like he hadn't had to deal with a hard time before.

He'd been dealing with it for the last nine years.

CHAPTER SEVEN

"No," Spencer said to Iggy, who was sitting, one eye fixed on his face, right by the door, "you can't go."

Iggy meowed loudly. Annoyed, clearly, by Spencer's refusal to let him go with him to the pickup game.

"Listen," Spencer continued, wondering when exactly it was that he'd lost his mind and capitulated to conversing with his cat like Iggy could understand everything he was saying. *But he can,* a voice in his head insisted, *he totally can.* "I know I took you out to the car wash yesterday, but that was a one-time thing, okay?"

Two days ago, when he'd taken his Tesla to get washed, Iggy had begged so plaintively at the back door that Spencer had ended up throwing on a baggy sweatshirt and tucking Iggy next to his chest, with just the tip of his head poking out of the zippered opening. Iggy had *loved* it, nuzzling into his warm chest, the buzz of his purring filling Spencer with a love and affection that he hadn't ever thought he could feel for another living creature.

The problem was that now Iggy wanted to go out *all* the time.

Iggy meowed again, reaching up and patting Spencer's leg with one dark paw.

"Gah," Spencer said. "I really can't take you. But tonight, we'll . . . we'll go for a walk, okay? As long as you're a good boy."

There had been a period when Iggy had wanted to shred every paper product in the house. It hadn't really *ended* per se; more like, Spencer had learned not to leave anything out that he wouldn't mind being torn up.

He swore Iggy nodded in agreement.

"I'm losing my mind," Spencer huffed under his breath as he picked up his bag and went to his car. "Talking to a goddamn cat like he can understand me."

The drive to the field wasn't particularly long, but Spencer didn't think he'd ever been in this part of Los Angeles before. It was on the edge of a light industrial district, about ten minutes away from the food truck lot, and as Spencer made the final turn, he didn't think he'd have ever guessed that there were sporting fields over this way. But there was a freshly painted, blue and white sign that proclaimed *Los Angeles Youth Sports Club.*

Spencer slowed, and double-checked the address that Alec had given him. This was definitely right.

He pulled into the wide entrance lane, the pavement also freshly done, and a few hundred feet away, the road split into a "Y." A pristine white sign directed visitors to the Youth Sports Club to the left, but Spencer took the right fork, which was labeled as *Mitchell Athletics Center.*

He hadn't known that Alec had his own facility. But then after the Super Bowl a few years back, they'd stopped chatting via text. It had been too hard, knowing that nothing was ever going to happen between them.

It was *still* hard, but at least Alec could be a friend. At least Alec could help him choose a different kind of life. It wasn't what Spencer had hoped for, all those years ago, but it was better than not having him in his life at all.

As Spencer drove along the road towards the medium-sized brick and glass building which looked practically brand new—it had to be, it couldn't be more than four years old, which was when he and Alec had stopped texting each other—he noticed the beautiful fields, all flawless green grass as far as the eye could see, with sheds dotted here and there, likely full of equipment.

He vaguely remembered something about Fisher revamping an old sporting complex, and he realized this must be the one. It made sense that Alec would be part of it—not only was Neal Fisher a client and one of Alec's best friends, Alec did an unsurprisingly large amount of charity work around the city he called home.

"Mitchell Athletics Center" was written on a discreet sign nearly tucked behind one of the azalea bushes dotting the front of the building. Spencer could see there was a large field behind, complete with field goal posts—which also made sense, since Neal Fisher was an ex-kicker and currently dating the Riptide's kicker—and as Spencer pulled into the small lot, he noticed there were already several cars here.

Chase's turquoise blue BMW was unmistakable. A navy blue Tesla, an Audi roadster, and several other expensive cars were parked next to it, as well as a Ducati, not unlike the one sitting in his own garage, except this one was a stark matte black finish. Not necessarily flashy, but it looked like a spendy custom paint job.

Spencer turned off the car, grabbed his bag from the passenger seat, and slid out. Locking the door, he dropped his keys into a convenient pocket on the outside of his bag.

"You can do this," he said under his breath with a quiet huff. "You can absolutely do this."

Walking into the Stars locker room the first time had felt overwhelming in the same way. He hadn't been sure of his reception back then, but it had quickly become obvious that he wasn't as welcome as he'd hoped he would be.

At first, he'd been able to fly under the radar, as there'd been a whole bunch of rookies. But after he'd made the team, and the season had started in earnest, so had all the shit.

He didn't think it would be quite the same this time. After all, these guys dealt with too much prejudice to truly bully him, but Spencer wasn't laboring under any false ideas of camaraderie and shared experience: he was not going to be welcome here, either.

Taking a deep breath, he walked up to the front door. There was lettering on the glass, proclaiming this building to be the property of Mitchell Athletics. Open, it said, by appointment only, but when Spencer pulled the door, it was unlocked.

There was a small entrance foyer, and Spencer recognized the same elegant touch that Alec's office bore in the reception desk, set to one side, next to the large double glass doors. Through them, Spencer could see various pieces of weightlifting equipment, as well as an open workout floor. It was well laid out, with plenty of room between machines, everything shiny and new.

There was nobody at the desk, though Spencer thought he saw a flash of Chase's blond hair through the glass doors. He'd just about given up waiting for someone to show up when he heard a voice behind him.

"What's this?" the voice asked, the faintest music of a Texas drawl still evident around the edges.

Of course the first person Spencer ran into was going to be Heath Harris.

He turned and tried not to tense. Heath wasn't going to throw him out. He *couldn't*. Not just because signing the contract in Alec's office last night gave him the right to be here, but because Spencer didn't think he *physically* could. Heath might still be a big, strong guy, despite his retirement a few years earlier, but Spencer was bigger and stronger.

And God willing, it definitely wouldn't come down to that. Though, Spencer had to admit the idea was a little tempting. It would definitely make any of these guys think twice about fucking with him again.

You're supposed to be making friends, not kicking ass, that voice that sounded so much like Alec's reminded him. *Be nice, and don't fuck up my new gym, okay?*

"Hey," he said, trying for friendly. "Alec suggested I come down and check out the facilities."

Heath's eyes narrowed. "Sam told me you signed with him. Why?"

"Why does anyone change agents?" Defensiveness crept into Spencer's voice, even though he tried to keep it tamped down. Harris didn't need to know *why*, only that Spencer was here now, and he'd better get used to it.

"Alec's a good guy," Heath said in that same casual drawl, which belied the obvious and intense interest in his gaze, "and the guys here are, too. But then, you already knew that, didn't you?"

You're trying to make friends, Spencer reminded himself, *not more enemies.*

"Yeah, I did."

"Hopin' it might rub off on you some?" Heath asked.

It wasn't as painful an insult as some of the others that Spencer had been subjected to over the years. But somehow, coming from Heath, it stung more, because he actually respected the guy. And *yes*, though he'd rather die than admit it, he'd always hoped that someday, Heath might respect him, too.

"Not exactly," Spencer said shortly. He didn't need to convince himself that he was fundamentally *good*. He just hadn't had many opportunities to demonstrate it over the years. But his career wasn't over yet, and there was still time. At least that was what he told himself, late at night, when he lay in bed and couldn't sleep and wondered what the fuck he'd been doing with his life. The reminder didn't exactly soothe the sting of Heath's insult, but it helped.

"Well, you might consider it," Heath said.

"I'll do that," Spencer retorted dryly. "I hear there's a pickup game today?"

Heath raised an eyebrow. "You here to play?"

"Yeah."

The ex-quarterback regarded him for a single, steady moment. Like he was trying to decide something. Then, to Spencer's surprise, Heath reached out and gave him a shoulder slap. "Well, those assholes aren't gonna expect you," he said, and even more shockingly, he *smiled*.

"Who do you guys play?" Spencer asked, following Heath as he approached the double doors and pulled them open.

"Alec didn't tell you?"

"No?" Spencer had wondered who it might be, but it had been impossible to guess. Was it other players? Alec had made it sound very competitive, so there would have to be some people on the team who could play.

"First off, we don't play our normal positions," Heath said as they walked into the main gym. "So you'll have to play offense. Neal's our quarterback. Jamie, Chase, Rashad, and Sam all play defense."

"What do you play?" Spencer hadn't played on the offense side of the ball since high school, but he could be an offensive lineman. That wouldn't be so hard.

Heath grinned slyly and Spencer remembered all the times they'd lined up opposite each other. How good Heath had been—all drive and focus and determination. "I'm the coach, of course."

"You guys have coaches?"

"This is supposed to be fun, but you know how it is. Nobody wants to lose," Heath said. "Especially the other team."

"Who *is* the other team?"

"Coach might be someone you recognize," Heath said, and to Spencer's shock, they turned the corner and the blond hair he'd seen hadn't been Chase's at all, but Colin O'Connor's.

"He's the other coach?"

"Yep," Heath said. They stopped in front of where Neal and Jamie and Colin O'Connor were chatting. "Hey, look who I picked up."

Neal and Jamie did not look particularly surprised to see him, though they didn't look *happy* about it either, but Colin O'Connor's jaw dropped open.

"Spencer Evans? You're gonna bring *him* in?"

When he'd first been drafted into the NFL, he and O'Connor had ended up together a lot. It had made sense, since they were the first two "out" football players. He genuinely liked the guy and couldn't help but admire him. The only problem was over time,

O'Connor didn't seem to feel the same way about Spencer, and Spencer wasn't sure he could really blame him for that. Way back when, O'Connor had tried to give him advice, had tried to help, but in the end, there hadn't been anything he could do.

If only, Spencer had thought so many times back then, he'd been drafted to the Piranhas. If only he'd been accepted in the same way O'Connor had. In the same way Crawford and Harris and Fisher and Wright had. Things would have been different.

Maybe Colin O'Connor wouldn't be looking at him now like he was a bug on the floor that he couldn't wait to squish with his shoe.

"Spencer is with us now," Heath said firmly. Heath might not have been happy about Spencer's addition either, but it was clear he wasn't going to show that in front of O'Connor.

"I'd heard a rumor you were finally signing with Alec," O'Connor said. "I see it was accurate. Unless," he added, raising an eyebrow, "you decided to finally bring in a ringer."

"Nope, he signed last night," Heath said.

"Just in time, I guess." O'Connor smiled, and held out a hand towards Spencer. "I'd say it's good to see you again, but I can already see you tearing through my players like wet cardboard."

Spencer shook his hand. Pleased that maybe it wasn't personal at all. That maybe O'Connor didn't hate him. That maybe he even understood, a little bit.

"I intend to," Spencer said. "Though Harris tells me we're playing different positions."

"Gotta keep it fair," Jamie said. "The first time we played, we didn't, and the score was . . ."

"No need to bring *that* old history back up," Colin cut in with a lopsided grin. "But it wasn't pretty. So we evened it up, some."

"Who else is on your team?" Spencer wondered.

"A few ex-players, like me," O'Connor said. "And some regular guys too."

"By regular guys," Neal said, "he means ex-military and some cops. Firefighters, too. Guys who've actually saved lives. Who've run right into the fire. Who could probably eat us up and then spit us out again."

"Just you, Fisher," O'Connor said with delight. "Just you."

"Hey, I had bruises for a *week* after that asshole Lennox grabbed me," Neal said.

"Who's Lennox?"

"He was a freaking *SEAL*," Chase said, approaching their group. "Great to see you, man." And he didn't get a handshake, Chase literally *hugged* him. "I'm so excited about you joining the team."

O'Connor's eyes narrowed. "I just bet you are. Where you gonna put him?"

"I hadn't decided yet," Heath drawled. "But maybe you could show him some moves, Riley."

"What?" Spencer spluttered. "I . . . I can't play *wide receiver*."

"Only way it's fair," Heath said. "Then these assholes can't whine like little sad puppies when they lose."

"You really want *me* to play wide receiver."

"You'd be the best blocking tight end in the league," Chase said with a laugh.

"With the worst stone hands," Spencer finished. "You guys aren't fucking around."

"Hell no. This is for bragging rights and who's gonna buy the first round," Heath said, even though they were all so rich they could probably buy the bar. He clapped him on the shoulder again. "Chase'll show you the rest of the gym. Get you acquainted with the rules."

Spencer nodded. "I'll see you out there, O'Connor."

Colin gave him a grim nod back. "I cannot fucking believe Mitchell signed him just to get you guys a ringer."

Chase was already walking away, so Spencer had no choice but to follow him.

He figured the moment he started making noise about being traded, it would be crystal clear that he hadn't just swapped agents to give Alec's team a better shot at winning, but that he had serious intentions about changing his life.

But O'Connor would discover that soon enough.

"I was so stoked when Alec texted me this morning and said you'd be here today," Chase said, as he led him through the rest of the equipment, then across a large exercise mat, lined on one side with medicine balls, and an enormous rack of weights. "You're gonna get us the win, for sure."

"Do you not usually win?" Spencer was surprised. They had a pretty good roster going, even with everyone not playing their normal positions.

"It goes back and forth," Chase admitted. "Lennox is tough."

"The SEAL?"

Chase nodded. "And some of the other guys on O'Connor's squad are just as hardcore, but we give them a run for their money. They've won the last two games we've played, but we won four straight before that."

"What changed?" Spencer asked as Chase approached a door at the end of the gym, and pushed open the door. They walked into a modern locker room slash shower facility, complete with custom lockers, emblazoned with names. Everything was shiny and new and in the same elegant style that Spencer had come to expect from Alec.

"They switched Lennox to offense. It's annoying as hell guarding that guy. He's *relentless.*"

"This place is sweet," Spencer pointed out.

"There's spare lockers down that way," Chase said, pointing towards the end of the locker room. "But I'm sure Alec will get you your own soon enough."

Spencer wasn't sure everyone was going to be good with that. Some of his uncertainty must have shown on his face, because Chase reached out and patted him on the back again. "Listen, man, I know things have been rough. But we're a family. We give each other shit, sometimes, but we don't judge."

Spencer raised an eyebrow. It sounded like a dream, like a fantasy that was too good to be true. "You sure about that?"

"It might take some time, but they're all gonna get on board the Spence train. Trust me." Chase sounded very sure of this, but Spencer wasn't sure he was right.

The wary, guarded look in Heath's eyes had been unmistakable.

"Thanks for the vote of confidence," Spencer said dryly.

"Of course, man," Chase said, but instead of Spencer's sarcasm, his tone was full of earnestness.

Alec had been right; the man didn't have a vindictive bone in his body. He was pure joy; open and generous and loyal. Even when he shouldn't have been.

When they'd had their run-in a year ago, and Spencer had insulted him to his face, he'd seen all of those things as negatives. All ways the world could reach out and hurt him. A slap in the face to all the pain that Spencer had endured.

But now, he looked at Chase and saw someone that maybe, with a little bit of luck and some work, he could learn to emulate.

It meant something that he didn't just *know* he could be better, be different, but that he *wanted* it, too.

Spencer cleared his throat. "Where's my locker? You said the spare ones are down at the end?"

"Oh yeah," Chase said. "When he texted, Alec mentioned that he stopped by this morning and set aside a jersey for you. So there should be one down there that has one, already."

"Alright," Spencer said, and headed down towards the other end of the locker room.

If he'd been worried that he wouldn't know which was his, he shouldn't have been. Alec *had* hung a jersey up, in the same bright white and blue as the sign outside, and to Spencer's surprise, not only was his name emblazoned on the back, Alec had taken some athletic tape, and stretched it across the top of the locker, and written, in sloppy capitals *Evans.* Just so, Spencer had to assume, he wouldn't feel left out for his first game.

Emotion swelled through him.

"Come on, guys," Heath said, pushing the locker room door open, followed by Neal, Sam Crawford, and Rashad Green. "Let's get changed so we can go over some of the new plays." He shot Spencer a look. "I wanna get Evans on the ball immediately."

Sam shot Spencer a much more dubious look. "You really think he can play wide receiver?"

"Hey, nobody thought you could play cornerback, either," Heath said, his gaze warming as he gazed at his boyfriend.

"Everyone *still* thinks you can't play corner," Rashad joked.

"Hey!" Sam said with a faux outraged tone. "I don't do half bad. I stopped Lennox last game, didn't I?"

"Yeah," Jamie said dryly. "He only scored twice. Great job on saving that third touchdown."

"That's why we're gonna be double-teaming him," Heath said calmly. "Chase and Sam are gonna run some plays together on him."

Chase groaned.

"Yeah, y'all suck at defense," Heath said. "But even though we gave up lots of TD's last game, if we'd managed to score some . . . we might have gotten somewhere. I want you"—he pointed to Neal—"and you"—this time it was Spencer in his sights—"gettin' together as soon as you're dressed and doing some catch and throw, 'kay?"

Neal grumbled under his breath, and it wasn't like Spencer felt much differently. When he'd walked in here today, he'd been expecting to be able to pull out some of his totalitarian defensive moves, and impress everyone. Now he was going to be catching footballs from Neal *freaking* Fisher of all people. He'd trust Fisher to kick a field goal in just about any situation; the guy was a shoo-in for the Hall of Fame, after all, even though he'd missed that one in the Super Bowl a few years back. But a quarterback?

If he wanted a quarterback, he'd go to Crawford or Aaron Rodgers. Hell, he'd even settle for O'Connor.

But today, he was going to be catching passes from Neal Fisher.

Wasn't that a fucking trip?

He changed quickly, and opened his bag up to grab his gloves, realizing at the last second that they weren't really the right kind of gloves. He knew the ones the receivers on the Stars wore were different. Thinner, tighter, grippier.

"Hey."

Spencer looked up, and before he could react, he was reaching up instinctually, catching a pair of used gloves as they flew towards his head. "I think those'll fit you okay," Chase said. "But if not, there might be some extras in the storage room."

He tugged them on, and to his surprise they did fit him pretty well. A little tighter, maybe, than he was used to, but then he could probably put that down to them being a different style of glove.

"No helmets?" Spencer wondered, when he didn't see any. He'd thought this might be flag football, but there were no flags in any of the lockers, either.

"We play touch," Heath said, looking up from his stretch. "Two hands, below the waist. Though," he added with a small smile, "you don't have to worry too much about the tackling, do you?"

"Nope," Spencer muttered.

"Let's go," Neal said shortly as he tossed a ball up in the air and caught it deftly. Maybe, Spencer thought as he followed him out of the back door of the locker room and out onto the field, this wouldn't be so bad.

Surely if Neal Fisher could play quarterback, he could catch a few footballs?

Separately they went through their warm-up, as the rest of the players began to trickle onto the field. Spencer saw O'Connor on the other side of the field with a *big* guy—tall and tough looking—and assumed that had to be the ex-SEAL that everyone kept saying was the best player on the other team.

"Come on, let's see some catches," Heath said, as he approached where Neal and Spencer were just finishing up their stretching.

Spencer eyed the ex-kicker, but before he could quite get himself ready, Neal had launched a missile in his direction.

It was an automatic reflex, especially playing defense. He saw a ball coming towards him and his hands were up automatically. He juggled it a bit but he tucked it under one arm and took off, sprinting towards the end zone.

Heath clapped, and called him back. "Not too shabby," he said. "I thought you were gonna drop it."

"I've got a few pick sixes under my belt," Spencer said with a grin. "But don't ask me to run a fucking route."

"Don't worry, we don't really do plays," Neal said. "I'll just chuck it and you try to catch it."

"Who plays running back?"

"Bran Phillips," Neal said.

"What?" Phillips was the Riptide's center. He was big and strong and anchored that line better than almost anyone else in the league, but he wouldn't be what Spencer called running back material.

Heath shrugged. "We throw a lot."

"You got anyone else catching the ball?"

"A few guys," Heath said. "But you're gonna be our number one receiver."

"What? *Why*?"

Heath grinned. "You're Spencer Evans, aren't you?"

He was, but he wasn't exactly renowned for his ball skills. This was going to be an interesting experiment.

Neal threw him a few more balls, pretty good spirals actually. He didn't catch all of them, but he thought by the time Heath told them to huddle up to kick off the game, that he wasn't half bad. And Fisher? He might have missed his calling completely.

"I wanna see some hustle out there today," Heath said, as they gathered around him in a loose semicircle. "Riley and Sam are gonna cover Lennox. Don't let him break away, we gotta contain him. Spence is gonna catch some passes today, so, Bran, you gotta cover him, and make sure he gets the blocks he needs." Spencer watched as Bran Phillips, big as a house and probably total shit as a running back, but *killer* as a blocker, nodded. "But yeah, just remember. We're gonna hustle, 'kay?"

Everyone nodded and echoed Heath's sharp clap that ended the huddle.

"You good?" Chase asked as they stood on the sideline, watching as Heath and O'Connor went to meet at the center of the field.

"Yeah," Spencer said. He was trying to focus—not just because this was a game, even if it wasn't his normal kind of game, but because he wanted to impress the other guys—but part of him was dying to ask Chase if Alec usually came to these.

It would make sense that he would. This was *his* field, after all, and the players he repped.

Spencer scanned the sideline, and he saw a few observers, but then suddenly, a man emerged from the parking lot, walking around the side of the building, and even though Alec was wearing shiny silver aviator sunglasses, Spencer swore he felt the jolt of their gazes connecting.

"Oh, look, Alec's here," Chase said, then glanced over at Spencer. He still hadn't managed to look away. Alec had left his suit jacket in the car, and he'd rolled up the sleeves of his shirt, pulling the tie out of its flawless knot as he walked over to the set of bleachers at one end of the field. "Oh," Chase added slyly, "I guess you've already noticed that."

"Yeah," Spencer said. He was probably giving himself away, if Chase hadn't already guessed there was something going on.

Except there was nothing going on.

Why didn't it feel that way, then?

He was just another of Alec Mitchell's clients, now.

"You're up," Heath said, clapping him on the back. "And keep your dick in your pants, okay?"

"Hey . . ." Spencer started to say, a little offended that *everyone* had guessed—though it was much more likely that Chase had actually told them—but Heath just held up a hand.

"Just go get us some points, tiger," Heath joked.

"Let's get on the Spence train!" Chase cried as he jogged out onto the field with Neal and the rest of the offense.

Nobody was playing with a full squad.

They had Neal, him, two other defensive players he recognized from the Cardinals who were playing receiver with him, Bran, and not a single offensive lineman.

"How is this going to work," Spencer hissed at Neal.

"You'll see," Neal said. "Evans, you're on the right. Let's do a button hook route, okay?"

Spencer had already told him he wasn't going to be much for running routes, but he figured they'd manage to find each other—or not.

The guy playing ref blew his whistle and the play began. Spencer took off, this big burly guy on his ass almost immediately.

He wasn't the fastest guy on the team, but that was something he and June had been working on—trusting his repaired Achilles, and pushing off the line with his trademark burst of speed—and he could definitely run faster than this asshole. He sprinted past him, off to the right, and a single glance back told him that he hadn't had to worry about the offensive line being nonexistent, because Bran Phillips was single-handedly blocking two guys who were trying to get to Neal.

Neal scrambled to the left, threw across his body, and Spencer tracked the ball through the air, shifting slightly to compensate for the ball, just as he noticed that the burly defender had nearly caught up to him.

The ball brushed the tips of his fingers and he reeled it in *barely*, pulling it against his chest as he took off. A moment later, before he could get the distance he wanted, he felt a single touch and then a second one.

"Down," the ref screamed out, and Spencer pulled up short, his breath coming in hard, fast pants. He hadn't run that hard in a year, but despite all the insane shit June put him through, somehow this dude had overtaken him. *Him*, Spencer Evans. He was gonna have to have a real serious talk with June about improving his speed before the season started.

"Good runnin'," the guy said, and to Spencer's surprise, he slapped him on the shoulder. "I didn't think I was gonna catch you."

"I didn't think so either," Spencer retorted.

The guy just grinned though. "Easier to do this than runnin' with fifty pounds on your back, like I did when I was smoke jumpin'."

Spencer remembered what Chase had said. That some of the guys on O'Connor's team were ex-firefighters. Ex-military.

And yeah, it was sure a hell of a lot easier to run without all that smoke and gear.

"Good hustle," Heath called out as they moved to the next down marker. At least, Spencer thought, he'd moved the chains. That was the important thing. *And*, he told himself, *at least you caught the fucking ball.*

In deference to Spencer's hard running, Neal called two running plays next, and Spencer blocked, something he was actually *good* at, as Brandon Phillips ran like a freaking bowling ball, knocking down anyone who might defend him. He might not have been very quick, but he was tough, and it took three guys to bring him down each time.

And the whole time, even though he tried to ignore it, Spencer could feel Alec's gaze on him. He was watching the *whole* game, Spencer tried to remind himself. Then he added an extra reminder that millions of people watched him play. He didn't need to let one freaking man make him nervous. But he *was*.

He wanted Alec to think he'd contributed.

He wanted Alec to think he was tough and competent and irresistible.

Even if that way lay certain disaster.

CHAPTER EIGHT

IT WAS ANNOYING HOW often Alec had to keep reminding himself that not only was the monthly off-season pickup game not just intended to be a fun, social activity he liked to organize for his clients, but that it also occupied an important place in his job as an agent.

It was a great way to spot if a player was sluggish or getting out of shape, or needed a new direction.

The problem with today's game was that Alec was flustered and distracted, and couldn't take his eyes off Spencer.

At first he told himself it was because Spencer was recovering from an injury, and as his agent, he needed to know, more than just talking to his physical therapist, that he'd really truly recovered. That he was going to be in top shape for the upcoming season, especially if Alec was going to be shopping for a trade.

But he knew better, because it had always been more than that.

He watched as Neal threw another pass, this one a little wobblier than the last, and it fell just out of Spencer's grip.

It was obvious from Spencer's frown that he blamed himself for not being able to catch the ball. That this mattered to him, already, even though he wasn't playing his normal position. Even though the game was ultimately meaningless, despite the way everyone bragged about it.

Alec had worried that he wouldn't take it seriously; that he wouldn't put the effort in or that he wouldn't play at all. But that, he realized, had never been who Spencer was.

He put himself, one hundred and ten percent, into everything he did.

It was why he'd refused to take Alec's initial no as his final answer.

He'd even recruited Chase Riley to help him, for God's sake.

But then, that was why, at the very beginning, Alec had wanted so badly to be his agent. He'd seen that crazy internal push and Spencer's undeniable drive, and couldn't help but wonder what it would look like applied to more than just the football field.

By then, Colin O'Connor had already begun to change the game, and Alec had been so sure that whatever he ended up doing, Spencer Evans was going to alter it forever.

He'd long given up on that dream, but he couldn't deny any longer that it was back. Maybe that was why he could pretend he found Spencer Evans so compelling, but deep down, he knew it was so much more than that.

"Come on, Riley," he shouted as his team changed to defense, and Chase jogged onto the field, game for anything. "Let's hold 'em!"

From the first play it was obvious that O'Connor had figured out the way to win: get Lennox involved early and keep throwing him the ball. Despite being a great wide receiver, Chase was miserable as a corner, and Sam wasn't much better. It didn't help that they were both athletic guys—strong and fast on their feet—but Lennox was a mountain of muscle and determination.

Alec sighed as he watched Lennox dodge Sam's grasp and then Chase's, as he ran for another twenty-five-yard play.

He pulled his tie off the rest of the way, after O'Connor's team scored a touchdown. Then his own went three and out, and the opposing team scored *again*.

But despite the frustration of possibly losing *again*, because O'Connor had outsmarted them, there was a silver lining.

Alec hadn't really believed that any of his guys—friends *and* clients—would ever truly bully Spencer. He knew they wouldn't have it in them. But he'd also worried they wouldn't accept him.

But Spencer inserted himself, becoming part of the team, even if they hadn't wanted him to be.

He was right there on the sideline, cajoling and yelling and trying to coach Sam and Chase. He was right there next to Heath and Neal, going over plays, trying to find a way to defeat that firefighter that O'Connor had just brought in.

When Spencer scored a touchdown, with a truly magnificent double fake that only Chase could have taught him, Alec found himself believing, against all odds, that this might actually work.

As the last few minutes ticked off the clock, Alec wandered down to his team's sideline, walking up next to Heath.

"You're gonna get them next time," he said consolingly.

"I think so," Heath said, and to Alec's surprise, he actually sounded optimistic about it. "I'm gonna have Fisher and Evans run some drills over the next few weeks."

"Really?" Alec raised an eyebrow. "You tell them this yet?"

"No, but they've got potential. And we've got to find a better pass rusher."

"You have Spencer Evans on your team. He's arguably the best pass rusher in the NFL," Alec joked weakly.

"Yes, but I can't use him the way he should be used." Heath ran a hand through his hair and his sigh was full of frustration. "We'll figure something out."

"You know, I started this to be a fun time," Alec reminded him. "I think you're going to get some guys balking when they find out you're starting a practice schedule."

"Maybe," Heath said, finally cracking a smile. He hesitated. "You know what you're doin' here?"

"With Spencer?" It was easier to pretend ignorance than to lie directly to Heath's face. Heath was so good at reading people, he'd never be able to pull it off.

"With him, and with him becoming your client. Trying to, I don't know, *change* him."

"He wants to change," Alec said simply. "He came to me and said he was ready to make a change, and I agreed to help."

Heath did not look completely convinced. "So that's a yes, then. You've figured out the can of worms you're opening?"

"Think of how good, for example, the Riptide might be if they had a player like Spencer Evans on defense. You gave up way more points than you could score last year. Even with Sam and Chase and Rashad. You guys need the help."

"We're gonna bulk up the defense in the draft," Heath said.

"Yeah, but those are rookies," Alec argued. "We're talking about one of the best defensive ends in the game. Someone who's *proven*."

"Someone who's proven themselves to be unsupportive of the way a lot of our team lives," Heath pointed out.

"He's not unsupportive. He just . . ." Alec sighed. "He never got a chance to prove it. You've heard how shitty the Stars can be. Close-minded assholes, all of them. What if you had been on that team when you'd come out? It would've been a hell of a lot different than it was. You know that."

"What about all that tough-guy shit? The posturing? The hyper-masculinity? The total lack of LGBT support he's given over the years? The shitty interviews he's given? *Gay guys don't have to wear pink* and all that garbage?"

"Gay guys *don't* have to wear pink," Alec said quietly. "You know that."

"Yeah, but his bullshit didn't help any of us. You know it. I know it's pissed you off on more than one occasion. He might not be straight, but he's been working against what you've been trying to accomplish. What we've *all* been trying to accomplish."

"Maybe he was. But he didn't have to tell me he's been unhappy. He *did* tell me that he wants to be different." Alec took a risk, a chance. "You were unhappy like that too, once. Did anybody tell you that you weren't allowed to try a different path? Say you couldn't experiment, because you might fuck your life up? Even if they had, you wouldn't have listened, because you knew if it worked out, you'd end up a hell of a lot happier."

Heath stared out at the field. The players from both teams were shaking hands, and O'Connor was heading towards them. Finally, Heath sighed and shook his head, albeit reluctantly.

"No," he finally admitted. "No, nobody stood in my way or told me I couldn't do it."

"I think Spencer deserves the same shot, that's all," Alec said. "And you've already given him part of it. You brought him onto the team."

"That was you," Heath pointed out wryly. "You invited him."

"Nope, I just invited him to play. *You* welcomed him onto the team."

O'Connor was nearly over to them now, and Alec assumed that at least for now, the conversation was over. He hoped he'd made enough of an impression. Heath Harris could be a damn tough nut to crack.

Heath stepped out and shook Colin's hand, and Alec took it next. "Good to see you both," he said. "Great game."

"Yeah," Heath said in a long, sarcastic drawl. "Real great."

"Hey, you'll get there," Colin said with a quick grin. "I fully expect to have a shit time covering Evans next game."

"You bet you will," Heath said, with a quick laugh.

Colin switched his attention to Alec. "I was surprised to see Evans out here."

"You shouldn't have been. Not if you'd been paying attention." Alec was tired of the questions already and this had barely begun.

"Oh?" Colin seemed interested now, the casual expression on his face sharpening.

"He was miserable. He doesn't want to be miserable anymore. It's not that much of a stretch."

The corner of O'Connor's mouth tilted up into a smile. "You gonna be his knight in shining armor, Mitchell?"

It wasn't that hard to answer. He'd been trying for nine goddamn years, after all. "Yes," he said in a tone that brooked no arguments.

"Well, then good luck," Colin said, and after shaking hands again, walked off to celebrate with his own team.

"You," Heath said, after he left, "have it *bad*."

"I don't know what you're talking about," Alec said primly.

"You absolutely fuckin' do."

. . . . ● . ● . ● . . .

The worst part was that Heath was *right*.

It was impossible to deny he had it bad when, after grabbing his workout bag from the car, he walked back into the locker room and came face-to-face with Spencer Evans' bare back.

When Alec had said that he was uneasy about posing naked with guys who looked like Greek gods, he'd meant Heath and Neal and Jamie and Chase, of course. But he'd really been thinking about Spencer.

How his wide, muscled shoulders curved and dipped, sinuously curving down to his tapered waist. Just looking at all that tanned skin on display, so hard and so soft, all at the same time, made Alec's palms sweat.

He wanted to touch, even though he knew he shouldn't. That he *couldn't*.

Alec set his gym bag down on the bench in front of his own locker. Spencer's head whipped over and their gazes met. "Oh," Spencer said. "It's just you."

"Just me," Alec said. "Since I was already here, I thought I'd get a quick workout in."

The corner of Spencer's mouth quirked up. "Now that you're thinking about stripping down?"

"Yes," Alec grumbled. "Wish I hadn't told you about that."

"No, you're gonna wish you hadn't told me about it when I've got you cryin' and hurtin'," Spencer said with a grin that set Alec's nerves alight.

"Is that starting today?" Alec pulled a t-shirt out of his bag, and after hesitating for a moment, decided that he didn't have much of a choice. He'd have changed in front of Heath or Chase. Spencer shouldn't be any different.

Unbuttoning his shirt, he hung it up in the locker, unconsciously sucking in a breath when he felt Spencer's eyes still on him.

Normally, he wouldn't have given a shit that he didn't have a six-pack. To do what he did, he didn't need one. None of the guys he occasionally slept with cared. But this was Spencer, and if he'd thought about Alec the way Alec had thought about him over the years, he'd surely wondered what he looked like under all the suits.

And if Spencer's fantasies had been anything like Alec's, this was definitely not how he'd have wanted it to happen.

A lot of things aren't how we pictured them, nine years ago, Alec reminded himself firmly, and reached for his belt, unbuckling it quickly and then shedding his suit pants, hanging them next to his shirt.

Clad in just his briefs—and for the first time in a very long time, aware of just how tightly the material clung to the curves of his ass—he dug through his bag, pulling out a pair of athletic shorts.

He couldn't look over at Spencer. Couldn't bear to see what was on his face. What kind of heat was in his eyes. Or, even worse, if he didn't see any, and he saw disappointment instead. But even the imagined warmth of Spencer's gaze was enough to heat his own skin, and a swath of goose bumps emerged over his chest and arms.

The tension strung somehow even tighter, and Alec's fingers trembled on his shorts as he pulled them on.

Why didn't Spencer say something? Why didn't *he* say something? Why didn't someone walk in and awkwardly interrupt them?

Finally fully clothed, he turned towards Spencer, telling himself the whole time that it didn't matter if he wasn't interested anymore. That it would be *easier* if he wasn't.

If this was all one-sided, he could move past it quicker, and they could get to the real work that needed to be done.

But it wasn't easier at all.

Spencer was frozen, his dark eyes somehow impossibly darker, his fingers clenched around the edge of his locker. Like that was all that was keeping him in place, and otherwise he'd be much, *much* closer.

"Oh." Alec considered himself both an intelligent man and someone who had a way with words. He was rarely speechless, but the small noise emerged from his mouth before he could stop it, like he'd been punched.

"Oh," Spencer said. Surprisingly grim about it.

Probably because of just how many times Alec had turned him down.

Probably because Alec had made it abundantly clear that nothing was going to happen between them, especially now.

Alec felt that same swirl of disappointment.

Maybe he shouldn't have gone to his room alone, that long-ago Pro Bowl. Then at least he'd know how it felt to have all that intensity focused on him. His fingertips would have already stroked all those mesmerizing muscles. Maybe they'd have exhausted the heat between them, once and for all.

But as they stared at each other, Alec knew, like he had then, that one night would never have been enough.

"Well," Spencer said, his voice deep and dark, the edges gravelly. "I don't think you need to worry."

It was reckless to continue talking like this, because Alec, warmed from the inside out by the compliment, knew exactly what Spencer meant.

But he couldn't help himself.

"Like what you see, huh?" Alec teased.

To his surprise, Spencer frowned. "Yes. But what I really want to know is who the asshole was who made you think you needed to work out for that stupid cover."

"There wasn't . . ." Alec hesitated. "I just . . ." He shrugged. The words felt thick and wrong in his mouth. "I just didn't want to look wimpy and scrawny in comparison. That's all. There's nobody . . ." *There's never been anybody like you, no matter who I've fucked, who I let fuck me. They've never been you, and that's all that matters.*

Spencer let go of the metal edge of the locker and suddenly he was right there, tall and big, with all this exposed skin, the ridges of his abs so lickable that Alec felt weak. It would be so easy to just give in, to push away all his concerns and his ironclad set of rules, and just fucking *let go.*

"You're not wimpy. You're not scrawny." Spencer's eyes were tracing his exposed skin—and he was a lot less exposed than he'd been five minutes before, but it was like with Spencer's gaze on him, he wasn't wearing a stitch—like he could still remember every inch of him. "You're absolutely fucking gorgeous."

This was so far over the line, already, and still Alec was almost unbearably tempted to just rise up on his toes and press his mouth to Spencer's. God, it had been so long coming. Surely he couldn't do everything he needed to for Spencer, surely they couldn't work together so tightly and frequently and *not* do this. He was reminded, almost unpleasantly, of why he'd originally told Spencer no.

He hadn't thought he could do this and keep his hands to himself.

He'd only changed his mind because he'd wanted so desperately to help him.

Desperation felt like an entirely different beast now, crawling restlessly under his skin.

"Maybe not." Alec didn't know where he'd summoned the casual tone he used from, but he was grateful for it. "But I still don't think it'd be a bad idea to fit a few workouts in, between now and then."

"I'm yours," Spencer said, and Alec felt his heart thud so loudly surely the other man could hear it. They could probably hear it in the other fucking room. "For whatever you need," he added, but the edge of his smile was sly. Knowing. Like he understood exactly what Alec wanted, and just like him, he was a breath away from just giving it to him.

Alec knew if he was smart at all, he would tell Spencer politely thanks but no, thanks, and he'd go put some very important distance between them. Only meet him in his office from now on, with a full suit on and his enormous desk between them and insanity. But he didn't, and he wasn't going to.

"Okay, lead the way," he said instead, and couldn't find an ounce of regret as Spencer nodded and turned to walk back into the weight room.

· · · ● · ● · ● · ● · ·

As he led Alec into the weight room, Spencer swore he could still feel his heartbeat in his ears.

He hadn't really expected to help Alec work out today. He definitely hadn't expected to see him strip down to just his underwear in front of him, and while he might have guessed, with all their history, such a moment might be fraught, he hadn't expected that it would set him on fire.

While Alec had been worrying that he was scrawny and out of shape, Spencer had been mesmerized.

He always felt bulky and almost *too* big. Strong, yes, but oversized in his own body. He'd done enough training that he wasn't clumsy, but occasionally he felt like he must be.

On the other hand, Alec was slim but perfectly formed, like one of those statues in an art museum. While he might be angsting about his muscle definition, Spencer looked at him, and thought he was absolutely fucking perfect just the way he was.

But then here he was anyway, internally panting like a dog in heat, as he watched Alec do a whole series of crunches with a medium-sized medicine ball.

"That's it," Spencer said encouragingly as sweat beaded on Alec's forehead and he slowed down his pace just a touch. "You can get through these. Four . . . three . . . two . . . one. Great job."

Spencer was trying to occupy the space of "supportive athletic trainer" but it was hard, because all he wanted to do was help Alec up and then walk him back to that conveniently placed wall and kiss him until neither of them could stand.

Alec groaned as he finished, collapsing back on the mat, a hand across his stomach.

"You're gonna kill me," he said.

If there were any deaths happening, they were definitely going to be mutual, and also pleasurable.

Spencer took a deep breath. "You good?"

Alec shot him a look. "Do I look good?"

So good I can barely stand it. How do you do it? Just sit there, like it's not killing you too, because I think it must be.

"You look tired." It wasn't what he really wanted to say, but he'd already pushed them right up to the line earlier, in the locker room. He'd made it absolutely clear what he thought of Alec's looks.

Alec groaned again. "I *feel* tired."

"One more set, and you can call it quits for the day."

"You calling it quits, too?" Alec asked.

He'd considered doing it. It wasn't technically his day to work out, but the game had left his muscles buzzed and engaged, and then there was all this sexual tension in the room.

Working out wouldn't leave him satisfied the way he wanted to be, but it would be better than nothing.

"Nah, I think I'm gonna get a little work in," Spencer said.

"After the game?"

Damn Alec, he couldn't leave well enough alone.

"Yeah, after the game," Spencer said, his voice rough and gravelly, even to his own ears. "I'm . . . keyed up."

"Oh."

"Yeah. *Oh.*"

"I'll leave you to it, then," Alec said, but even as Spencer went over to one of the weight machines, checking the calibration and the load, he could feel Alec's gaze on him.

"I'm gonna . . ." Alec waved absently towards the treadmills at the front of the gym, right by the bank of windows. "Get some cardio in." He proceeded to lift himself off the mat, and after wiping his forehead with a towel, walked over to the treadmill that would give him the best view of the gym.

And of Spencer.

Alec's gaze was flinty, almost *daring* him to say something about his choice of machine.

Well, Spencer thought, *you wanna play? We can play.*

He pulled his t-shirt off, wiping his own forehead with it, and leaving it on a heap on the floor. He heard, rather than saw, Alec start to jog on the treadmill, his feet making a rhythmic noise that Spencer decided he might as well use as his own meter.

It was a lot of weight, but even when he'd been hobbled by his torn Achilles, he'd still kept up on his upper body. Felt a drip of sweat form on his back, and wind its way down his flexing muscles. Hoped that maybe Alec was suffering even a fraction as much as he was.

And on cue, Alec's rhythm faltered just enough that Spencer felt a wave of exultation roar through him, giving him the last burst of energy he needed to finish the set.

Muscles aching, he let the weights fall to the base with a heavy clank.

He did two more sets, wiped his sweat off with his discarded t-shirt, and did the rest of his arms, enjoying not only the burn, but the heat prickling across his skin as Alec watched every single movement.

After Spencer finished, and moved to the mat to do his own ab work, something occurred to him that didn't make much sense.

Yes, he worked hard. He had a good, strong body. A lot of people had commented on it over the years, enough that he knew they weren't wrong. He even saw a fraction of what they did, when he looked in the mirror. But Alec was around football players *all the time*. Football players who were way hotter, way more built than Spencer was. But Spencer had never heard even a peep about Alec hooking up with a player—one of his clients or otherwise. Why, then, did it feel like every single goddamn time their eyes met, Alec was barely leashing his own desire in?

Could it just be . . . *him*?

The thought was revolutionary. He was just a guy. Just a guy who only knew what the fuck he was doing *on* the field. He had no personal life, whatsoever. He didn't even really have hobbies. He didn't have any cultured interests, like Alec did. He wasn't well-dressed or well-spoken, particularly, and he wasn't fancy or experienced, like all of Alec's exes probably were.

Then why was it he could practically feel Alec's longing from here?

Spencer finished his set of crunches and picking up the heaviest medicine ball, did a new variation of his normal routine, one that June taught him, one that tended to burn out, through pain and hard work, even the most persistent of mental questions.

When he finished, he was sweating freely, his fingertips slipping just a little on the ball, and yet, he still hadn't managed to dismiss the thought.

Could Alec . . . *care* about him?

Not just want to get him into bed. Not just want him for a night, even an unforgettable one.

Could he want the same thing that Spencer had always wanted?

Three Years Ago

Spencer was on his third beer, and despite his size, he was already feeling the alcohol moving through his veins.

He wasn't much of a drinker, normally, but if there was any occasion to make him break his normal habits, it was watching a team that wasn't his play in the Super Bowl.

They'd gotten close a handful of times, but the problem with his team was never the stifling defense that he'd spent the last few years leading, but the offense that never seemed to score enough points.

Every year began to melt together in his head—too many years of being good, but not quite good enough.

It made Spencer frustrated. It made him keep lifting a finger, one of the unobtrusive waiters arriving at his elbow a few seconds later with a fresh bottle.

It wasn't his normal habit, but if a guy couldn't get a little tipsy while mourning the slow, inevitable death of all his hopes, then when could he?

He'd been invited to watch the game from any of half a dozen of the luxury boxes that surrounded the upper tier of the stadium. He hadn't wanted to go at all, turning down all of the invitations, but then Larry, his agent, had called. He'd heard from the commissioner's office, he said. "They're going to want you there," Larry had said apologetically. "Looks bad if the reigning Defensive Player of the Year doesn't go to the Super Bowl."

"Looks bad when the reigning Defensive Player of the Year isn't *in* the Super Bowl," Spencer had muttered back.

"I know you're pissed about that," Larry said sympathetically. "But they want you to go."

"Then find me a box where I don't know anyone," Spencer said. "Or even better, get me a regular ticket. I'll sit in the fucking stands."

But the commissioner wasn't going to have Spencer Evans sitting in a regular seat, like he was just a fan, so he'd ended up in a box with various other NFL players. He hadn't really known anyone, so at least he hadn't had to send Larry an annoyed text.

With the detached veneer of alcohol, he could almost watch the game and pretend that he didn't care. Like most Super Bowls, it was an offensive blowout, which annoyed Spencer, but he wasn't surprised.

If it was you and your squad playing, it'd be a different story.

But it wasn't Spencer playing. They'd lost, again, in the first round of the playoffs. Not to the Riptide, at least, though it still stung that the other team based in Los Angeles was so goddamned good.

Sam Crawford was leading them down the field again, tossing pass after pass to Chase Riley, like there wasn't even a defense playing against them.

Spencer ground his teeth together as the defensive rushed against the offensive line and Bran Phillips, the center, easily sloughed off his equivalent on the opposing team.

If they kept giving Crawford all that time, he and Riley were going to continue picking them apart.

"You look pissed off."

Spencer glanced up and wished he hadn't drunk three and a half beers.

Alec was standing there, in one of his perfect three-piece suits, an aqua and baby blue striped tie proclaiming his allegiance to the Riptide.

If he'd known Alec was going to be here, he would have . . . Spencer mentally flailed a bit. What would he have done? He didn't know. He certainly wouldn't be sitting here, mouth open, a combination of surprise and arousal and *booze* running through his veins.

Football, he told himself, *you can talk about football. Not about anything you normally talk about. RuPaul's Drag Race and all that other stuff that makes you like him way more than you should.*

"Well, they're giving Crawford all *fucking* day," Spencer said, waving towards the field, because apparently his brain-to-mouth filter was broken today.

"Yeah, I can see that," Alec said smoothly, and then sat down, right next to Spencer.

Okay, so we're doing this again, Spencer thought. How many times had he sat alone in his house and wanted this?

He'd imagined it so many times, before and after that night. The texting was great, but it wasn't *this*.

It was impossible not to wish that things had been different—that *he* was different, and even if he wasn't, that Alec didn't care so much.

But Alec was incapable of *not* caring, which was even one of the reasons why Spencer liked him so much.

He was an agent not because of the money and the prestige, though he'd found plenty of both over the years, but because he wanted to make the National Football League a better place, and find guys like Spencer a place they could belong.

Well, the joke was on him, because Spencer was never going to belong anywhere.

Instead of putting the bottle into the cup holder, he lifted it to his lips, and took another long gulp.

When he glanced over at Alec, he had an amused expression on his face.

"I don't think I've ever seen you drunk."

"I'm *not* drunk," Spencer protested. "I can handle my booze, thank you very much."

Except he couldn't. He knew it. And even worse, now Alec Mitchell knew it.

The next time he got a text from Alec, there was going to be some sly comment about his drinking habits in it.

"Sure doesn't look like it," Alec said, nudging his shoulder with his own. "Guess I can't blame you."

"I didn't even want to come to this farce," Spencer grumbled.

Alec's bluish-gray eyes were sympathetic. "You threatened to sit in the stands, didn't you?"

It was annoying how well Alec knew him.

Like he could see right through all the walls he'd erected, the tough-guy act, and the way he liked to pretend that his life was *awesome*, and could see the truth, could see that scared kid who still lived deep down in him. The one who had taken one look at Alec and had wondered if he would ever be lucky enough to have a guy like that in his life.

You weren't lucky enough, Spencer told himself firmly. *There's nothing between you.*

He didn't even believe the lie.

But he understood why, despite the clear mutual attraction, nothing had happened between them.

"I did, but apparently that's unacceptable." Spencer drained the rest of his beer. He'd regret it in the morning, but right now, he didn't really give a shit, and that was nice.

"You're a big star, Spencer," Alec said sympathetically.

"And I should be at the biggest game of the year, *blah, blah blah*," Spencer retorted.

"Maybe it's not the victory lap you wanted . . ." Alec began.

"It's not," Spencer interrupted him.

Alec shrugged. "You guys had some tough breaks."

"We need a guy like *that*." Spencer gestured at the field with his empty bottle. To Sam Crawford. The Riptide had just scored another touchdown.

"Hey, I bet you that Harris'll be available after this game," Alec said, smiling. "No way the Riptide will keep them both."

"You think they'll commit to Crawford? Really? The rookie over the veteran?"

It was one of his fears. One of the many that kept him up too many nights.

Would he eventually be washed up and replaced, like Heath Harris had so obviously been?

Would he end up regretting every choice he'd made to prioritize football over everything else?

"In the NFL, change is the one constant," Alec said. "You know that."

He did know. He fought it every single day of his life.

So far, he'd been lucky. No major injuries. Nothing to derail his stratospheric rise. He faced each challenge and then defeated it, the same way that in a game, he mowed through offensive linemen.

Alec leaned forward in his chair as Neal Fisher kicked off for the Riptide, the ball sailing through the end zone.

"You got any other players in the game?" Spencer wondered. He was pretty sure he knew the answer, but he didn't want to admit to Alec just how closely he followed his career.

"Rashad Green, who just scored that touchdown," Alec said. "I keep trying to figure out Harris. He seems to want to switch, but then he always gets cold feet. We went back and forth about half a dozen times last summer, and then he ended up staying with who he's using currently."

"Too bad," Spencer said.

Alec shot him a wry look. "Don't get me started," he said.

Spencer wondered which elephant in the room Alec was referring to: that Alec still wanted to represent him, or that they'd spent the last two years flirting via text.

Larry was . . . well, he was *fine* and that was all Spencer needed. He'd gotten him a good contract after his rookie deal had ended. He'd even managed to get the management and coaching staff to make some half-hearted policies that of course nobody had ever followed.

Larry wasn't the problem.

Even Alec wouldn't have been able to change the way the guys in the locker room behaved. He wasn't *God,* even though he looked like an angel.

And speaking of looking like an angel . . .

Spencer thought of all those glorious selfies he'd gotten over the years. Alec mussed, Alec partially undressed, Alec considering all kinds of shirt colors.

He knew then, in that moment, that he couldn't bring all of that up. It was too close, too personal, and he was used to keeping it private. There were way too many players hanging around. So instead, he defaulted to the one topic that they usually discussed in person: his representation.

"Hey, you know I have considered it," Spencer said, even though that was not technically accurate. "I'm happy with Larry. You know that."

"You're settling," Alec said, but his tone was kind, at least.

Spencer could give him that.

"Is it settling if I just won Defensive Player of the Year *again*?" Spencer wondered out loud.

Alec rolled his eyes. "This is why we don't talk about football."

He was *right*, and it hit Spencer right in the gut.

"Well, we're at the Super Bowl. Kind of a requirement."

"True." Alec held up his hand and the waiter came over, bringing another beer for Spencer, even though he hadn't asked. He almost shook his head and turned it down, but they *were* at the Super Bowl, and talking about football was inevitable.

If he was going to talk football with Alec, he needed to maintain this blissful sense of false reality.

Everything was fine.

He was fine.

He didn't want to grab Alec's hand and take him into the nearest men's room and pull him into a stall and do everything to him that he'd ever imagined.

The waiter returned a minute later with a wineglass for Alec.

"Cheers," he said, tilting the glass, the red wine shifting.

"I could also mention it's the Super Bowl, so beer is *also* a requirement," Spencer pointed out.

"Ew," Alec said. "I hate beer."

"Amazing you ended up as an agent in a sport that is literally *sponsored* by beer," Spencer said. "Beer is football's drink of choice."

"Do you even like beer?" Alec asked, sipping his wine. "Or do you just drink it because you think you should?"

Now Alec's lips were tinted with the reddish hue of the wine, and somehow they were even more kissable than they had been five seconds earlier.

Spencer looked away. Back to the field. Back to sanity.

There was a reason they didn't do this.

It was like tempting fate. Or Spencer's utterly compromised self-control.

"I like beer," Spencer said shortly.

"You could try my wine," Alec offered enticingly, swaying an inch closer.

Spencer could feel his shoulder, surprisingly firm, under his jacket. He'd noticed, of course, that Alec had a slim but fit body. The fit of his suits left nothing to Spencer's imagination, and for a football player, he had a pretty good one.

"No, thanks," Spencer said. "I don't like wine."

Alec's expression made it clear he knew that Spencer was lying. He didn't know if he liked wine. He'd never had any. But trying it now, while they were sitting with about twenty other football players who would *definitely* notice him drinking Alec's wine, was a terrible idea.

Even if he was a little bit tempted.

"So, who do you think is gonna win this game?" Alec asked as the opposing team scored another touchdown, putting them up five points with two minutes left.

"Whoever scores the final touchdown," Spencer said. Still annoyed that this, like so many other playoff games, had turned into an offensive blowout. If he'd been playing . . . Spencer shook off the thought, because he *wasn't* playing.

"You think Crawford can pull this off?" Alec raised an eyebrow. He was clearly skeptical, despite obviously wanting the Riptide to win. He had *two* players on the team, and was even sporting that ridiculous tie.

"Yes," Spencer said. He'd been watching Crawford on the bench, even as the other team had driven down the field, scoring the touchdown that had put them up. His eyes had never left the tablet he was holding, and he and Harris—who Spencer had to admit wasn't the most likely candidate to be a backup—were deep in conversation.

Alec looked surprised. "Really? You think they're going to win?"

"Two-minute touchdown drill," Spencer said. "Defense hasn't gotten to him all fucking game. He can do it, if he can keep his cool and make his throws."

"If you were playing . . ."

Spencer shot him a look. "If I was playing, he wouldn't have a chance in hell."

"Next time, I'll definitely be at the Battle of LA, then," Alec said. "Because I'd love to see you flatten him like a pancake."

"Really?"

Alec rolled his eyes. "What, not you too? Just because I'm gay doesn't mean that I don't love a good tackle. Geez. You should know better, Evans."

Alec wasn't wrong. He *should* know better. But sometimes he spent so much time hearing the opposite that he almost forgot it wasn't like that at all. That liking men didn't make him a pussy or soft in any way, shape, or form.

"I should, you're right," Spencer admitted.

"It's that goddamned locker room of yours," Alec grumbled, taking a long gulp of wine. "They're fucking poison."

Spencer couldn't agree more. And yet, he was still trying to impress them.

He didn't understand it himself, but he kept doing it.

"Look," Spencer said, changing the subject and pointing at the field in front of them. The crowd was going wild, as Crawford hit Riley on a crossing route, gaining them an easy thirty yards. "They're gonna do it."

"I'm not convinced," Alec said. "But you seem to be. Wanna make it interesting?"

"Yes." The beer had loosened Spencer's tongue enough that he couldn't say no. Couldn't pretend he didn't know what Alec was suggesting. Couldn't ignore the one thing he wanted, desperately.

"I win, we have a serious conversation about you and Larry and what you're doing with your career. You win and . . ."

He wasn't just feeling *loose*, he was feeling downright reckless. That was the only explanation for the words that came out of his mouth. "If I win, we do it at dinner. A date. A real date."

Alec looked shocked. "You're serious."

He was, more than he'd realized. How long had he wanted this? Definitely since the draft, seven years ago, and even more since they'd become friends of a sort. Friends who flirted. Who ran right up to the line and teased it by sliding a toe across it occasionally.

"Yes."

"I can't go on a date with you," Alec said. "You're a player . . . it would be . . ." He moistened his lips with the tip of his tongue. "It would be a bad idea."

"Didn't stop you from coming over here and sitting with me, did it?" *Didn't stop you from texting me all those times.*

"No, but we're not on a date now," Alec hedged. "This is a work event."

"No date, no bet," Spencer said.

At least Alec looked like he regretted it. Maybe not as much as Spencer did, but at least that made his rejection—and his bullshit excuse—a little easier to swallow.

"Too bad," Alec said.

"Yeah," Spencer agreed, glancing over at the man next to him. "Too bad."

A minute later, they watched as Crawford connected with Chase Riley on a touchdown, essentially winning the game.

"Well," Alec said ruefully as the cacophony of the celebration made Spencer's ears ring, "I guess you would've won."

"I guess I would have." He'd never tell Alec how disappointed he was that they'd been *this* close.

They sat in silence a moment longer, watching as confetti fell down from the sky. All in shades that matched Alec's tie. Spencer swallowed hard. He wanted to wrap his fingers around the silk and tug him closer. Until there was no more room and no more lies between them.

But he couldn't. Not here. Not now. Probably not ever.

Suddenly, all those texts they'd shared didn't seem so special. They felt spineless, like something they both settled for.

"You think Green's gonna win the MVP?" Spencer said, his throat tight. "A hundred and ten yards rushing. Two touchdowns."

"Normally, yeah, but not after Riley caught that touchdown. Three for him. He's a shoo-in."

Alec was right, because a few minutes later, the stage was erected and there was Chase Riley, huge smile on his face, accepting the MVP award.

"I guess . . . I guess I should find a way out of here," Spencer said. He was about to stand, to escape, because all this fucking unrequited crap felt like it was strangling him alive, but then to his shock, Alec reached out and put a hand on his leg. Stopping him. He froze. Was he . . .? Had he changed his mind?

"Wait," Alec said, his voice strange. "Wait, I think something is happening."

Spencer glanced back down at the makeshift stage, where various players and personnel were passing around the Lombardi Trophy. Crawford had it now and he was making some point about how he couldn't have done any of this without Harris.

Spencer believed it.

Crawford hadn't been that good only a season earlier. But Harris, he was a machine. Until the injuries had sidelined him, he'd been one of the quarterbacks that Spencer was most cautious of.

"What's . . ." That was all the question that Spencer got out of his mouth before something *did* happen.

Sam Crawford reached out and pulled Heath Harris against him, and kissed him in front of a couple million people.

"Oh my God," Spencer exhaled sharply.

"I *knew* something was up with Harris!" Alec exclaimed. "I can't fucking believe this! The same team! At the Super Bowl!"

He turned to Spencer, who was still staring, dumbstruck, at the two players currently kissing on the Super Bowl victory stage. He'd never, not in a hundred years, ever imagined that something like this could happen. He'd have said it was impossible. But it was very definitely happening.

"You could do this," Alec said, but Spencer had heard—and seen—enough.

He rose.

"No, I couldn't," Spencer said, and this time, it was his turn to walk away.

The next time Alec texted him, a month later, he didn't respond.

And the time after that, and the time after that.

Spencer didn't know which was worse: not answering, or that Alec stopped after only three unanswered attempts.

Chapter Nine

Spencer woke up to a phone beeping with incoming texts and a mouthful of fur.

"Iggy," he groaned, rolling over carefully so he wouldn't smash the cat, curled up right next to his head, his long black tail wrapped around his chin.

Iggy chirped happily, and then stretching, planted himself right on Spencer's bare chest as he reached for his phone.

The texts were, unsurprisingly, from Alec.

It had been two days since the pickup game, and he'd spent them in a mix of emotional upheaval and undeniable hope. He couldn't help but think that if it was *only* sex, Alec would have been down for scratching their mutual itch nine years ago.

Spencer definitely wouldn't have been the one saying no. He'd have followed wherever Alec suggested, that night of the draft. If Alec had even crooked his finger, he'd have fallen to his knees, speechless but so fucking eager.

He wouldn't have been able to help himself.

But it hadn't happened then, or that night in Hawaii, or during those two years when they'd texted back and forth all the time, or even during that Super Bowl, either. It had *never* happened, even though Alec had, at points, been clearly, obviously interested.

Before, he hadn't even had the good excuse that he was Spencer's agent, either.

Spencer couldn't help but think that he must feel a little of the same fire burning through his veins. Not only a deep desire to get Alec naked and underneath and on top of him, but to kiss him and touch him and *talk* to him.

Those two years when they'd texted semi-frequently had been so incredible that Spencer still missed them.

He wanted that back. And he wanted *more*.

But this text wasn't a sweet nothing about how much Alec craved him.

It was a work text. Professional. Distant. Spencer knew it made sense, but he still had to fight the urge to throw his phone across the room.

First two steps in your education begin today, the text read. **Two PM, meet me at this address. Later tonight, we'll be going out.**

To dinner, Spencer thought with frustration. To a date that wouldn't be like a date at all. He wanted to scream, but this was what he'd agreed to, wasn't it? It was what he'd *wanted*.

But deep down, there was something he'd always wanted more. He'd long given up hope of getting it, but that didn't mean that the desire didn't beat, strong and true, buried so far down it was a miracle he still felt it at all.

But he did. He always had.

Going out where? he asked Alec, even though he didn't expect a less mysterious answer to be forthcoming. Alec was a lawyer, after all, and seemingly enjoyed being cagey about details.

We'll discuss it at our first appointment, Alec texted back almost immediately.

The reason why was not as secret as Alec probably hoped it was: clearly, Spencer was not going to like whatever it was.

He sent back what he hoped Alec would interpret correctly as a passive-aggressive thumbs-up emoji. Iggy meowed insistently, shifting on his chest as he set the phone down.

"Whatcha think, buddy?" Spencer said, rubbing him under his chin as he purred loudly. "You think Alec is gonna try to convince me to do something I don't want to do?"

Iggy regarded him knowingly. Even with one eye, he was unusually expressive. Way more emotive than Spencer had imagined a cat would be, but then he already knew Iggy was special. He'd known it from the first moment, the same way he'd known that Alec would mean something to him from their very first handshake.

Iggy's meow was insistent.

"Yeah," Spencer agreed, giving him one last rub. "Yeah, I know, it's breakfast time."

· · · ● · ● · · ·

Alec had spent the last two days working not only on the plan to get Spencer traded, but also various ways to keep a professional distance between them.

Today, he thought as he got out of the car, was the first step in that plan.

He wasn't happy about all of it—one part in particular left him feeling sick to his stomach, even as he kept trying to convince himself that it was necessary—but he was going to do it anyway, because this was too important to leave anything to chance.

Spencer was standing next to the doorway, leaning against the wall, arms crossed over his chest.

When would he stop feeling this visceral punch to the gut every time he saw Spencer? Was it *ever* going to get easier?

Alec took a short, calming breath. "Glad you're on time," he said.

Spencer shot him a look. "Did you think I wouldn't be?"

"No, but Ali is . . . particular and it's better not to start out on the wrong foot."

"Who's Ali?" Spencer asked as Alec pushed the door open.

"Ali is my tailor," Alec said shortly. "And no, you really don't want to piss her off."

"Clothes?" Spencer asked, his tone disbelieving. "We're here for *clothes*?"

"You need some suits for your interview and for the whole draft weekend. You know," Alec added, "the weekend where we're trying to change your life?"

"Right," Spencer said, but he still seemed skeptical.

They entered the shop, and it was just as neat and tidy as it usually was, the dark wood-paneled walls the one decoration in the austere room.

"I thought we were buying clothes?" Spencer asked.

Ali walked out then, her dark hair cut in her normal pixie cut, and perfectly styled, not a hair out of place.

"Alec," she said, nodding. "Good to see you." With her usual singular focus, she turned towards Spencer. "Yes, you *are* buying clothes. But not just the clothes you'd buy off the rack and pray fit you." She circled the other man, her dark eyes taking in every inch of him. "I bet you that you don't wear suits often because they don't usually fit you well."

"Well . . ." Spencer said, and then hesitated.

"He's worried the suits are gonna make him look too gay," Alec said, because suddenly he was very sick of continuing the charade.

"No," Spencer said staunchly, and from the determined expression on his face, Alec thought he might really mean it. To his own surprise. "I don't care how gay they make me look, even if a suit *could* make me look gay. I'm . . . I'm done with that bullshit. Forever."

Ali gave him a nod—not her nod of approval or disapproval, but one in-between. He had been going to her long enough that he could decipher her normally closed-off expressions and her series of nods, ranging from grudgingly accepting to downright disapproval.

"What does he need?" she asked, directing her question to Alec.

"Four suits, various fabrics, but all light, and shirts, ties, and a few pairs of casual slacks. We'll buy the polos off the rack."

"*Four?*" Spencer asked, sounding shocked.

"You can afford it," Alec said with a wave of his hand. "And this isn't just about you leaving the Stars. It's about more than that. You know it. Remember what Chase made you agree to?"

Alec watched as Spencer took a deep breath. "I still want those things. Regardless of who made me ask for them."

Alec wasn't quite sure that was true, but the problem was that he *wanted* to believe it was true.

"Okay," Alec said. "Then maybe you don't love the suits, but you don't really know if you do or not. Isn't that the point?" he added gently. "Trying new things?"

"Yeah." Spencer gave a nod. "Yeah, it is." He turned towards Ali. "I don't want to keep going into my closet and not being sure which t-shirt and jeans to pick out, or even worse, which sweatpants I should wear. I . . . I got stuck in a rut awhile ago, and it's time to move on. I just don't know how."

"Don't worry," Ali said, patting him on the shoulder, even though the diminutive woman barely came up that high. "We're going to take care of you."

It was by far the nicest thing that Alec had ever heard Ali say. Usually she was perfunctory at *best*, and Alec had been a client for over ten years now.

But Alec supposed he shouldn't be surprised. There was a genuine earnestness in Spencer's face, in his eyes, that drew people to him, even though he'd never been comfortable with the attention.

It was what had drawn Alec to him, from the very beginning.

Ali opened one of the panels in the wall and pulled out her book of sample fabrics, bringing it over to where Spencer stood, uncertainly.

"You said only summer weights?" Ali asked as she flipped through the book.

"Yes," Alec said.

"Must not be trying to trade him to Minnesota, then," Ali said with amusement.

Spencer opened his mouth and then snapped it shut again.

"Don't worry," Alec offered, because he had a feeling he knew what Spencer was worried about, "Ali's discreet. We're paying her enough that she wouldn't open her mouth even if she wanted to."

Ali shot him a look. "I don't open my mouth because that's not the kind of person I am," she pointed out frostily.

"Right, and there's that, too," Alec added with a smile.

"Yes," Ali said with an offended sniff. But he could tell, from long experience, that she wasn't even close to *really* offended.

"But no, he's not going to Minnesota, at least we both hope he isn't," Alec said. "Hopefully he'll be staying in the area."

"Good," Ali said. "Summer weight it is."

"And," Alec said, before he could overthink it, "you should add a tuxedo in there. He's going to need it. Lots of good LGBT fundraisers in the area, and he'll be going to every single one."

"I will?" Spencer didn't sound mad about it, just surprised.

"You will," Alec said firmly.

"I don't get invited to those much, at least anymore." Spencer sounded regretful about this. Alec wasn't sure he'd have gone if he was invited but surely it had stung when the invites had dried up.

It was probably hard enough to live on the outskirts of the gay community, and even tougher to realize that everyone resented him for the opportunity he'd squandered.

"That's going to change." He'd get invited, even if Alec had to bring him as his plus-one. That would inevitably cause a lot of questions, but it would be better than Spencer not going at all.

"How about this light gray?" Ali asked, holding up the swatch towards Spencer's face. "With a dark blue shirt perhaps?"

"That'd be good," Alec said. "I like that."

"Does it matter what I think?" Spencer wanted to know.

"No," Ali said, her tone leaving no room for argument.

"Spencer thinks gray is boring," Alec said before he could remind himself that he was supposed to be maintaining a professional distance. "Don't you, Spencer?"

Spencer shot him a look, making it clear he remembered the conversation Alec was referring to—though it was hard to say if he actually *wanted* to remember or not. Alec found himself wishing that Spencer looked back with even a fraction of the fondness that Alec did, when he thought of their texts.

When Spencer had stopped texting him, it had hurt, more than he'd expected it to. That was part of the reason why he'd only attempted it twice after, because if he was so keenly affected, it meant that he'd already lost his much-valued professional distance. It didn't matter if Spencer wasn't a client—and he'd thought Spencer wouldn't *ever* be, back then—he'd believed having an emotional affair with a player was the first step down the slippery slope to indulging in more.

Nobody had ever tempted him like Spencer had tempted him. In fact, nobody else had ever tempted him to break or bend *any* of his rules. But Spencer had always done it, as easy as breathing.

"Actually," Spencer corrected with a soft smile. An *intimate* smile that destroyed all the distance Alec had been trying to put between them. "I think I said I liked you better in blue."

Ali shot him a knowing look. They'd worked together long enough that she'd be far too aware of how Spencer's words sounded.

"The gray is fine," Alec said, hoping that he could cut Spencer off at the pass, before he decided that Ali's code of silence meant that he could divulge all the private things they'd discussed over that two-year period. "Also," he said, reaching for the book and flipping through it. "This tan, this pinstripe, and this medium blue. And black, of course, for the tuxedo."

Ali nodded, but the gleam in her eyes told him she'd figured out exactly what he was trying to avoid.

"Measurements next," she said, whipping her tape measure out of the pocket of her slim-cut trousers. She gestured towards a single wood block, set in front of a tri-way mirror at the other end of the room. "Strip."

"What?" Spencer gawked.

This was the moment Alec had been waiting for. He'd known it was coming, and he'd already planned on ducking out here, with an excuse that he needed to return some calls. He wasn't about to watch Ali measure every inch of Spencer's spectacular body.

It already starred in way too many of his fantasies.

"Measurements," Ali said in a tone that tolerated no disagreement and no discussion. "For the best measurements, I need you down to your underwear."

"I'm . . ." Alec cleared his throat. "Going to go return some calls."

Ali's glance over her shoulder made it clear she understood exactly why he was escaping.

Spencer, however, was too shocked and horrified to notice that Alec was leaving.

He hoped it would stay that way.

• • • ● • ● • ● • •

Spencer watched as Alec exited the room, letting the door close behind him, the bells on it jingling.

"Well," Ali said archly. "Are you going to strip or not?"

"I guess I am," Spencer said, toeing off his sneakers, and then his socks, and then pulling off his t-shirt, followed by his shorts.

He set everything in a neat pile and went to stand on the wooden platform she'd indicated.

"If it makes you uncomfortable to look in the mirror like this," Ali said matter-of-factly, "you can always turn around."

Spencer stared at his nearly naked body. He looked good. His right calf, which had been a sad emaciated thing after his Achilles tear, was nearly the same size as the left, now, after all of June's exercises, and the rest of him looked pretty good too.

"No, I'm fine," Spencer said. He kind of wished that Alec had stayed—though he understood why he'd left.

"Too bad you can't make Alec squirm," Ali said, and it was the least impersonal thing she'd said since they'd arrived.

Spencer looked down at her, kneeling at his feet to take leg measurements, and smiled. "He could use some shaking up, couldn't he?"

"I knew," Ali said briskly, "when he asked me if he could bring in a new client, it was not business as usual."

"Does he not usually bring in clients?"

"Alec has been coming here for ten years," Ali said. "Ever since I opened. He's never asked me if he could bring someone in."

Spencer's jaw dropped. "Really? Neal Fisher? Chase Riley? They don't get suits from you?"

Ali shot him an unimpressed look. "I don't like a bunch of people underfoot, all the time," she said. "I like my business to stay small. Personal. Attention to detail is my calling card. I don't accept just anyone, you know. Fisher's been trying to get one of my suits for ages, but Alec's never intervened on his behalf."

"But you took me," Spencer said uncertainly.

"Alec said you'd be a good challenge, and he's usually right about these kinds of things," Ali said. "Also, I could tell from his voice that you weren't just *any* client."

"Thanks? I guess?"

"You're going to have a dynamite suit for your interview," she said succinctly. "And an even better one for the draft. I know Alec's got big plans."

"You really won't make a suit for Neal Fisher? Is it because of the field goal?"

Two years ago, Neal Fisher had missed the winning field goal in the Super Bowl, ruining the Riptide's chances to be one of a few historic teams that had managed to win it all in back-to-back years. It had disappointed a *lot* of people in LA—more than Spencer had ever anticipated would actually give a shit about football.

Ali shot him a glare. "Of course not."

"Well, just saying that he's not a bad guy either." Spencer couldn't believe that he was really speaking up for Fisher like this, but they'd hit it off at the game, and developed, against all the odds, some decent chemistry as a quarterback and a receiver. Especially surprising considering that Neal had never been a quarterback, and Spencer wasn't a receiver.

"I'll think about it," Ali said.

"You should," Spencer said.

Instead of agreeing, like he'd hoped she would, Ali continued taking measurements silently, taking more than he'd ever before imagined would go into a suit—but then he'd never had a suit custom tailored to fit him either.

When she was finally done and Spencer had re-dressed, she stuck her head out the door, and beckoned Alec to come back in.

"He's all dressed now, don't you worry," he heard her tease Alec as he walked back in.

"That's not . . . I was . . ." Alec stumbled, which was unusual for him. He always knew what to say.

"I'll have a ready-made one tailored to your measurements—or at least as well as I can—and sent over to your house for tonight," Ali said. "Open white shirt. No tie."

"Perfect," Alec said.

"What?" Spencer interrupted. "What's going on tonight?"

Alec turned to him, as Ali went into the back. "I wanted to talk to you about that," he said, and the caution in his voice made the hair on Spencer's neck stand up. "I want you to come with me to Temple."

"The gay club?" Spencer asked incredulously. "Why?"

"Let's start with, it'll be good for you to be seen there. You've got to start changing your reputation at some point, and if the interview is airing a week and a half from now, it's not a bad idea to start laying some groundwork. I wish we'd gotten to lay some more."

"We could have," Spencer retorted, "if I hadn't had to spend a week convincing you to change your mind."

"Well," Alec said smoothly, "you *did*, so thanks for that. But yes, I need you to wear the suit that Ali's going to send over, and you need to come with me tonight."

"I've never been there." Spencer crossed his arms over his chest.

"I know." Alec sounded amused. "But I think you'll like it anyway."

Spencer doubted that. Even if he was fully able to embrace his gay self, he still didn't think he'd be much of a partier.

"A lot of high-profile guys go to Temple, especially on a Saturday night," Alec said. "You want to be seen by them. It'll make an impression."

"They're not going to spit in my face, are they?"

Alec smiled, and patted him on the cheek. "Honey, that's not what they're going to want to do to your face."

"Fine," Spencer said, trying not to think about Alec's words too closely. He didn't want anyone else. He never had. If this was about Alec trying to keep them professional, about trying to remind himself that they couldn't be involved . . . well, Spencer would have to cross that bridge when he came to it.

CHAPTER TEN

ALEC NOT ONLY HAD Ali send him over the suit, he also sent a car for him—a long, dark car, a Mercedes. It looked fancier than anything that Spencer even owned.

When he climbed in, already feeling out of place in the gray suit, with the white shirt, open at the neckline, as Ali had specified both in the shop and in the notes attached to the suit when it had been delivered, Alec was already sitting in the back seat.

"Is all this really necessary?" he grumbled. He might have agreed to go. He hadn't agreed to make a spectacle of himself.

Alec looked him up and down, and Spencer, who'd never been good at holding on to grudges, felt some of his tension melt, just under the heat of Alec's gaze.

He's just trying to make sure you look okay, that Ali did her job, he told himself. But as their gazes met, and he swore Alec leaned forward slightly, it didn't feel like this was about a job, at all.

"We're trying to make a good impression," Alec said.

"And?" Spencer raised an eyebrow, settling into the seat. Unlike other suits, where they'd felt like they were too tight, strangling him, or too loose, hanging baggy on his frame, this one fit him fairly well and he felt unexpectedly comfortable in it. He'd thought, when he'd taken a quick look at himself after dressing, that he actually cleaned up pretty good. The warm gray fabric suited his tan complexion better than he'd thought it would, and the white shirt, open at the collar, looked suitably casual, giving him a laid-back and relaxed vibe. Spencer thought if he ran into himself in a club, he'd take a second look.

"Did you look in the mirror before you left?" Alec asked.

"Of course I did. Had to make sure everything was zipped up and buttoned up, right?" Spencer retorted.

"Let's just say that you're properly zipped and buttoned up," Alec said. The cautious edge to his voice was completely at odds with the heat in his gaze.

The drive across town was short and quiet. Spencer didn't say anything else, still trying to figure out what the fuck Alec was up to, and Alec didn't say another word, probably because he liked leaving Spencer guessing.

It was annoying and frustrating and surprisingly hot as hell.

Spencer shifted in the seat and wished that Ali had left more room in the crotch of these pants, just in case he got an erection. If he was going to be wearing these suits with Alec around, that was going to be a situation he couldn't help.

They finally pulled up to the front door of the club, with its tall white pillars, a line of guys already snaking around them, waiting to get in.

Spencer opened the door, and climbed out, and immediately felt the weight of so many gazes. Maybe they didn't know who he was; maybe they were angry he was here. Maybe . . .

"Don't worry"—Alec's voice appeared behind him—"they're all staring 'cause you're hot."

"What?" Spencer barely stammered out the question, but then Alec was leading him towards the front door, with its enormous bouncer.

"Mitchell," Alec said succinctly, his voice cutting through all the low-level chatter surrounding them.

The bouncer waved a hand, and they entered.

It was dark and crowded and full not only of flashing lights but plaster angels, perching on all the corners, interspersed with writhing gargoyle types, with lots of red drapes and faux candles.

There were more angels than just the statues—some of them were real live men, wearing enormous feathered wings and very little else. Spencer swallowed hard.

He'd been hearing stories about this place for years; the kind that had both made him want to stay away, and also desperately curious to experience what the mystique was all about.

Well, you're gonna experience it now, Spencer told himself as he followed Alec through the crowds up a short flight of stairs to a platform running the back length of the club. The red velvet rope had a golden etched sign that proclaimed it "VIP" and Alec seemed to know where he was going, a waiter giving him a nod as they passed.

They settled down at a table at the far end, Spencer sitting gingerly on the red velvet upholstered low couch.

"Want something to drink?" Alec asked over the loud, pulsating music.

"A beer," Spencer said. He hadn't really wanted to drink at all, but his mouth was suddenly very dry, and maybe a drink would help dull his anxiety.

Alec opened a hidden panel on the dark glass table in front of them, and pulled a beer out. Just as he'd grabbed an opener from another discreet drawer, and handed both to Spencer, a waiter appeared holding a glass filled with red wine.

"Oh thanks, Chris," Alec said, giving the waiter a nod. "You always know what I like."

Chris smiled, in a way that made it clear that Alec could get *anything* he wanted from him, and Spencer felt ugly jealousy uncurl inside his stomach.

"So," Spencer said after popping the cap of his beer off and taking a long drink, "why are we really here?"

"To be seen," Alec retorted. "I said that. In fact, you should go downstairs and *be* seen. Talk to some people. Dance a little." Spencer watched as Alec swallowed hard, his Adam's apple bobbing. "Find someone to flirt with."

Spencer stared at him incredulously. *I have someone to flirt with. He's sitting right in front of me.*

"This is important," Alec continued, like Spencer had actually responded, "and you need to mingle."

"I don't like crowds," Spencer said.

"Then find someone you can talk to one-on-one. Trust me, it won't be hard. They're going to be lining up."

"You really believe that?" Spencer didn't think so. He'd burned so many bridges, he thought even if he *wanted* to go downstairs and find someone to flirt with, everyone would ignore him.

"I said it earlier. You're hot. Nobody gives a shit here as long as you're hot."

Spencer felt his temper spiking. "So I'm hot, but you'd be perfectly okay watching as I go downstairs and find some guy to grind against."

"I said . . ." Alec started to say but Spencer interrupted him.

"No, you said you wanted me to be seen, and yeah, I get that, but we could be seen in *lots* of different places."

"I want you to be seen, especially here." Alec waved his hand. "Lots of people like to escape their lives here, but nobody with a high profile is escaping here. Your presence will be noted. They'll think you're not ashamed. And you want to prove that you're not ashamed."

"I'm not ashamed." Spencer took a deep breath and a huge risk. "I'm also not going to be pushed into some kind of public scene with a random guy, just to change my reputation. There's a lot better ways to do that than dry humping some stranger." *Especially dry humping a stranger in front of you.*

Spencer watched as Alec's fingers tightened on his glass, the knuckles going white. There was tension around his mouth. Uncertainty in his eyes.

"Is that what you think I brought you here to do?"

"Yes," Spencer said. "Which is fucking insane, because that's not what either of us wants."

"What I want isn't relevant." Alec had retreated back behind his wall of vague, smooth professionalism, and Spencer wanted to take his fists to it, batter it endlessly until it came down and never went back up again.

"I disagree. I disagree a whole fucking lot," Spencer said. He drained his beer in one long gulp, and felt Alec's gaze on him the whole time, the heat of it completely opposite from all the crap he'd just said—that he *kept* saying. "I'm going," he said. "I don't need this shit."

He set his beer down and stood, walking away, weaving his way through the slowly filling VIP section, and back down the stairs, avoiding the stares and the looks and even a few of the guys who put a hand on him. He shoved his way out of the door, taking in a ragged breath of fresh air.

"What are you doing?"

Alec's voice, hissing behind him.

Spencer, feeling his temper rising, turned and took Alec by the arm and dragged him in the opposite direction of the line, to an alley on the other side of the bar, full of garbage cans and a few condom wrappers, and thankfully, no other witnesses.

"What are you doing?" Alec said again, this time his voice rising as he shook off Spencer's grip. But Spencer wasn't done by a long shot. He was done seeing the desire in Alec's eyes, and feeling the undeniable attraction rising between them and doing nothing about it. He'd yearned for this man for so many goddamn years, and had nothing to show for it.

He pushed Alec against the rough brick wall, not hard, but enough that hopefully Alec would understand that he wasn't going to go anywhere until they'd gotten to the bottom of this, once and for all.

"Are you going to tell me you *really* brought me here to hook up with some random guy? That you could actually watch me do that?"

Spencer watched as Alec swallowed hard.

"I wouldn't *like* it," Alec said cautiously.

"You wouldn't *like* it," Spencer repeated dumbly. "What the fuck is that even supposed to mean? Do you want me or not?"

"I'm not going to throw either of our careers away with two hands, just because I've got a hard-on," Alec shot back, his voice spiky with temper, echoing Spencer's own. "You finally know what direction you're going in, and I'm going to help you, and

I'm not going to let . . ." He gestured between them. "Let any of this inconvenient attraction get in the way."

Spencer stared at Alec, dumbfounded.

"Inconvenient attraction? That's all it was for you? A random hard-on?" Spencer didn't know whether he was pissed off or turned on. Could you be both, at the same time?

"You know it wasn't." Alec shot him a hot look. Hot with temper or with arousal? Again, Spencer didn't know.

But he was feeling all of it.

"It sure as hell wasn't just that for me," Spencer said. "You just . . .you caught me and you reeled me in and when I tried, I goddamn tried to make it more, to be with you, for real, you shot me down. Without even fucking blinking."

Spencer didn't think he'd ever seen that particular shade of desperation in Alec's face before. Maybe he'd always kept it hidden, but it was blatant now.

He took another step closer, his thigh brushing against Alec's. Felt his pulse accelerate even faster.

"I didn't like it," Alec said bitterly. "I wanted you. I . . ." He hesitated, licking his lips. "It's not as simple as you're making it sound, but if you want to boil it down to that, okay fine. Yes, I want you."

"You want me. You still want me." Spencer stated it, didn't ask. Didn't need to ask, because despite all the words, all the excuses, and all the bullshit that Alec had just spewed, that was all that mattered. That was all he'd heard.

"Yes, but . . ." Alec started, but he didn't finish.

Because there were no buts. Not after all those long years.

Spencer leaned closer, and before Alec could say anything else that was completely and utterly stupid, kissed him.

To his own shock, it was soft, almost *gentle*, at first. Uncertain, he realized. He didn't know how Alec was going to react, even though Alec had made it clear enough that the desire between them was mutual.

The fabric of Alec's jacket bunched in his fingers as they dug into his shoulders, and Spencer tilted his head, hoping for more. *Desperate for more.*

It was still unbelievable that this was happening at all. Those were his lips, weren't they? They were his lips and they were on Alec's lips, and maybe he wasn't responding as fast as he'd hoped, but maybe he was still in shock. *Spencer* felt like he was still in shock. He hadn't even meant to cross the line, but now that he was over it, he knew there was no going back.

He pushed his body against Alec's and then suddenly, Alec let out a ragged groan, and then he was kissing Spencer back. He could taste the rich red wine Alec had been drinking on his tongue, but it was the deeper, impossibly richer taste of *Alec* that Spencer couldn't get enough of. Breathing was overrated. They could just stand here, doing this forever, and Spencer wouldn't ever complain.

Nothing had ever felt as good as Alec's body did against his. He'd had his share of hookups, but they'd never been the man he really wanted, and the difference was blowing his mind apart. Alec was slim, but strong, and now that he was kissing Spencer back, his mouth nimble and passionate, there was an echo of that steely determination that Spencer had always adored about him.

His fingers pushed through Alec's hair, soft against his palms, and as he pressed him against the wall, his tongue diving into Alec's mouth, he felt his unmistakable erection pressed against his leg.

How had they never done this before? It felt like an impossibility that they hadn't, and it felt like a fucking miracle, now that they had.

Maybe, Spencer thought dimly, as he couldn't help his hips thrusting forward, his own hard cock searching for friction, the time just hadn't been right before. But he knew, not just because he wanted it to be right, but because it *felt* right, that everything had changed, and nothing was going to stop them now.

"God," Alec moaned against his lips. "We shouldn't . . ."

Of course, Alec was still going to try.

Spencer felt a rush of frustration move through him. Why was Alec still trying to deny this? Couldn't he feel how right it was? Couldn't he just let his concern go and focus on how fucking amazing it felt? Better than any of Spencer's fantasies, even.

He pulled back, just a fraction.

"Do you really want to stop?" Spencer asked.

Alec stared at him, flicked out his tongue and wet his bottom lip. Tasted Spencer on it.

"Do you really want me to go back in there and find some random guy?" Spencer kept going, because they were going to settle this once and for all. He'd thought he already had, but considering that Alec had interrupted the hottest kiss in history by proclaiming they should stop, maybe he hadn't been clear enough. "I'd look for a guy with dark hair, and maybe I'll even be lucky enough and he'll be wearing a suit. Of course, he won't be as hot as you, he *couldn't* be. And I won't want him, the way I want you, but . . ." Spencer took a ragged breath. "It'd be better than nothing. I'm . . . I'm done settling for nothing."

Alec *still* didn't say anything. Kept staring.

Finally, when Spencer thought the tension was so fraught that it might just explode between them, Alec pulled his phone out of his pocket. Typed a message.

"Come on," he said in a voice that didn't give any of his feelings away. "If we're going to do this, we're not going to do it in some dirty alley." He reached out and took Spencer's hand in his own, giving an insistent tug towards the street they'd come from.

Alec's fingers curled around his own, holding Spencer's hand tight and close, squeezing a bit as they emerged from the alley. He'd half-expected Alec to drop his hand and let him go, especially when the crowd came back into view, but if anything, Alec gripped his hand even tighter, like he wouldn't let him go for anything in the world.

As they approached the curb, it occurred to Spencer that the neutral, almost casual expression on Alec's face was the lie, was the front, and the way he wouldn't let go of his hand? That was how he really, truly felt.

A black car pulled up, the same Mercedes as earlier in the evening, and Alec opened the door, pulling Spencer in after him, still refusing to let go of his hand, even though it would have been way easier.

Once they were in the car, settling back into the cool, leather seats, Spencer chanced another look at Alec. The same smooth, inscrutable expression was on his face. But like Alec knew what Spencer was thinking, he shot a quick look towards the driver, only the back of his head visible, and gave a quick shake of his head.

Spencer understood Alec not wanting anyone to know what was happening between them, at least before they could figure it out. And he was probably right, Spencer thought, it would be better to have this conversation—or *not* conversation—in private.

But Alec still hadn't let go of his hand, and Spencer squeezed it, thumb cruising over the graceful curve of Alec's inner wrist, feeling the pulse begin to beat harder.

Spencer smiled. He might seem unruffled and undisturbed, but the blood thumping right under the skin, faster and harder, didn't lie. And even in the dark gloom of the car, Spencer thought he could see his erection, ruining the line of his slim-cut pants.

It had taken at least twenty minutes to go from Spencer's house to the club, but this time the driver took a different route and Spencer wondered where they were going. He realized, as the car pulled up to a private gated house only a few minutes later, it was clear that they weren't going back to his own house.

Spencer felt a swell of satisfaction and heat move through him. He'd had to fight for it, but Alec had finally let him in.

He took in the house, surprisingly small, made of stucco, with an immaculately tended garden around it, as he waited for Alec to exit the car behind him. Of course, Alec wouldn't dare to look too eager. Spencer heard him tell the driver that he wouldn't be needed for the rest of the evening, and offer him a goodbye.

When the car finally pulled away, leaving Alec behind, Spencer had approached the gate and was beginning to feel a few nerves.

The kiss had been so good. But what if the sex didn't live up to Alec's expectations? What if Spencer wasn't as skilled or as knowledgeable as some of the guys Alec slept with? Spencer hadn't had a lot of opportunities—which, he supposed, was his own fault—but the last thing he wanted was for the evening to be a letdown.

They'd been waiting for this for *nine years*. Surely it couldn't and wouldn't live up to their expectations.

"Well," Alec said, and for the first time in half an hour, Spencer could see the *real* Alec beginning to show through on his face, all eagerness and even a little uncertainty. He shrugged. "We're here." He went up and typed in the gate code, and it opened slowly.

"I like your house," Spencer said, reaching out and taking Alec's hand again. The hand-holding was new, and there was a sweet non-sexual component to it that he craved. A reassurance that this wouldn't just be one, unforgettable night.

Alec smiled, and said, "Yeah?" as they walked up towards the front door.

There was another door code, and then they were entering Alec's private sanctuary. Unlike some other agents—including Larry—who used their houses for big parties, Alec always rented a place out, never used his own.

Alec bringing him here had to mean something bigger than *I don't want to do this in some dirty alley*. After all, they could've gone to Spencer's. But Alec had specifically decided to bring him here.

The entry was dim, with only a small lamp in the corner, sending a warm glow up the walls. There was similar art to the pieces on the walls of Spencer's office, a beautiful curving sculpture sitting on the entry table.

"It seems like you," Spencer said. He didn't ever pretend to be good at words, and he'd already used a lot of them tonight. He must've not done too bad of a job, because he was here, wasn't he? Alec hadn't told him to fuck off, he'd brought him to his *house*.

Alec smiled again, and tugged him through the arched doorway, deeper into his sanctuary. "You want a glass of wine?" he asked, casually, like Spencer couldn't feel his pulse thrumming underneath his fingertips. Couldn't sense his tension, his *want*.

Like the same desires weren't rising in Spencer.

"No," Spencer said, and it was easier this time to pull Alec close, and kiss him.

There was none of the uncertainty this time around, and Alec melted like butter on hot toast, groaning against him as the kiss turned fiery almost immediately.

Alec's fingers dug into his shoulders, and then pushed, shoving off his coat, and before Spencer could find breath to protest, they were already working at the buttons on his shirt, leaving it gaping, delving in between the open halves, his palms pressing against his naked chest.

He'd imagined this so many times before, but it had never been so urgent, so desperate, the feeling of Alec's fingertips reverently tracing the lines of his muscles so consuming.

He'd never imagined it could feel like this. Then Alec's hands drifted lower, tugging his shirt out of his pants, and finally, landing right where Spencer craved his touch, his palm pressing insistently against his rock-hard erection.

"Fuck," Spencer panted, tearing his mouth off Alec's. His fingers were clever and teasing, giving him just enough friction, and not nearly enough, all at the same time.

"That's the idea." Alec's grin was sly and wicked. "Don't you want to? I thought that's what you dragged me into that alley to do."

"I dragged you to that alley to make sure what I wanted was clear."

Alec's pupils were shot, dark, with only a thin ring of grayish-blue around them. His chest was rising and falling rapidly, his cheeks flushed.

"I got the memo," Alec said. "Though, I'd gotten it awhile back, I just . . ."

"Yeah," Spencer interrupted, "you think it's a bad idea."

Alec sighed. "It's not bad, it's . . . complicated."

"More complicated than continuing to not do this?" Spencer dropped his head and kissed him again, gentler this time, sweeter and more determined. Alec unfolded, like he had every time before, like a flower, the desperate way he moved against him belying everything he'd just said.

Spencer lifted his mouth, and Alec took a deep, shaky breath. "No," he said. "Not more complicated."

"Then let's simplify it." Spencer reached down and took his hand again, squeezing it. "I don't want wine, I don't want a beer, even if you had one, and I don't want to stop. I don't want to overthink this. I just want you to take me to your bedroom."

Alec's smile was soft and set Spencer's heart beating faster with the promise in its curve. "Alright," he said, and pulled him across towards a staircase. "The rest of the house, all the public places," he said as they climbed the stairs, "are downstairs, but my bedroom, it's upstairs. Got a view of the ocean, but I don't think we're going to be looking out the windows tonight."

"No." Spencer couldn't believe how dark and rough his voice sounded. The nerves had disappeared, surprisingly, and all that was left was a deep, wide desire that threatened to overwhelm him.

Alec seemed to get that, and didn't let go of his hand. At the top of the stairs was a sitting area, with a small desk in front of a big bay window, and then through a pair of French glass doors, was an enormous bed, piled high with gray and blue pillows and a luxurious silk paisley coverlet.

Alec pushed him down gently, and Spencer sat on the edge, the man going to his knees in front of him. Spencer almost said something like *not like this, I want to touch you*, but then Alec was pulling off his shoes and socks, his touch light yet unbearably arousing, and Spencer leaned back and just let it happen. It felt too good, and he'd wanted this for so long. Would it be so bad to take a little pleasure for himself, if Alec wanted to give it?

Then his fingers were on his pants again, pulling off his belt and teasingly running along his straining length.

Spencer bit back a groan and a curse as Alec tugged his pants down, and then confidently laid a warm palm against his throbbing cock. "Yeah?" Alec asked softly.

He could only nod as Alec pulled down his boxer briefs.

"Don't be quiet," Alec said as he sank even lower, until he was eye level with Spencer's cock. The expression on his face wasn't anything like disappointment, but that was the last coherent thought Spencer had.

· · · ● · ● ● · · ·

Alec couldn't quite believe he was settling between Spencer's powerful thighs, his own arousal a throb in his blood, and in his cock. But *this* cock, it was one he'd wanted forever, and he was finally going to get to enjoy it.

It was long and thick, curving slightly, and when Alec curled his fingers around Spencer's length, it twitched, a drop of precome beading at the head.

He couldn't resist anymore, and he leaned forward, licking it off, groaning at the thought he was finally doing this, that he'd *allowed* himself to finally do this.

So far the experience had been an odd combination of potent arousal and a strange kind of hesitancy, but as he slid his mouth around Spencer, he felt the latter disappearing completely.

Spencer, taking his words to heart, moaned loudly. "God, *yes*," he said, the rough heat in his voice intensifying Alec's own lust.

He'd fantasized about doing this so many times that finally getting to do everything he'd ever imagined felt like coming home. He'd dreamt of him right here, just like this, on the end of his bed, with himself on his knees, his fingers digging into one of those muscular thighs, his mouth on Spencer's cock.

The reality was even better than he could've imagined. Spencer's sweet musky scent was intoxicating, and then there was the gentle way Spencer's hands drifted down to his head, tangling in his hair. Not forcing him, but just reassuring him. And his broken moans as he sucked harder and faster, one hand straying down lower to cup his balls as they tightened.

This wasn't going to last very long, but then Alec had a feeling when Spencer finally got a hand on his own cock, it was going to go even quicker.

They'd wanted each other for so goddamn long.

Spencer's fingers tightening on his skull, a long-drawn-out moan, and his cock twitching against his tongue were all the warning Alec got before he was coming. He swallowed, fingers stroking Spencer's thigh and his mouth drawing out the last of his pleasure.

His own arousal was a hard rhythm beating his blood as Spencer opened his eyes, dark and mesmerizing.

"Fuck, you're amazing," Spencer said, reaching down and lifting him up with almost no effort and very little obvious strain on all those muscles. Spencer naked was even more glorious than Alec had imagined and he hoped that this wasn't the only time, that someday he might get a real chance to explore everything he'd dreamed about.

There was so little thought in Alec's head, that he didn't register for a moment how surprised he was that Spencer was pulling him in closer, and then kissing him.

He'd wondered if tasting his own come on Alec's tongue would be too gay for him, but Spencer didn't seem to care, only kept pulling Alec closer and closer until he was practically on top of him, still dressed.

Alec wiggled out of his jacket, tossing it on the floor, for once not giving a shit if it got wrinkled. And then Spencer's fingers were at his belt, tugging it off, pulling his shirt off, buttons spraying everywhere, and unlike in the locker room, he didn't worry one bit about Spencer thinking he wasn't hot or sexy.

The eagerness in Spencer's kiss, the way his big, rough hands groped him all over, from his shoulders, to his chest, to his waist, and then down lower, sliding right over the curve of his ass, made it plenty clear that he found him *very* attractive.

If he'd had the thought in his sluggish brain, he'd have imagined that Spencer would pull down his briefs and wrap one of those crazy sexy hands around his cock and give him a few strokes and that would be enough to send him into bliss.

But instead, Spencer demonstrated that insane strength and flipped them, depositing Alec on the bed, naked except for his briefs, and then crawled up him with a predatory look in his eye.

Then, to Alec's surprise, he was pulling his briefs down with his teeth, and his mouth was on his cock, hot and wet and heady.

"Oh my God," Alec cried out, not expecting the blowjob, and not expecting that Spencer would be so good at it, fierce but teasing, his tongue curling around the underside as he sucked him hard and fast.

Alec dug his fingers into the coverlet and tried to hold on, but his orgasm was already shimmering in his blood, and the fact that it was Spencer who was so expertly sucking his cock was enough to just about finish him off.

He tried to warn him, but then Spencer was taking him even deeper, and Alec lost it, his orgasm overtaking him completely.

When he opened his eyes again, Spencer was licking his lips, looking *very* satisfied.

"You seemed to like that alright," he teased as he crawled up next to Alec and collapsed next to him, pulling him closer with one arm slung around his shoulders.

"More than alright," Alec said dryly. Then reminded himself that here, he could be himself. Here he could let some of his walls, fortified for so long, come down. "I . . . I loved it."

"You sound surprised," Spencer said.

"Well, you can't blame me. You haven't exactly been making the rounds of the hookup scene," Alec pointed out.

"I've got enough experience," Spencer said, self-deprecatingly. "At least you seemed to think so."

"Zero complaints here," Alec said, and dropped his head lower, resting it against Spencer's chest, right where his heart beat so steadily. "Give me a few minutes and we could try it again, even."

Spencer chuckled, a rumbling vibration Alec could feel through his whole body. "I was hoping you might say that."

CHAPTER ELEVEN

"Must've been some shitty winter," Alec said a few minutes later, breaking the silence that had fallen between them.

Spencer had a feeling he knew what he meant, but he asked anyway. "Why?"

Alec shifted, pressing a palm against Spencer's chest, right where his heart beat faster than it usually did, probably because he was still a little incredulous that they were tangled up together like this. "You came out of it and you changed your whole life. Your career. You're gonna blow it all up."

"*And*, I wouldn't let you get away with the bullshit tonight." Spencer heard how amused he sounded.

"That too," Alec added.

Spencer's fingers tightened, digging into Alec's skin. Wanting him to always be this close. "It *was* a shitty winter," he finally acknowledged. "I was hurt, and for some reason, maybe because of that, I felt alone, more alone than usual, and well . . .all I had was time to think about how I'd fucked it all up. Made sense to make some changes."

"And so you thought, *hey, let's storm into Alec's office and make some demands.*"

"I *did* storm your office, not like it did me much good."

Alec sighed, and pulled away, straightening. Spencer's first reaction was to grab him and pull him back. He wasn't ready for this lazy, tranquil post-sex haze to end. But then he realized Alec was moving so he could look him in the eye.

Whatever he was going to say was important.

Spencer felt his heart begin to beat a little faster.

"That day in my office . . ." Alec hesitated. "I didn't *want* to say no, Spencer. You weren't wrong. It was everything I'd wanted, way back before you were even drafted, for you to come to me and say that you needed me. My first reaction was to convince you to sign on the dotted line as fast as possible, before you changed your mind."

"But you didn't," Spencer said incredulously. "That's not what you did at all."

"No," Alec said softly. "I was . . . I was terrified . . . absolutely scared shitless that this would happen." He gestured between them, at their naked bodies.

"You thought we'd sleep together? That's why you said no?" Spencer frowned. This was not the confession that he'd been expecting Alec to make.

"This is coming out wrong," Alec said wryly, and Spencer knew why. Alec made a living with his words. Had made a career of saying the right thing at the right time. "You fluster me, even when I don't *want* to be flustered."

"Join the club," Spencer muttered. But he forced himself to relax, to listen to what Alec was trying to say.

"First off, I never rejected you because I wanted to. I felt like . . .like we couldn't have both, the sex and *more*, maybe even a relationship, not a few years ago, so I tried to stay away from you, but I'm obviously shitty at that. When you asked me to be your agent, I said no because I knew if I said yes, and you signed and then we did this—because it felt inevitable that we would, eventually—and then something happened, that if you got cold feet or you changed your mind, or . . ." Alec waved his hands in the air, like he was trying to pluck the right words out of thin air. "Or you ended up not wanting me, I couldn't deal with it."

"You couldn't deal with it."

Alec nodded, and then his eyes softened. "You know why, right? Why I couldn't deal with it?"

Spencer suspected he knew the truth, but he'd never imagined Alec would keep going, would keep talking, would say the thing he'd always dreamed that Alec might say to him, but that he'd never actually expected to hear.

"I love you," Alec continued, his eyes wide like he couldn't quite believe he was saying it either, "that's why. I . . . I've loved you for awhile. I didn't want to, it wasn't ever my intention to fall for you because it was so complicated, but . . ." Alec smiled suddenly, lopsided and adorable. "But it turns out that love isn't something you can choose."

Spencer felt a happiness he'd never experienced blossoming inside him. For so long he'd believed that he was more invested in whatever they shared than Alec. But Alec had been right there the whole time, hiding his real feelings, trying to avoid them.

Just like Spencer had.

Spencer wrapped his arms around Alec and pulled him back against him, feeling the man go soft and boneless. "It isn't," he agreed quietly. "I've never been able to choose. I just know what I felt."

The hope in Alec's gaze was nearly blinding. "You too?"

Nine years. Too many missed chances. For a moment, Spencer wanted to keep him waiting longer, to make him pay for the way he'd rejected him in Hawaii, at the Pro Bowl, for putting up so many roadblocks between them. But that wasn't what you did to someone you loved.

To someone you'd loved forever.

"Me too," Spencer said. "I love you, too. Of course I love you."

Alec laughed, free and wonderful and wild. Spencer felt the echo of it in his heart.

"You know," Alec said, pressing a kiss to Spencer's pectoral muscle. "It's why I said yes, too."

"Can you really use that as an excuse," Spencer teased, feeling lighter than he had in years, lighter than he had maybe *ever*, "for both saying no *and* saying yes?"

"Absolutely," Alec said, with all the confidence of a lawyer who could wiggle in and out of contracts. He gazed at Spencer, heart in his eyes. That's what that look was, Spencer realized. It was just beginning to dawn on him how long Alec had been looking at him like that. With hope and with trust and loyalty. "I can do whatever I want. I can even do this." He lifted himself up, and pressed his mouth to Spencer's.

Spencer was swamped with emotion as they kissed. It seemed unbelievable that their kisses could be hotter and sweeter and more amazing than they had been before, but knowing this wouldn't end, that they could keep doing this for as long as they were committed to each other, that Alec *loved* him, the way

Spencer loved him back, it was . . . absolutely fucking mind blowing.

Alec slung a leg over Spencer, and leaned down, kissing him harder, more insistently, their mouths sliding wetly together. It had been less than fifteen minutes since it felt like he'd come his brains out, but he already could feel arousal stirring in his blood, his cock struggling to get hard again. Alec's dick must have been on the same page, the *I can't believe we fucking confessed our mutual love and affection* page, because he could feel it half-hard against his thigh.

Even though it was too soon, it felt like a miracle that they were here at all, and Spencer decided they could just keep kissing like this, Alec's fingers framing his face, stroking his cheeks, his neck, his shoulders, like they couldn't figure out which part of him they wanted to touch first.

Alec pulled back a fraction, his lips slick and red from Spencer's mouth, and arousal flared through him, hotter and stronger. "I can't believe I can do this," he said softly, hands gliding down lower, a palm pressing against where Spencer's heart was beating. "It feels like a dream."

Tangling his own fingers in Alec's hair, loving the look of Alec naked and rumpled and all his, Spencer pulled him down into another searing kiss.

Time passed, and what felt like a million kisses later, Alec panted helplessly into his mouth as Spencer's hands slid out of his hair, and slid lower, and then lower still, right over the intoxicating curve of his ass.

"Yes, *that*," Alec mumbled against Spencer's lips. "God, yes, please."

Alec wasn't a guy who begged, or said *please*, except when he was being polite to a waiter or a driver—that knowledge filtered through Spencer's sluggish brain. And then, way too slowly, he realized what Alec was asking for.

And suddenly he went from mostly hard, to as hard as he'd ever been in his whole fucking life.

"You . . . really?" Spencer stuttered.

Alec's smile was soft and private. Spencer wondered if anyone else had ever seen it. "Yes," he said, and he took Spencer's hand and dragged it lower still.

Spencer didn't need any more encouragement, but he hesitated anyway. He'd been worried this would come up, especially with someone as sophisticated and comfortable with himself as Alec. He just hadn't anticipated that it would happen quite so soon. He hadn't really thought Alec would invite just anyone into his bed, and into his body.

Of course, he also hadn't expected that Alec loved him, either.

He could lie. He could pretend. He knew enough to not make a fool out of himself. But again, this was *Alec*. He loved him. He wasn't going to lie to him, even if it made him look like a stupid, uneducated idiot.

"I've never . . . not with anyone," Spencer admitted quietly.

Alec quickly smothered the shock on his face, but not before Spencer saw it. "Really?" he asked.

"I . . . there was never anyone I trusted not to babble about it," Spencer said. "I wanted to, don't get me wrong. I've done . . .a little experimentation, but not . . ." He took a deep breath. "Not with someone else."

"You're practically a virgin," Alec teased, not looking so displeased after all. Spencer took a breath, and then another, and realized that this was going to be fine.

He loved Alec, and Alec loved him.

Anything else was unimportant, and they'd figure it out.

"Would a virgin have sucked your cock like that?" Spencer asked, raising an eyebrow.

"No," Alec agreed. "You're not a virgin. Not . . . *technically.*"

"Technically, I guess someone could say I was," Spencer argued, to his own surprise. "You gonna pop my cherry, Mitchell?"

"It would be absolutely my pleasure," Alec said, and leaned over Spencer's chest, pulling open a drawer in the side table there.

"That's . . ." Spencer took another deep breath. "That's my concern, honestly."

Alec looked surprised. "My pleasure is what you're worried about?" He laughed. "Trust me, that's not going to be a problem. You've . . . I'm all lit up inside. You touch me, with just one fingertip, and I'm mush."

It seemed incredible, that it couldn't possibly be true, but Spencer couldn't do anything but believe it because every single time Alec touched *him*, that was how he felt. Like Alec had undone him effortlessly, without even trying.

"I don't want to hurt you. I want it to be good," Spencer said. If he was laying himself bare, he might as well go all the way. "I don't want . . . the worst thing in the world would be you regretting it."

"I won't, I promise," Alec swore. He set the bottle of lube and a condom packet on Spencer's chest. He was still perched, naked as the day he was born, on Spencer's lap, his cock an elegant curved line in front of him. Just as hard as he'd been when he'd first brought it up.

Maybe Spencer's inexperience didn't turn him off. Maybe it would be okay . . . maybe he could *make* it okay.

"Tell me what to do." Spencer's fingers, trembling with desire and nerves, struggled to open the bottle of lube. "What you like."

"You," Alec said, his eyes crinkling, the calm happiness in them radiating out so strongly that it would be hard to miss it.

And it seemed that was true, because when Spencer slid a finger damp with the lube he'd finally managed to get out of the bottle, through the valley of his cheeks, Alec trembled too, biting his bottom lip.

Spencer hadn't done anything particularly amazing, but Alec loved it anyway.

Maybe, he realized as he carefully slid his finger in, that was the difference between hot and dirty fucking and making love.

He'd never really been into the former, but the latter? He already could tell that it was going to take a disaster of epic proportions to separate him from Alec in the future.

He was going to want this all the fucking time.

"God," Alec said, his head falling forward, his fingers digging into Spencer's chest, as he carefully began to finger him. "God, that feels so amazing."

Spencer had, as he admitted, done his own share of experimentation, but it felt so different to do this to Alec, especially when he was loving it so much.

It was probably good that he'd already come once tonight, because he was going to finally get his cock into him, and it was going to feel so incredible, the chance of him exploding almost instantly was practically guaranteed.

It was hot to finger Alec like this, with him draped across him like Spencer's new favorite blanket, but he knew he couldn't get the right angle or do it properly, so he tensed his muscles, wrapping his free arm around Alec as he flipped them over.

Alec's eyes darkened as Spencer fitted a second finger along the first, thrusting slowly and carefully but inexorably.

"I've dreamed about your fingers forever," Alec groaned.

"Feels good?" Spencer checked, because even though that was clear ecstasy on Alec's face, he wanted to make sure.

"Better than the fantasies, even."

Spencer could feel the heat of Alec's body, his muscles relaxing around him as he took him in. "Good," he said, his own voice going darker, rougher. He already felt right on the edge of his self-control.

It was probably all those years he'd wanted to do this and hadn't.

"Come on," Alec moaned, picking up the condom package that had fallen to the sheets, pushing it towards Spencer. "You don't have to treat me like a porcelain vase."

"Maybe I like teasing you," Spencer said, drawing his fingers out slowly, and fumbling for the lube, got a third finger involved.

"Fuck," Alec swore as his cock twitched against his toned stomach, leaving a trail of sticky precome. *"Please."*

"I'm a virgin," Spencer said, batting his eyes, and unable to help the smile at the thought that in a few very short minutes he wouldn't be anymore, "do you really want to rush me?"

"Yes," Alec said on a hard exhale. "Absolutely fucking yes. Get your cock in me before I explode."

"You givin' the orders now?" Spencer ripped the condom package with his teeth, and even though he'd never done this before, it wasn't too hard to figure out how to roll it on. He hated leaving the hot clasp of Alec's body, but he wiggled his fingers as he pulled them out, loving the way the man moaned loudly when he did.

"I'm not the virgin here," Alec said, "you should be listening to me more." He panted as Spencer knelt in front of him, gripping his cock lightly with his fist, lubing himself up. He didn't want to come too soon, so maybe teasing them both hadn't been such a great idea in retrospect.

You're the most determined person in the NFL, Spencer reminded himself as he pressed the head of his cock to the entrance of Alec's body, the place he'd wanted to be forever. *You can do this right.*

As he pushed in, Alec's eyes went wide and shocked, not in pain, Spencer hoped, but because it felt implausible, impossible, and utterly inconceivable to finally be inside of him.

"Maybe," Alec groaned, "you're not that clueless."

"Feel good?" Spencer checked, even though it felt fucking unbelievable to him. He wanted it to feel the same for Alec. Wanted it to feel even better.

He rearranged his grip on Alec's legs, and dragged him closer, fulling seating his cock inside of him. It was the hottest, sweetest pressure that he'd ever felt, the pleasure searing and, Spencer realized, changing him forever.

Maybe he hadn't really been a virgin. What was virginity but a societal construct anyway? But whatever it really meant, he was happy that he could give this to Alec, could show him that of all the men who'd drifted in and out of his life, there had been only one who stuck.

Who he'd never been able to forget.

He gave a slight, experimental thrust, and watched as Alec's head fell back, pleasure glazing over his handsome face.

"Feels . . . fucking amazing," Alec groaned. "Give me some more, please."

The begging was new, but the drive to give Alec what he wanted wasn't, so Spencer began to thrust harder, faster, gathering up every single moan, every single way that Alec trembled around him, every curse that fell from his mouth, the way his cock twitched and held them close.

He reached down and gripped Alec's dick in his fist, pumping along his own thrusts, sliding his thumb through the pre-come bubbling in the slit.

"Yeah, baby," Spencer groaned. Alec's body was so tight around him, clenching up, he knew he was about to come, and then when it hit, that was it for him too, his orgasm exploding through him with a fierce intensity that he'd never experienced before.

"Well," Alec said as Spencer pulled out, his knees—and frankly every joint and muscle in his body—feeling like Jell-O, "that was . . . well . . ."

Spencer couldn't help his smile as he slid off the bed, heading in the direction of what looked to be the bathroom. He tied up the condom and tossed it in the trash, opening a few cupboards, looking for a spare washcloth. He found one and wet it, using the fancy-ass sink sitting in Alec's even fancier countertop.

"Did I render you speechless?" Spencer asked, coming back into the bathroom. His own words weren't coming all that easily. It was far easier to tease Alec about his lack than to admit the sex had blown his own mind.

"Pretty much," Alec admitted, plucking the washcloth from his hand and cleaning himself with a few perfunctory strokes. He tossed it on the side table, and glared when Spencer shot him a questioning glare. "Okay, I just want to cuddle a little? We'll deal with it later."

Spencer wasn't going to argue with that. He climbed back in bed, and Alec draped himself over his chest again. "I'm glad you liked it," he said into the contented silence that followed. "I hoped you would."

"And now you're not a virgin anymore," Alec teased quietly. "How does it feel?"

How *did* it feel?

Like Spencer's life was still sitting in front of him, when only six months ago, he'd felt so sure the whole thing was one big dead end.

"When I was going through that really shitty winter," he said cautiously, "there were a few nights I almost texted you, and told you to come over."

Alec smiled. "If you'd have asked, I'd have come."

"Really?" Spencer hadn't thought he would. After all, they'd stopped texting years ago. There hadn't been anything between them anymore, officially or unofficially.

"Yeah," Alec said, resting his hand over his heart. "I couldn't have said no. You were hurt. Struggling."

"You knew I was hurt. You didn't know I was struggling," Spencer pointed out.

"I knew you," Alec said. "I *know* you. I hoped I was wrong, but well . . ."

"You weren't?"

"I'm rarely wrong, except I was tonight," Alec admitted. "I shouldn't have tried to get you to hook up with a random guy at Temple. It was the last thing I could do to try to put some distance between us."

"Didn't work," Spencer pointed out.

"Because you didn't let it," Alec said with a chuckle.

"I don't want anybody else," Spencer confessed. "Just so we're clear."

"Well, that's good, because neither do I."

Spencer realized that he was actually pretty tired. He could probably fall asleep right here, with Alec a warm and reassuring weight against him. He'd just begun to drift off when he heard Alec speak again.

"Do you think this is what Chase meant when he said he wanted you to experience new things and I needed to assist you?"

The last thing Spencer remembered before his eyes fluttering shut and sleep overtaking him was the sound of Alec's warm chuckle and the last thing he felt was love.

Chapter Twelve

"Maybe *this* is more what Chase intended," Alec suggested, leaning back in his chair and shooting Spencer a wry smile.

It was late afternoon, and they were sitting in the outdoor courtyard at the Wine Cavern, his favorite wine store in LA. He had a regular standing appointment here every month to try new wines for his personal cellar. He'd always intended to bring Spencer here, but as it happened, this appointment had been some of his first free time in days. Perfect for their first official date.

It had been five long days since the kiss that had changed everything. Outwardly, nothing much had changed. Alec still got up way too early, went to the office, went to breakfasts and lunches and dinners with his players, with scouts, with executives, wrangled Kyle, reviewed contracts, and yet, despite everything seeming so incredibly normal, inside he was a big mushy pile of goo.

Because when he glanced at his phone after a marathon afternoon of meetings, he might have a text from Spencer, a picture of him sweat-slicked and bright eyed from one of his workouts. For someone who apparently didn't do much dating—or much hooking up—he knew exactly how to make Alec smile and exactly how to make him squirm. And maybe, Alec mused as he gazed at him from across the little wrought iron table, it wasn't about how much Spencer knew about dating, it was about how well he knew *him*.

He knew that Alec would want to talk to him before he went to bed, and if they weren't together, they would FaceTime. The texting had resumed in earnest, and now instead of mildly overt flirting, Spencer was now bordering on the outrageous.

Just this morning he'd sent a pic of himself, bare chested in all his incredible glory, sheet riding low on his hips, with Iggy draped over him. It had been the best way to wake up that Alec could remember—except, of course, if Alec had been there.

He'd wanted to be, but as he'd told Spencer the night they'd finally cleared the air between them, his schedule running up to the draft was always insane and this year it was extra insane, because the draft was being held here, in Los Angeles.

On top of all the normal craziness that he went through, he was trying to do something agents rarely succeeded at: getting their client traded away from a team that didn't want to let them go. And not just to *any* team, but the team that Spencer wanted.

Alec knew he could do it, but that didn't make it any less tricky.

"I think this is *exactly* what Chase intended." Spencer grinned. "And not just you bringing me to a wine tasting. All of it. The guy's a great wide receiver, but he missed his real calling."

Alec suspected the same thing. "Matchmaking?"

"Yep," Spencer agreed. "He'd give Lady Danbury a run for her money."

Alec raised an eyebrow. "You're watching *Bridgerton* again, aren't you?"

"It's really good, okay?" Spencer said a little defensively, which made Alec's heart ache. Spencer could decide to change his life, play for a different team, and finally do something about his feelings for Alec, but it would take time to undo all those years of trying to be someone he wasn't. All those years of pretending weren't going to be reversed in a moment or a week or even a month.

They hadn't discussed what—if anything—they would say about their relationship. Spencer had never dated anyone publicly. He'd never allowed even so much as a hint to escape. And Alec? He hadn't either, though for very different reasons. This was going to be a first for both of them, and likely tough for both of them, but Alec was worried it was going to be the biggest struggle for Spencer.

Alec knew it and he was already beginning to dread it, the one dark cloud in all these blue-sky, full-of-sunshine days.

"You've got great taste in matchmakers *and* binge-watching," Alec said. "I knew I loved you for a reason."

The joy on Spencer's face pushed the dark cloud away, until Alec could barely feel it, hovering on the edges of his consciousness. He'd never seen Spencer so happy or so content. Alec wasn't sure that *he'd* ever been this happy.

They had both wanted this for so long, and considering how much they cared about each other, surely they could figure it out.

The sommelier approached the table, a welcoming smile on her face. "Hello, welcome back to the Wine Cavern, Mr. Mitchell," she said. "Not sure if you remember me, but I'm Gwen. We've worked together in the past."

He'd actually requested her personally because she was way less snooty than the other sommelier who normally worked at the

Wine Cavern, and he'd wanted Spencer to give tasting a fair shake. "Hi, Gwen, of course I do," Alec said. "This is Spencer, and it's his first time, so take it a little easy on him, okay?"

"Sure thing, Mr. Mitchell," Gwen said. "What tasting menu were you thinking about today?"

Alec saw Spencer mouthing *tasting menu?* out of the corner of his eye.

"We just sat down, we're going to need a minute, if that's alright," Alec said.

"Of course, take your time! Just wave when you're ready to make a selection," she said.

"I thought you brought me here because *you* were buying wine," Spencer said as soon as Gwen had moved on to the next table.

"I brought you here because I missed you and it was the first open spot on my calendar for *days*. But technically, I *do* have a standing reservation here," Alec said. "The third Thursday of every month. I figured, *two birds, one stone*. After all, we've both got to keep your promise to Chase." Alec shot him a warm smile. "Might as well do it on a date, right?"

"I've already tried the wine though," Spencer said, sounding uncertain. "Don't we need to do something else?"

"I thought you liked it," Alec said. "If you didn't, it's alright. I can do the tasting by myself."

"No, no, I did like it, I just . . ." Spencer smiled boyishly, almost like he was embarrassed he'd misunderstood. "I know I'm not an expert, not like you. What if I don't like something?"

"Here's the thing," Alec said, leaning across the table, "you don't *have* to like everything. Wine tasting is about trying something on for size. If you don't like it? You can dump it out."

"They won't be offended?" Spencer sounded skeptical.

"That's what this is for," Alec said, pointing to the silver bucket that was on the end of the table, "you pour out whatever you don't want to drink."

"Huh. I thought that was like … the ice bucket or whatever."

"Nope," Alec said. "You can even spit it out if you don't want to swallow."

Spencer grinned. "Oh, is that right?"

He couldn't help the laugh that bubbled up out of him. It was glorious seeing Spencer this way, the way he'd always imagined he *could* be, if he felt free enough to be himself. And having Spencer be this way with *him*? It was beyond anything that Alec had even hoped for.

"You're gonna take to wine tasting just fine," Alec said. "Now," he added, pushing the menu over towards Spencer, "which flight do you want to try?"

Spencer shot him a tentative look. "I think you should pick. You should know what I like. I liked the red wine you brought over, and the champagne, too." He hesitated. And then to Alec's surprise, reached over the table and took Alec's hand, squeezing it. There was some uncertainty in his eyes, like he wasn't sure if this was okay, but there was determination too. Like he intended to take this step, even if he was unsure, and even if he was afraid. "You know me," he said quietly. "You know what I like."

Alec squeezed his fingers back. Hoped he wouldn't take them back immediately.

But he didn't. He kept them there, loosely connected to Alec's.

"Alright," Alec said, and waved an arm towards Gwen.

"That was quick!" she exclaimed as she approached the table. If she noticed they were now holding hands, she didn't look even the tiniest bit surprised. "What did you two decide on?"

"We're going to do two flights, the specialty sparkling, and the European red," Alec said. "Which would you recommend doing first?"

"Hmmm," Gwen said. "I'll bring some cheese and crackers to clear your palate after the first flight, so either way would be fine. Do you have a personal preference?"

Alec turned to Spencer. "You want to start with the reds or the sparkling wine?"

"Uh." Spencer looked surprised—and maybe a little uncomfortable—that Alec had asked him. "I'm not sure . . ."

Gwen shot him a sympathetic smile. "There's no real right way to do this." She paused. "Well, *technically*, there is, but it's different depending on who you are, and how formal you like your tastings to be. Mr. Mitchell doesn't really stand on formality."

"He wouldn't," Spencer said, shooting him a hot look from under his lashes.

"Alec, *please*," Alec reminded Gwen. "Remember, I don't like formality."

"Fine, *Alec* doesn't really stand on formality," Gwen corrected.

"I think . . . I think I'd like to end with the sparkling wine. Feels . . . kinda like a celebration, yeah?"

Gwen gave Spencer a soft, reassuring smile. "Of course, I totally get it. I'll get the European red flight ready."

"You okay with that?" Spencer said as soon as she was out of earshot. "I didn't want to do the wrong thing, but you said you didn't care, and she said it didn't matter and . . ."

Alec squeezed his hand. "It's all good."

"I wasn't going to let you put me on the spot." Spencer's expression was wry. "But I've been realizing more and more that not hiding means a lot more of this, and I'd better get used to making decisions and putting myself out there."

It was exactly what Alec had been thinking, and he'd been worried that pointing it out would freak Spencer out—but not only had it not seemed to freak him out, he'd gotten there on his own.

It was a really good—and important—reminder that Spencer wasn't helpless, and while he'd buried the core of who he was behind walls so thick and impenetrable that most people didn't realize they even existed, he was also surprisingly self-aware.

"You're not wrong," Alec admitted. "But I'm glad you see it."

Gwen showed up at the table then, two glasses in one hand, and a bottle of red wine in the other, the ivory label covered in a scrawling fancy script.

She set the glasses down, and then Gwen poured out the wine with a practiced flick of her wrist, only an inch or so of the jewel red liquid in each glass. "This is a Sangiovese from Tuscany, from the *Montalcino* region. It's got a great fruit aroma, dark cherry, prune, and plum, with a lot of oak on the finish. I think you're really going to like this one."

"Thanks," Alec said, and Gwen departed, leaving them to their wine.

"This," Alec said, turning towards Spencer, "is as good a time as any to talk about the big interview that's coming up."

"Don't you want to taste the wine?" Spencer asked, frowning.

Alec had a feeling that it wasn't that Spencer was that eager to try the wine; it was more that he didn't want to talk about the interview.

"It should breathe a few minutes," Alec said, "and I'd like to get this out of the way so we can enjoy our afternoon." He hesitated. "I've got to be both, Spencer, your agent and your lover. Let's get the former out of the way, alright?"

"Okay." Spencer sighed, then, clearly resigned to it. "What about the interview?"

"Have you considered what you're going to say?"

· · · · ● · ● · ● · ·

"Some of it, yeah," Spencer said. Alec had forwarded over the list of possible questions two days ago, and even though a very big part of him had only been able to focus on Alec and their burgeoning relationship, the other part of him had been thinking, the last forty-eight hours, on how he'd answer them.

He'd sworn to himself during the last shitty winter that he wouldn't pull his punches; that he'd finally be honest about who he was and about what he'd experienced. But while it was easy enough to make that promise in the safe cocoon of his warm bed, to actually sit down in front of a camera and repeat things to millions of people that he'd never intended to say to a single soul?

That was a different matter entirely.

Alec lifted his glass with his free hand, and Spencer followed suit, picking up his own.

"How do I do this again?" he asked.

"We look at the wine first, admire the rich color," Alec instructed, holding his glass up to the late afternoon sunlight. "And then we do a little swirl, to release the aroma."

"I feel silly," Spencer admitted as he tried to follow the quick swirling motion that Alec had just done so effortlessly. "This is part of why I thought I wouldn't like wine."

"You said you wanted to know how to do this right," Alec teased.

He had. He *did*.

The part of him that was afraid of looking silly—AKA too *gay*—was screaming, but he wasn't going to listen to that part anymore. He'd already told himself that he wouldn't. But when he'd made that promise, he hadn't anticipated that the voices would be so loud or that the fear would be so crippling.

He'd been afraid like this a hundred, a *thousand*, times before, from the first time he'd walked into the Ohio State locker room after posting his coming-out statement on social media, to the draft, when he'd been terrified that being gay would sink his stock, and every single fucking time that Shaughnessey made a derogatory comment about taking it up the ass.

But every time he'd felt this particular brand of fear, he'd turned and hidden in his cave. Hoped that nobody would notice. Hoped that nobody would see.

Thought that if he kept his head down, it would pass.

Spoiler alert, he thought to himself, *it never fucking passed.*

There was only one thing to do. Press forward, even if it scared the shit out of him.

"I want to do it not just because it's right," Spencer said. Alec's hand was grounding him. It was just a glass and some wine. Nobody was going to lurch out of the bushes, screaming at what a gay fairy pussy boy he was, and logically he *knew* it, but it wasn't his head he was trying to convince—it was his heart.

And Alec? He already knew that Alec had his heart.

"Why do you want to do it, then?" Alec's expression was empathetic and endlessly patient. Which was why he'd fallen in love with him; not because he was the hottest guy he'd ever been privileged to meet, but because Alec was a fucking good person. The *best* person.

"Because I *want* to," Spencer said, the words spilling out of him before he could hold them back—and then he realized, he was *done* holding back.

"Good." Alec gave him a slight nod. "I'm really proud of you, you know."

"Why?" Spencer gripped Alec's hand, squeezing it hard. He hadn't done much in his life to be proud of. Yeah, he'd won some awards. He'd changed the game of football. But what had he *really* done?

"It's hard as hell to confront this," Alec said softly, "and you're doing it anyway."

Spencer cleared his throat. "It helps that I'm not alone."

Alec's eyes were so warm, so full of love. He'd thought, nine years ago, that they were fairy-tale blue, full of impossible dreams, but now he looked at them and realized that the dreams weren't impossible, not if they tackled them together.

"You're never going to be alone," Alec promised. "Not ever again, not if I have anything to say about it."

There was nothing Spencer wanted more than to lean forward and close the distance between them, press their mouths together, because mere words didn't feel like enough—but they hadn't talked about what they were going to do in public. Yes, they were holding hands, but that wasn't *kissing*.

But before he could clear his throat and ask what they were doing, Alec resumed his instructions. "Okay, so once you give the wine a swirl," he said, "you're going to hold it back up to the light, and admire the legs."

"Legs? You want me to admire your legs?"

Spencer was rewarded with a dry chuckle from Alec. "No, not *my* legs, the wine's legs. The sweeter the wine, the higher alcohol content, the slower the swirl you made with your wine will return to the bottom of the glass."

"Huh," Spencer said, swirling his glass again, and watching as the rivulets meandered down to join the rest of his wine. "Interesting."

"And then, the third *s*," Alec said, "we sniff the wine, to ascertain the aroma."

"Is that really different from tasting it?" Spencer asked.

"Absolutely." Alec sounded dead serious. "Wine can often taste very different from how it smells. Also your olfactory senses are connected to your taste buds. Smelling the wine first will enhance its taste when you finally take a sip."

"Do you do all this when you drink wine?" Spencer wanted to know. "I didn't see you do any of this when you drank wine before."

"Not always," Alec admitted. "Sometimes I'll give a quick swirl and then a sip, but I drink wine because I *like* wine. I don't need to make a production out of tasting it."

"Huh, okay," Spencer said.

"But you," Alec offered lightly, but with a grave expression in his eyes that showed just how serious he was, "are free to do whatever *you* like."

"Thanks, I will," Spencer said and realized that he actually meant it. He was going to do whatever the hell he felt like. If he didn't like the wine, then that was fine. Beer was perfectly okay. And if he liked the wine, then he'd drink it however he wanted to.

The only person he was answering to going forward was himself.

It was the most freeing realization he'd had yet.

And it made him wonder if Chase hadn't just set him on this course because he'd been playing matchmaker—which he absolutely had been—but also because he knew that Spencer needed this push. Otherwise, he'd still be just a guy who only wanted to play football, and the last few weeks had opened his eyes.

He wasn't even the same guy who had walked into Alec's office and asked him to be his agent. He definitely wasn't the guy who'd hosted Alec for dinner and claimed that he didn't want to eke out a pound of social justice on the Stars.

He'd changed, irrevocably.

He wanted that pound of flesh.

And he was going to take it.

"About the interview," Spencer said, after taking a nice deep sniff of the wine. It smelled really rich and fruity, just like Gwen had said it would.

Then he took a sip.

"One more, remember?" Alec pointed out. "Second sip is the best representation. Sommeliers call it the *savor*."

"Right," Spencer said, and took another one, still blown away by the explosive flavor on his tongue. "Anyway, about the interview . . ."

"What about it?"

"When you said you wanted to make the Stars pay, I said I just wanted to play football." Spencer took a deep breath. "I think . . . I think I'm on the same page now."

Alec's smile lit up his face.

"Nobody should look that happy while planning to take down a whole NFL team," Spencer teased.

"I'm just happy to see you embracing yourself," Alec said. "I want everyone to see who you really are, because I *love* who you really are."

It was unbelievable how those words felt, rocketing through him. He'd heard them over the last few days, each time feeling even better than the last, but nothing seemed to compare to this moment.

"I think . . . I think I might be loving who I really am, too, *finally*," Spencer said.

"I haven't heard better news in ages," Alec said, sipping his wine. "So tell me, what are you going to say?"

"I'm going to tell the truth." Spencer hesitated. "The whole goddamn truth."

Alec looked surprised. "Really? That's not what . . ."

"You probably just wanted me to drop a few damning anecdotes," Spencer said, "and I thought, maybe I could do that. But I don't want to do that. I want to draw a line in the sand, once and for all. This is me, and this is what I want."

"It's your choice," Alec said, "but I'm gonna give a heads-up to the reporter. Jordan's going to want to know you're blowing the top off this."

"You said he played football, the reporter?"

"Yeah, he was a receiver for the Bears for a few years, then got traded to the Stars. This was . . . ten years ago? Fifteen? I can't remember if he retired before or after O'Connor came out of the closet, but after he did retire, to become a writer, he did a big spread in *ESPN Magazine,* with his boyfriend, who's a chef."

"I remember that," Spencer said. "It was a good story. Well, I'm glad he's the one telling it."

"When I brought it to them, they jumped on it, Jordan could barely contain his excitement," Alec said. "This is going to be good for everyone, not just for you. Good for football."

Spencer drained the rest of his wine. He'd never wanted social justice. Never dreamed that he could have both, even though Alec had always believed that he could.

Now he was going to grab on to his career and his sexuality, and never let them go.

"You should bring Pru here for the interview, and the draft," Alec said after Gwen had been by to refill their glasses with what she called "a nice Barbera." "You could use the extra support."

"I don't want . . ." Spencer hesitated. His aunt had always been there for him. Had never failed him. It wasn't so much a question of her not supporting him now, but Spencer knew this could get ugly. The Stars wouldn't take his accusations lying down. When it had just been about getting traded, not about laying his truths bare, Spencer might have invited her to come stay with him, would definitely have wanted to introduce her to Alec. But things had changed. "I don't want to drag her into this. This isn't her fight. She's got her life, still, in Ohio."

"Don't you think she's the best judge of what she should and should not be dragged into?" Alec said, swirling his wine.

"She thinks the best of everyone, kind of like someone else I know," Spencer said wryly. "This might get dirty. Ugly. You know that."

"I'm fully prepared to play just as dirty as they are," Alec said.

"But I'm not prepared for her to have a front row seat to it, or be dragged into it," Spencer said.

"Alright," Alec said, reaching over and putting a reassuring hand on his thigh. "But just so you know, I'm going to be here, and I know my other clients will too. Chase, of course. And Neal and Jamie and Heath and Sam. They wouldn't leave you high and dry."

"Even if they don't want me traded to the Riptide?"

"They don't . . . *not* want you to be traded to the Riptide," Alec said cautiously. So cautiously that Spencer wondered what they'd said to him. But he wouldn't ask, because like Alec had said earlier: they were agent and client, and they were also lovers. It was probably good to do as much as possible to separate them.

"I get it, it's a lot of scrutiny, suddenly."

"They want to win football games," Alec said simply. "And you're going to make that happen for them. As for the rest of it? They'll come around."

Spencer secretly was not so sure they would, but, he thought a little bitterly, that had always been the case with his teammates. They'd always wanted him around to help win games, but for the rest of it? They hadn't given a shit about him.

He'd wanted different. *Better.*

Spencer had to remind himself that this was never going to be easy. He'd have to win them over. It would take time. Their approval wasn't just going to be handed to him on a silver platter.

It should be enough that he had their support.

"I hope so," Spencer said softly. Hopefully.

It had been so long since he'd had hope that he'd forgotten what it even felt like.

"Come on," Alec said, raising his glass, "let's toast to your future. It's never looked brighter."

Spencer raised his own, and couldn't help the thought that echoed through him.

You make anything and everything possible.

CHAPTER THIRTEEN

ALEC LOOKED CRITICALLY AT Spencer's reflection in the mirror.

They were standing in Spencer's walk-in closet, which was huge, but barely filled. Alec didn't know why he'd been surprised. But then his surprise at the nearly empty closet had been dwarfed by his shock when Spencer had pulled on the baby pink shirt he'd picked for the interview tomorrow.

"You're really serious about this, aren't you?" he asked. watching as Spencer tugged on the neckline.

"What gave it away?" Spencer's tone was dry.

Reaching up, Alec smoothed down a wrinkle on Spencer's shoulder, but then his hand lingered, just because he wanted to touch. Just because he *could* touch, now.

"You don't *have* to immediately confront all the shitty things you've said. That's not a requirement. You realize that, right?"

"I know." There was a stubborn angle to Spencer's jaw. "I'm not doing this because I have to. I'm doing this because I want to."

"Jordan wasn't going to ask about it," Alec pointed out. When he'd arranged for this interview, for Spencer to tell *his* side of the story, he'd made sure to pick a journalist who wasn't known as a shark. Someone who was also queer, who'd also been an athlete—someone who might know a fraction of what the last nine years had been like for Spencer.

Alec knew Jordan had no intention of digging too hard or asking any difficult questions. When he'd arranged the interview, they'd both been on the same page.

But of course, Alec should have known that Spencer, once he made up his mind, wasn't ever going to take the easy way out, because that wasn't who Spencer was.

It was one of the reasons Alec loved him.

It was also one of the reasons why he'd always been such a pain in his ass.

"He *should* be asking about it. I was . . . well, you know how stupid I was. How many stupid things I said over the years."

Spencer *had* said a lot of stupid stuff, including the infamous quote that was still making the rounds. The infamous quote that led to Spencer picking out this pink shirt to wear tomorrow.

Gay men don't have to wear pink.

At the time, Alec had sort of understood what he was trying to say: that being gay didn't mean that he couldn't be tough. But there'd been a terrible backlash against the statement, and Alec hadn't blamed the queer community for being really pissed.

He also hadn't blamed Spencer for saying it, because it was clear Spencer was trying to build an impossible image of unrelenting toughness.

And pink? It didn't have a place in that image.

"I'm not going to explain it," Spencer said, "God knows I tried that enough times afterwards and it never got any better, but I think just the shirt sends the right message."

It certainly drew the kind of line that would leave no doubt as to Spencer's intentions.

"You really want to do this, don't you?"

"Wear pink?" Spencer turned, and the edge of his mouth quirked up. He began to unbutton the shirt. "Actually, I don't care either way. I just . . . I figured it would be the best way to not talk about it again."

"You must not know journalists very well," Alec said wryly. "That's all they're going to want to ask about, after you wear this."

Spencer finished unbuttoning the shirt and carefully hung it back up, the muscles in his back flexing as he reached up.

Swallowing hard, Alec tried to keep his mind—and his dick—on track. This was too important. Spencer was depending on him to make the right moves. He couldn't let himself get distracted with sex.

"I don't have to answer," Spencer said bluntly. He wrapped one big hand around Alec's waist and tugged him closer. "I think I'm being plenty clear enough."

"Yeah?" The question came out breathless and full of anticipation.

Like his body already knew his mind was going to be overruled.

"Yeah," Spencer said, and leaned down, brushing his lips across Alec's. Soft and sweet.

Alec had imagined about a hundred thousand times what sex with Spencer Evans would be like. He'd never guessed it would be so romantic.

"I think . . ." Alec cleared his throat. "I think it's a good idea."

"The shirt or . . ." Spencer pulled him close, right against his firm body, so close that Alec could feel his erection.

There'd been a part of him that had known, when he'd found a spare hour in his schedule tonight to go over some last-minute interview details with Spencer, that he'd end up disheveled and blissed out.

He told himself it was a good stress reliever, and then Spencer kissed him again, hotter this time, and more insistent, and Alec let himself stop thinking.

"God, I missed this," Spencer groaned, pulling Alec's polo off as he reached down, undoing the button and zipper of his slacks, fingers trembling with need. Alec wanted to just rip them off, and get his mouth on Spencer's cock, but Ali would kill him if he showed up early tomorrow morning needing a repair before the interview began.

And even worse, she'd know why.

"We did this two days ago, after the wine tasting." They'd both been half drunk and giddy with love and desire, barely making it into the foyer of Alec's house before dry humping against the wall, coming before they'd even managed to get undressed.

Alec wouldn't ever be able to look at that particular statue again without thinking about the way Spencer had groaned, his fingers digging into Alec's upper arms, the look on his face pure ecstasy.

The problem with the sex being this good and this all-consuming was that Alec wanted it all the time. Clearly Spencer was on the same page.

"Wasn't enough," Spencer mumbled into his neck, hands already in Alec's gaping pants. He pressed a palm against Alec's hard, straining cock and he gasped as the pleasure rocketed through him.

"Never enough," Alec groaned in agreement. He tugged Spencer's briefs down and wrapped a hand around his dick, feeling it twitch as he began to jerk him off.

Spencer matched his rhythm, his big, calloused palm the perfect pressure, and it didn't take long. Alec might be embarrassed that it was only a minute or so of frantic making out and a hand job to make him come so hard, but when he caught his breath, his forehead pressed against Spencer's, he realized that it wasn't about what they were doing at all.

It was just Spencer, and the huge, all-encompassing way he felt about him. He couldn't get close enough.

At least this time they'd mostly gotten their clothes off.

After cleaning up, they retreated from the closet and headed into the dimly lit kitchen. Spencer grabbed two bottles of water and tossed one to Alec. He caught it, and opened it, draining half in a single, long gulp.

"You seem really relaxed about tomorrow," Alec said.

Spencer, leaning over the counter, shot him a look. "That's typically what orgasms do," he said.

"No, I mean," Alec said, hating how flustered he felt, just because Spencer had said *orgasms*. Spencer had just had his hand on his cock, and yet the word made his blood heat up and if he could've gotten hard again, he would've. "I mean, you did *before* the uh . . ."

"Orgasms?" Spencer grinned.

"Ugh, you are the worst," Alec said with a groan. "Yes, the *orgasms*. I can say the word, too, you know."

"Can you?" Spencer teased. "Seems like you were having some trouble with it."

"I'm not so buttoned up."

"No, you're not." Spencer reached over and pulled him against him. "Not even close. Last time, we didn't even get our pants off."

"Believe me, I'm still trying to figure out what I'm going to tell my dry cleaner," Alec said dryly.

"That you have a super hot boyfriend who can't wait to rip your clothes off?"

There were plenty of moments during the last ten or so years where Alec had wondered if all the crap they'd been through had been worth it. Seeing the happiness in Spencer's face now, how his dark eyes practically glowed with it? Alec realized now that not only had it been worth it, it would've been worth *more*.

"You *are* super hot," Alec conceded, "and I think it's fair to say we can't wait to tear each other's clothes off."

"Fair," Spencer agreed with a grin. "Totally fair."

"But you *are* feeling good about tomorrow?" Alec said. It was his job to make sure that Spencer felt supported in this crazy time—and not just because he was his "super hot boyfriend."

"I don't know about good," Spencer said. "But I'm ready."

Looking at the determination on his face, Alec believed him.

· · · ● · ● · ● · · ·

Typically, Spencer avoided interviews and reporters like his life depended on it. He'd never been easy talking about himself, because before he'd come out, there'd been so much to hide, and then after? That was all anyone wanted to talk about, and he never knew what to say.

Which meant, of course, that he inevitably said the wrong thing.

There was a whole slew of bad soundbites—him putting his foot in his mouth, and then doing it again and again. At first he'd tried to downplay his sexuality, but when it felt like that was all anyone cared about, he'd gotten defensive and combative. He'd said some stupid shit, hoping to take some of the heat of his homophobic shithead teammates off him. All it had done was bring him more attention—*unwanted* attention—and further alienate him from the people who might've supported him.

He'd dug himself a hole, and though he'd avoided looking at or thinking about the hole forever, he didn't have any choice but to confront it now.

And to start digging his way out of it.

"We're going to start out with some nice slow pitches, okay?" Jordan Christensen, ex-wide receiver and current sports journalist, shot Spencer a friendly smile. He was tall, not quite Chase-tall, but still tall, with kind green eyes. "Just try to relax, and talk to me like the camera's not rolling."

Just because he was committed to this, one hundred and ten percent, didn't make him any less nervous. What if he fucked it up? What if he wasn't convincing? What if nobody gave a shit because of all the idiotic asinine crap he'd said over the years?

Spencer felt himself begin to sweat under his arms, the dampness causing his shirt to stick to his back.

At the time, it had seemed like such a good move, wearing the exact same thing that he'd once decried.

Gay men don't have to wear pink.

"I wish it was that easy," Spencer said wryly. "I'm . . . well, I haven't been very good at this."

Jordan shot him a sympathetic smile. Spencer hadn't expected him to be so nice, but then Alec had arranged this, and it wasn't like he was going to pick someone judgmental and rude. Especially when he knew how nervous Spencer was about it.

"It's okay," Jordan said. "It must've been tough." He leaned forward. "But you know what the best part of this is, today?"

"What?" Spencer wiped his damp palms on his dark gray dress pants, that Ali had tailored flawlessly. He'd looked in the mirror today and thought he really looked like the polished, best version of himself.

Finally someone he could be proud of.

Jordan grinned. "You can tee off on all those assholes who made your life so shitty. Expose the hell out of 'em, okay?"

A voice inside Spencer's head told him that of course Jordan wanted him to be as shockingly honest as possible. After all, that would get him the most views and the most clicks, and ultimately, the most exposure for this interview.

But then, Spencer realized, they wanted the same thing, anyway. He wanted to put the Stars on blast, and the more people who saw that, the better.

He straightened. "I plan to," he said, surprising himself with how hard his voice sounded. "I'm done with letting them get away with this crap."

Jordan nodded approvingly. "You've put up with it for a long time."

"No more," Spencer said. "It ends here."

Alec approached the two couches they were sitting on, shaking hands quickly with Jordan, before turning his attention to Spencer. "You ready?"

If Alec had asked him five minutes ago, he wasn't sure what his answer would have been. Maybe he'd have lied and said *yes*, he was ready to go blow up his life.

But now, with the realization that the life he'd led hadn't exactly done him any favors burning through him, he knew he *was* ready.

"Yep, I'm good," he said. "Ready to burn it all down."

Alec smiled at him. Professional, around the edges, maybe, but Spencer felt the soft, sweet, ultimately gooey love in it. Felt Alec's support bolster him the last little bit of the way.

He could do this.

He was *gonna* do this.

"Okay," the producer said, "we're ready to roll."

Alec gave him one last look, patted him on the shoulder and faded into the darkness surrounding the interview set.

The producer called for the camera and then Jordan was introducing himself, and Spencer was trying not to squirm in his seat.

Not because of nerves. No, suddenly he felt *eager* to do this. To get it over with. To draw the line in the sand, once and for all.

"Hi, I'm Jordan Christensen, and today I'm here with Spencer Evans. You may know him as one of the most knockout, punishing defensive ends in the NFL. But he's here to tell you that you don't know him, not really. But you will after today." Jordan shifted his gaze to Spencer.

Jordan had already told him that he was going to ask some questions, but that Spencer, as requested, was going to be mostly leading the interview. "What's the first thing you want us to know?" Jordan asked.

"To know what it's been like," Spencer said. "I know I've said a lot of stuff . . . but not enough of it was the truth."

"What's the truth?"

"The truth?" Spencer hesitated, then knew what he needed to say. "If you want the truth, there's nowhere else to start but at the beginning. I was honored to play college football. Honored to get a scholarship. I knew . . . I'd known for awhile . . . that I was gay, but I thought. nobody else has to know. Surely if I keep my head down and play hard, nobody will even care."

"I remember feeling that way, too," Jordan said empathetically. "Like if I got enough touchdowns and kept us moving the ball, nobody would care who I loved."

Spencer nodded. "That's not how it works though. You know that. For awhile, it *was* okay though. Until I met this guy in my Intro to Marketing class. His name was Eric, he was cute and funny, and we started hanging out. I was lucky enough that it turned into more, and then . . ." Spencer took a deep breath. "Then one night, we were kinda goofing around on campus, by the dorms, kissing and stuff, and I didn't think anyone saw us, but I was wrong."

Spencer remembered how it had felt when he'd gotten the first anonymous email. Shock and horror. Terror. And ultimately, so much anger pouring out of him.

He'd tried talking to Eric about it, who hadn't understood what his issue was. "Just tell everyone, okay? It's not a big deal. Didn't O'Connor already tell everyone he was gay and nobody gave a shit?"

Maybe it hadn't been a big deal to Eric, who'd been out of the closet since he was fifteen, and was already beginning to chafe at the restrictions that Spencer felt like he was forced to set on their relationship so that nobody would know—but Spencer hadn't been ready.

"I got an anonymous email, with a picture, and the person claimed they had more. Claimed they had personal details. I didn't know who'd betrayed me, but whoever wrote the email claimed they'd post about it on social media. Make sure everyone knew exactly who I was."

Spencer paused, and then continued wryly, "The problem was, *I* didn't know who I was. I was just trying to figure it out. Eric was my first boyfriend, and I wasn't ready to come out of the closet yet."

"But you felt you had to," Jordan said.

"I didn't feel like I had a choice. I thought it would be easier if I did it on my terms, instead of being outed." Spencer sighed. "In some ways, it *was* easier. I got to tell everyone the way I wanted. I thought Eric might stick around if I was out, like he was. But one of the hardest days of my life was walking into the locker room for practice the day after I posted about my sexuality."

"Other players gave you crap about it?"

"Yes and no." Spencer hesitated. "I want to say first, the coaching staff was supportive. They made a public statement, that bullying wasn't accepted or allowed. That I was to be treated like I had been before my announcement. But . . . you know how it is in a locker room. It's not . . . the coaches don't know about everything. The coaches don't *want* to know about everything."

"Nope, they don't," Jordan agreed. "So shit happened, but it was under the radar."

"I didn't know the right way to fight back, so I didn't," Spencer said. "I showed up at practice and gave a hundred and ten percent. I became a better football player, because that was really what I wanted. And for awhile, that helped. It did. We won a lot of games, and the more games we won, guys mostly left me alone."

"Mostly?"

"You know guys. They start stupid shit. They mutter things under their breath. Insults. Shitty comments. Leave used condoms in your locker. That kind of crap. It was actually . . . I couldn't believe it at the time, but it was easier when Eric and I broke up. They knew I was gay, of course, because I'd said so, but they didn't want to see it, right in front of their faces. So after, when I didn't have a boyfriend anymore, they almost forgot about it." Spencer breathed out. *One word at a time*, he told himself. "What that taught me was to keep my life hidden. Not private, *secret*. Like I was still in the closet."

"But you weren't," Jordan pointed out, not unkindly.

"No, I wasn't. I wasn't in someone else's closet, I had built my own closet," Spencer said dryly. "I'm not sure if that's better or worse. But that's how I got through college, and that's how I approached the NFL. I would keep my head down, I would play really well, and nobody would give a crap who I was."

Jordan tilted his head. "You've played for the Los Angeles Stars since you were drafted. What has that been like?"

This was it. The moment of truth. Spencer took a deep breath. "The Stars gave me a lot of opportunities. A lot of education, a lot of coaching, and invaluable training. They helped me become the player I am today. But I'll be honest, I've hated playing for them every single minute I was on the field."

Jordan was either a very good actor or he hadn't imagined that Spencer would go for it like that, because he looked surprised. "You hated playing for them? Why?"

"I was just a cog in the wheel for them. Other players, players they didn't worry about embarrassing them or looking too *gay*, those players mattered. I only mattered when I did something good. They made token statements about acceptance and equality, but they weren't ever sincere. They never checked the toxicity in the locker room. They let it happen. They *encouraged* it, because they thought it would make us better players."

"That's . . . well, that's just terrible," Jordan said. "If it was that bad, why did you sign a second contract with them?"

He expected the question. Why *had* he signed that second contract? Spencer knew Alec had never understood it. To Alec, that had been his chance to get out.

"I wanted to be the best. I thought . . . I stupidly, naively thought that they'd make me the best." There was no other truth than that, though Spencer already knew that some people would see this, would read the quote, and not believe it. They'd assume it wasn't as bad as Spencer said, because he'd chosen to stay.

At the time, it was all he knew. He didn't think it could be any different.

"They sure did, though, you can't deny that," Jordan said. "Your list of accolades and awards is long. You've got a legendary reputation."

"For a long time, all I wanted to be known for was being the best defensive end in the league," Spencer said. "And then I realized that's cold comfort when you're hiding everything you are. I don't want to do that anymore. I want to be myself. I want . . . I want to play for a different team. A team that actually appreciates me."

"You could have asked for a trade before now," Jordan pointed out reasonably.

Spencer made a face, making sure that the camera picked it up. "They'd never trade me willingly," he said. "I make them too much money. But they've made their last cent off me. I want to be traded," he said, slowly, clearly, so there was not an ounce of doubt, "and if I'm not traded, I'm not sure I'll be playing another down of football."

"You'd sacrifice a career, a career where you're in your *prime* for this?" Jordan asked.

"If I'm afraid to be who I really am, afraid to explore who I really am, what's the point of being the best?" Spencer asked. "I took a long hard look at myself when I was injured this winter and realized that there isn't one. Or if there is, it's not a price I'm willing to pay anymore."

"You were injured," Jordan pointed out, "in the Battle of LA last year. Is that why you're considering retirement? You aren't *sure* you can play anymore?"

"I'm in the best shape of my life," Spencer said, confidence ringing in his voice. "I guarantee whatever team I go to, they'll see that. Whoever I play for, they'll be getting my very best."

"I see." Jordan smiled. "Rehab went good, I guess."

"I've got a physical therapist who could double as a drill sergeant. She made sure I was in fighting shape."

"So, Spencer, you've said you want to be traded. Sounds like you're really wanting to change your life around."

"That's the plan," Spencer inserted. Afraid, suddenly, of where this was going.

"Is that why you've signed with a new agent?"

"Yeah," Spencer said, "Alec Mitchell is not only queer himself, but he knows how to get the best for his clients. That's the representation I'm looking for, which is why I signed with him."

"No other reason?" Jordan smiled conspiratorially. "Not because he's got so many clients who play for the Los Angeles Riptide?"

Spencer let out the breath he'd been holding. He'd worried that maybe Jordan was hinting that there was something more going on between him and Alec—after all, the man wasn't blind, he must have seen the way they were looking at each other—but it turned out, he was just trying to prove that the team Spencer really wanted was the Riptide.

He wasn't wrong, but Alec had insisted that it wasn't the right time to show their hand yet.

"They have a great track record of on-the-field excellence," Spencer said. "And off-the-field excellence, as well. They support their players. They have a very clear, *enforced* no-tolerance policy. If I had a chance to play for the Riptide, I'd be honored."

"They're a great team," Jordan agreed with a nod. "What if the Stars told you that they'd make changes? Would you reconsider your stance?"

"No," Spencer said firmly. "They've made promises before, when I signed my second contract, and I figured out later they didn't ever have any intention of keeping them." He took a deep breath. "Jordan, I should have done this years ago. Is it hard to do this now? Honestly, it really sucks. But I'm going to do it anyway, because I'm not going to let any more time pass before doing the right thing."

"It sounds like you've thought it through," Jordan said. His expression was sympathetic.

"It's time," Spencer said. "Long time coming."

Jordan reached over and shook his hand. "I know how tough it can be to play in the NFL and not be a cookie-cutter player," he said, "so I'm rooting for you, man. It's not gonna be easy."

"According to my aunt Pru, nothing worth doing is," Spencer said wryly.

"Your aunt Pru sounds like a smart woman," Jordan pointed out.

Spencer nodded. "The smartest," he said. "She's gonna be really happy I'm doing this."

"I think . . ." Jordan hesitated. "I think a lot of people are, to be honest."

He segued into the closing, and then it was over.

Spencer sank back into the stiff couch cushions, feeling relief flood him. He'd done it. He'd made it through the interview, and not said anything stupid. He hadn't dug the hole any deeper, and he'd also faced it straight on. He'd done everything he could, and if people didn't want to believe him, and if the Stars wanted to call his bluff . . . well, Spencer was ready.

He stood, and Jordan did, too.

"Great interview," Jordan said, and this time he didn't shake his hand, but reached out and gave him a tight hug. "I'm so sorry for all the shit you've been through."

"You didn't do it," Spencer said, surprised at how supportive Jordan sounded.

"No," Jordan agreed. "But we didn't give you the benefit of the doubt. And we should've."

We, like he wasn't just referring to himself, but the entire queer community.

Spencer wasn't just surprised, he was shocked.

"I didn't give you all that many reasons to," Spencer admitted. "But thanks . . . that . . ." His brain was screaming at him, *Jordan's part of the community here, he might not be a current player but he's an ex-player and he's queer, just like you, and he not only believed you, he wants better for you.* "That means a lot."

He hadn't really believed it would happen.

He still wasn't sure that the rest of the community would come around.

Maybe Heath Harris would still look at him like he wasn't quite sure what to make of him, and keep him at arm's length. Maybe Neal would toss him passes, but not ever become a friend.

Or maybe he was wrong.

"Of course," Jordan said, and then grinned widely. "Reed and I are gonna be rooting for you. Off the record, of course, but it's the Riptide you want, isn't it?"

Spencer hesitated, not quite sure how to answer. "Well . . . let's say you were playing still, and you were out. Who would *you* want to play for?"

Jordan laughed. "Understood, I get it. Don't want to tip your hand."

"No, we don't." Suddenly Alec was there, shaking hands all around, looking like the perfect no-nonsense agent. "Great interview, Jordan, I appreciate it."

"You told me I just needed to listen"—Jordan shrugged—"and that's all I needed to do."

Alec turned to him. "You ready to go?"

"Yes." Suddenly Spencer felt a little lightheaded and floaty, like he couldn't quite believe what he'd just done. Suddenly, he just wanted to feel Alec's arms around him. Grounding him. Reminding him that however this went, there would always be one person on his side.

"Alright," Alec said, and then he was leading him out of the studio, and then through the winding hallways, but, to Spencer's surprise, they were detouring into a bathroom.

"What . . ." Spencer started to ask as Alec pushed him in and closed the door behind him, locking it.

He didn't get the chance to finish his sentence, because suddenly Alec's arms were around him and he was hugging him so tightly, Spencer could barely breathe.

"You . . ." Alec murmured into his shoulder, a note of wonder in his voice, "you . . . amaze me."

Spencer let his eyes close and leaned into the embrace of the man he loved. "I didn't do anything amazing," he muttered.

Alec pulled back, and to Spencer's shock, there were tears in his eyes. "You survived," he said simply. "Why didn't you ever tell me about college?"

"I . . ." Spencer stuttered. "I try to forget about it a lot of the time, to be honest. And it's not some amazing inspirational coming-out story, like the ones that everyone wants to hear. I was scared shitless and I didn't want to do it."

Alec's fingers tightened. "That doesn't make you any less."

"Sometimes it makes me feel like I am," Spencer admitted.

"God," Alec said, his voice breaking. "I knew you'd had a hard time. That wasn't a surprise, but then I heard all that, and I thought of how shitty I was to you, how judgmental, and it made me sick. I should've been supporting you, this whole goddamned time, not being a snotty asshole." Alec sighed deeply. "You shouldn't love me, you should hate me."

Spencer reached up and cupped Alec's cheek with his palm. "No," he said simply and honestly. "I couldn't ever hate you. You didn't know. Nobody knew. And that was the way I wanted it to be."

"Not anymore," Alec said. "I'm so fucking proud of you."

"You know what? I'm proud of me, too."

Alec laughed, and that was a sound that Spencer would never get tired of hearing. He wanted to hear it every day, for the rest of his life.

"You know what else?" Spencer continued. "I love you a whole fucking lot." He pressed his lips to Alec's and felt the man melt underneath his touch.

It was such a turn-on, knowing that under all his fancy suits and professional demeanor, all his notorious efficiency and brilliance, Alec was *his*.

Alec's kiss, hot and heady, reminded Spencer almost immediately that it had been too damn long since they'd been able to be alone together. "Tell me," he said between kisses, "tell me that you're free tonight."

"I'm actually having a late dinner with Phillip Reynolds," Alec said, sounding disappointed.

"Wait," Spencer said, the realization taking its sweet time to process. Must be all the blood that wasn't in his brain. "Phil Reynolds? He works for the Riptide. He's the VP of player personnel."

"Yep," Alec said with a smile and nod.

"Don't tease me," Spencer said, sliding a hand down Alec's chest, resting it right above his heart. "Is this about me or is it about Chase or Rashad?"

"It's about a lot of things." Alec's voice had gone serious. "But I'm really hoping to talk about you."

"Really?" Spencer couldn't help the hope that was billowing in him now.

"I fully expect, because I told Jordan to make sure they did, that a few snippets of the interview are going to leak ahead of time.

Maybe even tonight. I want to see what Phil's reaction is to the fact that you might be available soon."

Spencer took a deep breath. "Wow, this is really going to happen, isn't it?"

Alec's smile was fond. "I'm going to do my best. But yeah, everyone's going to know. Soon."

"Before the draft, even."

"The draft is only a few days away," Alec reminded him. "Whatever Jordan leaks won't be the big stuff, but enough that everyone is going to know something huge is coming down the pipeline. But remember what we said? Keep your head down. And if anyone from the Stars calls you . . ."

"Tell them they'll want to talk to you," Spencer finished for him. "I remember."

"Good."

Spencer hesitated. "I know you're so busy and you're working hard for me . . ."

"A lot of what I'm doing is because of you," Alec teased. "But yeah, I want to spend more time together too. I'm . . . this is serious for me."

Spencer felt the worry he'd refused to give voice to virtually evaporate. "I'm serious, too."

"We've been dancing around this for a long time," Alec said. "I don't think we could be anything *but* serious. But yes, after the draft, I'll have more time."

"All for me, I hope?"

"All for you," Alec confirmed with a sweet, secret smile. "We'll celebrate the draft properly after it happens, I promise. The draft *and* your emancipation."

My emancipation. The words felt right as they echoed through Spencer's head.

"I can't wait," Spencer said, leaning down to kiss Alec again.

CHAPTER FOURTEEN

ALEC WAS ENJOYING AN excellent dinner of grilled swordfish with lemon and a red pepper aioli when suddenly, as Alec had expected, Phil's phone started going crazy.

"Excuse me a moment," he said, and Alec merely smiled and nodded. Fully prepared to wait for Phil's reaction.

Whatever it was, it was going to be worth waiting for.

A minute later, Phil looked up from his phone with a shocked glance, set his glass of wine down on the table with a decisive click and shot Alec a half-hearted glare.

"You're always full of surprises," he said without heat. "I've given up trying to predict you. Spencer Evans, really?"

"Really," Alec said. "Great guy. Great player."

"Now, I'd a hundred percent believe the latter. But the former?" Phil frowned. "That's why I'm so surprised. Not that apparently he's got shit to say, because God knows, I don't like the way the Stars run their organization, but that you think he's a great guy. After all the ways he's hurt what you're trying to do." Phil paused, and Alec braced himself. One of the reasons he liked and admired

Phil so much was that he rarely held back the truth. "What *we're* trying to do."

"I think you forget that four years ago, the Riptide was a different organization," Alec pointed out.

Phil leaned back in his chair, his shrewd gaze not leaving Alec's face. "I remember," he said.

"Do you? I remember the way everyone tripped over themselves, trying to figure out what to do in the aftermath of the Super Bowl. You weren't ready. You weren't prepared. You supported Heath and Sam, sure, but you also didn't expect the first Super Bowl win in the franchise's history to be overtaken by arguably the biggest coming-out statement the NFL has ever seen."

"We weren't ready. But we *got* ready."

"Maybe you did, but then you let Michael terrorize Neal the very next season."

"You know that we took care of that mess."

"*Eventually,*" Alec pointed out and took a sip of his wine. It was a stainless steel Chardonnay—crisp and the tiniest bit sweet on the palate. An excellent choice with the swordfish. He'd have to call the Wine Cavern and put in a special order for a case.

"Yes, *eventually*. But we did take care of it. We let Michael go. Is there a point to this?" Phil sounded grumpy that Alec had gone out of his way to remind him of all the Riptide's failures.

"You haven't always been perfect. Neither has Spencer Evans. But you both have something in common. You're *trying* to be better." Alec paused. He'd never thought he'd use his law school classes in opening and closing statements when he became an agent, but he'd learned that you had to position your pitch even more carefully when it was to one person, rather than a jury of twelve. "And you could have even more in common. I know you're shopping for some defensive help."

Phil shot him a look. "Cut the bullshit. The Stars are never going to let Evans go."

"Maybe. Maybe not. But I'm not sure it's going to be up to them."

He and Phil had been working together for years now. He'd spearheaded the efforts to convince the Riptide that even though it couldn't save their Hall of Fame kicker's career, it was worth cleaning house to avenge what had happened to Neal after he'd missed the kick in the Super Bowl. They'd worked together on Heath's coaching contract, and then he'd persuaded Phil and the rest of the Riptide front office that they didn't need to trade Chase either, that he'd be willing to restructure his contract.

Alec had never wondered if they would or wouldn't get something done; he'd always been confident that they'd figure something out that both parties could be happy with.

But now? With the career of the man he loved resting on his persuasion and negotiation skills? He felt uncertainty and fear in a way he hadn't in years.

What if he couldn't convince Phil that Spencer had changed? What if he couldn't convince Phil that Spencer had *never* been the guy he'd presented to the world?

Even worse, what if the Stars, angry at Spencer for exposing their ugly, dirty laundry to the public, refused to trade him?

Spencer claimed he was willing to retire, but Alec knew how much being a football player meant to him. If the Stars called Spencer's bluff and he actually retired rather than play another down of football for them, Alec knew he'd see it as a personal failure.

He'd had others. Players he'd never been able to sign. Contracts he'd never convinced teams to ink. Promotional deals that had fallen through.

But if he failed Spencer, Alec already knew it would haunt him forever.

"The Stars aren't going to let Spencer Evans retire, of all players," Phil scoffed.

"Again, it's not going to be up to them," Alec said. "Spencer is resolved. When the interview comes out, you'll understand why."

"I don't doubt they were assholes," Phil said. "But Spencer Evans is the jewel in their crown."

"Yet they're not winning Super Bowls. You are."

"We've only won one," Phil pointed out dryly. "You know that."

"And you're going to win more," Alec said smoothly. "You've got Crawford and Rashad and Chase all locked up for years. Your offense is the best in the league. Nobody can score more points, more easily, than the Riptide. But you know what you can't do? Stop the other team from scoring just as many."

Phil set his fork down with a click. "You're playing hardball."

Alec forced himself to shoot the other man the most charming smile in his repertoire. He *was* pushing hard. Harder than usual. Was it because he felt the fear of failure so much more acutely than he normally did? Had his feelings for Spencer already begun to interfere in their professional relationship?

"Am I?"

"You know you are," Phil said decisively. "You're pushing this."

"Spencer Evans came to me because he wants results," Alec said. "You've known me a long time, Phil, and you know that's what I deliver: *results.*"

"What do you want?" Phil asked baldly. "Plain and simple. You want Evans on the Riptide? Is that what *he* wants? Wants to be on a team that doesn't give a shit that he's gay?"

"That'd be a good start," Alec said. "He wouldn't mind a few rings, while you guys were at it."

"There's a reason you invited me to dinner, and not Marcus Branson." Marcus was the GM for the Miami Piranhas, the other NFL team that was considered most accepting of alternative sexualities and lifestyles. But the Piranhas were in the middle of a major rebuilding phase. They'd only won two games last year, and had just hired one of the biggest hotshot college coaches to turn their team around.

"That's right."

Alec, trying to pretend like this wasn't killing him, dug back into his swordfish. It was just as good as it had been before, but he'd lost his appetite. He'd expected Phil to be a lot more excited and far less reticent about the possibility of Spencer Evans playing for the Riptide. He'd expected, like all the other times they'd teamed up to get something done, for him to say, "Sure thing, let's make it happen."

But he hadn't.

Alec supposed he couldn't blame him. This was a fluid situation with a lot of question marks, and Phil made a lot of money doing what he did best: protecting the Riptide from the very thing that Alec was trying to bring to his doorstep.

"If, and I say *if* because we don't even know if the Stars are gonna come to the table, if the Riptide decide to pursue Evans, it won't be a popular locker room decision." Phil sighed. "Basically, you're handing me a gift that I sure want, but we both know it's got strings."

"He knows he's not the most popular player in the NFL, but he's working on that," Alec said. "*I'm* working on that."

"You got him in that pickup that I pretend not to know about?" Phil asked.

"He was catching Fisher's passes like he's been playing wide-out for years," Alec said with a grin.

"And Harris?"

"What about Heath?" Alec asked innocently, even though he knew exactly why Phil was asking.

Heath was always the toughest nut to crack, the most fanatically loyal, the most difficult mind in the room to change.

"He's . . . well, you know how he can be," Phil said. "It's his greatest strength, and sometimes his biggest flaw. His stubbornness. It kept him playing even when his heart wasn't in it. It was what kept him coaching Crawford when he wanted to wring his neck."

"I don't think that's all he wanted to do to Sam," Alec teased.

Phil chuckled. "No, no that's not all. But you know what I mean. He's *your* client, Mitchell, you know how he is. And despite that he's a coach, and not even the *head* coach, he's the guy that the whole locker room listens to. If he's not on board, I can't sell this."

"What if the Stars want something you aren't willing to give up?"

For the first time, Alec saw the gleam of excitement—the possibility of winning multiple Super Bowls, with Spencer Evans leading a revamped defensive line—in Phil's blue eyes. "I'm sure we could come to some kind of agreement," he said, his tone contradicting the undeniable look that Alec had just spotted.

"For Spencer Evans, you could," Alec said bluntly. "Because he's Spencer Evans."

"Like I said, he could be a gift. But those strings . . ." Phi said regretfully. "I don't know what to do about them."

"What if the strings were . . . less of an issue?"

Phil shot him a look. "You know Heath."

"I can convince him to come around."

"You're good, but you're not *that* good," Phil said, laughing.

"It's not me that's going to be doing the convincing," Alec said confidently. "It's going to be Spencer."

Phil did not look convinced, but that didn't matter, because Alec had gotten what he wanted.

If the Stars relented, and between the combined persuasive power of Alec and Spencer, they could convince Heath to get on board, the Riptide were interested.

Later, when Phil excused himself to go to the bathroom, Alec checked his phone. Wasn't even the tiniest bit surprised to see four texts, all increasingly anxious as the news began to filter in, and Spencer waited to hear what happened during the dinner.

Alec's fingers paused on the screen. What *should* he say? The Riptide was on board, if they could convince Heath it was a good idea?

Heath made Spencer antsy, and justifiably so.

It wasn't that he was a bad guy; actually, it was the opposite. He was so loyal and so steadfastly supportive of the community the Riptide had built that he was going to be a tough nut to crack.

Alec *loved* Heath and yet he knew the very things that made him so great were going to make this so much more difficult.

Finally, he settled on, **Phil interested. Opening negotiations have begun. Just have to convince the Stars to let you go.**

Then he added in, **and take a deep breath. You're good.**

Spencer answered almost immediately. **You really think so?**

Yes, Alec typed back, **you're totally good.**

It was the same kind of reassurance that he'd have given any of his other clients, but he still felt slightly uncomfortable as he put his phone away, Phil returning to the table a moment later.

He would go into detail about the situation with Heath when the right moment presented itself, Alec reasoned. There was no need to freak Spencer out, when he was already halfway there with everything else.

"Your phone must be blowin' up," Phil said with a conspiratorial smile. "Not every day you manufacture the trade of one of the NFL's best defensive players."

"I'm sure the panicked calls are going to start coming in any second," Alec said with a grin.

• • • • • • • • • •

But they didn't, not really, not the way that Alec had anticipated.

He'd been sure that he'd have half a dozen calls and texts from Roddy Murphy, the GM of the Stars, by the time the dinner ended, but there was a curious silence from Spencer's current team.

Everyone else, though? They *all* called.

Once they scented the story, the sports media salivated for four straight days.

Alec didn't think they'd ever fielded more calls in his office than they did from the moment the first rumblings about the interview came out to the morning of the draft, when the full version was released.

Kyle was so busy that he hadn't even had time to obsess about his ex-boyfriend in days. Alec had almost considered hiring another person to help, but Kyle had gotten that stubborn, implacable look in his eye, and he'd decided to just let his assistant handle it.

He'd never had a major player on the trading block before, and he'd heard situations could go crazy when that happened. But Alec reasoned that Spencer wasn't even technically *on* the trading block yet, as the Stars had yet to publicly—or privately—respond to any of the accusations or demands he'd made in the interview, and he also just wasn't any major player.

He'd won *three* Defensive Player of the Year titles, had overcome a debilitating injury just last year, and he'd just called out one of the NFL teams for an epic ton of bullshit.

Alec fully predicted that things were about to go from insane to nuclear.

Still, despite his packed schedule, he'd made the time to take a detour to the airport.

He'd arranged to make his pickup in the private, VIP section of LAX, but even then, there was a mass of photographers. Likely, he thought with a grimace as he fought through them to the steely-eyed woman with the no-nonsense gray bob and the sweet smile, they'd been following his car.

Things were really getting out of hand, and they'd barely begun.

"I see you've shaken things up quite a bit, young man," Pru said to him as she slid into the passenger seat of his Mercedes. "I sure hope you two know what you're doing."

Even though Spencer had told Alec that he hadn't wanted his aunt to be there for the draft, and the media circus that was sure to follow, Alec hadn't listened.

He'd known, even if Spencer hadn't, what this would really be like, and he'd known that even if he'd wanted his aunt out of the fire, she'd never want him to go through this alone.

"I hope so too," Alec agreed.

"I am glad you called me, though, I had three people walk up to me in the bathroom and demand to know what Spencer is doing." Pru's nephew—for all intents and purposes, her *son*—had been an NFL player for almost ten years now, but Alec would put good money on everyone having left her alone until now.

Spencer had never done anything particularly newsworthy, other than play lights out for the last ten years.

He'd certainly never made a stink like this one.

"Ah, well, things have gotten a little wild already," Alec agreed, switching lanes, and beginning to merge onto the freeway. "That's why I wanted you to be here."

"You made the right call," Pru said unequivocally. "Spence likes to pretend that everything is fine, he's made a pretty good career out of doing that, but he shouldn't get away with it so often."

"He shouldn't," Alec agreed. "I have you booked in the Four Seasons . . ."

Pru shot him a look. "You didn't tell him I was coming."

"Neither did you," Alec pointed out.

"Larry certainly never called me up out of the blue," Pru said. "What exactly is going on between you and Spence?"

The few times that Spencer had mentioned his aunt and legal guardian through most of his childhood, her fierce intelligence and incredible garden had been part of the conversation. How she'd never let him get away with a single thing; she'd always managed to nose it out first. "I think," Spencer had said with a laugh, "she knew I was gay before I even did."

Despite Spencer's clear warning, this was a rather rude awakening. Clearly he'd never be able to manage Pru the way he managed most players' relatives.

"Ah, well, you know, we've known each other for a while," Alec prevaricated.

"That's right, you have." Pru paused. "I remember the first time you met. Spence walked around with stars in his eyes for *weeks*."

Alec swallowed hard. "I think that was because he'd just been drafted in the first round."

"No, it was because he met you," Pru said with finality. "Are you going to lead him on some more? Spence is a good boy. He deserves someone that will really love and accept him."

Alec didn't want to admit it, but he was definitely sweating. He cranked up the air-conditioning and told himself it was because it was an unnaturally warm May for LA. "I think he deserves that too, Mrs. Evans," he said.

"It's Pru," she repeated firmly. "I never married, I was too busy raising Spence, and you know what? I never missed it. I had enough love in my life. But Spence? That boy needs his fair share."

"He does." It was impossible *not* to agree with her, when she was so obviously right and Alec had thought the same way for ages.

He'd long since given up hope of being the love that Spencer needed so badly, but now that it had actually happened, all he felt was gratitude to a fickle universe.

"Well, then." Pru smiled, looking very pleased with herself. "I won't ask when the wedding is, because I know that's not always important to you folk, but I want to say, I'm pleased."

Alec felt a wave of surprising relief. It wasn't like he'd expected Pru to dislike him, but hearing her approval felt unexpectedly nice.

"I'm glad," Alec said. "Even though it's a conflict of interest?"

Pru shot him a level stare. "Are you going to do the best you can for him?"

"Of course. Always."

"Even if you break up?"

"Even if we break up." Though Alec could hardly imagine such a thing happening. They'd already been through all the difficulty of a relationship, before they'd ever been in one.

"Even if he ends up in Minnesota or Florida?"

"He's not . . ." Alec protested.

"*Even* if he ends up in Minnesota or Florida? Or God forbid, *Buffalo*?" Pru stressed.

"It won't matter where Spencer plays," Alec said, "or if the Stars call his bluff and he ends up retiring. I'll love him no matter what."

"Good." Pru looked very pleased by *that* statement.

Maybe he'd never met the "parents" before, but it turned out that he actually knew just what to say. He'd been trained as a lawyer, hadn't he?

But truthfully, he knew that wasn't why he'd been able to give Pru an answer that settled her fears. The real reason was because he loved her nephew, and she knew it.

"But I'm pretty determined to make this work out," Alec said.

"How's it looking so far?"

"Not too bad," Alec said. "I'm slightly concerned about the lack of response from the Stars." He was a *lot* more concerned than slightly, but anything he said to Pru was sure to make it back to Spencer, and he was still managing Spencer's anxiety about the whole situation.

There hadn't been a good opportunity to tell him about Phil's concerns about Heath, which Alec thought was actually a blessing in disguise. Spencer would want to try to fix things right away, in the midst of everything else that was going on, and Alec had decided it was better to let the interview release, the draft happen, and *then* deal with Heath.

The Stars clearly weren't going to make any moves anytime soon, and Alec decided that he might as well use the extra time.

"They haven't said *anything*?" Pru sounded just about as concerned as Alec was, deep down. "Is that what you expected?"

"It's a rather . . . unexpected situation, all around," Alec hedged. "I'm not sure they know what to say. They might be waiting until this afternoon, when the full interview comes out. The good news is that Spencer has a lot of public support."

"Of course he does," Pru replied crisply. "He's the victim in all this."

Alec agreed, but saying so in front of Spencer? He'd *hate* knowing that people felt sorry for him. He'd argue that wasn't why he'd revealed all his years of mistreatment.

He'd done it to guarantee himself a better life going forward, and to prevent anyone else from dealing with the same crap.

"Yeah, but don't say that to his face," Alec joked lightly.

Pru nodded seriously. "He'd *hate* it." She gave him a small smile, her expression thawing another fraction. "You really *do* know him."

"And care about him," Alec agreed. "A lot."

For a minute or so, as they approached the enormous draft complex that had been erected in downtown Los Angeles, Pru was quiet. Then she finally spoke again, right before Alec pulled up to the valet station that had been set up.

"I didn't think you two would ever get your heads out of your asses," Pru said succinctly. "I'm very glad to be wrong."

Alec gaped. "You knew about . . . well, about everything?"

"Not everything, I'm sure, but enough. Spencer likes to tell me things." Her gaze narrowed. "I know he's always liked you way too much."

"I'd . . ." Alec hesitated. "I'd argue that he likes me just the right amount."

Pru smiled then, a full-blown smile that reminded him so much of Spencer, when he let his guard down, that Alec couldn't help but smile in return. "I was wrong about you, Alec Mitchell, and that's a relief, plain and simple."

"I'll never hurt him," Alec promised.

Pru reached over and patted his hand. "Of course not. Now, let's go find my nephew. Where is he in all this mess?"

Chapter Fifteen

"See, not so bad at all," Chase said confidently as they sat in one of the temporary green rooms that had been set up adjacent to the makeshift television studio, all prepped and ready for the draft, which would be starting in a few short hours.

"Alec didn't need to ask you to come babysit me," Spencer grumbled.

Chase shot him a look. "I *wanted* to come hang out with you, man. You're gonna hurt my feelings."

Six months ago, Spencer would've argued that wasn't possible, but in the last few weeks, he'd learned that Chase Riley hid a sweet, sensitive soul under his brash, charming exterior. And, he'd discovered, he really just plain *liked* the guy.

"So, there's no possible way that when I told Alec that I was worried I'd be mobbed down here, with people I didn't want to talk to, that he didn't ask you to come sit with me?" Spencer asked, arching an eyebrow in Chase's direction.

"Hey, you try one of these root beers?" Chase said, waving the bottle in his hand. "It's this craft shit, but it's really good. You should try one."

"Root beer?"

Chase nodded vigorously. "A good root beer fixes all your problems." He stood. "Let me go grab you one."

He headed over to the snack bar, with its glass-fronted fridge and large woven basket full of snacks. "You want something to eat too?"

"No, thanks," Spencer replied. He didn't really want a root beer either, but if it would make Chase happy, he'd drink it.

"Here," Chase said, returning not only with two root beer bottles, handing one to Spencer, but a whole armful of bags of chips and pretzels and mixed nuts. He spread out his bounty on one of the large stuffed ottomans that were serving as tables, scattered throughout the green room.

"Give me some of those nuts," Spencer relented, and Chase tossed him a bag. He opened his root beer and popped a few cashews into his mouth. Nuts weren't messy like chips or pretzels—he couldn't imagine how pissed Alec would be if he showed up, and Spencer had made a mess out of his suit.

In a few hours, this would turn into the spot where the prospective NFL players waited to see where they'd be drafted. Right now? It was serving as the waiting area for everyone who was appearing on the pre-draft coverage.

That had been Alec's big one-two punch plan. First the interview, which had come out an hour before—Chase had already confiscated his phone, because he hadn't been able to stop refreshing, reading the comments, both the good and the bad—and next, a special appearance on one of the big Sunday game panels.

Incidentally, the very same one that Neal Fisher had joined after his retirement.

Just like Alec picking the perfect journalist to conduct Spencer's interview—someone objective but empathetic, who'd been in Spencer's shoes—it wasn't an accident that the show he'd ended up on had a client who Spencer maybe didn't consider himself *friends* with yet, but that he'd developed a semi-friendly acquaintance with.

He'd always known that Alec took care of his clients, but Spencer wanted to believe that this time, Alec was working extra hard, not just because this was an extraordinary situation, but because he really cared about Spencer.

"Oh good," Chase said, looking up from his phone. "Alec's here. He said he just parked and he'll be here in a few."

"Not fair you get your phone and I can't have mine," Spencer said, though he *had* been feeling better once Chase had forcibly removed the temptation to look at what people were saying about him online.

Chase shot him a look. "You gonna be good and stay off Instagram? Twitter? Facebook? Pinterest? Google? Email?"

"What's even left if you remove all those?" Spencer rolled his eyes.

"There's this great app that has old-school comic book strips," Chase said. "You could always check *that* out."

"Root beer and comic strips," Spencer grumbled. "You're a freaking piece of work, Riley. What does Tate even see in you anyway?"

Chase flashed him a bright grin. "Oh, wouldn't you like to know?"

"Ew, *no*," Spencer said, but Chase just laughed.

What would he have done if Chase hadn't stopped by, unexpectedly? Sat here in the green room and angsted over all the shitty things people were saying about him? Stressed about who might come up to him and confront him? He knew the Stars front office contingent was somewhere in this complex, getting their draft room set up for the upcoming weekend.

Plain and simple, he'd have been miserable.

But Chase had made passing the last hour less stressful, and extra bonus, he never failed to be entertaining.

"So," Chase said, before Spencer could thank him, *properly*, for keeping him from going out of his skin, "you gonna tell me how the whole 'learning about yourself' thing is going? Is Alec treatin' you good? Giving you lots of new and different experiences?"

His expression was sly and amused, and Spencer laughed.

"Oh yeah, definitely," Spencer said, thinking of the wine tasting, of Ali, and last but not least, of the first time they'd fucked. How good it had felt. How right.

"I bet he is," Chase teased. "You ever gonna tell me what's going on between you two?"

"Nope," Spencer said cheerfully.

"Aw, no fair. You're a real hard-ass, you know?"

"You'd better bet I am, when I start playing for the Riptide next year," Spencer pointed out. "You know, this is actually a really good root beer."

"See! I told you so. I introduced you to that root beer, I deserve to get at least a few details about you and Alec. He's so annoying and won't talk about it at all."

"I won't talk about what?" Spencer glanced up and nearly dropped his root beer. Alec was standing in the doorway and next to him was his aunt.

"Hello, dear," Pru said, giving him a warm, crinkly-eyed smile. He was up and over to her in a split second, hugging her tightly against him.

He'd told Alec that he hadn't wanted her to come to LA. That he hadn't wanted her to get involved in the messiness that was sure to follow, but now that she was here? He could acknowledge just how much he'd wanted her here.

"I'm so glad you came," Spencer mumbled into the top of her gray hair.

Pru pulled back, giving him a no-nonsense look. "Your boyfriend had to call me, Spence, that's not alright. You need to tell me when you need help. You *know* that."

"I know," Spencer said. "I'm sorry . . . I just thought . . . I thought I could handle this."

"This is the biggest thing you've ever done. I wasn't there for you when you came out, but I'm not going to let that happen again," Pru said firmly.

Spencer had never been happier that Alec knew what he needed before he needed it. When he finally got his guy alone again, he was going to show him just how grateful he was.

"Boyfriend?" Chase piped up.

Alec shot his other client a glare. "Don't you dare get started."

"I won't! Not me!" Chase threw his hands up in mock surrender.

"Who is this?" Pru demanded to know. "A friend of yours?"

"Chase Riley, ma'am," Chase said, walking over and sticking his hand out to shake before Spencer could intervene. "One of Alec's clients, and *hopefully*, soon to be one of Spence's teammates."

Pru shook his hand and took a closer look at him. "Aren't you that boy who danced when you lost the AFC Championship? All over the stage?"

Chase looked sheepish. "That'd be me."

Pru smiled, patting him on the chest. "Makes me feel better too."

"Dancing?" Chase perked up.

Pru nodded.

"Not now," Alec hissed under his breath. "We've got to get Spencer ready."

"Spencer is right here, and he's plenty ready," Spencer said dryly about himself.

"Good." Alec's expression softened. "Really?"

Spencer wanted to reach out and just touch him, but while they were surrounded by friends right now, anyone could wander in and see. Even he knew it wasn't the right time to tell everyone that he'd fallen in love.

"Really," Spencer said, discovering that he was actually telling the truth. "Chase was . . . well, between the phone confiscation and the root beer, he was great."

"I'm glad," Alec said.

A guy wearing a headset and carrying a clipboard poked his head into the doorway. "Spencer Evans? We're just about ready for you."

Spencer took a deep breath. "I guess," he said to Alec, "this is the moment of truth."

He watched as Alec hesitated, and then clearly threw caution to the wind, pulling him into a quick, tight hug. "You can do this," he murmured into his ear. "You've got this."

And with the feeling of Alec's arms still lingering and his words in his head, Spencer followed the assistant to the set.

. . . .

"So, son, we hear that you've been unhappy with the Stars."

Terry Bradshaw had perfected the *oh shucks, it's just ol' me* routine a long time ago, but Spencer knew that underneath the *good ol' boy* exterior, he had a razor-sharp mind.

"Yes, sir," Spencer said politely. He was sitting between Terry and Neal, and Jerry Rice and Jimmy Johnson were seated opposite them.

"Anyone ever blackmail you, Fisher?" Terry asked, turning to Neal. "Because let me tell you, my blood pretty much boiled when I heard that part."

"No," Neal said. "And mine did, too. Did you ever find out who sent you the email, Spencer?"

Spencer tried not to squirm uncomfortably in his chair. He'd expected these kinds of questions. He'd prepared for them. That didn't make them any easier to deal with. "No, never."

"Real damn shame," Jimmy said. "You should've gotten the chance to do it on your own terms."

"I appreciate that, I do, but here's the thing," Spencer said, "I'm doing it on my own terms now. Maybe a little late, but better late than never, right?"

Terry nodded at his words. "You serious about not playing football anymore?"

"What I'm serious about is not playing for the Stars anymore," Spencer said clearly. According to Alec, they still hadn't reached out, and they'd been conspicuously, painfully silent on every single one of the accusations that Spencer had leveled in their direction.

They hadn't said anything about the treatment he'd received over the years, or about his trade request.

If he was being honest, Spencer was a little pissed.

Thought they could ignore him, could they?

"I know you touched on this a little in your interview with Jordan Christensen," Neal said, "but what about helping the Stars change from the inside out? I know my old team, the Riptide, wasn't always great at inclusion and representation, but they've gotten better, with a lot of help along the way."

"They'd have to want to make changes, and from my experience, the desire just isn't there. I'm tired of playing for an organization that doesn't respect me, but wants to profit off me." Spencer hesitated. "If they were serious about changing, they'd have contacted me about my concerns. But they haven't."

Everyone around him looked downright shocked.

Alec was probably going to murder him. Or kiss him.

Spencer continued, feeling reckless, and surprisingly, loving every second of it. It felt so freeing to no longer give a fuck. "Before I signed my second contract, we had a lot of meetings, facilitated by my old agent, Larry Nicholson. Even though the Stars had helped craft me into the player I'd become, I wasn't interested in staying the locker room punchline. I was done. They knew it, they said everything I wanted to hear, and I should have believed my instincts when they screamed that it was too easy, too simple. That they didn't mean anything they said."

"What happened after you signed?" Neal asked.

"First day of OTAs, I walked into the locker room, and someone had written a nasty word inside my locker, in permanent marker. I reported it, as we'd discussed during the contract negotiations, and suddenly, it was just too much work, too difficult." Spencer took a deep breath. "I played the whole season looking at the word every time I came back to the locker room."

Spencer could hear a pin drop.

He'd known that his vague words would only be enough for so long; at some point he was going to have to lay down some real factual events, things that he'd hidden forever, that he'd sworn he'd go to the grave never telling a soul.

But things had changed. *He'd* changed.

"Wow," Neal said softly. "They really refused to clean it up?"

"Finally, last day of the season, I came to clean my locker and I brought one of those magic erasers," Spencer said, "and I scrubbed it off myself. So when I say they really don't give a crap, they *really* don't give a crap."

"They're probably gonna give a crap now," Terry said sagely.

"Yeah, I think the sound we just heard was the PR team for the Los Angeles Stars scrambling for the Xanax," Jerry joked weakly.

"There's more I could share, but . . ." Spencer hesitated. "But I don't want everyone to think it was all bad either. Just . . . just bad enough that I'm done, and that I'm not willing to listen to pretty promises."

"I get what you're sayin'," Terry said. "They supported you as a player, but not as a man." He cleared his throat. "You deserve better, son."

"Thanks, that means a lot." It *did*, more than Spencer had thought it would.

"The draft is startin' tonight," Jimmy said, "what would you say to some of these guys, coming in fresh to the NFL? Any advice for them?"

Spencer hesitated for a moment. What *would* he say to them? What would he say to himself, if he could go back to nine years ago?

He remembered a man who'd tried to give him some advice, back then. But he'd refused to listen. As the years had passed, he'd gotten angry, and then sad, and then depressed, and eventually resigned.

And a hundred times, a *thousand times*, he'd wondered what would have happened if he'd approached his career differently. If he'd accepted, early on, that he wasn't ever going to be "just" a football player?

"I think"—Spencer cleared his throat—"it's important not to dismiss how important each and every one of you are. I had someone tell me once that all things are possible if you work hard enough and believe in them enough. At the time, I thought he was full of fairy tales, but now? I believe that all things are insurmountable if you never try. So *try*. And don't ever let anyone tell you that you aren't important, because the NFL needs *you*, not the other way around."

"That's a great reminder," Neal said, nodding. "I remember when I was drafted, my agent at the time told me that I was lucky enough to be drafted at all as a kicker, I shouldn't press my luck and come out, too. But I wish I had. I wish I'd shown everyone what's possible. Instead, I lived in fear."

"Hey, I lived in fear for eleven years," Spencer said. "I was out of the closet but I was still locked inside. We can't judge ourselves on yesterday, only tomorrow."

"Great advice, great advice," Terry said supportively. "We should have you runnin' the rookie camp."

"Ha, *no*," Spencer said. "They'd hate me within hours."

"Minutes," Neal said, laughing.

"Hey now," Spencer said, all faux offense. But by the time the interview ended, a minute later, he was feeling lighter than he had in weeks.

Months.

Maybe even years.

It was amazing how much telling his side of the story freed him.

"You were right," was the first thing Spencer said when he rejoined Alec and Pru in the green room.

Alec raised an eyebrow. "Yes, I know. But about what?"

Spencer laughed. He couldn't help himself. He loved this infuriating, stubborn, know-it-all optimist who believed that even the sky wasn't the limit.

"I should've done this ages ago."

"Yes," Alec said simply, "but you weren't ready. Now you're ready. It wouldn't have felt this way if you'd rushed it."

"You think so?" Spencer wasn't convinced. Hadn't Alec been pushing him all this time?

"Listen," Alec said. "I was right, maybe, but I was wrong, too. It would've been a disaster if you'd forced yourself to do something you weren't ready for. You weren't ready in college. Did you really want to do that again?"

"No," Spencer agreed quietly.

"I never should have let you do that," Pru said, wrapping a hand around his arm, squeezing reassuringly. "I know you don't think you had any choice, but we always have a choice."

"I've got a choice now," Spencer said. "And I'm using it."

"Speaking of choices," his aunt said pointedly, "when were you going to tell me about this one?" She jerked an elbow in Alec's direction.

"Uh," Spencer said. "Soon?"

"Not soon enough," Pru said.

"Really, I've been telling you about him for years. This can't be that much of a surprise."

Alec grinned. "Really? What did he say about me?"

Pru shot him a look. "Wouldn't you like to know?" She turned towards Spencer again. "It's not a surprise, and it's not unwelcome, but I don't want to be some old, forgotten relative you keep in the dark in Ohio, alright? You know how I feel about this."

He did. And he'd done it anyway, because it had been easier.

Pru was always so comfortable with who she was, and what she wanted. She was forthright and often disarmingly honest. It had been easier for him to keep her in Ohio. Away from all the decisions she could question; the decisions she *would* question.

He still remembered when he'd signed the second contract with the Stars and she'd been so angry she'd yelled across the phone line and then wouldn't talk to him for a week.

"Why did you do it?" she'd moaned at the time. "This was your chance to get away from them!"

He'd decided that she wouldn't understand, so he'd refused to talk about it.

What he'd really been afraid of was her holding the mirror up so he could see the stupidity of his choices.

"I'm sorry," Spencer said. "It won't happen again."

Pru looked very determined that it wouldn't. "See that it doesn't," she said, and added, turning towards Alec, "And you too, young man."

"Of course," Alec said, barely smothering an amused chuckle.

"Where'd Chase go?" Spencer wondered as they got ready to leave the green room and Alec finally handed him his phone back.

"He ran into Jamie, who was here with Neal," Alec said. "Who knows what kind of trouble they're off causing."

"Ah," Spencer said.

"You going to drop me off at the hotel?" Pru asked. "I hear the pool is great and I want to take a dip."

Spencer was surprised. "You're not staying with me?"

"I thought about it," she said, shaking her head, "but you've got a boyfriend now, Spence. Need your privacy."

"But . . ." Spencer tried to argue but Pru just held up her hand.

"You gonna deprive me of a chance to stay at this fancy-pants hotel that your boyfriend is paying for?"

Spencer glanced over at Alec, who was smiling. "Nope, I guess not," he said.

• • • ● • ● • • •

After they dropped an excited Pru off at the Four Seasons, Spencer fully expected Alec to drop *him* off, and then head back to the draft, but instead, Alec pulled into a local Coffee Bean.

"Need a pick-me-up?" Spencer asked. In all the times they'd been together, he'd never seen Alec drink coffee. Did he even drink coffee? If he didn't, why were they here?

"I don't drink coffee, makes me too shaky," Alec said, but continued to pull into the drive-through. "Except today, maybe I could use some shaking up."

Spencer shot him a look. "What's going on?"

"Nothing . . . and everything?" Alec said with resignation as he drove up to the speaker. "You want anything?"

"Iced tea?" Spencer said.

Alec ordered his iced tea, and then some long complicated coffee order that Spencer didn't even quite understand.

After they collected their drinks, Alec drove around the building and got out, walking over to a picnic table on the side. He took a sip of his coffee, but didn't sit down.

Instead, he just started to pace.

"Alec, you need to chill, okay?" Spencer said. "So the Stars haven't said anything yet. They will. I think the interviews went well. Public opinion is on our side."

Alec paused in his pacing. "Listen," he said, "you've done great. Everything I've asked of you."

"I know," Spencer said warily. Why did he suddenly feel like the other shoe was about to drop?

"I'm . . ." Alec gave a heavy sigh and plopped down into the chair next to Spencer. "This is hard for me. Harder than I thought it would be, and I already thought it would be difficult."

"What's hard?"

"Being your agent and your . . . boyfriend." Alec's voice was wry. "I'm not used to this. It's why I turned you down to begin with. I don't know which hat I'm wearing, sometimes, and it seems this is one of those times."

"Oh." Spencer didn't know what to say. He hadn't meant, ever, to put Alec in a difficult position. But he supposed, it *was* awkward. He even felt an echo of it.

"There's something I need to tell you, something that isn't . . . *great* . . . and I need you to not freak out, okay?"

"Okay . . ." Spencer said hesitantly. "For the record, saying I can't freak out immediately makes me want to freak out. It's like telling someone to be calm. It never works."

Alec cracked a smile, but still looked nervous as he sipped his coffee. "That I'll agree with. You know I had dinner with Phil Reynolds."

Spencer nodded. "You said it went well? That they were interested, if the Stars were willing to let me go."

"They *are* interested. However, there's a catch. They want Heath and the other queer players on the team to be a hundred percent on board with you coming into the locker room. They don't want any issues. Heath might not be QB1 anymore, but he's the heart and soul of that team. Everyone follows him, they always have. And now that he's a coach, on the fast track to being offensive coordinator? He sets the tone for the locker room."

"Why would I make an issue?" Spencer asked and then realized, with his stomach dropping to the ground, exactly what the issue would be. It wouldn't be something he'd do *now*, it would be everything he'd represented—all those stupid quotes coming back to haunt him, *again*—in the past.

This was why Alec hadn't wanted to tell him.

Why he'd avoided it until he couldn't anymore.

Why he'd found it difficult, especially in this instance, to balance their professional and their personal relationships.

"It's not that Heath isn't sympathetic. It's not that he hasn't been through his share of shit, because he has," Alec said, "but here's the thing about Heath. He doesn't like change. He's got things just the way he wants them, and he's not going to want to shake things up, even to get a player as good as you on the defensive side of the ball."

"So what? Everyone is still mad because of before? Heath didn't seem all that mad when we played together a few weeks back." But then, Spencer remembered how he hadn't been all that happy to see him either. He'd been reserved. Guarded.

Glad to see him playing for his team when it didn't really matter, when they were playing for pride.

But when it really mattered?

Spencer swallowed hard.

He hoped that maybe things would be a little easier, maybe he'd softened Heath up with his latest revelations, but considering Heath's reputation as a hard-ass, that was not necessarily true.

"Honestly," Alec said, "I love Heath. He's the most loyal, most hardworking, most dedicated person I know. And those things can all be positive. But they've got a negative side, too. It means he's stubborn. It means he doesn't like to change his mind. It means he *doesn't* change his mind."

"So what are we going to do?" Suddenly, the future, which had looked so sunny only a moment ago, seemed cloudier.

"You're going to convince him," Alec said firmly. With confidence. Sat down next to Spencer, and put a hand on his knee, squeezing reassuringly. "I know you can do it. I know if I get you two in the same room, and he *listens,* he's going to remember what it was like for him. How scary it was. How terrified he was. How it turned out the right way for him, and how easily it might not have."

"But you just said he doesn't change his mind," Spencer pointed out bluntly.

"He will," Alec said. "And I know he will, because *one*, I love you and I have faith in you and *two*, because you've done an absolutely unbelievable job of changing everyone else's."

Chapter Sixteen

If Alec had thought in the week after the draft that things would calm down, he soon learned that wasn't exactly true.

He'd started negotiations between the three players he'd had drafted and the teams they'd been drafted to, and he'd answered about a million questions about Spencer and his career.

But none of those questions had come from the Los Angeles Stars.

Alec had ended up reaching out a few days after the draft, trying to get someone to talk to him about Spencer's status, but he'd gotten stonewalled. In fact, the entire organization had been bizarrely silent on every single accusation that Spencer had leveled against them.

Of course that didn't stop the sports journalists from endlessly speculating—or Spencer from continuing his slow freak-out.

Still, he'd promised Spencer more personal time after the draft, and he'd made good on that promise tonight, agreeing to meet him for dinner. Originally, they'd talked about eating at Spencer's house, but then Kyle told him, when he got out of his last meeting, that plans had changed, last minute, and had texted him a new address.

Alec hadn't known what to expect, but he was used to improvising.

He just wasn't quite as used to improvising where Spencer was concerned, so when he pulled up to the address—a popular restaurant in Malibu with people already milling about outside, clearly waiting for a table—he couldn't help but feel apprehensive.

Going to the Wine Cavern was a far cry from this *very* public establishment, but then Spencer had picked it, so Alec could hardly argue.

He tossed his keys to the valet and approached the host station. "Hi," he said, feeling that weird pull between his agent self and his boyfriend status, "I'm Alec Mitchell and I'm meeting . . ."

He didn't even get the whole sentence out before the blond hostess gave him a smile. "Spencer Evans? Yeah, he's here already, and waiting for you on the back patio."

"Oh." Alec felt even more astonishment. The back patio? He'd eaten there, plenty of times, usually with people who he could safely say *wanted* to be seen.

Was that what Spencer wanted? They hadn't talked about it. There hadn't been much time to discuss it, with everything they had going on. But Alec thought about it briefly, as he followed the hostess through the restaurant, and onto the patio, and realized that he wouldn't mind it.

If everyone knew, he wouldn't be afraid or ashamed. Not anymore. He knew what he wanted. He'd known what he wanted for a very long time, and there'd been plenty of lonely, empty nights to come to terms with it.

And really, in the end, Neal was right after all. Nobody was going to "forget" to return his calls because he was dating Spencer Evans.

Nine years ago? Maybe. But not now. He'd worked hard, and that hard work had paid off.

He'd been assuming that if they didn't immediately reveal their relationship, it would be because Spencer wasn't comfortable with that yet.

After all, the reason why he'd never gone public with someone was totally different from why Alec had never done it.

Spencer was sitting at the far end of the patio, his table spaced out from everyone else's slightly, giving the illusion of privacy. But there wouldn't really be *anything* private happening, not in the full view of Malibu.

He was in jeans and a baby blue polo, tight on his biceps, staring out at the ocean, his eyes covered in silver aviator sunglasses. He was hot and sexy and absolutely fucking edible, and Alec felt a pulse of disappointment that he wouldn't get to eat him up before dinner.

"Hey," Alec said as he sat down. Spencer turned and smiled.

"Hey back," Spencer said, and to Alec's shock, he reached out and under the tablecloth gave Alec's knee a quick squeeze. He felt it, all the way through the wool of his slacks, in his bones and his muscles and *definitely* in his cock.

"This is a . . . surprise," Alec said, "I thought we were eating at your house, but then Kyle told me differently."

Spencer shrugged, and to anyone else, it might look casual, like changing venues was no big deal. But Alec knew him better than that. Could see the slight hesitation in his eyes.

This *wasn't* easy for him.

But he was doing it anyway.

"I thought it might be nice to get out of the house," Spencer said. "I've been, well, *Pru* told me I'd been hiding again, after the interviews, and I don't want to be that guy. The one who hides."

"So we're not hiding, then?" Alec said breezily.

Spencer smiled. "You've got more to lose than me."

The last few weeks had been such a whirlwind that Alec had barely had time to think about when—and *if*—he'd want to handle the public side of their relationship. Was he prepared for the possible backlash that he was dating a client?

Truthfully, he'd never worried about *that*, because he'd always assumed that Spencer wouldn't want to tell anyone for some time.

"I . . . uh . . ." Alec didn't know what to say.

"I think that's the first time I've ever caught you speechless," Spencer said, picking up his glass of wine—he was drinking *wine*, out of choice, in *public*, and Alec's brain was an absolute fucking mess. "If you want, we can keep this a friendly meeting."

"A friendly meeting?"

Spencer leaned closer, and Alec's heartbeat sped up. "On the surface, anyway," he teased, "nobody needs to know what we're doing *after.*"

"Is that what you want?" Alec asked.

Spencer leaned back. "I don't think it should matter to anyone what we're doing here, but I know there will be some inevitable questions. Questions you'll probably have to deal with. So if you want to give it some time, think about it, I'm fine with that. I know you were worried about that before."

"Really? You'll be fine with it?" Alec knew he sounded skeptical and maybe he should take Spencer's words at face value but it was so surprising that they were coming out of his mouth at all, he found he couldn't.

"Don't worry about it," Spencer said, and there it was, Alec could hear the self-consciousness creeping into his voice. "Let's just enjoy our evening."

"I'm glad you picked this place," Alec said, determined to change the subject. "I'd tell you all about their fantastic wine list, but it seems you've already discovered it."

"Oh, yeah, well, some really cute guy thought I'd like wine, and it turns out he was right," Spencer said.

"He's happy to hear it," Alec said, picking up the wine list. "What did you get?"

"Here," Spencer said, setting the glass down in front of Alec. "It's a viognier, the waiter recommended it, and he was right. Just the right amount of tropical fruit on the palate. Really refreshing."

Alec shot him a dubious look. "Tropical fruit on the palate? You doing some reading on your own?"

"Not much else to do, right now," Spencer admitted.

"Before you ask," Alec said dryly, "nothing from them today. I've got a loose contact in the front office, I didn't really want to reach out unless we didn't have any other choice, but it looks like that's where we are."

Alec picked up the glass of wine, and after taking a sip and then another one, decided he liked it. "We'll get a bottle," he told Spencer, nodding his approval. "It's a great choice."

"I don't know why they're being so difficult," Spencer said with frustration.

"Yes, you do. You made them look bad. Then you made them look *worse*. They've clearly decided to wait til the furor dies down before dealing with you. My guess is they have no intentions of letting you go and hope that once you get all this out of your system, you'll reconsider."

"I'm not going to reconsider."

"Yeah, I know," Alec said with a soft smile. "But they don't."

"So not only do I have to convince Heath Harris that I'm not a bad guy, I have to convince the Stars that I'm serious."

"If they think you're serious, they *will* trade you, because they'd rather get something rather than nothing for you," Alec pointed out. "And now, with that said, I'm declaring this a work-free zone."

"I thought this was a friendly meeting," Spencer teased.

"Hey, that was *your* idea," Alec said, leaning forward, almost close enough to press his lips against Spencer's. Knowing that it would probably give the wrong—or the *right*—impression, but he decided that he wasn't sure he really cared all that much. Seeing that smile, the contented happiness that had settled deep into Spencer's bones, was everything, and Alec would do anything to keep experiencing it.

"It was a stupid idea," Spencer said, the love in his gaze unmistakable.

"Tonight, I'm just wearing one hat," Alec said softly, "and it's my boyfriend hat."

"I didn't know you had one of those."

"It's new, and I think I like it."

Spencer's grin was infectious. "I think you're gonna like it a lot more after dinner."

"Probably, but the dinner's pretty nice too," Alec pointed out. "It's a beautiful evening, and it's going to be an even more beautiful night, and there's nobody I would rather share it with than you."

"Am I finally going to get some Alec Mitchell Sweet Noth-ings?"

"You keep looking at me like that, you sure will," Alec teased right back.

Their gazes caught, and for a breathless moment, Alec won-dered how he had ever lived without this. He'd gotten little glimpses, tiny tastes of what could be, but he'd never allowed himself to just wallow in it. Now that he had, and he was lucky enough to be doing it on a daily basis, he wasn't sure how he'd ever resisted.

Spencer was like the sun, and he was helpless to do anything but orbit around him.

"I really want to kiss you right now," Spencer said, shrug-ging helplessly. "We don't need to, I get why you don't want to, it makes sense, but I thought . . . I thought I should tell you. You should know."

Alec didn't say anything for a long moment. "Did I ever tell you that sometimes I'd go to dinner alone, and sit there, often on a patio like this, and drink my wine and think about what it would be like if you were with me?"

Spencer looked surprised, which was crazy, because surely he knew how Alec had felt. He hadn't exactly made much of a secret of it. "No," he said. "No, you never told me that."

"At the time," Alec said wryly, "I told myself it was because I'd never really had a serious boyfriend, and even though I was satisfied with my life the way it was, it was like a latent desire to have some kind of commitment. A person I could share a meal with, tell about my day, someone I could go home to, but deep down, I always knew it was more than that. I could've done it with any number of guys, but I didn't, because I always wanted it to be you."

Spencer didn't say anything, not immediately, his eyes growing soft and loving. He reached out, and this time when he touched Alec's knee, Alec dropped his hand and tangled their fingers together, squeezing.

"Why don't you tell me about your day, then?"

"I thought this was a work-free zone?" Alec joked lightly.

"If you can have your boyfriend hat on, so can I," Spencer said. "What did you do today?"

"I'm negotiating a new Adidas contract for Chase," Alec said. "And you know how he is. One minute he wants one thing, the next he wants something else. The good news is that they're desperate enough for him that it hasn't fazed them. But *ugh*, why does he have to be so difficult?"

"It's Chase," Spencer said, leaning back and taking a sip of wine, his smile making it obvious how much he was enjoying this. "He follows his heart."

"He does," Alec grumbled. "I wish he would follow his heart into becoming decisive."

"You knew what you were getting into with him," Spencer pointed out.

"That I did," Alec said.

The waiter approached then, and Alec ordered wine, and the squash blossom appetizer and Spencer added a large tossed green salad, and they promised to examine the menu more thoroughly.

"Do you think he knows?" Spencer asked a few minutes later, after the waiter had brought their bottle of wine.

Alec realized he hadn't even been thinking about it, and when he'd been standing there, laughing at them about how they'd literally not even *looked* at the menu, if the waiter was observant at all, he'd have noticed how Alec had touched Spencer twice on the shoulder, and then on the upper thigh.

"Uh, probably?" Alec acknowledged. "I guess I wasn't thinking about it."

"*Worrying* about it," Spencer said. "You weren't worrying about it."

"I . . ." Alec hesitated. "I really wasn't, I guess. I wasn't even thinking about it. That's okay, right?"

"I brought you here, didn't I?" Spencer asked.

"That's right, you did," Alec said. He hadn't ever expected to be the one who was putting the brakes on their relationship and it was freaking him out a little.

"Seriously, don't worry about it. Now stop flirting with me and look at the menu before the waiter kicks us out for wasting his time," Spencer said, leaning in, and tempting him more than he should be. How insane would it be to just lean in and kiss him now? *Absolutely fucking insane* and yet he was still thinking about doing it.

Even though he picked up his menu and started scanning the dishes listed, he couldn't quite banish the thought the way he wanted to.

· · · ● · ● ● · ·

Spencer knew he had no right to be disappointed, but it was hard not to be a little bit bummed that even though he'd landed on the "let's do this" page, Alec wasn't quite there.

It wasn't Alec's fault; this had been quick, and the date at the public restaurant sudden.

He'd had too much time over the last few days to think, and instead of overthinking, and worrying, and agonizing about what people might think about him if he dated his agent, he found himself actually *wanting* people to know that he was in love for the first time in his life.

"That was really delicious," Alec said, and he looked relaxed and even a bit sleepy under the string of lights hung above the patio. Over the course of their meal, the sun had set, providing them with an incredible view. Now, with the dusk slowly slipping away, the edges of Alec's dark hair were gilded with the glow from the lights.

"Yeah, really good food, and . . ." Spencer paused, because he'd discovered just how enjoyable it was to give his boyfriend a hard time. "Ehhh, *decent* company, I guess."

Alec grinned. "Oh you think you're pretty cute, don't you?"

"Yep," Spencer said. "And you think so too."

"Ehhhhh." Alec's smile grew impossibly wider. His gaze was soft and sweet, and yet when it fell on Spencer, it felt like it burned him wherever it went. "Just decent, I think."

Despite his teasing words, Spencer had to admit he'd never felt sexier.

It turned out that this being-open thing was pretty great.

He felt free, and somehow impossibly safer than he had when he was desperately trying to hide everything. And on top of everything, he was happy and hopelessly, madly in love—more, it seemed, with every passing day.

Pru, before she'd left, had cautioned him. "It probably feels really good right now," she'd said when he'd driven her to the airport, "but what if he doesn't get you the deal you want? What if you have to retire to get what you want? How are you going to feel about him then?"

Spencer had been shocked that she'd worried about that. Because he hadn't. Alec had been honest and upfront about the chances. He'd always believe, no matter what happened, that Alec would do everything he could. And not just because they were in a relationship, but because Alec was one of the most honorable, hardworking people that Spencer had ever met.

He wouldn't leave a single opportunity unexplored because that was who he was, not because Spencer was giving him mind-blowing orgasms.

He'd told her that—minus the "mind-blowing orgasms" part—and she'd seemed satisfied by the time he'd dropped her off at the airport.

But now, sitting here with Alec, Spencer suddenly wondered if his aunt wasn't the only one who was worried about that.

"You know, if the Stars don't call you back, and just expect me to show up for OTAs, it's fine," Spencer said, and he'd been saying it all along, and he'd been okay with it, but now that the possibility was looking stronger, he was fully prepared to retire.

"Of course, we've talked about this," Alec said, half his attention on the dessert menu that the waiter had dropped off a few minutes earlier.

"Yeah, we did," Spencer said firmly, "but not recently, and not seriously. I don't want you to think I'll blame you if it doesn't work out. I knew it was a long shot, but I was miserable before, and now I'm not, so whatever happens, I'm good with it. If that means no more football, then I know I'll find something else that makes me happy."

Alec set the menu down and shot him a surprised look. "This isn't over, you know that, right? We're just getting started."

"Maybe," Spencer said, "but I was thinking about that conversation we had the other day—when you said it was awkward for you to be both my boyfriend and my agent, and I just want to let you know . . . there's no pressure just because you care about me."

"Are you . . ." Alec hesitated. "Are you really worried about this?"

"I'm not worried about me, I'm worried about the kind of pressure you might feel," Spencer confessed.

"Right now, right in the middle of the biggest situation in your entire professional career, you're worried about *me*," Alec said bluntly.

"Yes."

Spencer watched as several emotions flitted across Alec's face. Disbelief, first, and then fondness, and then finally, a love and an affection that Spencer had never really believed that *anyone* would feel for him.

But before he could really absorb the reality of it, Alec was standing, and his fingers were not quite steady as he reached into his wallet, pulling out bills without really looking at them. Alec was always generous, but that was at least five hundred dollars he was leaving the waiter. Spencer almost opened his mouth to say something, but something about the desperation in his boyfriend's eyes stopped him.

"I think . . . I think we don't need dessert," Alec said unsteadily, and when Spencer stood, hoping it was dark enough that nobody would spy his erection in his jeans, Alec leaned closer. Wrapped a hand around Spencer's bicep and then leaned in the rest of the way.

Their lips brushed once, and then twice, and then Alec groaned a little into his mouth and the third kiss was soft and lush and so goddamned sweet.

It had been twelve years since Spencer had kissed someone in public.

The last time he'd done it, the worst thing he could ever imagine had occurred.

It felt right that today, twelve years later, Alec kissing him in this restaurant felt like the very best thing.

Too soon, Alec pulled away. Spencer almost chased his lips, pulling him in tighter, closer, but they *were* in public. Maybe better to save that for when they were alone.

"Every time," Alec said softly, "every fucking time I think I know you and how your mind works, how your heart works, I'm always surprised. I can't believe you're worried about *me*."

"I wouldn't want you to think I'd resent you if you failed."

"Listen, you hot, sexy, incredible hunk of a man," Alec said, "if I do fail, I'll feel it, I won't be able to stop myself. But I'd never believe you'd think less of me, okay? But it doesn't matter, because this isn't going to fail. You put yourself out there. You applied an unbelievable amount of pressure to the Stars, and you were honest with the universe. I can't believe that it's going to pay us back by refusing to play nice."

"Still believing in fairy tales?" Spencer said, reaching out and tangling Alec's fingers with his own.

"Yes," Alec said firmly, "and I think I'm not alone, anymore."

• • • ● • ● • ● • • ••

Spencer had his hand on Alec's upper thigh, squeezing with the perfect amount of distracting pressure as he pulled into his driveway.

"Aren't you glad I thought ahead and took an Uber to the restaurant?" Spencer asked, his voice low and gravelly in the dark of the car as Alec turned off the ignition.

"So you could torment me all the way home?" Alec asked.

Spencer's smile practically lit up the inside of the car. "Oh, was I doing that?"

"You were," Alec said, grinding his teeth as he opened his door. "You totally were, and you know it, you sadist."

"You sound unhappy about that." On the other hand, Spencer sounded delighted. Probably because after their kiss, Alec had been subject to all kinds of casual touching. A hand on his back, sliding low, nearly cupping his ass, as they waited for the valet to bring Alec's car around. A hand on his shoulder, squeezing with the perfect pressure as he'd opened Alec's door for him.

And then there was the hand on his thigh on the whole drive home, until it felt like all Alec could do was stare at the road and hope that he wouldn't lose control or concentration—when that was all he was dying to do.

Now that they were finally at his house, Alec could turn the tables and extract a little sweet revenge.

"What . . ." Spencer began as they walked through the front door, pushing it shut behind him.

But before he could get any more words out, Alec had him pressed up against the wall. He might not be the strongest guy in the world—certainly not as strong as Spencer, but they'd been working out together, and Alec knew he wouldn't be embarrassing himself at the photo shoot in a few weeks—but he was definitely strong enough when he surprised Spencer.

"Oh," Spencer said quietly, his eyes huge and wide in the dim light of the foyer. "What do you want?"

Alec pressed his thigh harder into Spencer's erection, hard and hot even through his slacks. "You," he said, sliding his hand up, behind Spencer's neck, and pulling him down sharply until their mouths met in a hot, heavy kiss. He pulled away, breathless, his pulse thrumming with need. "Always you."

The way Spencer's eyes glazed over, the way he practically melted like taffy on a hot day in Alec's hands, it was never going to get old.

"God," Spencer groaned, head falling to Alec's shoulder, his lips finding the most sensitive patch of his neck. "Why are you like this?"

"Like what?"

Alec asked the question but it wasn't like he didn't wonder the same exact fucking thing, all the time. How was Spencer so goddamned perfect? And so goddamned perfect for him? It was why he'd thrown everything to the wind, bowled over by Spencer's generous heart, and kissed him at the restaurant.

How could he have done anything else?

Spencer made him crazy with love and lust and every other emotion in between.

"Like you're so hot and so perfect and smart and . . . *ugh*," Spencer said. "I don't even have fucking words for it. But you always do. And that just makes me love you even more."

They were just going to end up making out like two besotted idiots in his foyer if he didn't get them moving upstairs. To the bedroom. Alec was burning for it.

"I do have the words," Alec agreed. "You going to let me call the shots, then?"

Spencer's gaze was worshipful. "Anything you want," he said, and Alec knew he would do it. Anything he asked. The power—and the trust—was incredibly heady.

Taking a step back, Alec gestured towards the stairs. "Let's go upstairs," he said. "You go first."

"You gonna be ogling me?" Spencer asked as he walked over towards the staircase.

"Absolutely," Alec said. There was just enough light to see the curve of Spencer's ass in those jeans, the play of his back muscles in his polo shirt as he began to climb.

They reached the top of the stairs, and impossibly, just watching Spencer had made Alec want him even more.

His control was slipping.

Maybe he wanted to let it off the chain completely.

After flipping on the light in the corner, Alec walked over to the bed and sat on the edge of it. When Spencer moved to join him, like he had the very first time, he held up a hand. "You said I could call the shots," he said in a low, resolute voice. "I want you to stay back there. And take your clothes off. Slowly."

Spencer looked surprised. "You want me to do what . . . *strip* for you?"

"Yes," Alec said.

He toed his shoes off, and then his socks, and then moved back, settling against the massive headboard. Far enough away that he wouldn't be tempted to touch Spencer and ruin this before he could really enjoy it.

How many times had he lain like this in his bed and imagined that Spencer was right there, dark eyes intent on his, all that glorious muscle being revealed one piece of clothing at a time? He couldn't even remember, because it had been one of his favorite fantasies.

And, he thought, what was the point of having a boyfriend as hot as Spencer Evans, who worked as hard as he did in the gym, if he didn't get to enjoy it?

"Okay," Spencer said, suddenly sounding unsure. "I . . ."

Reaching down, Alec cupped his hard cock, hissing a little under his breath at the sudden pleasure. "Do you know what seeing you like this does to me?" he asked.

"Show me," Spencer said, his gaze a burning brand against Alec's skin.

That hadn't been part of the plan, but Alec was basically just as helpless as Spencer was to resist any of his suggestions. So he yanked his belt loose, his zipper down, and scooting slightly, pushed down his pants and briefs, cock bobbing hard into the cool air of the room.

If he touched himself too much, he was going to come, and there was so much he wanted, that would be disappointing.

He watched as Spencer reached for the bottom of his polo shirt, raising it up one tantalizing inch at a time, revealing his chiseled abs, then his pecs, until finally, Spencer lifted it over his head, his arms flexing.

Alec felt his pulse, impossibly, accelerate even further.

"I thought I told you to show me," Spencer said, fingers paused on the fly of his jeans.

Alec opened his mouth, and then snapped it shut again. He could do this. He *had* to do this. First he pulled off his shirt, tossing it to the side, and then, carefully he wrapped his fingers around his cock, stroking it gently. Spencer gave him a little nod of approval, his tongue flicking out to lick his bottom lip, like he couldn't wait to taste his cock again.

Spencer leaned down, all coiled strength, and as slowly as Alec had insisted on earlier, began to untie his shoes. First one, and then the other.

And suddenly, just his hand, pumping his cock excruciatingly slowly, wasn't enough. He leaned over and rummage around in the drawer in the table next to the bed.

"What are you doing?" Spencer's shoes were off now, and he had lifted his head, hand drifting down to his own dick, a hard, undeniable outline in his jeans.

Alec popped open the lid of the lube and slicked up his fingers, pulling up his knees, and circling his hole. He hadn't really thought about what he really wanted tonight—the beat of his blood was just *Spencer, Spencer, Spencer*, and he wouldn't have cared if he'd ended up finishing himself off on Spencer's broad, muscular chest—but he'd realized he needed *more*.

"I want you inside me," Alec said, surprised at how guttural he sounded as he sank a finger in, "*now*."

"But," Spencer teased, the edges of his lips curling into a smile, "I'm not done stripping yet."

"Well, then get finished," Alec barked out. He pushed in a second finger alongside the first, forcing himself to relax. Spencer was a *lot* bigger than just two fingers.

"But you said slowly." Spencer's hands drifted down to his zipper again, and he pulled it down, so leisurely that Alec swore he could hear every single click of the metal.

Alec sank a third finger in, the pleasurable stretch lighting him up inside, making him desperate, and more than a little unhinged.

"Need you," he breathed out unsteadily. "Need you *now*." Especially now that he could see the thick length of Spencer's dick, outlined in tight black cotton. He wanted to lick it, suck it, and he absolutely wanted it to fuck him senseless.

"You want this?" Spencer licked his lips again and cupped his dick.

Alec stared at him, feeling the desire rise so hard and fast he wasn't sure he could push it back down again.

Like he knew he'd pushed him just about as far as he could, Spencer pulled down his briefs, hard cock bobbing in front of him.

"Come here and lie down," Alec said.

He'd wanted to set the tone, and he'd done it, and it had already been mind blowing.

"One thing," Spencer said softly, as he slid up the bed.

"What?"

Spencer kissed him hard, tongue delving into his mouth, brushing up against his own, and Alec felt himself just fucking *melt* into the mattress.

What had he been thinking? All he needed was this . . . Spencer all around him, a warm, muscular cage, pinning him down, fucking him until he grew hoarse screaming about how good it was.

He tightened around his fingers, feeling his orgasm begin in the base of his stomach.

It's not time yet, you want more. You need *more.*

He pulled them out, just in time, wrenching his mouth away from Spencer's, panting hard. "Lie down," he repeated again through clenched teeth.

Spencer grinned, like he enjoyed just how close to the edge he'd pushed Alec.

"Sure thing, boss," he said, lightly, but when Alec reached out to stroke him, to put the condom on, he hissed under his breath.

"Goddamn," Spencer spit out. "I'm . . . you gotta be careful here. You got me all wound up."

Alec shot him a look as he finished unrolling the condom and then fished for the lube, lost in the bedcovers. He finally found it and slicked Spencer up, loving the way he groaned as Alec's fingers stroked him.

"Trust me," Alec said, throwing a leg over Spencer's waist and settling down, right where he belonged—on top of all this beautiful human male. "You're not alone."

"You gonna tell me about it?" Spencer's question ended in an abrupt groan, as Alec began to sink down onto him.

"Nope," Alec said, breathing through the stretch, tugging on his own dick as he settled down. "I'm gonna show you."

The moment Alec began to move, Spencer's fists curled in the coverlet, his face a mask of ecstasy, he knew he wasn't going to be able to last.

Spencer's cock was so deep inside of him, and it felt so good, so fucking *right*. He'd already pushed himself, wanting it all, wanting to show Spencer just how good it could be between them, but he'd worked himself up so much, it was going to be a miracle if he lasted a handful of strokes.

So he moved his greedy fingers away from his cock, nearly crying out at the loss of it, braced his hands on Spencer's stomach and began to ride him. Slowly at first, because it had been forever since he'd done this—forever since he'd even wanted to—but then quicker, his thrusts becoming harder, more forceful, pushing the most gorgeous sounds out of Spencer's throat.

Maybe, he thought dimly, as he slammed down on Spencer's cock, feeling the pleasure radiate through him, it wasn't only Spencer who was making a lot of noise.

That was definitely him who was screeching in tandem, possessed almost, by the way it felt to take him inside.

And then suddenly, it was happening, and it was almost too much, and it had *never* happened like this before. He'd never come from just a cock rubbing up against the spot inside of him, the one that made him yell even louder, but he was, he was right there, on the edge, and then he wrapped his fingers around his cock and pulled *hard*, and he was falling over it. Spencer was groaning too, his hands reaching up and pulling Alec down, closer to him, and bracing his feet on the bed, he thrust hard, once, twice, and then bellowed out his own orgasm.

For a long moment after the pulses of pleasure ended, Alec didn't think he could even move.

"Wow," Spencer said in a surprised voice. "Just . . . wow."

"Yeah," Alec mumbled into his chest.

"If I'd known it could be like that . . ." Spencer trailed off.

"You'd have done this a long time ago?"

"Well, *yeah*," Spencer said, and his outrage made Alec smile even though he wasn't sure he'd be able to find the energy to move at all.

"I'd have taken you back to my room in Hawaii, and not let you walk off alone, for sure," Spencer said. "And the Super Bowl? Yeah, no way. You'd have taken that bet. I could've convinced you."

"You weren't ready. And . . ." Alec hesitated, propping his head up, resting his chin on Spencer's pectoral muscle. "And maybe I wasn't either. But we're ready now."

"Are public kisses always gonna get you this worked up?" Spencer wondered after a long moment of silence.

"I just . . ." Alec reached up with a clean hand, and stroked Spencer's face. "I just like knowing you're finally mine."

"Trust me," Spencer said, his eyes glowing with a soft, radiant happiness, "the feeling's mutual."

Chapter Seventeen

Two days later, Alec and Spencer were eating lunch in the former's office, when Kyle came to the door, a concerned expression on his face.

Alec set down his club sandwich. "What is it?" he asked.

"It's the Stars," Kyle said. "They want a meeting."

Spencer had always known it would begin like this.

He just hadn't ever known how it would end.

"Alright," Alec said. "Give me a minute. Are they on the phone now?"

Kyle nodded wordlessly.

"Transfer them through in a minute," Alec said, carefully wiping his fingers on a napkin. He glanced over at Spencer, who realized he hadn't moved since Kyle's pronouncement. "You ready for this?"

"What do you think did it?" Spencer hadn't known the question he was going to ask until he was in the middle of asking it. Realized it had come up, unbidden, from some secret, hidden part inside of him that he hadn't even known really existed. Some angry, furious part, that wanted to rage and scream and clear Alec's desk with his fists, even though none of this was Alec's fault.

It was all the people on the phone.

"What do you mean?" Alec was all business now. He'd put his agent hat back on, and maybe that was just as well.

"I wonder if kissing you did it," Spencer said unapologetically. "Is that what made them finally call?"

Alec waved a hand, clearly unconcerned about why it was happening, only that it was happening. "Does it matter?" he asked.

Did it matter?

Spencer wanted to say no. But then, he remembered all those early conversations, when Alec had said very clearly that he knew it was going to take some real leverage to get the Stars to move on this issue. That they wouldn't want to let him go, even if he made them look bad.

And clearly, that had not been enough.

Nope, Spencer had had to go out and be *gay*.

At least he'd done it with someone he really, truly cared about, who cared about him. So, maybe, it didn't matter. Not the way that he'd been worrying about, deep down, in that place he hadn't known was even there.

"No," Spencer said finally. "No, it doesn't matter."

"Good." Alec nodded sharply just as the phone rang. "Because it *doesn't* matter."

He picked up the phone.

"Alec Mitchell," he said into the receiver with a crisp confidence that made *Spencer* feel confident, too.

For nearly a minute, Alec just listened, and Spencer felt like crawling out of his skin. What were they saying? Were they telling him to fuck off, that they'd trade him over their dead bodies?

Even examining Alec's face didn't help, because it was frustratingly blank. There was an intense focus in his eyes, as he absorbed what he was being told, but other than the fierce intelligence there, he didn't give a thing away.

"Alright," Alec said. "We'll be there."

There was another long pause. "And please," Alec said, still polite, but his voice turning firmer, more inexorable, "be ready to actually discuss the many issues my client has."

Ten seconds later, Alec hung up the phone.

"Well," he said slowly, "you're not going to be happy about this, but they actually want to get together to discuss your problems, which they claim are mostly 'misunderstandings.'"

Spencer had known they wouldn't give a shit. The callousness of the statement still took him aback.

"What?" he demanded.

"Hey, hey," Alec said soothingly, reaching out and gripping one of Spencer's hands with both of his. "They're blustering. They're bluffing. They're reeling, and upset, and don't know what to do. It's why this took them so goddamn long. And all they have now is an offer to discuss your 'misunderstandings'? Yeah, you've got nothing to worry about. We'll go, we'll listen, and then we'll annihilate them. Okay?"

Spencer wasn't sure he quite believed that annihilation was possible. It was much more likely that they'd go and listen, and then he'd have to be the one taking the final step. Removing himself from the National Football League so the Stars didn't have any way to control him anymore.

But Alec still looked *very* sure. Surer than Spencer had ever seen him before. He'd agreed to leave the negotiation in this man's hands, even if it was tough. So he would.

"Alright," Spencer said after taking a deep breath. "We'll go."

· · · ● · ● · ● · ·

The next day, Alec picked Spencer up. He'd sent him very specific instructions on which suit to wear, which Spencer begrudgingly agreed to.

We're sending a united front message, Alec's text said, **so don't grumble, even though I know you will want to.**

It had made Spencer smile, even though it felt like nerves were going to eat him up from the inside out.

Surely, nothing could be worse than walking into that locker room, week after week, year after year, believing that nothing would ever change, never knowing what new fresh bullshit he was going to have to endure. But somehow, walking into the glass-fronted building that housed both the Stars front office and their practice facility, was harder this time.

Maybe because he'd grown and changed so much since the last time he'd been here.

He'd become a new, better person. Someone who wouldn't just tolerate the newest bullshit with a pained smile and an agonized chuckle.

"You okay?" Alec said as Spencer opened the door for them.

"As okay as I'm going to be, coming back here," Spencer said. "But I know we need to do it."

Alec nodded, paused. "You let me do most of the talking, okay? I've got this. You can just sit there and glower."

"Glower?"

Alec cracked a smile. "You're doing a pretty fair job of it right now."

"Okay, good," Spencer said. At least he was encouraged to glower. If Alec had told him to smile and look happy to be here, that was going to be an impossible task.

Alec approached the front desk. "Hi there," he said to the young lady. "I'm Alec Mitchell, this is Spencer Evans, and we're here for our meeting with Mr. Murphy."

"Mr. Murphy?" Spencer questioned under his breath, and Alec shot him a look.

Roddy Murphy wasn't one to ever stand on ceremony. He might have been in charge of the front office of one of the more lucrative NFL franchises, but in Spencer's opinion, he'd never acted like it.

He'd been a player himself, ages ago, and still acted like he needed to prove how tough he was.

Roddy was one of the biggest problems that Spencer had never figured out a way to circumvent. Because Roddy, not even very deep down, was undeniably homophobic, and he set the tone for the whole organization.

In his mind, men were men, and they weren't sissy gay boys who liked to fuck other boys. And if you weren't a man, you couldn't play football. Not the "right" way, anyway.

For a time, Spencer had tried proving Roddy wrong, had even gotten some small satisfaction out of doing it.

The problem was that Roddy had never wanted to draft Spencer for exactly that reason, but they'd needed a defensive end, he was right there, and despite his beliefs, he never wanted anyone to know about them.

So he'd made the final decision to draft Spencer, wished he could have regretted it, and then spent the next nine years being pissed off that Spencer had proved him wrong.

"Just this way," the young woman said, and led them, to Spencer's surprise, not upstairs to where he knew the large spacious conference rooms were, where they usually held these meetings.

Instead, she took them downstairs, winding through the hallways of the secondary meeting rooms, the ones the players used to hold positional meetups, and review film.

Finally, she opened a door down a hallway that Spencer didn't think he'd ever been in once during the last nine years.

"Roddy will be down in a minute," she said, and shut the door behind them, leaving Spencer to watch Alec's incredulous expression emerge.

"What is this?" he said, more to himself than to Spencer, taking in the simple table, with three chairs, two on one side, one on the other. "I told him to come to the table, expecting to talk. And this is what he does? This is the disrespect he shows me? *You*?"

There were huge conference rooms upstairs, all light and glass and expensive red and goldenrod yellow furnishings.

This was definitely not one of them.

"Roddy is an asshole, he probably thinks being tough at the outset will impress you somehow," Spencer said, taking a seat.

Alec dropped down next to him. "I can't fucking believe this," he said. "I hate to sound like an egotistical dick, but this is *not* how I'm usually treated."

Spencer believed it. Just like he believed this was some kind of move designed to provoke a certain response. Fear, maybe? Or confidence in squashing their ego? Roddy clearly hadn't had much interaction with Alec over the years because otherwise he'd realize that it would take a lot more than a shitty room to put Alec off.

"Of course it isn't," Spencer said. "Don't let it bother you."

Alec's gaze narrowed as he set his laptop on the table. Took a pad and a single expensive-looking pen out of his bag. "Oh, don't worry about it bothering me," he said. "Roddy Murphy wants blood and someone's head in a bag? I'll make sure it's *his*."

"Should I still sit here in silence and glower?" Spencer wondered.

Alec smiled evilly, which would have been a turnoff, except that Spencer knew exactly who all that animosity was directed at, and it turned out that it was actually kind of hot to know that Alec had every intention of destroying their enemies with the fierce brilliance of his mind.

"Yes, absolutely. The more sour the glower, the better."

"That shouldn't be too tough," Spencer said.

Before he could say anything else, the door opened and Roddy, accompanied by nobody else, walked in. He was wearing shorts and an ill-fitting polo shirt with the Stars logo on it. There was a bright red stain on the collar, like he'd spilled ketchup on it from his daily breakfast sandwich.

"Mitchell. Evans," Roddy barked out, taking a seat opposite.

Alec raised a perfectly groomed eyebrow. He always looked good, but there was an extra gleam to him today, in his three-piece suit, flawlessly tailored by Ali, the starched blue of his shirt which matched his eyes, the silvery tie, the coordinating pocket square. He was handsome and urbane and everything Roddy wasn't.

Spencer sat back and prepared to watch two very different men do battle.

"Is this your normal accommodation for guests?" Alec asked.

Roddy grinned. Spencer had been tempted to punch him in the face half a dozen times before, but never more than in this moment.

He'd have to settle for Alec mentally throttling him, and it was absolutely a sign of just how far gone he was that the thought filled him with an unexpected anticipation and even more satisfaction than using his fists would have given him.

"Don't want anyone to know about this," Roddy said. "No good parading our pariah through the offices upstairs."

"He's not a pariah," Alec said, "he's a victim."

"Six of one, half dozen of the other," Roddy said, still grinning. Like he believed he'd already won. "In the end, it doesn't matter. What does Spencer want to shut his mouth?"

"He's already made that perfectly clear, as have I, in many messages sent to your office," Alec said crisply. "He wants to be traded."

"And he just thinks that he can make demands, after signing a very lucrative contract, and we'll just . . . *bow* to his pressure? His very public pressure?"

It turned out that it was pretty easy for Spencer to sit there and glower.

It was harder to stay quiet. A *lot* harder.

"There's nothing stopping Mr. Evans from expressing his displeasure with his treatment publicly." Alec paused and the silence felt weighty, significant in his masterful hands. "If you didn't want him to say anything unpleasant about the Stars organization, then perhaps you should have treated him better."

"We didn't treat him bad, we made him a *man*." The expression on Roddy's face made it crystal clear that he didn't think Alec knew what that was.

Roddy was wrong; Alec was a hundred times the man Roddy was. A *thousand* times. But this was exactly why Spencer hadn't wanted to have this meeting. It was fucking pointless. Roddy was never going to change his mind. Not today. Not tomorrow. The best they could probably do was negotiate with him to finally just let Spencer—and the publicity nightmare—go.

"You made him an excellent player, while also making him absolutely miserable as a person."

"Wasn't aware that was part of our job, to fucking coddle them," Roddy said.

"It is," Alec said. "And you've failed. Utterly."

"Listen," Roddy said before Alec could say anything else, "you can take your fancy law school words and overpriced suits somewhere else. I want to know what it'll take for Spencer to shut his mouth. That's why you're here. To find a way for us both out of this situation."

Alec put both palms flat on the table and regarded Roddy with a killing stare. Anyone else—someone else *smarter,* definitely—would have flinched. But Roddy still didn't seem to understand who he was dealing with.

"We have made it clear what the price of his silence is," Alec said. "A trade, preferably to one of a short list of teams."

Roddy let out a sharp bark of disbelieving laughter.

"And you think I'll just ... *let him go*?"

"You either trade him, and receive compensation for his loss, which considering his elite status, will be considerable, or he will retire and you'll get nothing."

Roddy switched his gaze from Alec to Spencer. "You really gonna sit there and let him talk about you like this? We both know you aren't gonna retire. You belong on the field. You worked your ass off to get back in shape, I got all the reports. Am I supposed to believe you did that for nothing?"

"I didn't do it for nothing," Spencer said. He felt Alec tense next to him, and knew that he was supposed to say quiet, but he'd stayed quiet for so *goddamn long*, and he couldn't do it anymore. "I did it for me. I did it because that's what I *do*, not because I was dying to come play for you anymore." He could hear the disgust in his voice, and maybe he should have tempered it a bit, kept the veneer of professionalism that Alec was maintaining, but he couldn't do that either. Not anymore. Something had broken in him, and when he'd fixed it, he'd lost the ability to just let insulting shit like this pass him by.

"What Spencer is saying . . ." Alec started to continue, but Spencer nudged him under the table.

"What Spencer is saying is that this meeting is a waste of all our time. We came down here, as a courtesy to you, even though you don't deserve one. You never wanted to draft me. You definitely didn't want me to become the player I did. Well, guess what, you get your wish, Roddy, I'm gone. Just say the word."

Roddy opened his mouth and then snapped it shut again.

Alec shrugged. "Alright, that works too." He wrote a few names down on a list, and slid it across the table. "These are the teams that we're interested in Spencer being traded to. The first is, obviously, the best choice. For everyone. They're willing to pay top dollar for a defensive player of his talent and skill, and you should know that better than anyone else."

Roddy glanced down at the paper and frowned.

"You gonna let him lead you around by the dick?" he finally said, and yes, the veneer was totally obliterated now. He was openly sneering, the disgust showing on his face.

Spencer had already known that it was the rumor that they were involved that had made Roddy finally return Alec's calls and messages. But it hurt more to know it for sure.

"For the first time, nobody is in charge but me," Spencer said bluntly. "And if someone *did* have a hand on my dick, at least this time it's gonna be someone's hand I want to be there."

"I know," Alec inserted smoothly, "that there are many, many more stories than the ones that Spencer has already told to the media. He doesn't want to exhume all those painful memories, but he will if you force his hand. Is that really what you want? For your organization to get dragged through the mud, just because you're not willing to take viable compensation for him?"

"I don't know if it's viable yet," Roddy said, stubborn to the last.

"It will be." Alec slid his laptop into his bag. "I've already seen to that, as you're seemingly incapable of running your organization properly."

"You started negotiations on our behalf?" The chair screeched as Roddy suddenly stood, looming over the table. He was not a small man. At one point, all the bulk on his large frame had been muscle, but now it was more sheer heft than anything else. Spencer could take him, if it came down to that, but he discovered that the last thing he wanted was to touch the man.

Still, Alec didn't flinch. Didn't even blink.

"I paved the way," he said bluntly. "What Spencer wants is important to me, more so because it hasn't seemed particularly important to anyone before this."

Spencer had known that Alec would fight tooth and nail for him, with every weapon in his not inconsiderable arsenal. He hadn't known how it would feel to sit here and listen to him fling argument after argument at the architect of all his misery for years.

If he thought he'd loved him before this, it paled to the adoration flowing through him now.

"I'm sure it is," Roddy muttered.

"Is there something else you wanted to discuss?" Alec asked.

Roddy pointed at Spencer. "He's never gonna retire. If I wanted to keep him here, I could."

Spencer stood too, now. "No," he said finally, inexorably. "No, you couldn't. I only let you before, and now I'm done and you won't get another second of my time." He turned to Alec. "I think this conversation is over."

Alec nodded slowly. "I suppose it is."

"Hey," Roddy insisted, "it's over when I say it is. We're not done here."

Spencer gave him one last look. "Actually, we've been done a long fucking time."

• • • ● • ● • ● • • •

That had not gone quite like Alec had expected it would.

He'd done quite a bit of research ahead of time, on Roddy and the way he liked to do business, but the audacity of the man had still almost caught him off guard.

Almost, because to his complete lack of surprise, Spencer had stepped in.

He'd never really anticipated that Spencer would be able to stay quiet, and he was glad that, in the end, the person who had fought the hardest for Spencer was Spencer himself.

But after fighting, he was clearly ready to get away. Or maybe ready to bash some heads in. Alec wasn't sure.

Spencer was walking fast, through the hallways and up the stairs, and he didn't even pause when they hit the front desk. Alec was struggling to keep up, but he kept his legs moving so that he wouldn't get left behind.

He wasn't willing to leave Spencer alone in this building.

Not just because a confrontation might actually hurt now more than it would help, because God knows how pissed Roddy would be if Spencer actually took out one of his players.

As for Spencer, Alec had always believed that he could take care of himself; he just hadn't done a very good job of it up til now. But the man was capable of anything, and he'd just proved that, staring down the person who'd made his last nine years a living hell.

"Wait," Alec huffed under his breath and then suddenly, as they neared the front door, he saw the confrontation before it even happened.

Shaughnessey, the player that Spencer had mentioned once or twice as the biggest bully in the locker room, the one who had spearheaded all of the shit that Spencer had endured over the years, was approaching the front of the facility. Alec could see him in the front windows, but Spencer hadn't yet, because he was too focused on getting out of the building.

Alec nearly called his name, and insisted he stop, or change directions or something, but in the end, he kept his mouth shut because there was no avoiding this.

Maybe it would even be good—and cathartic—for Spencer.

He knew the moment Spencer came face-to-face with him, because he watched his shoulders tense under his flawlessly tailored jacket, and he hesitated, his fingers just brushing the door handle.

Shaughnessey pulled it open and the two of them stared at each other.

Alec could feel the animosity bubbling in the air.

"Come to grovel?" Shaughnessey said, breaking that tight, painful silence.

Spencer didn't answer.

Alec approached, knowing that it was a bad idea to get between these two, and knowing that there wouldn't be anyone else.

"Spencer," he hissed under his breath, but Spencer didn't say a word in return, and didn't flinch, his gaze never leaving Shaughnessey's.

"Hey, you can come crawlin' back all day long, no sweat off my back," Shaughnessey taunted him again.

Spencer still didn't answer, but instead, he reached out and took Alec's hand, holding it tight, squeezing it with all his strength. Alec had developed a damn good poker face over the years, but it took real effort to keep his expression blank as Spencer nearly squeezed his hand off.

"Nothin'?" Shaughnessey asked again. "Well, can't say I'm surprised. You always were a big fat pussy when it came down to it."

Impossibly, Spencer's fingers tightened even further on Alec's. But instead of replying, he turned and pulling a shocked Alec after him, pushed open the door next to Shaughnessey and walked through it.

They were a hundred yards down the vast concrete entrance dotted with benches and enormous planters overflowing with plants matching the Stars' red and yellow color scheme when Spencer stopped abruptly and began to tremble.

Alec faced him and hated to see the pain in his eyes.

"I wanted to kill him," Spencer said, his voice shaking. "I really, really wanted to."

"But you didn't," Alec said, "you didn't even touch him. Listen, nobody would've blamed you for punching the shit out of that asshole, and frankly Roddy fucking Murphy either."

Spencer's smile was wry. "I know I was supposed to be quiet."

"You said it better than I could," Alec said with finality.

"I wanted to say a lot more."

"And you still can, if you want to. You can tell everyone all the shitty things they've done to you over the years and nobody would blame you for doing it."

Spencer let out a shaky breath. Then again. And then again. "No," he said and he sounded resolute. "I got what I needed. If I hold on to this forever, it won't make me any better. I need to move on. I *want* to move on."

It was everything that Alec had ever hoped for. He reached up and tugged Spencer into a tight hug. Right here on the doorstep of the Los Angeles Stars.

Normally he'd have rather chopped his own arm off than do something so unprofessional, but he was learning and growing. Discovering that not being so rigid came with its own set of rewards.

"I'm proud of you," Alec murmured into Spencer's ear. "And I love you. A whole fucking lot."

Spencer's fingers tightened around him. "I'm proud of you too. I thought you'd reach across the table and strangle Roddy, but you didn't."

"Oh, I was plenty tempted."

Alec let go of him, and still holding hands, they walked to the car.

"Now what?" Spencer asked after they'd slipped inside.

"Now," Alec said with a resigned sigh, "we do my least favorite part of this whole thing. We *wait*."

"You think Roddy'll call the teams on the list?"

"He's curious, so yeah, I think he will." Alec glanced over. "And if he does, we need to make sure everyone's on board. So that's one thing we *could* do. Tackle that other problem."

Spencer sighed. "Heath?"

Alec gave a nod of agreement. "Heath."

CHAPTER EIGHTEEN

"Do you usually go to these pool parties?"

Spencer was walking up the front path to Heath and Sam's house with Alec and hating how nervous he felt.

He'd heard about Heath's famous pool parties, but he'd never imagined that he'd be invited to one.

Technically, he hadn't been invited to this one, but Alec had decided that the best way to get Heath on board was for Spencer to crash his party.

"No, not usually," Alec admitted. "I'm usually too busy, though Chase and Neal are always giving me shit about missing them."

"So at least they'll be happy to see you," Spencer said morosely.

"They're going to be happy to see you too." Alec sounded stubbornly confident. "Trust me."

"I do," Spencer said as Alec knocked on the door. "I just . . ."

The door swung open before he could finish his sentence. Which was actually a real relief, because Spencer hadn't been sure how he was going to finish that sentence.

"You came!" It was Chase, with Tate tucked under one arm, and he looked absolutely delighted. "Both of you!"

"You sound surprised," Alec said dryly.

"Well," Chase said, beckoning them into the house, "you never come to these, and Spencer . . ."

"Has never come to one of these?" Spencer spoke up.

"That's right," Chase said with a megawatt grin. "I don't think you've met my boyfriend, Tate, yet. Tate, this is Spencer Evans."

Tate clearly knew their whole history, because though he shook Spencer's outstretched hand, he didn't look quite convinced that he *liked* doing it.

"It's nice to meet you," Spencer said, and meant it. Hoped that Tate realized that he did. "Your guy's been . . . well, way too fucking generous."

The corner of Tate's mouth quirked up in a smile. "That he is. Can't even help himself."

"I'm . . . I'm relieved he can't, because I could sure use the support."

Tate's expression softened more still.

"I've watched the interviews," Tate said. "Sounds like you did. Too bad that you didn't get any til now."

"Too bad he didn't get any *what*?"

The Texas drawl of Heath Harris was too distinctive to miss, and Chase and Tate melted away, clearly not wanting to be in the path of Hurricane Heath for what might happen.

It was clearly one thing to be on Heath's team for the pickup games—it was entirely another to come to his home. Technically uninvited. Spencer forced himself not to squirm under that dark brown unrelenting gaze.

Alec broke the silence. "Heath, my man, it's good to see you," he said, and approached him, casually performing one of those complicated half-handshake, half-hug combinations that Spencer had never learned to master that well.

"Good to see you, too." He actually sounded like he meant it, and then Heath's gaze returned to Spencer.

"I hear you two are involved now," Heath said slowly.

"That's the big rumor," Alec said, chuckling.

"It's not a rumor," Chase said. "I saw pictures."

Alec didn't look surprised—not like the shock Spencer was currently experiencing. "Oh, were there pictures?"

He sounded the opposite of shocked; he sounded bored.

Spencer was kind of in awe of his poker face. It was extraordinary.

"Come on, Spence here is *big* news," Chase said. "And you guys dating, well, it's not even *bigger* news, it's just fucking great news. Period."

Heath rolled his eyes. "You *would* think so, Riley."

"You don't think so?" Sam appeared, next to his boyfriend. He was wearing a pair of sky blue board shorts, and his blond hair was pulled back in a bright pink scrunchie. "Hey," he said, immediately extending a hand towards Spencer. "Don't think we've ever met. I'm Sam Crawford. Welcome to our house."

The way Heath's jaw tightened made it clear that he was rather less enthused about his boyfriend's welcome. But Spencer wasn't going to turn it down. "Thanks," he said. "I'm fucking glad to be here, honestly."

"Bet you are." Sam's expression was pure sympathy.

Spencer thought he'd hate that. But he discovered that it was actually sort of soothing, like a balm on feelings that had been mistreated for far too long.

"I was saying that I'm glad Chase supported Spencer," Tate added into the uncomfortable silence with a clear purpose on his face.

Spencer shouldn't have been surprised that Chase would end up dating a guy who had zero compunction about going toe-to-toe with Heath Harris. Even with the storm-cloud look on his face, and his big, strong arms crossed over an equally strong, bare chest.

For a second, Spencer felt like everyone in the foyer was holding their fucking breath. And then Heath chuckled lowly, and reached out and clapped Spencer on the shoulder. "Course," he said. "I'm glad, too."

As the group headed towards the big open-floor-plan kitchen, Spencer felt Alec brush up against him. "Well," he said, under his breath, "that could've gone better. Also could've gone *worse*."

"I'm gonna have to talk to him, alone," Spencer said, already dreading it. "Here's the thing, I don't even blame him for not wanting me here. If I was in his shoes, I wouldn't want me here."

Alec paused and pulled Spencer against him. "Listen," he said, urgently, "you aren't an interloper here. I brought you. I *love* you. Chase supports you. Tate surprised the hell out of me by backing him, though I guess it shouldn't have, because they fucking adore each other. But you aren't in the wrong. Maybe you were, once, but you've made an effort to leave that behind. You're making amends. You're changing your life. Don't let Heath go all hard-core on you. Because he might. Not because he doesn't care, but because he cares too goddamn much."

Spencer nodded slowly. "You really believe that."

"Heath had . . . we'll say a difficult childhood. And adulthood too, for that matter. He's very possessive of the family he's built, and the happiness he's found, because he had jack all during the first twenty-seven years of his life. He can see you as a threat only because he doesn't know you." Alec poked him hard in the bicep. "But once he does, he's going to realize how great you are. I did, didn't I?"

"Yeah," Spencer said, "but you're special." He smiled, trying to hide his nervousness. But Alec saw it, of course, because Alec saw everything.

"Give Heath a chance to be special, too," Alec said seriously. "He's a good guy. The *best* guy, and part of why is this bullshit. Loyalty, friendship, family, etcetera, etcetera."

Spencer understood better than Alec realized. "I know he is," he said.

"Alright," Alec said. He reached down and squeezed Spencer's hand.

"Were there really pictures?" Spencer asked as they walked into the kitchen.

"Oh, *yeah*," Chase interrupted. "You didn't see them?"

"Kinda been keeping off social media lately," Spencer said. "Though," he added dryly, "it's not like I've ever been very *on* social media."

"That's the fucking truth," Chase said.

"Yeah, there were some pics," Sam said, casually entering into the conversation as they grouped around the enormous marble-topped island. "Blurry. Dark. But uh . . . you could definitely see everything you needed to."

"Yeah, *you*," Chase said, smacking Alec on the shoulder with a hearty laugh, "apparently are a real romantic bastard. Who'd have guessed that?"

"Not me," Neal said, as he and Jamie walked in, hand in hand.

"Hey." Alec's voice was full of faux offense. "I can totally be a romantic."

"Let's just say," Jamie said, "that I've *never* seen you treat Neal like that. Or Chase. Or Heath."

"Probably better for all of us," Sam said dryly.

"Actually, that wasn't me," Alec pointed out, after a quick glance over in Spencer's direction. "That romantic-as-hell dinner? That was all Spencer."

Chase's eyebrows shot up.

"You, Spence? Wow, I'm impressed." Chase put out his hand and Spencer had no choice but to smack it in a high five—and try not to die of embarrassment.

The romantic dinner *had* been his idea, and it's not like it hadn't turned out well, but he also hadn't anticipated there would 1) be pictures or 2) that he would end up getting mercilessly teased over it.

Still, getting teased was a hell of a lot better than being shut out or stonewalled.

The only one who'd mostly done that was Heath.

And conveniently, Spencer realized, glancing around, he wasn't even in the kitchen to witness him fitting in with a room full of his hopefully soon-to-be teammates.

"Listen," Jamie said, "I lost ten bucks off this whole thing." He shot a wry grin in Alec's direction. "Neal was convinced that it was like that, and I wasn't. No offense," he said, "but you *never* date."

Alec shrugged, taking this whole thing a lot better than Spencer. "Maybe I was waiting for the right guy."

"We've known each other for years," Spencer inserted, because as much good as this was probably doing, he was done being talked about like he wasn't even here. "I just finally wore him down, got him to go out on a date with me."

Alec looked amused. "We almost bet on your first Super Bowl, Sam."

"What?" Sam squawked.

"We were in one of the player boxes, watching it, and what . . ." Alec turned to Spencer. "What was the bet again?"

"You definitely bet against the Riptide," Spencer said. This was perhaps slightly more performative than he felt comfortable with, but he knew Alec had brought it up for a reason. And for so many reasons, he was helpless to do anything but play along.

First, because he loved Alec.

Strong second, because Alec was a fucking genius.

"What?" Sam squawked again. "Seriously? I can't believe you'd bet against me and Riley."

"That was why I bet that you'd win," Spencer said. "You guys are dynamite out there. A literal fucking nightmare for me."

"Maybe not for much longer," Chase said speculatively.

"So what did you win?" Sam asked. "Because I'm pretty sure we won that game." He turned towards the patio, which the kitchen opened out onto, the long windows pushed to the side, and yelled, "Heath, we won the Super Bowl, didn't we?"

Heath approached, a soft smile that Spencer had *never* seen before on his face. "Yeah," he said, his voice suddenly rough, as he pulled Sam into a tight embrace. "Yeah, we sure fucking did."

It was a side of Heath that Spencer had never actually witnessed, had only heard about it in bits and pieces, since Heath was one of the more notoriously private ex-players. He coached for the Riptide now, but he rarely shared anything about his personal life, even though everyone on the fucking planet knew he was dating the Riptide's QB, thanks to that kiss they'd shared at the Super Bowl.

"Best day of your life," Sam teased, pulling back an inch. There was a similar happy peace on his face.

"Best day of *your* life," Heath dished right back.

Anyone who could love like that, with it written all over his face, with the sheer joyous ecstasy of it, couldn't possibly be a bad guy.

Spencer had never really thought so. He'd known Harris was a hard-ass, but seeing him like this? It was hard to even hold on to that impression of him.

"So, what did you win?" Chase wanted to know. "Because yeah, we goddamn won that game."

Spencer shrugged. "Alec reneged, in the end."

Chase shot Alec a dirty look. "You really did that?"

"What can I say?" Alec said, grinning. "He wanted something that I wasn't quite ready to give up."

Chase's smile grew downright dirty. "Yeah, I bet you weren't."

"It was a date," Spencer spoke up. "Just a date. But don't worry, I got him in the end."

To Spencer's surprise, Heath let go of Sam and approached him. "You want a beer?" he asked.

Wine was growing on Spencer, but there was nothing like a can of cheap, cold beer for a summer afternoon at the pool. He nodded. Heath reached into one of the coolers, and grabbed two, and glanced back over his shoulder. "Come on, then. I know you're here to talk to me."

· · · ● ● · ● · ● · ● · · ·

Spencer felt cautiously optimistic as he followed Heath out into the backyard. The pool dominated the yard, all aqua blue and pristine. But scattered around the landscaping were chairs and tables. There were a few people Spencer thought he recognized there, but other than a smile and a nod as they passed, Heath didn't acknowledge them. Instead, he led Spencer to a pair of chairs and a small table set back a ways.

He set the beers on the table and sat down, fixing Spencer with his trademark hard stare.

"Just tell me one thing," Heath said. "You're not using him, are you?"

Spencer's fingers froze on the can. "What? Using who?"

Heath leaned forward. "Alec. Tell me you're not using him to get to me. To get on the Riptide."

"No!" Spencer was shocked. Is that what people thought? He couldn't help but be absolutely fucking horrified. "I would never. I . . . I love him. I've loved him for a long time."

"You have history." Heath phrased it like a statement, not a question, his hard stare not really easing up, necessarily, but his face softened a fraction.

"We have history. A lot of history. Way back to, well, way back to when I was drafted. He wanted to be my agent."

"Alec wanted to be a lot of players' agent back then."

If Heath was trying to corner him into admitting it was because they were both gay, he wasn't going to play that game.

He'd spent enough fucking years apologizing for his sexual proclivities.

"He wanted to be mine because he thought I could do some good in the world." Spencer heard how wry he sounded. "That was his mistake, thinking that I was interested in that, back then. But I guess better late than never."

"I guess." Heath sounded dubious about that.

Spencer thought of what he knew about Harris. "I would've thought that was *your* motto," he pointed out.

Heath looked surprised. He probably wasn't used to anyone else calling him out. For a long moment, he stared at Spencer. Then he popped the lid on his beer, and to Spencer's surprise, knocked it quickly against his own before taking a long drink.

Mirroring Heath's actions, Spencer wasn't sure what else he should say.

But before that could be a problem, Heath spoke up again. "Yeah, you're right, though not many people have the balls to say it to my face." He grinned then, suddenly, and Spencer was reminded of the version of Heath he'd seen just a few minutes ago—the one who was wildly in love with Sam. "But *you*, man, you've got no problem with that. I shouldn't have been so surprised."

"You should have been." Spencer hesitated. "I haven't ex- actly stood up for myself in the last few years."

"Yeah, you have," Heath argued, looking mildly shocked that he was taking Spencer's side. "You'd have to be tough as fucking nails to make it through that gauntlet, year after year, and never break. I . . . I couldn't have done it. I wouldn't have wanted to do it. I'd have quit playing."

"That might be happening, still," Spencer said. Blown away by Heath's confession. *I couldn't have done it.*

The toughest fucking player in the NFL, and he had just told Spencer that he'd have broken.

"Phil told me you want to come to the Riptide. You gotta know, they'd pay just about anything for a player like you."

Spencer nodded. He knew it. He'd worked so hard to be the kind of player that no team would ever turn down.

"But . . ." Heath hesitated, fingers tapping against the side of his beer can. "I gotta know. Is this all legit? Would you really take a stand and hang it up?"

"You should know I'm serious. You did it."

Heath shook his head. "I never loved playing football. That's not why I played. Once I realized that I was trying to prove something to someone who didn't matter, it was easy enough to hang up my cleats. And I like coachin', especially coachin' Sam. At least when he listens." He shot Spencer a lopsided smile that he hadn't even realized Heath Harris possessed. "He can be a real stubborn sonofabitch, sometimes. I love him, every single fucking day, but wow, sometimes I wanna take him apart."

Spencer swallowed hard, and refused to flinch or react. Show in any way, shape, or form just how hot that would be to watch. Heath Harris, with all that legendary focus and toughness, taking Sam Crawford—hardly a slouch in the looks department—apart.

It would be epic.

"But you, you're not ready to retire, not really," Heath said, dragging the subject back to what mattered right here, right now.

"You're in the height of your career. You really willing to take that step?"

"I've thought about what I might do. I've thought for years about starting a really high-end skill camp for defensive players. You've got your quarterback camps, your wideout camps, your running back camps. We need a really solid camp for defensive players. I'd be happy doing that."

Heath nodded. "You'd be a good guy to teach 'em. Coaching isn't always easy, but I get a lot out of it."

"Except when Crawford makes you want to destroy something?"

Heath threw his head back and laughed. "You are *not* what I thought you were, Evans."

"You know, I get that a lot," Spencer retorted dryly. "I guess that's not much of a surprise."

"Well, hopefully, not so much in the next few years," Heath said. "Anyway, Phil was concerned that I'd be concerned about you, and well . . . I'm not gonna lie. I wasn't a fan of the idea, when he first brought it to me. But it's . . . well, it's growin' on me now. You think the Stars will let ya go?"

Spencer supposed they were both being really honest now, so he might as well unburden his whole truth. "I don't know. They hate me but they don't want to let me go, either."

Heath nodded sympathetically. *Empathetically*, Spencer realized. That was the way he was looking, and the difference left Spencer feeling that maybe, just maybe, this might work out after all.

"Roddy may not get his head out of his own ass, which considering how homophobic he is . . . is interesting."

Heath chuckled.

"But I'm resolved either way," Spencer continued. "I won't play for them anymore."

Heath finished his beer and set it down with a metallic click on the table.

"We've built a good thing at the Riptide. It wasn't easy. Things weren't always perfect. But it was probably loads better than anything you ever got before. If . . . if it comes down to you coming to us, I won't fight it."

Spencer felt his heart beat twice as fast. "But you won't support it."

Heath's gaze was still relaxed and easy. Nothing like it had been when he'd first spotted Spencer in his house. "You know? I was all prepared to dislike you, and I'm only annoyed now that I don't, not anymore." Heath sighed. "I see way too much of myself in you, which that bastard Alec probably knew."

"He's brilliant."

Heath smiled. "Spoken like a man in love."

"You asked me if I was using him. I'm not. I'm lucky he's willing to even give me the time of day after everything."

"Alec's got good instincts. The best instincts. I was sure that this time he was wrong, but goddamn it, it appears that he wasn't." Heath shot Spencer a look. "Don't you dare tell him that."

"Wouldn't dream of it."

Heath stood, stretching. "Chase keeps telling me he's gonna organize a legit game of Marco Polo. Let's go see if he's gotten a game off the ground."

"Marco Polo?"

Spencer followed Heath in the direction of the pool and stopped when Heath turned abruptly. "You gotta keep an eye on that dude," he warned, "because if you give him an inch, he'll take a mile. I once caught him opening his *eyes*."

"Chase?"

Heath nodded vigorously. "We play to win here."

And Spencer could hardly argue with that principle. After all, the yard and the pool were slowly filling up with a ton of current and ex-NFL players.

If anyone knew anything about playing to win, it was gonna be them.

• • • ● • ● • ● • • •

"I can't fucking believe you convinced me to play that game, you sadist," Alec groaned as he collapsed into a lounge chair, his naked chest glittering with water droplets.

Spencer didn't think he'd smiled or laughed so much in forever. Chase had indeed tried to cheat, but Bran Phillips and Jamie had ended up tackling him in the pool, teasingly splashing him in the face. Then Heath had taken over, and they had all been reminded of how tough and how focused he could be.

"Oh, you had fun," Spencer teased, because they *had*. They'd both let go for an afternoon and just played around in the pool, and he knew that was something they'd needed.

They'd been dealing with so much stress, and they'd been undeniably tense, even alongside the sheer happiness he knew they both felt at them finally figuring their relationship out.

"Actually," Alec said, leaning over and flashing him a quick, happy grin, "you might be right. The best part was when I caught *you*."

"You'd say that," Spencer scoffed, but Alec's joy at catching him off guard and tagging him had made him feel lighter too, lighter than he'd felt in forever.

Almost like . . . maybe he'd finally found a group of people that he could be himself around. Maybe if he was truly forced into retirement, into giving up his career, it wouldn't be so bad if he still had these guys as friends. Neal didn't seem unhappy, and Heath certainly didn't either.

It wasn't the first time he'd thought that he'd be okay if he never got traded and his career ended. Sure, he'd never win a Super Bowl. That would be disappointing. But the clearer and clearer the picture became of how happy he could be without being constantly degraded and insulted?

Nothing was worth that. Not even a ring.

"You didn't tell me how your talk with Heath went," Alec said.

"Yeah, he basically dragged me right into the pool," Spencer said sheepishly. "Sorry."

"And then you dragged *me* in," Alec pointed out.

"Hey, you wore a swimsuit, did you think I'd let you get away with not using it?" Spencer teased.

"I should've known better."

"You really should've," Spencer said. Paused. "Well, I think it went okay, actually. The talk with Heath, that is. He didn't seem particularly pissed off. We talked a little about when he retired."

"Really?" Alec raised an eyebrow.

Spencer had a feeling Heath didn't talk about that with very many people. He'd always been very private, but when he'd quit the NFL and started dating Sam, he'd locked it *all* down tight, as tightly as he could.

"Yeah," Spencer said. "Technically, he didn't really *want* to, kept going on about how we were so different, and you know, that's not true. We're not really all that different."

"You're not," Alec agreed. "But I'm surprised he let you get away with it."

"I am too. And so was he," Spencer said, chuckling. "But yeah, I think it'll be fine. He said he was on board."

Alec reached over and Spencer wasn't quite used to being so open, but here, in the backyard of people he trusted, it was easy to lean in and kiss him back.

Alec tasted like the rosé he was drinking, smelled like sunscreen and chlorine, and felt like *love*.

His skin was warm and still damp against Spencer's palms as he curled his fingers into him.

"If I haven't said it," Alec said as he pulled back. "I'm very proud of you."

"You are?"

Alec smiled. Soft and sweet and private, like this was meant just for Spencer. And maybe it was. "None of this was easy. But you did it anyway."

Flopping back onto his own lounger, Spencer said, "I didn't think it would be like this, at first. But every time we came to a crossroads, and I had to make a choice, it felt like it got easier. None of the other options seemed legit, not anymore. It was more about keeping on the path, and not letting myself get distracted by what could have been."

"And today?"

"Not as bad as I thought it'd be," Spencer admitted. "Heath's . . . well, we get each other now. I respect him. I think he could learn to respect me. And that's all I can ask of him."

Alec reached out and gripped Spencer's hand and squeezed hard. "We're going to make this happen, still."

Spencer hadn't given up yet—not by a long shot—but he already knew that if it came to that, he wouldn't cry over it.

And he wouldn't be alone. Not ever again.

Chapter Nineteen

SPENCER WOKE UP SLOWLY, aware first of a warm body pressed close to his, and the bright sunshine hitting his face as his eyes opened.

Third, the alarm was loud, unbelievably fucking loud, and it was impossible to ignore.

"What is that?" Spencer asked, his voice cracking. "What the ever living . . ."

"My alarm," Alec said.

Spencer, with his eyes open exactly a quarter of an inch, could see Alec fumbling for his phone on the bedside table. Finally, after an obscene amount of time, the sound stopped.

"What the fuck," Spencer groaned, rolling over. "Do you have a death wish?"

"No," Alec said with annoying amusement in his voice, "just an early meeting."

Spencer opened an eye again, taking in Alec's nakedness, from when they'd fooled around the night before. They'd both been tired from the pool party, and from a round of really hot sex, and it hadn't been that hard to convince Alec that clothes were overrated. *Good call, Spence, you need to make this happen every morning going forward.* "How early?"

Alec laughed. "Not that early," he said, and climbed on top of Spencer with a nimbleness and a coherency that Spencer didn't quite feel.

"Are you telling me that all this time has gone by, and I never knew you were a morning person? How did I miss this?"

Alec laughed. "It's never come up before?"

They'd spent a few nights together, but on those days, maybe Alec hadn't had an early meeting. Or Spencer had, so it had been a moot point.

But then Alec rotated his surprisingly limber hips, and suddenly Spencer wasn't sure he cared.

"If you keep grinding on me like that," Spencer said roughly, "it's not going to matter *who's* the morning person."

"That's the idea," Alec said with a teasing smile. He leaned over to kiss him, but instead of their lips touching, Alec's phone blared out again.

Somehow, this time around, the noise was impossibly even louder.

"What the fuck is that?" Spencer asked, as Alec climbed off him and went in search of his phone again.

"I've got a few people on ring alert," Alec said, the undercurrent of his voice excited. "People I'm looking forward to hearing from, specifically." When Spencer glanced over, he was staring at the screen. "Phil Reynolds is one of them."

Spencer opened his mouth to ask what Phil could possibly want so early in the morning, but Alec answered the phone before he could.

"Phil, it's pretty early to be hearing from you," Alec said casually, like this might not be the phone call they had both been waiting for.

Alec listened for a few moments, nodding along with whatever Phil was saying. "Yeah," he said. "Wait just a second, I happen to be here with someone who might want to hear this, too. Do you mind me putting you on speaker?"

Glancing up at Spencer, the joy and triumph in Alec's eyes said it all.

Spencer dug his fingertips into the bedding and tried, very hard, not to cry.

"Sure thing, but you know, I'm going to get you back for *that* comment," Alec said with a jovial tone. "Yeah, we're just working out together. Early morning, best time to exercise and all that."

Spencer laughed, because he couldn't keep it in anymore. It exploded out of him, happiness and relief and something else, unnamable.

Hope.

That was what it was. The first time he'd felt an overwhelming sense of hope in as long as he could remember.

"Great," Alec said, and pulled the phone away from his face, hitting a button on the screen. "Yeah, Phil, you're live. Spencer's right here."

"Hi, Spencer," Phil said. "I got the strangest call from Heath last night."

Spencer felt his breath catch. Maybe, despite the look on Alec's face, this wasn't what he thought it was. What if Heath hadn't said good things? What if he'd told Phil that he didn't approve after all?

"He told me that if I didn't do everything I could to sign you, you'd be the player I'd regret losing forever," Phil said. "Got me thinking. I called up Roddy after that call, real late, and it turned out, he's been thinkin' too."

"Yeah?" Spencer said when Phil paused, clearly waiting for an answer. A reaction. But Spencer didn't have anything. It felt like his voice had dried out in his throat. Like speaking was impossible.

"He's been thinkin' he doesn't really like you much," Phil said, clearly amused, while Spencer just wanted to die.

"Yeah, that's probably true," Spencer had to admit. Not the best thing to admit to someone who might be your future boss—that your current and possibly former boss didn't like anything about you.

"Well, to be honest, I don't like him very much either," Phil said, sounding amused. Hope and fear were warring inside Spencer now, making it nearly impossible to concentrate on what the other man was saying.

Still, he did his best, because whether he was traded or not, this could be the phone call that changed his entire life.

"We're still working out the last details," Phil continued, "but I wanted to be the first to tell you: welcome to the Los Angeles Riptide."

Spencer's eyes met Alec's, and there was that feeling again, fizzing through him like the fine champagne that they'd shared together: hope.

"Really, sir?" Spencer choked out. Suddenly, he *was* near tears—tears of relief, tears of disbelief, because he hadn't been sure that this would happen at all. It had been such a long shot, fueled by the most acute kind of desperation: the desperation of totally losing himself in the hundred insignificant yet vitally important compromises he'd been forced into making.

"Really." Phil sounded very certain. "We're over the moon here at headquarters. Alec?"

"Yes, yes, I'm here." Alec had to clear his throat twice, and unless Spencer was mistaken, there were tears in his eyes too.

"Bring him in tomorrow, for a press conference," Phil said. "PR is working on the details, but it's gonna be a big deal. Huge celebration. Rainbow balloons. We'll send over some Riptide gear. PR will be sending you an email all about it. Now, I gotta go convince Roddy that the third-round pick he wants is *really* a fourth."

"You think Spencer's not worth a third-round pick?" Alec asked archly.

Phil chuckled. "Oh, he's worth a *first*-round pick, but I'm not gonna let Roddy get away with that shit."

"Go get 'em," Alec said. "I'll look for your email."

"Can't wait to shake your hand, Spencer," Phil said. "I think this is going to be great for both of us."

"Me too, sir," Spencer said.

"It's Phil to you, now, Spencer," Phil said kindly. "I'll see you tomorrow."

Alec said his goodbye, and then it was over, and the phone was on the bed and suddenly Alec was in Spencer's arms and they were hugging each other so tightly that Spencer wasn't sure he could even breathe.

Not sure he even wanted to.

"We did it," Spencer murmured into his shoulder. "We fucking did it."

Alec pulled back, staring at him straight in the eyes, and Spencer couldn't miss the tears welling in them now. "No," he said. "You did. This was all you, Spencer. You put yourself out there and then held out your hand and said, *you've taken all this but you won't take another single thing*. And you *stuck* to it."

"It wasn't hard, not with you behind me," Spencer said with blunt honesty.

"Next to you," Alec corrected softly, pressing a kiss to his mouth. "I'm always going to be next to you, holding your hand, reminding you that you're never alone."

• • • ● • ● • ● • • •

"Mr. Mitchell, *Sunday Morning Football* is on, and they're addressing Spencer's situation," Kyle said over the intercom.

"Okay, thanks, Kyle," Alec said, looking up from the contract he was reviewing with a fine-tooth comb. He'd been at it for hours, and he was still only halfway done, but he'd told Kyle to let him know when the special OTA edition of *Sunday Morning Football* was on, because he'd known that they'd definitely be discussing Spencer's trade, and he was curious to see what was being said.

He pulled the TV remote from his top desk drawer and flipped on the TV, then tuned to the network *Sunday Morning Football* aired on.

Neal was in the middle of talking, a huge graphic of Spencer at the press conference from two weeks ago up on the screen behind him.

". . . and we know," Neal said, "that Evans made it clear that he was either going to be traded or he was retiring, plus he was injured in the last game he played in, at the end of the season, so these first practices are super important. He needs to establish that not only can he pass the physical, which we're told he did with flying colors, but that he can play up to the high bar he's set for the last nine seasons."

"Oh he's ready to prove you wrong," Terry Bradshaw countered.

Neal laughed. "I'm not thinking he's washed up, if that's what you thought I meant."

Alec couldn't help the chuckle that escaped him. There was no way Spencer wouldn't be texting Neal right now, outraged that he'd even vaguely insinuated that Spencer was washed up, that his best days were behind him.

"I'm thinking you're prodding the beast," Terry said sagely.

"Maybe," Neal said with a quick grin at the camera. "But, guys, he does have some stuff to prove. Is he back in playing shape?"

He'd know just about better than anyone else, because at the last pickup game, he and Spencer had connected for three touchdowns, including the winning one.

Alec's phone dinged, and he looked down. It was a text from Spencer. **What the fuck is Neal going on about my fitness?** Accompanied the outraged comment was a picture of Spencer, shirtless and pants-less, flexing just about everything. Making Alec's mouth dry out very suddenly. He cleared his throat, fingers trembling slightly as he texted his boyfriend back.

We still on for dinner?

Spencer's reply was nearly automatic.

If you're the first course.

Alec chuckled to himself again. **I think we can arrange that.**

Text me when you're on your way, and I'll get ready . . . I mean the GRILL of course. Preheat the grill. Right?

Alec forced himself to put the phone down and turn his attention to the screen, and what the five guys were saying about Spencer.

"The real question," Jimmy Johnson said, "is what is the Riptide defense going to look like now that they have Spencer Evans? He can't transform an entire defense, and let's face it, the Riptide defense needs a major transformation."

"He's the kinda guy who elevates everyone else he plays with," Terry argued. "He's going to make everyone on that whole team better."

"You think so?" Neal sounded dubious.

Alec had a feeling the only reason Spencer had stopped sending him quasi-dirty text messages was he was currently busy texting Neal, letting him know just how he felt about Neal's stance on the Riptide defense.

"They also got some pretty good players in the draft," Jimmy said. "And geez, imagine turning Spencer Evans loose on some rookies. He's gonna make them better. Just by standing next to them."

"Well, I guess we're gonna see," Terry said. "I can't wait for the first preseason game, it's gonna be real interesting what this team looks like. Are they the Super Bowl contender we think they are? What about the addition of Evans? How's he gonna gel with the rest of the players? Will there be a locker room problem?"

"There won't be a locker room problem," Neal said confidently. "Harris is totally on board. You saw his posts about Evans getting traded. He doesn't speak up on social media much but he did for this, which I think says volumes about how he feels."

"That's true," Jerry Rice agreed. "I was surprised to see Harris being so public about his feelings on the issue."

"Probably because the Stars were so crappy to Evans," Neal said. "I played for the Riptide. That locker room is tight. Evans could be an interloper, but what I think is gonna happen? He's going to be embraced. Riptide take care of our own, and Spencer is now one of us."

Alec nodded in approval. He'd reached out to Neal, talked over with him what the segment might go like, what he might say. What Neal *had* said was a lot more decisive and positive than even Alec had suggested.

He leaned back in his chair, pleased.

Doubly pleased because the next subject the panel turned to was the Stars defense without Spencer, and they weren't the only ones who were already predicting it wouldn't be nearly as good this year.

Losing Spencer would be a blow.

A blow, Alec was convinced, they deserved a hundred and ten percent.

He flipped the TV off, feeling satisfied in a way he'd never experienced before.

A long time ago, ten years ago to be precise, he'd hoped that one day he might feel like this. Know what it was like not only to change the world but to change players' lives, one at a time.

Nothing would ever be the same for Spencer after this, and Alec was going to be lucky enough to not only have a front-row seat to the rest of his career—and the rest of his *life*—but he'd get to hold his hand through it.

. . . ● ● ● ● ● . .

The name above his locker was written in big, declarative turquoise letters.

Staring at it as he finished his preparations for practice—his very first practice with the Riptide—settled Spencer.

He hadn't been on a football field in months. Not a real football field, anyway, and he found that as he got ready to jog back on, he was ready. Not just ready, but *excited*.

He'd never been excited to start a season before.

He'd also never walked into a locker room before and been ignored, in a *good* way.

Like he was just another guy, just another teammate, nothing special about him, just a cog in the wheel.

Nobody sneered. Nobody catcalled. Nobody made any comments under their breath.

Spencer wanted to fall to his knees on the cold hard tile and thank God or whatever deity had given him the strength and the fortitude to do this. Because when he'd first begun, he'd not even been sure that he *could* do it.

And then, he'd realized, right in the middle of it, that he didn't have any other choice.

"Hey, Evans," Sam said, approaching him and pulling him into a quick hug. "Great to see ya."

He was absolutely not lying when he responded, "Actually, it's fucking wonderful to see *you*."

"No kidding," Sam said. "Now try not to demolish me more than like . . . a handful of times today, okay?"

Spencer grinned. "What? It'll be just like old times. Me tackling your ass to the ground."

"You'd better not take it easy on *any* of us," Chase chimed in. "I want to see the Spence Train in all its glory."

"Don't worry," Spencer said, clapping Chase on the back. Hard but not as hard as he intended to take him down, when they were out on the practice field. "I don't do soft."

"Nobody ever doubted you," Sam chuckled. "Now let's go play some football."

"I'll be out in a second."

Spencer turned back to his locker. Trying to get his heart rate under control. Trying to get his *emotions* under control.

He'd never had friends in the locker room before. There'd been players, like Blaze, who had tried to support him, but who hadn't, through no fault of their own, wanted to stick their necks out for him.

Spencer couldn't blame Blaze or anyone else. Who'd *want* to bring the focus of the shitty locker room vibe squarely onto their own shoulders? And he'd borne it so long, it had almost begun to feel normal.

But this? This, Spencer realized, this was what normal really was.

Being a fucking *team*.

He took a deep breath, grabbed his gloves, and headed towards the doorway, jogging through the tunnel, done up in gaudy turquoise and aqua stripes, and then finally, emerging onto the Riptide practice field.

"Evans!" A shout came from the other side of the field. It was Coach, waving him over. He changed direction, and a moment later was standing next to Coach Rodriguez, one of the best coaches in the NFL. Coach Schaffer was next to him, the defensive coordinator.

"Evans, great to have you on board." Schaffer looked thrilled, which made sense. In the last few weeks, Spencer had taken time to watch a lot of film of the Riptide's defense, and though they hadn't always had the best players to execute the plays, the plans were solid. He could help, he could *really* help, and he could make this team better. He knew it, and clearly Schaffer, who wasn't a fucking moron, knew it, too.

"I'm ready to get to work," Spencer said. "Whatever you need me to do, I'm there."

"Yeah," Coach Schaffer said happily, like he'd just won the lottery jackpot, "yeah, I just bet you are." Casually, like he had zero issues touching Spencer—a completely brand-new sensation to Spencer, since the Stars coaches had always avoided touching him if they could, like he could fucking *infect them*—Coach patted him on the back. "Yeah, you're gonna be our guy. Don't you worry about that."

And suddenly, just like that, he wasn't just an island.

He wasn't alone.

He wasn't isolated.

He was *our guy*.

Spencer lifted his head and decided it was time to get to work.

The rest of his career had finally arrived.

EPILOGUE

"Don't tell me you're gonna hide in there," Chase said, pounding on the door. "It's time to get your naked ass out here."

Alec met his boyfriend's gaze and tried not to cringe.

"I really thought this was a good idea, didn't I?" Alec said, raising his eyes to the ceiling in a mock plea. "Why did I think this was a good idea?"

Spencer was grinning at him, his bright, free smile something that Alec was lucky enough to see all the time now.

Chase pounded on the door again. "The photographer says it's time to get your asses out here." He paused. Alec could practically *hear* his amusement. "Your *naked* asses. You feelin' a little self-conscious, Spence Train?"

"No," Spencer called out. "Give us a minute."

"Oh," Chase said loudly. "So it's Alec who's freaking out. I'll let *you* deal with that."

Spencer was still grinning when he turned to Alec again. The robe he'd been given to wear was tight on his shoulders, barely containing them.

Any other day, Alec would've been thrilled down to the soles of his feet to see his boyfriend naked.

Just not when he was naked. And the rest of his clients were naked, too.

"I just . . . don't *do* this, not like you guys do, on a daily basis," Alec hissed under his breath. Was he a little worried that Chase would hear and tell everyone? Absofuckinglutely.

"Hey, you had no problem stripping down in the locker room that one day," Spencer pointed out.

"That was . . ." Alec cleared his throat. "I was trying to impress you."

"Well, it worked," Spencer said, leaning down and brushing his lips across Alec's. "I was suitably impressed. And horny as hell, after that."

Alec found himself smiling, even as his nervous stomach threatened to expel the egg white he'd eaten for breakfast.

"Trust me," Spencer continued, "there isn't going to be anyone judging. You look gorgeous."

"I don't look like *you* or Heath or even Neal," Alec said.

"You look like yourself, the guy I love," Spencer said confidently.

Give Alec a contract to negotiate or fine print to review, and he'd feel just as confident as Spencer did. But naked, in front of a camera?

Legitimately, what the fuck *had* he been thinking?

He'd been thinking how great it would be for not only his career and the National Football League, but the careers of all the guys he managed.

That hadn't changed.

Alec raised his chin. "I guess I do," he said. "I'm just used to . . . well . . ."

"The three-piece suit, AKA your battle armor?"

"Yes," Alec said with a resigned sigh. "But I push you guys out of your comfort zones all the time, I suppose it's only fair that I do it to myself every once in awhile."

"Yep," Spencer said. "You could always put the modesty patch . . ."

Alec shot him a glare. "Hell no. You're not wearing one. I doubt anyone else is either."

"I doubt it too," Spencer agreed. "But we get naked in front of each other all the time."

"Ugh, don't remind me," Alec complained as he headed towards the dressing room door. Why had they even needed dressing rooms? Surely they could've just shucked their clothes off right there, next to the camera.

He opened the door and was relieved to see that Chase wasn't still hanging around, waiting to see him emerge.

"Come on," Spencer said, reaching down and taking his hand. "This is gonna be fun, right?"

"Fun," Alec muttered under his breath as they approached the main studio, where the photographer was set up.

Neal and Heath were already standing on the marks that the photographer had made on the ground, naked as the day they were born, lounging confidently in the way that only someone who knew they were in killer shape could.

And they weren't even playing football anymore!

Spencer shed his robe on the chair and just as confidently walked over to where Neal and Heath were standing. They greeted each other, and then the three of them glanced over at Alec.

"You comin'?" Heath asked, raising an eyebrow.

"Yes," Alec said, dropping his robe before he could panic about the fact that this was happening and joined the trio.

Alec heard a wolf whistle from the side, in the dark part of the studio, away from the bright lights.

"Don't tell me you brought *Sam*," Alec hissed to Heath, who just shrugged.

"He wasn't going to miss this," Neal said. "And neither was Jamie."

"Oh God," Alec said.

"Lookin' sharp," Jamie called out.

"Oh good, you're all here," the photographer said, straightening from his position in front of the camera. "Let's get you positioned. Alec, you in the middle."

"Right, of course," Alec said awkwardly, stepping into the middle of the group. He'd kind of been hoping that he'd be in the back, mostly hidden from view, but clearly that didn't make any sense.

He was the reason this was happening at all.

"Come on, you big dork," Heath said, slapping him on the back. "Get in the middle of this."

"Get it, Mitchell!" Sam called out.

"Heath, you over here," the photographer said, and Alec almost felt sorry for him, desperately trying to maintain his professionalism as the four naked men in front of him devolved into twelve-year-olds.

"Chase, in the back," the photographer continued, "and put your hand on Alec's shoulder. Yeah, just like that."

"I can't believe I waxed my chest if it's gonna be all hidden," Chase grumbled.

"You waxed your chest?" Heath demanded in disbelief. "Were we supposed to do that?"

"No," Neal said, eyeing him. "Though maybe *you* should've."

"It's okay," Chase said with an unrepentant grin. "I think Tate enjoyed doing it."

"What about me?" Spencer asked the photographer.

Next to me, God, please, Alec mentally begged. He was about five seconds from panicking about all of this, and having Spencer close . . . it would help.

"We should've brought scorecards," Jamie said to Sam, loudly. "Like, a solid fucking eight for Neal over there."

"I'm just an *eight*?" Neal squawked.

"You're a kicker, it's alright," Heath said, patting him reassuringly. "Nobody's gonna judge."

"Nine point five for Harris," Sam offered.

"You sure weren't subtracting half a point last night," Heath said slyly.

"You missed leg day last week," Sam said. "I think you might be losing some of your definition. Now, the Spence Train, that is a tall drink of water. I definitely think he gets a ten. Don't you think? I bet you Alec gives him a ten."

Alec ground his teeth together. The photographer had put Neal next to Heath, partially in front of him, blocking the parts to turn this from soft porn to an artistic statement.

Then, Spencer got positioned next to him, putting an arm around Alec's waist, and he felt like he could properly breathe again.

"A couple of shots like this," the photographer said, stepping back and giving a nod of approval. "Make sure you keep everything . . . covered."

"Yeah, don't want to give baby gays all over the world jackoff material or anything," Sam crowed.

"Just the baby gays? I bet they'd move a few guys on the Kinsey scale," Jamie said.

"Let's focus here," the photographer barked out. Alec was a hundred percent sure he was regretting every single one of his choices.

Alec sure was.

"Give me some Blue Steel, guys," the photographer added with a grin.

Okay, maybe he wasn't having such a bad time after all.

Fifteen minutes and three poses later, they had just about wrapped things up.

Alec was *almost* used to standing around naked, letting everyone in the room get a nice good look at his junk.

"I think that's about it," the photographer said. "But I do have one more idea . . . if you're on board."

At this point, Alec wasn't sure there was something he wouldn't be on board with.

"What is it?" he asked.

"I know you and Spencer are dating," the photographer said, almost apologetically, like he felt guilty for reading gossip sites. "Would you like a few pictures, just the two of you? Real classy and stuff, don't worry about that."

"Uh," Alec said, and for the first time, he was almost worried that he *might* get a little too excited. "Let me talk to Spencer about it."

"They probably won't make it in the article," the photographer pointed out. "But it might be nice to just have them, you know? For posterity."

"Yeah," Alec said, realizing that he was probably right.

"What's up?" Spencer asked, walking over. "Everything okay?"

"He suggested we get some pictures of just the two of us," Alec said. "What do you think?"

"I'm down," Spencer said with a fierce grin. "You okay with this?"

"Surprisingly," Alec said slowly, "I think so?"

"Well, let's do it." Spencer actually looked *eager*.

"You don't think the others will feel left out?" Alec glanced over to where Heath and Neal were lounging with their respective boyfriends. They'd all put on their robes, but Chase hadn't even bothered to tie his.

"This story's about *you*," Spencer reminded him. "I think if they want a naked photo shoot, they can do it on their own time."

"Alright," Alec said, turning to the photographer. "How do you want us?"

"Like this," the photographer said, mimicking them holding hands. "Facing the back wall there, yeah, turn just a little bit, and look at each other."

They posed as asked, and when Spencer glanced over at him, love and amusement brimming in his eyes, he squeezed his hand. Alec didn't need him to say what he was thinking. They were in this together, a thousand percent, and this was the perfect representation of that.

"Lookin' good," Heath called out. "Now you gotta get a little closer. Give us all a preview of coming attractions."

The photographer raised an eyebrow. "You want to do that?"

"Yeah," Alec said, surprising himself. "Yeah, we can do that."

And without being bidden, tugged Spencer closer, using his body to shield his own from the camera, and running his fingers up Spencer's arms, laid his head on his chest.

"Oh, just like that, don't fucking move," the photographer called out. "I think you're gonna love this."

Spencer's head dipped towards his, just a fraction and he murmured, "I don't think I ever want to. Now that I've got you just where I want you."

"Naked with a bunch of other guys watching?" Alec teased.

"No," Spencer said seriously, "completely and totally mine."

"You've always been mine," Alec echoed. "From the very first moment."

Later, Alec would not be surprised at all that the artistic black-and-white shot, with them gazing at each other with nine years' worth of love in their eyes, would end up being their engagement portrait.

· · ● · ● · ● · ● · ·

Want to read a *very* sexy scene about Spencer trying something new in the bedroom? Check out the bonus scene, available to download here.

· · ● · ● · ● · ● · ·

Don't miss the Miami Piranhas, the next chapter in Beth's football universe. *Playing for Keeps* is available on Amazon, KU, and Audible.

INTERESTED IN READING MORE OF
BETH'S BOOKS?

CHECK OUT A FULL LIST OF TILES
BY SCANNING THE QR CODE
OR VISITING HER WEBSITE

WWW.BETHBOLDEN.COM/BOOKLIST

WANT TO FOLLOW BETH?

MAKE SURE YOU NEVER
MISS A RELEASE?

SCAN THE QR CODE BELOW
OR VISIT HER WEBSITE
FOR A SOCIAL MEDIA LIST,
NEWSLETTER SIGNUP,
AND SO MUCH MORE!

WWW.BETHBOLDEN.COM/ABOUT

9 781964 691282